MW01164931

# SUMMER
## Vacation

# SUMMER
*Vacation*

LINDA GEE

Copyright © 2017 by Linda Gee.

| Library of Congress Control Number: | | 2017907674 |
|---|---|---|
| ISBN: | Hardcover | 978-1-5434-2330-3 |
| | Softcover | 978-1-5434-2331-0 |
| | eBook | 978-1-5434-2332-7 |

All rights reserved. No part of this book may be reproduced or transmitted
in any form or by any means, electronic or mechanical, including photocopying,
recording, or by any information storage and retrieval system,
without permission in writing from the copyright owner.

This is a work of fiction. Names, characters, places and incidents either are the
product of the author's imagination or are used fictitiously, and any resemblance
to any actual persons, living or dead, events, or locales is entirely coincidental.

Any people depicted in stock imagery provided by Thinkstock are models,
and such images are being used for illustrative purposes only.
Certain stock imagery © Thinkstock.

Print information available on the last page.

Rev. date: 05/12/2017

**To order additional copies of this book, contact:**
Xlibris
1-888-795-4274
www.Xlibris.com
Orders@Xlibris.com
760411

*To Sia, my husband Sia of Forty-two years,*
*To my children,*
*and to*
*Aaron, for giving me such cute ideas.*

*Some of the stories in this book*
*are actual events that happened.*
*Some things our precious*
*daughters did to make me laugh.*
*I love them more than they will ever know*

# CHAPTER ONE

My name is Samantha Lord, I just turned eighteen years old, and my friends and family call me "Sam". I have a black cloud over my head. I am misunderstood and feel unloved. My only salvation is I have three great friends; three of us have been close since kindergarten.

My best friend is Veronica, but she goes by Ronnie. My father works for Ronnie's father along with many other attorneys. I consider my family middle class, but my Dad is always complaining they aren't paid enough. We live in Minneapolis, Minnesota decent summers but cold winters.

I have a younger sister, Alexandria who is fourteen. I also have a younger brother, Raymond who is eight years old. They are the favorites in the family. They don't get in trouble, they mind our parents, they do what they are told which is a lot less than what I am expected to do.

I seem to be in trouble often. Okay, maybe I am somewhat of a trouble-maker. I don't care what people think about me or who I hurt in most of the choices I make in life or what comes out of my mouth. My mom says I need to learn to think before I speak. I have little to no patience for anything that happens in our home with my siblings.

We live in an average two story house. There were three bedrooms; my sister and I share one, which I think is ridiculous. I am a senior in high school but, none the less, that is the way it is. I have dreams like any other teenage girl. My brother gets a room to himself. I want love and happiness. I even want a family someday.

I need freedom. I need to see where life takes me without having to take care of my brother and sister. I want to see the world. I want to see if I can be "me" without feeling bad about it or thinking I am useless, unwanted and unloved. I need to know someone is out there for me. Maybe there is and maybe there isn't that perfect someone, but I have to try.

My friends and I are about to graduate from high school. We have been planning our senior trip for over ten years. We have been working part-time. We save our allowances, our Christmas money and, even birthday money. I even begged, borrowed and stole for this trip. We have worked hard preparing for our summer fling.

Of course, Ronnie, who I sometimes call 'Ron', comes from a wealthy family, so she didn't have to work. She did work and saved her own money to prove a point to her father. She is not like what you would think a "rich girl" would be. She is down to earth, very giving, and kind.

Ronnie's parents are divorced, and she lives with her father. Ronnie's mother moved to Florida a few years ago and Ronnie visits her a couple times a year, but they are not close. Ronnie loves animals and plans to attend college to be a veterinarian. The idea appalls her father. He wants her to go into law, like him and his father before him, but Ronnie has different plans. Ronnie's decisions usually are anything her father disagrees with.

She has three step siblings with her father's new wife. They are total brats and get anything they want. Her stepmother or 'stepwitch', as we call her, treats her civil but distant. I mean she doesn't beat her but she feels more like their housekeeper's daughter. Their housekeeper/cook, Mabel, took pity on Ronnie when her mother left. Her father was gone most of the time, so Mabel taught her how to cook, clean, and keep house. Ronnie loved helping her. Mabel loves Ronnie and has given her more attention and love than anyone else. Ronnie spent as much time as possible at our house while we were growing up. Ronnie is my best friend, we are "BFF's".

Katherine Patterson is the oldest of the group, as she always reminds us. We let her think she runs the group it keeps the peace between us. She hates her name so she has always been "Kat". Kat's mom is a single mother, and Kat has never met her father, she tells us he lives out of the country somewhere. He sends her mother money occasionally and sometimes exotic gifts.

She has done without the nicer things most of her life. So her attitude is she takes what she wants and says what she pleases, no matter what. Don't get me wrong, we love Kat. She is a lot like me, but I don't think she knows who she is yet, well, neither do I, chuckling to myself, nor do Ronnie or Abby.

Abigail Hall lives just around the corner from me. Her father owns the local grocery store. Their finances are kind of up and down, but mostly in the same financial bracket as my family. As her friends, we all call her

'Abby'. She worked part time for her father as well as working as a waitress on weekend to earn money. She has a younger sister, Ashley who is the family princess. She has been in beauty pageants and won most of the local ones.

Her father is a cranky old man and rules the house with an iron fist. Her mother adores Ashley. Abby feels inferior and left out most of the time. She considers herself the ugly one; she is built like her mother - small waist, and larger hips. She has a pretty face but doesn't think so. She hides it with her long bangs and rough hair cut which always hangs in her face. She studies very hard and is a straight-'A' student. Her parents never make a big deal out of her grades or her achievements.

Kat, Ronnie, and I bonded the first day of kindergarten. We were the misfits. We were mouthy little girls who didn't let anyone push us around. The teacher made the mistake of putting us together in a group. We ruled the group; the boys in our group didn't stand a chance. We pounded their egos and threatened to do bodily harm to them if they didn't do as we said.

For a while, it worked well, until one of the little piss ants told on us. Little did we know then, he would grow to be the hottest boy in our class. He was the most popular, and he loved to put the three of us down every chance he got, as long as he had friends around to protect him, that is. I guess our lives could have been a lot different if we had treated him nicer, but little girls didn't like dirty little boys at five years old.

Abby joined our group near the end of our kindergarten year. She was quiet and no one ever noticed her. No one even knew her name until she joined our group. We changed her life. Well we didn't change it, but we gave her someone to cling to. She felt like we did; out of sorts, unwanted, unloved. We stood by each other and when one was in trouble or down, we were all there to help. We never abandoned each other, ever.

We talked about college and our futures. We spent time together as we grew up telling each other our deep dark secrets, at least most of them. We planned college together but our senior year our plans changed. Our career choices changed. I planned to go to college at the University of Tulsa, in Oklahoma; Ronnie was going to the University of Oklahoma, in Norman.

We wanted to be far away from home but the career I wanted and the career she wanted didn't seem to work out college-wise. We would be close. The reason I chose Tulsa was for a law degree, and it wasn't because of my father, it was because I could make enough money to get away and stay away.

I told myself I would never be like my parents; I would be independent and work for the homeless and unemployed. Oh, hell, I don't know who I was kidding most of the time. I didn't like law; I just didn't know what

I wanted. I don't even know who I am yet. I finally chose law just to shut my parents up. I can always change courses later on. First, no matter what I have to get my basics.

Abby's plans are to go to Cornell; she is smart and worked hard to make the best grades possible. It still wasn't good enough to get the so-wanted attention from her parents. Her father was just happy Abby got a full scholarship so he didn't have to pay for it. He was so mean and the most selfish dirt bag of our fathers.

We never stayed at Abby's house, never, not one time, do I remember ever spending the night there. Maybe because he wouldn't allow it, I'm not sure. We stole what we wanted from him most of the time; it was easy; Abby knew when her father was out doing errands or not watching when he was in the store. We were drinking beer by fourteen years old. Too bad, he didn't have liquor in his store.

Kat, well she was accepted to several colleges but isn't sure what she wants. I believe she plans on a local college, the University of Wisconsin. She thinks her mother needs her to stay close to help her. Kat wanted to be loved so badly, she accepted any attention she got from her mom.

She acts tough to hide that pain deep inside her. We were afraid she would miss out on the college life by being so close to home. Her mother works two, sometimes three jobs to give Kat what she wants. She also gets money from her boyfriends when they move in for a while, which is kind of creepy.

Her mom loves her but she is rarely at home. They never did anything together. When we stayed at Kat's house, we were always unsupervised and got in a lot of trouble, that's when the drinking part came in, along with smoking and other things.

When Kat's mom wasn't working, she was at the bars with men. She brought so many different men home. By the time Kat was ten, she had watched her mother have sex and she knew every part of a man's anatomy and she told us all the gory details. Sometimes the men knew she was watching and even preformed for her. She had some scary episodes where those scumbags went for her. She always seemed to get away. Kat's mom did try to protect her from them.

Kat was smart too; she had a lot of common since. She did well in school. She studied, and she wanted her mother to be proud and she always told her how proud of her she was. But her mother drank a lot and forgot about Kat. Sometimes she'd leave her waiting at school or movie theaters for hours.

We planned months before graduation where we would spend our summer of freedom. We all wanted different things, we all wanted sun and fun but wanted different places. We had different reasons for our choices. We had to draw lots to see where we would go.

We each put in our desired destinations. We had to research the route to get there, the highways and how long a drive to get there. We had to figure the cost of the trip, housing and food, and the sites to visit in the area. We put our choices in a box and, we let my little brother draw. He pulled out Florida, which was Kat's choice.

We each agreed upon the choice and did further research. We chose an affordable condominium that would sleep four in Clearwater, Florida. We hoped we could find part-time jobs to help once we got there.

The condominium on line looked great online. It had two bedrooms and two bathrooms, a small kitchen, and a dining area. It was fully furnished, including a television, pots, pans, and dishes, and even a washer and dryer. It worked out to be a little over $1,500. each for the whole summer, all bills paid.

Of course, Kat was the one most lacking in funds. Now we had to decide who got what bedroom. One bedroom had two twin beds and the bath was in the hall. The other bedroom was a king-size bed and the bath was in the room.

We talked it over deciding on the two in the master bedroom would pay the entire amount above the $1500, that made it easier to choose who went where. So, Kat and Abby chose the bedroom with the twin beds. Ronnie and I would share the king. Ronnie came up the idea so she could actually help Kat out on cost.

Now, our plans were set. We would leave on June 1, and arrive there in two days. Ronnie had a SUV, and so we decided to take her car only, so we would all have to rely on her to get us around. But we found out we could rent scooters for a nominal fee daily, weekly, or monthly, so we thought we would be fine.

We only had to take our clothes and personal effects for the trip. The condo supplied hair dryers in both bathrooms. We would be on the Gulf side at Clearwater Point. It was a beachfront condo with a swimming pool and a hot tub, and we were to be on the third floor. We were so excited we could hardly contain ourselves.

We had been taking nonperishable food from Abby's father's store for months., non perishable items, canned meats, cereal, rice, canned vegetables, and anything that would not spoil or go bad for some time. We decided to hit it the last week and get things like chips, sodas, water, candy bars, and snacks for the trip. We figured we would have food to last a couple of weeks or longer at least.

My parents weren't happy about the four of us going without an adult, but three of us were already eighteen. My parents couldn't stop me from going but they didn't like our plans at all. They wanted me to save my money for college.

Of course, my mother ranted and raved for days but finally let it rest hoping the experience would be good for me, to live on my own and be responsible for myself. I got Mom's final okay by telling her we would write home often. Kat's mom was more open-minded than the rest of the parents. Abby's parents acted like mine, they wanted her to save her money for college. That way her cheep father didn't have to pay anything. I bet he wouldn't anyway, I am sure Abby would have to work while in school. Ronnie wasn't eighteen yet, but she had written permission from her father to go. Her 'stepwitch' was so excited to get rid of her for three months.

Besides, when we returned, we would all be off to college. My brother and sister were excited I would be gone too. I liked to pester them most of the time. I was the instigator instead of the little sister or brother being the pest it was the opposite in our house.

I thought of myself as average looking, I was five feet, seven inches tall, I weighed about 120 pounds, sometimes more, I had boobs, and they were just a little on the small side. I wore my hair short, it was blond and curly. I had tons of freckles across my nose and cheeks, and I hate them. The more I was in the sun the more freckles showed up and the blonder I became.

I didn't like the guys in high school; I never had a serious boy friend and didn't go to parties. I wasn't asked out and no dates for dances or prom. I was Abby's companion when Kat and Ronnie were on dates. I don't mean we were gay but we kept each other company on those lonely nights. We drank too much beer, ate too much junk food, and partied by ourselves. Abby and I had low self-esteems about ourselves. I was depressed so much of the time growing up I was a trouble-maker. Any attention I got, good or bad was good for me.

Abby was built different than the rest of us. She wasn't fat; she had her mother's wide hips, a small waist and small top, but she was only five foot four inches tall. Her height made her look larger than she really was.

Kat was the tallest; she was about five foot nine inches and a little larger frame than me, but some things of mine she could wear and vice versa. She had huge boobs, and an awesome body, with an athletic build. Boys loved her body. She was, I will say just a little bit promiscuous.

Ronnie was the cutest of of us with a tight little body. Boys adored her too. She had the cutest face and no freckles or blemishes. She had a sweet smile, with perfectly white, straight teeth and large brown eyes. Her hair always looked great even messed up. Her perfect complexion was obnoxious to me. She was flirty with the boys; she got what she wanted and sometimes unwanted attention. I think I should hate her but I love her, she was my best friend. It seems the rich girl is the cute slender one who seems to have it all, but she didn't have it all.

Abby and I bonded because we didn't know how to talk to people, and Kat and Ronnie did. They bull shitted their way through life. They weren't included in the popular groups but they seemed to manage to smash parties and make the best of it.

Most of the girls resented Ronnie because she was wealthy, and wore cute fashionable clothes and boys always looked her way making their girlfriends furious. She drove a decent car but she didn't have that cheerleader attitude. She pissed most of the popular girls off.

We didn't care what those girls said or did. We assumed they were jealous of us. Kat wanted those girls approval though but they didn't want her, she was from the wrong side of town. Kat was poor and needy and had a bad reputation. Kat and Ronnie were known for sleeping around. Especially Kat sleeping with guys who had girlfriends just to make a point

We had all brought CD's to play, and we had mapped out our route and, planned where to stay at night. We were on the road and so excited. We sang and played games. We took turns driving and paying for gas, but Ronnie filled it up before we left. She had a credit card from her father for gas so that would be a lot of help for us.

Ronnie's father also booked our hotel for the trip and paid for it as a gift for us. He tried to act the nice man, but I think he was happy all the quarreling and usually problems in the house would subside for the summer.

Ronnie is so kind hearted and I knew it hurt her feelings so often, the way he doted on his three other kids and not on her. I mean, he loved her I think. He took care of her and gave her anything she asked for, but Love and attention was the one thing she lacked. She confided in me, but I know she held so much back as I did, and I am sure as Kat and Abby did also. We all had our secrets, our dark cloud that we told no one about, parts we kept to ourselves. We shared almost anything except our shame.

We had our stuff packed and loaded into Ronnie's car by 6:00am. The drive went smooth with no unexpected concerns. We arrived in Knoxville, Tennessee, about ten o'clock that evening. We were all exhausted from the drive. We had stopped for food a few hours earlier, so we went straight to bed. We slept sound all night long.

We woke about six o'clock, had our continental breakfast, and were back on the road by seven o'clock, heading for Clearwater, Florida. We were so tired and talked less. We even were a little cranky with each other.

Ronnie tried to keep spirits up by telling jokes and making plans for our summer holiday.

We arrived at seven o'clock that evening at our condo. We weren't quite as excited as we were seeing it on the internet. It was okay but not as nice as the pictures were. The twin size beds were a little lumpy. It had a balcony that over looked the Gulf of Mexico. The beach was not far away, but we didn't see any people on the beach, perhaps because it was seven o'clock in the evening.

We noticed two good looking guys at the pool when we were bringing our stuff in; they watched us, laughed, and waived. We got all our stuff upstairs, carrying that much stuff up three flights of stairs wasn't as easy as we expected. I was definitely out of shape. We unpacked and made a grocery list for fresh fruit, vegetables and meats.

There was a list on the table for us to check over the condition of the condo. We had to mark if anything seemed damaged then return it to the condo manager. We put all our groceries in the cabinets and we thought we would be fine food wise.

We decided to look around the area to see what was around and how far stores were. We checked liquor stores first, Ronnie, Kat and I had fake ID's so we could get liquor. We were driving through town looking around, when we saw a pizza parlor, and decided we would have pizza tonight and buy groceries the next day, giving us more time to plan meals later. We all ordered what we wanted, and Abby was still standing at the counter. She walked to our table smiling.

"Guess what"?

I looked at her, "What Abby"?

"I have a job, I start on Friday".

We were amazed, quiet, shy Abby had a job when we had been in town less than three hours.

"That is great Abby, do they need anyone else"? Kat asked.

"By the way, they do. They are looking for one more. Hurry and the job may be yours" Kat ran to the counter, filled out the application, and came back with a smile. "I got it""

Ronnie said, "I am happy for you two. Now Sam and I need to find one, and we will be set".

This was a great pizza parlor. This pizza had awesome crust and you could buy it by the slice. It was the best pizza I had ever ate. We went back to the condominium to sleep because we were exhausted. It felt good to be here, we were happy and excited for what lay ahead of us.

We agreed that there would be no stupid stunts. We hoped to meet boys, but if we decided to sleep with them and brought them to our place we all had to agree it was okay. We figured with the two bedrooms it wouldn't be a problem unless we brought two guys in at once. I was still a virgin, so was Abby. Ronnie, and Kat were both on the pill and had been sexually active for some time, but Abby and I held out. We wanted the right one and the right reason to have sex, and Abby, preferred marriage. For me it would happen when it happened.

We slept in the first morning. We put on our swimsuits, grabbed our towels, and headed for the beach. No one was on our beach, not a single soul. Why not? I wondered. We saw a couple in the pool area with a small child and decided to ask them.

"Hello, we just arrived last night. We were wondering why no one is on the beach". Kat was the brave one.

The gentleman laughed, "Yeah, we have been here two days and no one has gone to that beach. If you want to swim in the ocean, I suggest you go further up north to where the hotels are. It is just a mile or so up the beach. The beach here drops off quickly, and the undertow is awful. It isn't as it showed in the brochures".

"Wow, we have found a few things that were misrepresented from the web site". Ronnie said.

"Yeah, we did too. Fortunately, we are only staying two more days. The pool is nice and the hot tub does work. Good luck, ladies." He nodded at us and we began to walk away.

We all looked at each other. Now what do we do? We prepaid for three months. We were stuck with it. So what if we had to drive a bit, as long as we had a place to eat and sleep we could handle driving to a nice safe beach. We did place a letter of complaint in the manager's box. We wrote him, we would be sending one to the National Tourism Guide as well.

We all jumped into the car and drove north. We found a dead end street on the beach with parking. We had to pay for parking but we would be on a nice beach where we saw many people seeming to have fun, and we wanted to have fun. We walked out to the shore and the sand was so soft beneath our feet. It wasn't hot as I had expected; it was rather nice. We laid out our towels and refreshments and headed toward the water. The water felt great. It was comfortable.

We played and splashed each other; we ran and pushed each other under the water. You could see the bottom pretty far out. We had a blast. We got out for a while, drank some sodas and ate some snacks. Then we buried each other in the sand. Abby made a mermaid out of Kat.

We took lots of pictures. It was so cute. We had Ronnie's lap top and mine, so we could send pictures to our families. We lay in the sun, turning from side to side. We had on our protective sun-block, but we played in the water so often that it didn't stay on. We spent all afternoon playing in the water getting burned but having a great time.

We headed back to the car with all our stuff in tow wasted from exhausted from playing in the water and the summer sun. When we hit the pavement bare-foot it was like walking on coals. It was flat hot. We jumped back in the sand, and put our shoes on, got in the car and headed back to the condo.

We saw a few signs in storefronts for 'Help Wanted'. We made some notes for Ronnie and me to come back and apply. We stopped at a quick stop and got a local paper. We looked for entertainment and possible employment.

Ronnie and I went over the paper and marked several positions we might like. Most of the jobs were part-time, which was good, as we didn't want anything to keep us away from having fun over the summer. We just wanted some extra spending money or emergency money.

We spent some time at the pool that evening, talking to some of the residents about places to go and see. There were a couple of nice guys that gave us information. They were staying here for the summer also, but they had already been here for three weeks; they were older guys, on summer break from college in Virginia.

We met a young couple from Texas, It was so funny to listen to them talk. They were friendly and told us everything they had done on their vacation. Most people stay here by the week, they told us, so we would be meeting many new people all summer.

We made our plans for the next day. We were going to drop Abby and Kat off where we were yesterday at the beach, and Ronnie and I were going looking for jobs. We had cell phones so if they wanted to leave they could call or text us. We hit probably twenty places for jobs. Ronnie even checked one at the Humane Society, which was her most desired place. I kind of liked it too, but didn't have the experience she had with animals.

One of the businesses was a law firm. They offered the job right away to Ronnie, but she turned it down. She only came in for my benefit. They then offered me the job, and I accepted it. I would have to dress office casual, I didn't bring many dress clothes with me, but Ronnie had some for me to wear. I would work three days a week, four to six hours a day. I would work Monday, Tuesday, and Wednesday, from nine o'clock to one o'clock or later if need be.

It sounded easy and a new experience for me. I would be filling, running errands, doing some Internet research, etc. It seemed right up my alley. They offered $10.0 an hour, which was great. I thought I shouldn't tell Abby and Kat how much I would be making. Ronnie didn't care if she made anything; she didn't need the money only something to do with her time.

We found a place that rented scooters. We rented two of them for the summer. Abby and Kat worked usually the same hours so they rode together. I could use the other one to go to work. If we all wanted one to ride around on we could rent them by the day or week later. We thought we were set.

# Chapter Two

We were having a great time in Florida. The guys in our condo unit, Steve and Trent, were so much fun. They took us to a party and introduced us to their friends. We were hanging with college kids and being treated just like them. We were given drinks, guys were talking to us, and girls were pleasant completely, unlike high school girls.

One guy, Mick really liked Ronnie. He followed her everywhere she went. I didn't know if she was playing hard to get or wasn't sure about him yet. I watched and laughed.

Abby stayed close to me. She was uneasy at this party. Kat was off with a boy she had met; she was already laughing, dancing and drinking with him. I saw Ronnie finally in a serious conversation with Mick and knew then she liked him.

A couple of young men came over to Abby and me, asking how long we were here, what we did, and so on and so on. Only one of them was doing the talking, the other one was restless and kind of a jerk. He kept looking over his shoulder all the time. I told them we would be starting college in the fall, and we were here for three months, the four of us.

One was cute the other guy was standoffish, he had a hard face, and he was tall, broad shoulders, and looked kind of mean. He had a shadow of a beard, dark complexion, and he had deep, dark eyes. I kept looking at him, and when he looked at me his eyes where shinny and scary but then he would look away, he wanted to leave. It seemed as if he didn't want to be seen with us, so I started acting disinterested in them, they finally left.

I noticed Abby was not having a good time. I told Ronnie and Kat we were leaving, but they both wanted to stay. We walked toward our condo;

thank goodness, we didn't have to walk too far. The temperature was nice and cool, the sky was full of stars, and the moon was bright, so we had lots of light.

We were walking on the beach when we heard a car, which sounded out of place on the beach. I turned around, and it was a dune buggy, with two guys in it. When they got close, I recognized them from the party. It was the cute boy and his freaky friend.

They stopped beside us, asking why we left the party and where we lived. I told them Abby and I just lived up the beach and didn't need a ride. I couldn't remember their names, the freaky guy told his friend to move on, I laughed. The cute guy got out of the dune buggy and asked us to sit and have a drink with them. We were leery and scared of them, because no one else was around.

We looked at each other then nodded. The cut guy introduced himself as Sam. He sat next to Abby. Abby started laughing at things Sam was saying. Sam moved closer to her. They seemed to like the same things, reading, tennis, and they both sang. They sat on the sand facing each other.

The freaky guy finally got out of the dune buggy and stood beside me. Freaky guy was what I called him in my mind because I still hadn't heard his name mentioned. So I didn't know what to call him. I was afraid of him but I knew I had to be cool and not let them see my fear. He was nice looking, but I didn't know what to say.

I crossed my arms across my chest. So, I said my voice cracking some, "Hey man, are you here for the summer?"

He said with a smirk on his face, "Yeah sort of, I go in college, but I was born and raised in Florida, in Ft Lauderdale Area. My parents lived there. Well my Dad does now."

"Cool, why here then instead of there?" I inquired.

"I am here to get away from my Dad." He said quickly.

"Yeah, that is what we are doing too." I laughed.

I continued, "Where do you go to school?"

"I go to Harvard Law School." He was only answering what I asked, not adding anything. He seemed disinterested and anxious.

I was afraid he was thinking me to be an idiot now, but I couldn't stop myself. The words kept coming out of my mouth. "Wow, that is where I wanted to go, but I was accepted at the University of Tulsa instead."

I hesitated feeling my face flush, why I couldn't just shut up I didn't know. These guys may want to hurt us. Looking around the beach, it was deserted. I memorized his face. He had a scar over his right eyebrow; deep laugh lines, or frown lines which made him, look dangerous. He had a strong square jaw line, and at least a day's beard growth.

He noticed my expression, looking around, "Are you scared of us"? He smirked.

I laughed, and then snorted, "No! Yeah, I am a little".

Smirking again "Don't worry; we are not killers or anything.".

My voice squeaked out. "I am working for a law firm part time this summer doing odd jobs for them."

"That sounds good. Get your start, and get experience anywhere you can, if you really want to go into law." He looked down at the ground, and then he smiled. He pointed to the sand like asking me to sit. I hesitated but sat down and he sat beside me.

I relaxed some and saw he did too.

I sighed, "Yeah, my Dad is an attorney in Minnesota. He actually works for Ronnie's Dad, one of my other friends. They are still at the party."

He nodded his head, taking a deep breath before speaking. "I wanted something else when I started college, but you know how parents can be? My father and his father before him were attorneys or judges, so that was what I was raised and primed for. Not much choice you know." He hung his head picking at the sand on the ground. Occasionally throwing pebbles or sticks out toward the water.

"Yeah, I do." I paused, "What did you want to do?"

He looked off into the ocean, he sighed, and said, "I want to help people, low income people, give back instead of taking all the time. I live a privilege life, and I want to know what it is like to be normal." He was interesting; I liked listening to him talk. He had a nice deep voice with authority; he was somewhat relaxed, and actually trying to hold a conversation. I found myself flushed now for a different reason. I liked him.

"That sounds like Ronnie. She wants to be a veterinarian. Her father hates the idea." I laughed.

"Sounds right. Attorneys think their way of life, their job choices, or any choice is their way or the highway is the only right way. I guess that is why they are such good arguers."

"My dad is okay as far as a dad goes. He does some pro bono work, while working for the Ellsworth Law Firm. I am not a favorite child". I hit my forehead with my palms; "I didn't mean to say that. He gives me a place to live and feeds me. He works hard, he's gone a lot, we are not wealthy, but we get by okay. My mom works also. Sorry, I don't know what normal is." I felt so stupid with my blabbing.

He looked at me now. "All attorneys aren't the same that is why I decided to stay in law. I want to help the less fortunate. I want to work with the district attorney's office or be able to do pro bono like your father does." He smiled at me. I looked away.

"Well, you have to do what is right for you. How far into law are you?" I was still looking down the beach not at him.

"This is my last year." I still felt his eyes on me.

"Have you applied for a position anywhere? I mean, looked where you might want to be located? Maybe here in Florida?"

He laughed out loud, "Hell No! I definitely do not want to work in Florida. I have looked in the Mid-west and the central part of the US, even as far as the West Coast."

"Do you have a large family?" looking back at him now.

He had his arms around his knees and his head rested on his shoulder looking at me. "No, I am the only child. I just don't get along with my dad." ... "My mom died, several years back. She was an attorney too and did nothing but pro bono work."

He looked down a moment I guess remembering her. "I remember she was kind and everyone liked her." Shaking his head now, "Hell I was so young. I want to believe she was kind."

"I'm sorry." This guy should be one of the misfits. I like him. He is nice, and I shouldn't have judged him, I knew better, I have been judged, it hurts, and it is wrong.

"It is okay, enough talk about that. Why did you leave the party?" looking back at me.

"We, Ah . . . Abby and I weren't enjoying ourselves there." I felt nervous again.

With a huge smile, on his face, "So you walk home on a deserted beach. Do you know any pervert or stranger could accost you out here"?

"Well . . . we didn't think that way. Ah . . . not until you . . . and . . . your friend, came barreling up the beach toward us."

He laughed, a booming laugh, looking up, "Ha. . . . Ha . . . Ha . . . So, you thought we might be the bad guys. Why did you sit with us then?" Ah, that smile and laugh changed everything. He was adorable; he was so handsome when he smiled. Those deep dimples made me smile back at him.

"We . . . I mean I . . . were more afraid not to . . . Where could we run? You had a vehicle; we didn't have much of a choice." He shook his head. I looked at Abby and Freaky guys' friend.

Freaky guy looked over at them too, "He's an okay dude. We go to school together. We came here to spend the summer, and we live up the beach a ways."

"I am sorry, but I don't know your name."

He laughed again. "My name is Edward, Edward Anderson III."

"It is nice to meet you Edward. My name is Samantha 'Sam' Lord." I stuck my hand out to shake his.

"'Sam', that is a good name for you. My friend's name is also 'Sam', hope I don't get confused," Laughing.

"Me too!" I blushed, I was glad it was dark so he couldn't see my red face. I was beginning to feel comfortable with him.

He lay back on the sand then turned over his on elbow, and rested his head on his hand. "You are from Minnesota that is a long way from here. What made you choose Clearwater Beach?"

"Well, we, you know the four of us . . . we all wanted different places. So we put our choices in a box and drew one. Clearwater won."

"So how is it so far?"

"Our condo isn't what it was advertised to be, but it is okay. We have a roof over our heads, a kitchen, it's clean, and we have a place to sleep. Three of us have jobs."

"Sounds good, you have thought this all out. Good luck."

"Are you working while you are here?"

"No, I don't have too, Daddy pays for everything. I have trust funds from my grandfather, from both sides, actually." He rolled onto his back crossing his arms across his face. "You know it would be nice to have something to do besides sit on the beach and look pretty. Maybe I will look for a job. What Law Firm are you at?" He laughed.

Smiling, "I am at McCray and Neill." I looked at that little scar above his eye, following it down his face, such a nice straight nose, full lips. I lingered, on his full kissable lips moving down his rock hard chest. I could see through his t-shirt, and then a trim waist and hips. My eyes roamed down to his crotch, smiling, lingering too long, his legs seemed to go stiff.

I looked quickly back at his face and he was watching me. I gasped, "Oh my God!" I buried my face in my knees I was hugging so hard I almost cut off the circulation.

He chuckled, "Sam, I looked you over earlier at the party. Thank God you didn't catch me or you might not be sitting here with me now." He laughed again. "I know where McCray and Neill Law Firm are." He said trying to change the subject, you could hear the laughter in his voice, "Do you mind if I apply for a job there?"

I shook my head, "Of course not. It would be nice to have a nice face around," I gasped again swearing at myself, "I mean a familiar face."

He laughed again, "Great, Monday I'll be in, Can I use your name as a reference?"

I was still hiding my face, "If you want to, but I don't have any clout, I just started."

"I bet you will love it and I bet they will love you."

I raised my head with just my chin now on my knees. "I already like it; I file and do odd jobs, you know but they let me do stuff for them on the computer, and I enjoy it. I like the people there."

"Good deal."

I heard Abby laughing, and then she called out to me, "Sam, it is late, shouldn't we get going?"

"Okay Abby." I looked at Edward; "I guess Abby is ready to go."

"Yeah, I heard that. Does she always tell you what to do?" He shook his head, "Sorry, I didn't mean anything by that. Can I call you?" He stood up holding his hand out for me, then pulling me up gently. I was looking up at him, standing too close. I could smell his scent.

I sighed, "Yes she does, and yes, I would like you to call me. Are you sure you want too?" He turned his head to the side smirking. I gave him my number and Abby and I walked down the beach. I turned around, and they were watching us. I waived and they waived back and then I saw them drive away as we reached our condo. When we walked in, Ronnie and Kat were furious with us, wanting to know where we had been, what we had been doing and so on.

"Hey, we are big girls, just like you are. We wanted to leave and you didn't. We told you we were leaving, and you seemed fine with it. We were stopped on the beach walking home, by a couple of the guys from the party. We sat and talked awhile with them and had a beer. Is that a problem with you?" saying by raising my voice with too much attitude.

"No Sam, but we were worried. You left over an hour ago."

"Well don't worry." I was being too short with Ronnie. I was angry with her at the moment or maybe myself for saying such stupid things on the beach. I was afraid he would never call, no, I knew he wouldn't call. I was an idiot.

"Okay. We agreed no bosses. No one tells the other what to do or when to be home. We wanted our freedom from our parents, but it seems as if I brought mine with me, Ronnie." I glared at her.

She looked down, "You are right, Sam, I am sorry."

"Okay." Looking over at Abby and she looked in a daze or something. "Abby, are you okay?"

"Yes Sam, I liked Sam… the guy Sam . . . you know . . . on the beach?"

"Did you give him your number?" we all asked at once.

"No... he didn't ask."

Kat raised her arms in the air. "Well I guess we all had a good time tonight."

We laughed and went to bed.

# Chapter Three

We slept in on Sunday, hearing the rain outside and. knowing we wouldn't be spending the day at the beach or the pool. I heard Abby and Kat stirring in the other room. I yawned and stretched, it felt so good, waking when I wanted and, being lazy if I wanted to, with no one to yell at me when to get up. It was a wonderful feeling. I looked over at Ronnie, and she was snickering at me.

"What?"

"You looked like you did when you were little, stretching, and rolling all over the bed."

"So, what is wrong with that?"

"Nothing, it just reminded me of those days. I guess I miss them, you know."

"Not me, I was thinking about how nice it is to be my own boss."

"Sorry about last night."

"It's okay, I understand, I overreacted too. I'm sorry too Ron."

"Friends?"

"Of course Ronnie, you know I love you and always will." We both sat up. I knew if she beat me to the bathroom, I would be waiting for a long time, so I jumped up and ran. When I got to the door, I turned around and stuck my tongue out at her and shut the door.

I heard her laughing, telling me to watch out. I brushed my teeth, showered, and shaved. Damn, I forgot my clothes. I would have to go out and get them. I put my T-shirt back on, and when I was completely ready except for dressing I left the bathroom. Ronnie was lying in bed, waiting her turn. I had only been in there about twenty minutes, and I knew she would take an hour.

She stood up, stretched, and went to do her thing. "You know payback in hell." I dressed, brushed my hair again adding only mascara. I was ready for the day.

Abby and Kat were still in their pj's eating cereal when I went in the kitchen.

"Good morning, ladies. Well, afternoon I guess."

"Yeah, what's so good about it?" Kat said.

"We are alive and living in Florida, where we can do anything we want."

"It's raining on a Saturday, you idiot." Abby remarked.

"Hey, that's not nice. I like the rain. We can still do other things. Remember those museums and bookstores? Shopping? There is a mall."

"I just feel lazy with the rain." Abby said.

Kat just made a noise. "Humph . . ."

"Come on guys, let's do something."

"I don't want to," Kat replied.

"Maybe Ronnie will have a good idea when she gets in here." I fixed myself a bowl of cereal and sat with them at the table. Kat went into the living room and turned on the television. She was surfing channels but couldn't find anything she wanted to watch, so she clicked it off.

"We could play cards or some game." I suggested.

"Nah," they both remarked in unison.

I finished my cereal and took my bowl to the sink, picking up Kat's and Abby's too. I rinsed them out and put them in the dishwasher. I walked out onto the balcony, through the living room, sitting and watched the rain. I thought I should wait for Ronnie, before I got into a book or something else. A book, and sitting on the balcony could last all day.

I heard the guys downstairs yelling and laughing. I looked over the edge watching them. They were chasing each other in the rain. They were such goofy guys, like big kids. I mean, they were older than we were, but had no maturity about them at all.

I saw Trent pull Steve close to him and kissed him on the mouth. Oh, I got it now. I watched them and laughed. They were at least having fun, no matter what. The girls up here all acted as if they had PMS or something. I heard Ronnie come out of the bathroom, and I knocked on the sliding door, just off our bedroom, so she would open it.

"Hey Ronnie, what do you want to do today?"

"Nothing, it is raining."

"You are just like those two in there, dead beats. Look outside at the guys; they are having fun in the rain."

"Yeah, tomorrow they will probably be sick."

"I don't want to just sit here all day, Ronnie." I went back into the living room and stood there with my hands on my hips looking at the two lazy girls. Kat was on the couch, and Abby was lying in the floor, hugging her pillow, as they watch television.

"I can't believe you two."

"What? We worked all week; we just want a day to do nothing, just rest."

"Rest, I work too, and you were off yesterday." I don't want to sit here all day. I went back into the bedroom.

"Ronnie, it is raining, so I can't ride the scooter. Can I borrow your car? I want to go to the library. If you rather take me, and pick me up, that would be okay."

"Sure. No one else wants to do anything?"

"No they are too lazy to do anything. They don't even put their dirty dishes in the sink."

"Sure go ahead." I got my bag with my laptop, camera, and bag and headed for the public library.

The library was nice, it was easy to find and pretty inside. I found a couple of interesting books, so I signed up for a temporary card, and checked out the books. I decided to go to the coffee shop, next door, to read. I turned on the laptop, set my phone out on vibrate, and checked my email. I had one from Mom and replied to her telling her I was fine. I had a couple from other friends, well school chums, but I replied to them, telling them about all the fun we were having in Florida. . . . lie, lie, and lie. Ha! They didn't need to know it was raining and I was sitting in a coffee shop alone.

I ordered a Chai Tea Latte and checked out places to visit in our area. There were a couple of interesting places. The Lowry Park Zoo in Tampa, the Clearwater Marine Aquarium, plantation all over the area, boating, shopping, balloon flights, nightclubs, and so on. There was an app for The Plantations, wasn't sure about that one. We could go boating, shopping, Fantasy Flights Balloon Rides, nightclubs, and so on. Some of these might be fun to do on a sunny day.

I wrote down addresses of interesting sites. I thought we would have to do other things besides just laying on the beach. I decided to read a while. I was getting into the book when someone tapped me on the shoulder and said, "Hey good looking." I jumped clear out of my skin. It was freaky guy, Edward, just not so freaky anymore. He was smiling at me and I was staring at him.

"Hi, how are you?" blushing thinking about looking him up and down and getting caught.

"I'm great, what are you doing here?" He asked.

"I couldn't stand to sit at home with nothing. So, I went to the library and checked out a couple of books. Then I came here to drink coffee, well actually, tea and check the internet out. What are you doing here?"

"About the same, no books but coffee and internet surfing was on my agenda." He stood there not saying anything. I thought, dang I guess I had to ask him to sit down, but I wasn't sure what to do, but I did want him to stay.

"Do you want to join me?" I asked with a shaky voice.

"Yeah, sure that sounds okay." He sat and looked at my books, turning them over to read the back covers and laid them down. "What are you drinking?"

"Chi Tea"

"Is it good?"

I shook my head, "Yeah, I like it. Would you like to try it?" He took a drink of my tea, dang he actually took a drink.

"That is pretty good. I think I'll get one." He walked over to the counter, ordered his drink, waited for it then came back and sat down. "Here, you can take mine and I'll take yours, since, I took a drink."

"No, that's okay. Mine is half gone." That was nice of him, but I should have taken him up on it.

Looking around the room then back at me, "This rain makes it kind of a sad and lazy day."

"Yeah, my friends wouldn't get out at all. They all stayed home, lying around doing nothing."

"My roommate is at home too, watching television. I was bored, so thought I would get some coffee here and saw you in the window."

"Oh." I felt like an idiot, I just say "Oh." Man, what should I say to him? He seems nice but a little scary. I didn't know, but there was something different about him, I didn't know if I trust him or not. He was watching me. He didn't smile often, but when he did it pulls me toward him.

"I still plan to apply at the law firm tomorrow. I look forward to have something to do with my time besides lying on the beach. That gets old real quick."

"Well, the beach isn't old with me yet, but yeah, I need something to do, or I go nuts. I guess a little too much energy sometimes." Bouncing in my chair, dang, that didn't come out right.

"Where did you say you were going to school?"

"I am going to the University of Tulsa, my friend Ronnie will be at the University of Oklahoma, so we will be close to each other, well about a hundred miles."

"Yeah, I remember you telling me that."

"You are at Harvard, right?"

"Yeah, that's right."

"Do you like it?" Looking up at him through my eye lashes while taking a drink of my tea.

His smile was nice and I loved those dimples, "Yeah, it is a good school. I really like a couple of my professors. They push me hard. One in particular, she thinks I have great potential and pushes me way beyond my limits. She makes me use my brain and think outside the box. I make okay grades."

"That's good." Now we sat again with nothing to say. I sighed looking outside, then back at the people at the counter.

He rested his elbows on the table, "Are you board?"

"Oh no, I just don't know what to talk about. I enjoy talking to you, really I do. I am not great about being interesting, I guess."

"You are interesting to me, Sam. I like you." He said in his husky voice that made me tingle.

I spit some of my tea out. "I'm so sorry about that. I didn't expect you to say that." I felt y face redden, "Thank you, I like you too." I knew he saw my red face. What was he thinking about me? I wished I could just talk to him like I do Ronnie. I can tell her anything. I thought Edward was a nice guy. He is nice looking, tall and intriguing. I hope working with him we will get to know each other better. I didn't know what to say now.

"Sam!"

"Yeah?" I looked up at him, worried I had been quiet too long.

"Will you go out on a date with me? I mean like to dinner, not anything fancy or serious, just dinner. Maybe go to the park and talk, something like that?"

I giggled; I was so embarrassed, red face getting redder. I bet my freckles were even blushing now, "Edward, I would like that."

He smiled at me, "Great! Tonight?"

"Wow, ah . . . sure, that will be fine. What time?"

"How about seven o'clock."

"Okay, do you want to meet somewhere?"

"Can I pick you up?"

"Okay... sure."

"I know you live on Gulf View Dr, but what apartment?"

I laughed, "Yeah, 3rd floor, 310."

"So okay, I will pick you up at seven."

"Casual?"

"Yeah, comfortable. Nothing fancy, like I said, wear what you want."

"Okay, sounds great." He then said he had a few things to do and left. I watched him walk away, and he turned around and smiled at me. He saw I was watching him walk away. I blushed and giggled. He waved bye to me. He had a nice body, and nice butt, too. I read for a while and then my phone vibrated. It was Ronnie, wondering where I was and what I was doing. I told her I was on my way back in a few. She said there was a party tonight at the beach. I told her I had a date.

She paused, and said sarcastically, "A date?"

"Yeah, is that a problem? He will be picking me up at seven." She didn't say anything. "I'll be there in a few, okay." I hung up the phone, smiling from ear to ear. Ronnie was always the one that got the date first, all the guys went crazy for her. Ronnie was so pretty and just a classy girl.

I drove to the condo, and when I opened the door, they bombarded with questions, what, who, where, etc. I told them it was Edward, and Abby had a fit.

"Freaky Guy" I told them he was nice, that we talked on the beach the other night and today at the coffee shop. I told them they could go to the party, and I might meet up with them later.

They were all ready for the party, wearing bathing suits, T-shirts, flip-flops, and coolers of beer. Thank goodness, it had stopped raining late this afternoon. They headed out on foot.

Ronnie told me I could take her car so I would have my own transportation, but I informed her I would be fine, as Edward was picking me up. They didn't want to leave until they saw him and made sure they all approved, but I told them to go on and leave me be.

They left reluctantly, at least they were gone. I sure didn't want them to make a big deal out of our date and embarrass me. I wore a pair of khaki capris, a white shirt tucked in, and a pair of tennis shoes. I had my wallet and money in my pocket, along with my cell phone. I was ready to go by six-thirty, so I sat and read my book until just before I thought he would arrive. I was so anxious and nervous at the same time. Man, I hoped I had the right opinion of him. I hope I was looking beyond his looks and more at what he had told me about himself.

The more I sat and waited, for what seemed like forever, the more nervous I got. I was ringing my hands when I heard a car pull up outside I looked out over the balcony windows and saw him get out. He was here.

I ran to the bathroom, checked my makeup, what little I wore. I turned around to make sure my clothes looked okay, took a deep breath, and heard him knock on the door. I turned off the lights, left the hall light on, and opened the door.

# CHAPTER FOUR

He was wearing khaki shorts, a white shirt, and tennis shoes. I burst out laughing, looking him up and down so did he look me up and down. That broke the ice. I knew it was going to be all right. He asked if I was ready, and I told him I was, unless he wanted me to change clothes. He told me I looked fantastic.

He was so cute when he laughed or smiled, but he didn't do it often I asked him to come in, but he motioned for me to come out. I was glad he didn't want to come in. We were still looking at each other; I was smiling about our clothes when we got to his car. He opened the door for me, shut it, and then walked around and got in.

"Where are we going?"

"It's a surprise." He looked over at me. "What kind of food do you like?"

"Well, I love Italian, Mexican, and hot dogs," I said laughing. "I am not much of a steak eater. I prefer vegetables and fruit to meat, usually. I mean I eat meat, I am not a vegetarian. Hot dogs seem to be my vise, I don't know why. What about you?"

"I hope what I chose is to your liking."

"Oh, okay. What did you choose?" I was smiling at him.

"I am not falling for that. Let me ask you about some different foods, okay?"

"Sure."

"Do you like Middle Eastern?"

"I don't know."

"What about Chinese?"

"Oh yes, I like some oriental foods. I even like some sushi, but it is usually with cream cheese and vegetables." I was laughing aloud.

"How about Indian food? You know, from India? Not American Indian?"

"Well, I have eaten Indian food; I know they use a lot of curry. Some of it is good, and it is rather hot, what I have tasted. I know they use goat, so I chose careful when I eaten it."

"Good"

"Is that where we are going?"

"Nope." We drove across the bridge to Tampa. We were winding through town, places I had never seen. He pulled into a parking lot that was empty. I thought, Man, this may not be a good restaurant if no one comes here.

He got out, came around, and opened my door, holding out his hand to help me out. I giggled, and then took his hand standing up. He shut asked. "Ready?" I looked up at him. Oh my, he was a very handsome man when he smiled, beautiful white straight teeth, and dimples on each cheek. I smiled at him, and then we headed for the front door. The name of the restaurant was Guido's Pizza.

I smiled, "Italian my first love. How did you know?"

"So, it's okay?"

"No one seems to be here, why?" I looked around, and the sign said closed. "Edward, the sign, look."

"Don't worry." About that time, a man opened the door saying, "Good evenings, Edward, how are you?" I looked up at Edward.

Edward replied to him, "Guido, I am excellent. Thank you so much for doing this for me. I just had to make our first date a memorable one. I wanted her to taste the best food she's ever eaten."

"It is my pleasure to do so for you, follow me, please." We followed him to the back of the room, and he sat us at a table all prepared for us. He said he would be right back. He walked to the front door, locked it, and then went behind the counter, and brought us water and menus. "What would you care to drink this evening?"

Edward said, "We would like a bottle of Shiraz, and the water is fine." He left the table, and I looked over at Edward amazed. I didn't know what to say.

"Edward . . . this is nice, but. . . . what, no why, is no one, no . . . I mean they are closed and going to serve us dinner. Why?"

"Because Guido is a friend of sorts of mine, and he is returning a favor. They have the best pizza in the world here. They have great lasagna also, but I love the pizza." He opened his menu. "Look over the menu, and you can have anything you want. If it is not on the menu, Guido will make it for you anyway."

I made a nervous giggle. What's with all this giggling? It is embarrassing me. "I like pizza, what kind do you like?"

"I like anything. My favorite is a pizza made with pesto sauce instead of marinara, topped with grilled chicken, mozzarella cheese, feta cheese, goat cheese, artichokes and secret spices."

"Wow that sounds good."

"I am happy to hear that. Anything else look good to you?"

"Yes, the fried mushrooms. Are they good?"

"Yes, they are wonderful."

Guido came back with a bottle of red wine and two glasses he placed on the table. "Have you decided what you would like to eat?"

"Yes, Guido, we want the artichoke pizza with pesto, an order of mushrooms, and garlic bread, please."

"Wonderful, Edward. Your favorite meal." He bowed toward me, took the menus, and left the table. Edward poured the wine in his glass, swirled it around, smelled it, took a small sip, and then swallowed. It was so romantic, so sexy the way he did that. He knew about choosing wines that would pair with certain foods, he was very proper,

He poured my glass and then his. I picked it up, and he toasted me, "To our first date." We clicked our glasses lightly and drank. It was wonderful. I liked this wine; it was dry with a hint of peppery spices, very mellow and easy to swallow."

"I like this wine; it is good, very smooth."

"I hoped you would like it, I prefer red wine usually to white. I like it dry."

"Me too. What little I drink, anyway. I am only eighteen remember?"

"Yes, but don't say that too loud, or Guido may come and take yours away." He laughed, and so did I. I was feeling comfortable with Edward; he was nice and polite. We talked about so many things, and laughed. Before I knew it, Guido had brought out some fried mushrooms and garlic bread. The mushrooms were very hot, they had just come out of the fryer, and I burned my mouth. Edward laughed at me again. I blew on it and stuffed it in my mouth again.

The spice on the crust tasted like cayenne, and some other savory spices. They were salty and so good. I didn't use the dips he had brought; I think it was ranch dressing and a red sauce, until I had eaten a couple of them. Edward was chomping down on them also. I was hungry; I hadn't eaten lunch today, so I was being a glutton.

Edward broke off a piece of the bread and offered it to me. I took it and it, was heavenly. It was toasted, with garlic and real butter which you could taste, rich and savory. There was basil and Italian seasoning on it, and loaded with cheeses. It was 'to die for' good. I was afraid I would be full before the pizza came. Guido brought the pizza and put it on a stand between us. He put a slice in my plate and a slice in Edwards's plate, and told us to enjoy, and if we wanted anything else to ring the little bell, he had placed on the edge of the table. He told us he would leave us to enjoy and walked back into the kitchen.

I looked at this pizza, it smelled marvelous. I cut it with my fork, and the crust was crisp, just how I like it. I took my first bite, and Edward was watching me, It was so good. The artichokes were fresh and tender, the chicken had a smoked taste, the pesto was great, and the blends of cheeses were the killer of it all. Those three cheeses together would make dirt taste good, I think.

"Oh Edward, this is great, this is the best pizza I have ever had, thank you."

"I was hoping you would agree with me on that." I liked this guy more and more. We got along so well, we agreed on foods, except he liked red meat, and liked it rare. We agreed on politics, books, likes, dislikes, even music. He was this freaky guy who rarely smiled, but when he did, my world seemed to get better. Wow, this was the man I was afraid of, wouldn't have taken a second look at, and almost told to get lost.

We ate until we were stuffed. I drank three glasses of wine, and I was tipsy. Edward drank only one, he was drinking water now. He was being responsible, since he was driving. Edward rang the little bell, and Guido came out.

"Thank you so much, Guido. This was the perfect meal, and we will definitely be back during your regular hours."

"Edward, for what you have done for me, I will cook for you anytime, anywhere, anything. Thank you, my boy." I looked a little puzzled, but didn't say anything.

Guido took our food to the back and returned with them boxed up to go. He told us to have a nice evening and he hoped to see us again soon.

"Thank you, it was delicious," I said.

Guido pulled out my chair, and Edward stood up. "Guido, you out-did yourself as usual. Tell your family, hello for me." He left a hundred dollar bill on the table, Guido tried to argue with him, but he held his hand over Guido's hand. This is for you, my friend. You deserve it.

"Thank you again."

"Yes, of course Edward." Edward took the boxes and we headed for the door. Guido unlocked it and we left as he re-locked the door behind us.

"Wow that was nice, Edward."

"Yes, Guido is a great guy. He had some problems with the owner of this building, and I helped him legally with some stuff. He then bought the building, and since then his business has been booming. I asked him for a favor, and he was happy to do this for me. He is a great guy and has a nice family."

"You are a smart man, and make great choices in restaurants."

"I like to think so. I am not a licensed attorney yet, so I did it pro bono of course, just for the experience, and it worked out great. I helped a great family who needed it."

"You are a nice guy, I knew it." He just shrugged. We talked and drove back toward Clearwater. We had the windows down and the radio on. It was so nice outside, and the music was playing softly. I would look at him occasionally, and he would be looking at me. I giggled repeatedly. I was not usually a giggler, but with him, I just couldn't quit.

"What would you like to do now?"

"I don't know that meal was so great, can you top it?"

"Probably, not"

"My friends are at a party on the beach, do you want to go there?"

"If you want, but I don't like the party groups. I am not much of a drinker and don't do drugs, and some of those people are just stupid."

"I agree with you on that. I am usually not much of a drinker until tonight. You got me almost drunk on wine."

"I am sorry; I didn't mean to do that. Are you alright?"

"Yes, I am fine, just a little lightheaded now. The wind helped a lot."

"How about a walk on the beach away from the party?"

"Okay, sounds good." He drove to my condo and parked before getting out to open my door. He grabbed the food.

"Hey let's put this in your fridge so it doesn't spoil. Your friends can try it tomorrow."

"Sure." We went upstairs, and I was a little reluctant now. I was woozy, and we were going into my apartment without my friends there. I was hesitant. I smiled up at him.

"I promise I am a good guy, I won't try anything. I will wait outside for you."

I looked at him, and said, "No, it is okay. Come in, I am not afraid of you." But I really was scared to death. He came in with me. I put the food up and told him I was going to get a jacket just in case. He waited just inside the apartment door. I returned and he looked so nice standing there in the low light of the room. I smiled at him; he seemed to smile back, but only a lift of his mouth on one side.

"Are you ready?"

"Ready." He opened the door. I shut it and locked it, and we headed for the beach. I told him the party was to the right, so we walked left. I decided to remove my shoes, and so did he. We carried them, sometimes stepping in the water that was washing up on the beach. We walked and talked for an hour. We found some rocks, and sat down, and listened to the waves hitting the beach and the rocks. It was so peaceful and relaxing. His hand touched mine. I jumped.

He said, "I'm sorry. I didn't mean to scare you."

"It's alright, I just wasn't expecting it." He touched my hand again and held it. We entwined our fingers together, and it was nice.

"I wish we had brought a blanket, maybe a radio."

"I could sing to you."

"Great, go for it."

I laughed, "No you don't want to hear me sing."

"Ah, I thought you were serious." He let go of my hand and sat on the sand, so I moved down beside him. The cool breeze was blowing our hair, and you could smell the salt water. He lay back with his hands under his head. I looked down at him, I wanted to kiss him, but I would never make a move like that. I lay back and put my jacket under my head. We looked up at the stars. They were so bright.

He gasped, "Look there is Jupiter, the largest planet in our solar system. First, the moon is the brightest, and then Mars, and then Jupiter".

"Wow, I didn't know that."

"Jupiter and Mars are basically the only planets you can see without a telescope."

"How do you know so much about so many things?"

"I read. I never had anyone to talk to growing except Cook and Granger, so I spent my time in libraries with books. My dad was gone most of the time, with his young new girl-friends. The girl-friends didn't much care for me until I was older, and then they wanted to sleep with me too. I hated them. I hated him too." He paused. "I am sorry; I didn't mean to say that."

I turned on my side facing him, with my head resting on my hand up on my elbow. "Edward, it is okay, you can say anything you want to me. I am not a gossip, and I don't betray my friend's trust or secrets, okay."

"It is not a secret, me hating my father, but I just don't tell everyone about my family life." He looked up at me, leaned in, and kissed me.

I jumped back, falling on my back and, trying to get up, but I was so stunned, feeling clumsy and stupid as well.

He jumped up, trying to help me up, but I stumbled around, falling back on the sand.

"Sam, please let me help you up, I am so sorry."

I lay still and let him help me. We were standing facing each other. He was looking down.

"Sam, I just wanted to kiss you, I have all evening. I am sorry for being too forward. Can we maybe forget that happened?"

"Edward, it is okay, I don't know why I am acting like I am tonight. Yeah, I do. I haven't gone on many dates. I don't know what to expect or what to do. I like you. I wanted you to kiss me, but at that moment I was. . . . I guess . . . concerned for you, and not expecting it. So . . . do you . . . maybe think . . . you could try it again."

He looked at me with amazing bright eyes, leaned forward, and kissed me ever so gentle.

"Now that was a nice first kiss. Can I do it again?"

"Yes." He kissed me again, but not too deep or too forward, just nice kissing. His lips were soft and warm. I opened my mouth, slightly but he did not ravish me. He just was kissing nice, soft, even kisses. He pulled away.

"Sam, I like you. I like you a lot. Will you go out with me again?"

"Yes, Edward, I would love to."

"It is late, we should be heading back." I didn't want to go, but we did. He took my hand, and we walked back to the condo. I heard laughter when we got close to the apartment. I knew my friends were back and with a crowd. He looked at me, and I sighed.

"I think your friends are back from the party."

"Yeah, I think so too. They brought company with them." Ronnie saw us walking up and ran to me, hugging me.

"Man, you missed a great party, you should have come." She looked questionably at Edward.

"Ronnie, this is Edward. Edward, this is my best friend, Ronnie."

"Hi, it's nice to meet you."

"Hey, Abby, Kat, come here. Kat, this is Edward. Abby, you remember him, don't you?"

Kat said, "What's up?" Abby stood back. She didn't like Edward from the party, the first time we saw him.

"We had a lovely dinner and went for a walk on the beach."

Ronnie asked, "Where did you go?"

"We went to a restaurant in Tampa. It was great. I . . . I mean, we brought you guys some food."

Abby said hatefully, "Yes, Sam I remember Edward and his friend from the party and the beach.

Kat looked confused. "Come meet the guys and join us." We walked up to the pool area, and they were all drinking and partying. There were three guys waiting for the girls. I didn't want to party with them. I knew Edward didn't either. Edward nodded at the guys, and they called out his name, saying "hey" to him. Well, I guessed he knew them. We all sat around the pool area, and they were all drinking, laughing, and talking. Edward and I were talking quietly.

Someone yelled, "Turn some music on." When the music was playing, Kat and Ronnie were dancing, so two of the guys joined them. Abby looked miserable as usual, she didn't like the guy she was paired with.

Edward whispered to me, "The guy by your friend sitting there is a jerk. Watch her, okay. He is a bully and pushy."

"Okay, I know . . . I mean, I can tell by her actions she doesn't like him."

"Good, she is safer not to like this guy. Sam, the guy with me the other night, likes your friend. He is a decent guy as far as I know."

"She liked him too, I could tell. I am so glad he started talking to her. It helped her self-esteem."

"I think I should go." He said as he squeezed my hand.

"Okay, I understand."

"Sam, will you walk me to my car?"

"Yes of course." We walked hand in hand to his car. He placed both his hands on my face, looked into my eyes, leaned in, and then kissed me. I sighed.

"Sam, I like you. I will see you at the Law firm tomorrow. Hope I get a job."

"Yeah, I'll be there."

"Good, remember we can't act too friendly at work."

"I know."

"I am going to want to kiss you every time I see you." I smiled. He got in his car and drove off. I went back to my friends and sat by Abby. I butted in when the boy beside her was talking, and she looked at me and said, 'Thank you' without making a sound.

The boy was getting pissed. I told him not to be such a jerk. He stood up, called out to his friends, and said let's go guys. The two with Ronnie and Kat weren't ready to leave, but Kat told them she needed to get to bed because we all have to work the next day. Ronnie agreed, so the boys left.

We went upstairs and talked for hours about Edward and my date, and they ate all the food we brought back. They told me about the party, and I warned Abby about the guy that was sitting by her. She said he wouldn't be around again. Abby was hard on herself, and it made it hard for boys to notice her. She was meticulous and opinionated, making it difficult for anyone to like her sometimes. I guessed it was her protection mode. We had to try to help her have a good time this summer.

We went to bed around two-thirty. It was going to be difficult getting up tomorrow and working. I showered and went to bed so Ronnie could have it in the morning. Besides, I had been lying in the sand on the beach and felt miserable. I slept well and dreamt of Edward, kissing me. Oh, he had fangs. He was a vampire chasing me through the woods, and I was running but laughing. I wanted him to catch me. He was so good-looking and so sexy. Then I jumped and woke up. Whoops, wrong Edward. I snickered to myself and went back to sleep.

# CHAPTER FIVE

I woke up before the alarm went off. I stretched and jumped up, I was in a great mood. The sun was shining, and I felt wonderful. I thought about Edward and smiled to myself, taking a deep breath. I looked at Ronnie, and she had her head covered.

I brushed my teeth, washed my face, and went through all the clothes in the closet. I decided on wearing some of Ronnie's clothes, trying to look as cute as I could. I went to the kitchen to fix myself a piece of toast and drank some milk. Abby and Kat were still sleeping too; they didn't have to work until eleven.

I got my bag, putting my phone and stuff in it, strapped it over my shoulder, and headed out the door. I rode my scooter to work. When I arrived, I saw that Edward's car was parked in the lot, so I parked next to it. I felt even better knowing I was going to see him in a moment.

I pulled myself together, straightened my clothes, entering the office, saying 'Good morning' to everyone. I sat at my desk, put my bag away, turned on my computer, checked messages, and went to the file cabinets. There was stuff already there for me to do, so I got busy filing. I finished quickly and went back to my desk. I was looking around for Edward but didn't see him anywhere.

My boss came in and remarked on my prompt arrival and the work I had already done. She told me I was doing a great job, and she appreciated my attitude and work performance. I was so pleased. She went into her office. I was checking to see if I had received any new duty requests, but nothing popped up. I didn't know what to do. I looked around and then went to Renee's office.

"Excuse me, Renee, I don't seem to have anything to do right now. Is there anything you have for me?"

"Well, I hired a new guy, Edward. He is in the conference room. You can tell him about our procedures and check to see if he needs anything or has any questions regarding the forms he is filling out. Here is our procedure book, take it with you, and if you need anything, let me know. This is a great help I can call some clients back. Thank you, Sam."

"I am happy to be of assistance, Renee." Whoopee, that was where Edward was hiding. I took the book, grabbed a pen from my desk, and went into the conference room. I thought, *I was going to do this as a professional.*

I stuck my hand out to Edward to shake. "Hello, my name is Samantha Lord. Everyone calls me 'Sam'. It is nice to meet you Edward." He smirked. "Do you have any questions regarding the forms you are filing out?"

"No ma'am, I am doing fine."

"Oh, I guess there is no reason then for me to stay."

"Oh, wait . . . I have lots of questions."

I sat down, "Hi Edward."

"Hi, Sam".

"Renee asked me to come help you with your forms and tell you our procedures here at the firm. I was thrilled to do this small favor for her. I looked all over for you. I saw your car but didn't know where you were."

"I got here early"

"Me too, but you still beat me here."

"I am happy to see you. Did you miss me?"

"It has only been a few hours since we last saw each other. Yes, I have thought about you. I even dreamed about you."

"Ooh, that sounds interesting."

"It wasn't what you are thinking." I was embarrassed. I felt my face turning red.

"And what am I thinking."

"I mean . . . never mind, let's just change the subject, okay."

"No, I want to know what you dreamt about."

"Edward, I can't tell you. We are at work and this is business."

"Okay, then you must tell me later." I blushed even more. He laughed aloud and I had to turn around.

"Ah . . . would you like a drink, some water, or something?"

"No, Sam I am fine. Let's talk about procedure, okay." I opened the book, and we went over everything that I recalled they told me about when I started. He reached out and touched my hand. I pulled back. He completed his forms, and then we stood to leave the conference room, pulled me close and kissed me.

I smiled and pushed him back, I shook my finger at him. I opened the door and took him and his paperwork to Renee's office. She greeted us, asking Edward to sit down and thanking me for helping her out. I left and went back to my desk, without a backward glance at Edward, but I was smiling inside.

I heard them laughing and her telling him what she expected of him. It was a businesslike conversation. I finished the filing again that had built up. I went back to my desk, checked messages, did the two requests I had, and sat back. It was going to be a long day with nothing to do I was afraid.

Renee and Edward came out of her office. She called me over to where they were. She told Edward she wanted him to go to the courthouse and look up some stuff, and then to the library. She wanted me to go with him so he could do the research and I could do the coping. She wanted us to get back here as soon as possible. She wanted this taken care of today and not dragged out it had to be perfect. We left in his car. He turned his head finally looking at me. He nodded, just nodded and I just nodded back. This felt great, The first day on the job, and Edward and I were together alone in his car, off going to do research work at the courthouse and library. It could take hours.

He pulled into a space at the courthouse, and we entered. We had to go through metal detectors and they searched my bag. He told me what we were looking for. We went to the records department, where he looked around, and when he found files he needed copies of, he gave them to me to copy. It was all business-like. For about thirty minutes back and forth, this went on. He was working fast and being precise on what he was looking for. I asked him what the hurry was. He said he wanted more time at the library so we could talk, and here there were too many people watching us. I understood and kept working whatever he told me to copy I copied.

We left the courthouse and went to the library. He called Renee, telling her what he had found and what we had copied, and she was so pleased. She told him a couple of things, so he had to pull over to write them down. I heard him say, "Sure, that will be great." Then he told her we should be done by one o'clock.

He asked her if we could stop for lunch and if she wanted us to bring her anything. He was listening to her and I heard him say he would see her then, and he hung up. He turned and looked at me.

"Okay, Sam, we go do our research, and then we will go to lunch. On Renee, of course."

"It is your first day, and we are already going out to lunch."

"Great, huh?"

"Okay, what should I look for, or how do I help you?"

"Well, I will check the index. I know what books I think I need, but I have to wait until I read certain cases to make sure. I know the case she is working on and what it is about, so. I understand what she wants."

"How do you know the case if it is your first day?"

"Well, I watch the news, I read the papers."

"Okay. Just point me in the right direction." I blushed for being an idiot and asking such a dumb question.

He worked diligently, reading, searching, and giving me stuff to copy. He asked for other books in the area. I found them and brought them back, and he read them over. He didn't let up. He asked me to follow him back to some old article bins down stairs. There wasn't anyone else around. He turned and kissed me as soon as we entered the room.

"I have wanted to do that since we left this morning."

I blushed, "What do I say to that."

"Ah . . . do it again' would be nice." I made a face, and he smiled, and did it again anyway. I loved seeing him smile. It was so rare. Those dimples just did something to my gut. I felt funny and weak. I don't know how to explain the feelings I felt when he looked at me, let alone touched me.

"What if someone catches us?"

"So what if they do? They don't know us or who we work for?'

"Sam, will you walk on the beach with me again tonight, to the rocks where we were last night?"

"Edward, I can't tonight, how about tomorrow night?"

"Okay, I will miss you tonight. I want to spend lots of time with you, if you let me."

"Yeah, Edward, that sounds nice to me too. Maybe we can take our own wine and food and eat on the beach tomorrow."

"Sounds really good. Okay, I could just look at you all day but we have to get back to work. We don't want Renee keeping us apart because we don't get stuff done, we want her to trust us and see how well we work together, right?"

"Right." He started looking through articles and found a few things he needed copied. We finished by twelve-fifteen.

"Okay, now lunch, Sam. What would you like?"

"Well not pizza. Nothing compares to what we had last night. How about the coffee shop. They have sandwiches?"

"No, there is a great sandwich shop down the road a couple of miles. We will go there."

"Okay, whatever you say." We went to the sandwich shop and I had veggie sandwich, with bean sprouts, onions, tomatoes, avocados, and mayonnaise on a wheat bun. Edward got a grilled steak sandwich. We sat, ate, and talked for about half an hour. I asked if we were to take Renee something, and he said she had to go to court and would get something on the way. We had a great time today; I enjoyed helping him, even if it was just coping stuff. It was fun just being with him.

We went back to the office and didn't see much of each other the rest of the day. He had to process all the stuff we gathered from the courthouse and the library. When Renee came back in, she was thrilled with what he had for her. She said he was the best decision she had made since she started work here. He told her how well I noticed things and how much help I was to him and how we really worked well together.

She said we did it faster than anyone else had done before, and she was happy with his performance. She said he saved her hours of work. I was ready to leave, and Edward was still with Renee, so I just waved to them as I was leaving. Renee yelled out to me 'Thanks' as I was leaving. Renee yelled "Thanks!"

Edward just waved and nodded. I knew I would hear from him later, or I hoped I would anyway.

I went home, brushed my teeth, and watched television. All my friends were out, so I took a short nap. My phone started buzzing. I picked it up and it was Edward.

"I miss you already."

"I miss you too. I will see you at work tomorrow. I promised my friends dinner tonight. I am cooking, I am sorry. We are just staying in, it is nothing big, but I promised them. Will you forgive me?"

"Sure, it is good to spend time with them. I didn't know if you had a date or something, I was hoping it wasn't a date with another guy."

"No, of course not, Edward. I have only been here a week. You are the only guy I have met so far that I like anyway."

"I will see you tomorrow. Bye."

"Bye, Edward. I fixed dinner for us, and we had a great time. We played cards and drank margaritas. I went to bed early; I was so tired. I knew the others were too, but Kat and Ronnie could party all night, work the next day, and do without sleep. I wasn't like that, I needed sleep.

The next morning at work, I looked for Edward. I saw him standing up against the wall looking at me. He saw me frantically looking for him. He was going to think I was nuts most of the time. I guess I was of nuts most of the time. He nodded at me and I nodded back with a smile. I saw him occasionally throughout the day. He even walked by me a couple of times and reached to touch my arm. I would get goose bumps and want him to come back by again soon.

I caught him smiling, looking at me in the afternoon. When he saw me looking at him, the smile fell off his face, and he turned around and walked away. I wondered why he didn't smile more. He had such a nice smile, pretty teeth and dimples. He usually had a grumpy or pissed off look on his face, as if he didn't want people to see the nice guy. I saw the nice guy and it was too late for him to try and hide it.

I left about Four o'clock, and Edward was still working. He looked up when he saw me leave. He nodded, and I shook my head slightly and walked out the door. It was hard seeing him, and being so close to him but not able to touch him or talk to him, afraid to make Renee curious about our relationship. Wash there even a relationship yet?

He called me before I got on my scooter.

"Hi."

"Hi, Edward. You okay?"

"Sure, why wouldn't I be?"

"I don't know, just asking." He wanted to know when to come over and I told him anytime he wanted to. He told me since we had sandwiches for lunch yesterday; he would bring something a little different. I told him I wanted to do something, and he told me next time I could. He said he would bring a couple of bottles of wine, and he would have everything for us, including a blanket whenever I was ready.

I told him I would be ready when he got there. He told me then he would be at my place in an hour to an hour and a half. I drove home, ran to the bedroom, put on shorts and a tank top, grabbed my bigger bag, and put a jacket, and some flannel pants in it in case it got cold. I had a radio, a flashlight, and my camera. I was ready so I sat and waited.

# CHAPTER SIX

I was watching the parking lot, when Edward arrived right on time. He ran up the stairs and knocked on the door just as I was opening it. I was smiling, and he grabbed me and kissed me.

"Are you ready?"

"Yes! Hi! How are you too?"

"Sorry, Hi. I was just anxious."

"Okay, I am ready to go. Do we need anything from here?"

"Yeah, do you have a radio?"

"Got it."

"Wow, you are good. Let's go." He grabbed my hand, and down the stairs we went. He went to his car and got the basket of goodies he had brought with him. I tried to look in the basket, and he slapped my hand and told me I had to wait.

We walked down the beach to the rocks, and he spread out the blanket on the sand. He put the basket on one corner to hold it down. I placed my bag on one corner and took the radio out and placed in on one corner, so it was secure on three corners at least. He bowed and motioned for me to have a seat. I sat down and he sat down across from me as I giggled like a little girl.

He asked if I was hungry and I told him not yet really. He wasn't either. He took out a bottle of wine and opened it, giving me a plastic cup and taking one for himself. It was Shiraz, but a different brand name. We drank and leaned on our hands, watching the waves and the birds. The sun was still up high and would be for a couple more hours. I took some pictures of the area and some of Edward. He took the camera away from me and held it out, taking pictures of both of us. He even kissed me while taking a picture. It came out pretty good.

We drank a bottle of wine and I was feeling good. We laughed and told each other stories about our childhood, about friends we had, (he had many friends), things we did, places we'd been.

He began telling me about his mother. He became weary and sad. He told me how he missed her and wished so many times that; she was still there just to talk to. He was only eight when his mother died, and he felt his father avoided him from that day on. He felt his father, deserted him most of his life, and Edward had no idea why. He said he and his father would sit in the same room for hours and never say a word. He felt his father left him when his mother died.

He said he felt alone, growing up except for the cook and her husband. He tried to get his father's attention, but his Dad would get angry with him, and he had no idea why. He said he remembered, one day holding his father's hand, looking up at him smiling. The next day he felt the love was gone. He said he remembers loving his father and going places with him and being happy as a small boy and then it just ended.

I just sat there.

"I'm sorry Sam, I didn't mean to depress you or make you feel sorry for me. That is not what I want from you at all. I mean, I don't want anything from you. I like you, and I like being with you."

"Edward if you want to talk, I will listen. If you don't want to talk about her, it is okay too. I like you too, you know that. I enjoy talking to you about anything and everything." I raised both my arms up over my head and pointed around. He leaned in toward me. He had such scary eyes sometimes; they were seductive and drew me in. He was looking at my lips, and then I was looking at his, and he kissed me. He pulled back, looked at me, and let out a deep breath of air.

"Sam, tell me more about your sister and brother."

"Oh my gosh, they are such brats. They are younger, so they get their way about everything. My mom and dad are constantly on my back about them". I changed my voice, holding my nose, to sound like my mom. "Sam!'You need to appreciate your brother and sister, one of these days you will wish you spent more time with them.' 'Sam, fix your brother and sister something to eat.' 'Sam, drive your sister to the mall,' and so on and so on."

Shaking my head, "My Dad doesn't even talk to his brother and hasn't for years. My mother is an only child, so no family there. My grandmother, on my mother's side was the only one who made me feel good about myself." I paused feeling tears in my eyes, I missed her she was gone and I didn't want to think about her now.

I paused looking down the beach away from him. Then I took a deep breath and went on. "One time my little brother climbed up a big tree in our back yard and he fell out and broke his arm. We had to take him to the hospital. He had a cast on for six weeks. I was watching them; I have never been able to live that one down."

Snickering, "My sister was angry at me and I don't even recall, why, now. But she was chasing me with a baseball bat through the house when my parents weren't home. I was so scared she was going to hit me. I ran into the bathroom and locked the door, and she hit the door so hard it went all the way through it. When my parents got home, and found me in the bathroom and her outside the door crying, I was the one who got yelled at. They said, I antagonized her! They said, I was supposed to be watching them! I was supposed to be the responsible one! It was my job to watch them after school! I should have done a better job!" I shook my head thinking about it.

I looked up at Edward kind of appalled at myself. "I think she would have hurt me, or killed me if she had hit me with that bat, but I was at fault of course. Those are just a couple of the reasons I hold grudges against them."

He laughed and took my hand in his. I continued talking, "I think my parents love me, or cared about me at least. They don't tell me they love me, but I want to believe they did. I smart off to them, talking back all the time. They knew I pushed my little sister until she would get so angry she could spit fire. I don't know why I do it, but I do."

I stiffened remembering one occasion. "Once I was sitting on the steps lacing up my tennis shoes when Alex walked up behind me, plopping a hard plastic brush on top of my head. It hurt so bad I thought I was going to pass out. I just grabbed my head and rolled onto my side screaming. My mom came running out of the house and grabbed me, asking what was wrong. My sister told her what she did. Mom checked my head and I had a knot that was about an inch in diameter and stood at least a half-inch tall. My Mom held me rocking me and telling me it was going to be okay." I couldn't even speak it hurt so badly, I cried and cried.

She rocked me until I stopped crying, "That time my sister got in trouble. I played that for what it was worth too. Her punishment was to clean our room for a week, and she had to do my choirs. When I was punished, I would be grounded for weeks, or months sometimes. I did most of the choirs anyway, because I was the oldest." He laughed at me again. I was getting angry. I started to stand up and he pulled me back down.

"I'm sorry for laughing at you; I miss not having brothers or sisters around. I would have loved to have someone to play with, or fight with. Please tell me more."

I nodded. "Once… we were walking through Wal-Mart. Alex was walking backwards begging Mom for something, as usual and Mom kept telling her 'No' and telling her to be careful, Mom yelled at her she was going to get hurt. About that time she, turned around and ran right into a six inch diameter metal post. It knocked her back and almost knocked her out. She shook her head, and Mom had to help her get up. Employees were running around, wanting to call an ambulance but my mother said she was fine. I was rolling in the aisle laughing, holding my sides, they hurt so badly. I got in trouble when we got home, and I was grounded for the next two weekends for laughing at her."

I shook my head, "I mean something was just wrong with my family." He was laughing and rolling around on the blanket. I was happy he was back in a good mood, even if it was at my expense. Actually, it was funny about some of the situations I had told him. The sun was starting to set, and it was beautiful. I took several pictures of it. He held the camera out again and took a picture of both of us with the sun setting behind us.

He picked me up and twirled me around, saying; he hadn't felt this happy in a very long time. He felt carefree and alive, something he had missed, and he never wanted it to end. I guessed I stiffened because he was scaring me, not actually scaring me.

It was just emotions were on the surface I had never felt before, and I didn't know how to handle them. He made me feel things I didn't quite understand. He put me down and hugged me, telling me he didn't mean anything bad. He just liked the way things were going with us. I had never liked anyone like this before. I liked him and trusted him, and I didn't want this to end either.

He and sat back down, asking me if I would like some cheese and crackers. I told him that sounded nice. He had cheeses, crackers, sliced meats, grapes, apples and strawberries, in the basket. We had a light meal, the kind I like to have. It was refreshing especially with the wine. He opened the other bottle and we drank it. I was getting drunk. I put my hand on his neck and pulled him toward me. I kissed him. I fell backwards pulling him with me. He kept kissing me, deeper and more passionately.

I didn't know exactly how to handle this but I liked it, liked it a lot. He kept kissing me, deeper and deeper, and oh so passionate. His hands were moving up and down my arm, and then they on my side, I felt him touch my breast, and I didn't pull away. His fingers were moving across my nipple.

I felt an urge growing in my belly and wanted him to be closer. I felt a need that my body was aching for. No fully understanding these needs, this ache, and I was so confused, I wanted more. I was kissing him, moving my hands up, and down his back felt nice.

He suddenly pulled away, jumping off the blanket, and stood a few feet away. I was just looking at him. I was shocked. What did I do wrong? I was offering myself to him; I had never done that before.

"Sam, we shouldn't do this. I don't want to hurt you. I know you are a nice girl. This is your first time away from home on your own, and you need to be careful. You need to protect yourself. Men different, and well, younger boys think that way too, but older guys know how to get what they want. Guys like me, Sam."

I just watched him and wondered how I was supposed to respond to him. I felt embarrassed. I sat up and held my head down. I was thinking that he saw me different than I saw him. A young, inexperienced, stupid girl and I was a naive stupid girl. He doesn't want this from me. I thought I have made a fool of myself, again as usual. I thought he liked me; he kissed me, was it more as a friend, or someone to hang out with, but not someone to be romantic with.

I couldn't say anything. I knew I was drunk, and I was having difficulty thinking. I can't believe I did what I did. I couldn't look at him, and now I would see him every day at work and he would be thinking of how stupid I was. I stood up trying to get my nerve up to hold my head high, and look at him. My head was spinning, I felt like I was going to throw up.

"Edward," in a whispered voice, "I am sorry I put you in a position you didn't want to be in. I promise it will never happen again." I tried to stand up, but was having a difficult time getting off the ground. I picked up my bag, once I was standing or weaving on my feet. Tears ran down my face.

I looked at him, "How could I be so gullible to think you liked me?" and took off running up the beach. I was crying, I left my shoes there, my camera but I didn't care. I wanted to go home, and cry by myself. He was yelling for me to stop, to wait, he wanted to talk to me. I am a fast runner, which is one thing I am good at. I was on the track team, and knew he would never catch me. I guess he didn't even try, when I looked back I didn't see him.

I figured he would gather up the stuff and leave. I made it to the condo and ran inside, locking the door. I ran to the bathroom and cried my eyes out. I sat in the bathtub, letting the water pound me, I didn't want the others to know when they came back, I had been crying. I kept the washcloth over my eyes to keep them from getting too red.

I heard someone knocking on the door, but I did not answer it. I heard Edward calling out to me, but I stayed where I was. I finally came out, and watched him get in his car and drive away. I opened the door and found my shoes and other stuff there. I locked the door, ran back to the bathroom, and cried some more, until I was all cried out.

My phone kept ringing; it was Edward trying to reach me. I couldn't answer it; I was so ashamed at what I had done. I felt awful and wondered what I would do at work. I felt so stupid. I didn't know how to act, what to do, or what to say. I had feelings for this guy I couldn't understand. I liked him so much, and he didn't want me, Rejected again.

Rejected and unloved, as I felt I would always be. No one will ever want me, why would they? That black cloud was hovering over my head. I grew sadder and sadder, thinking about what I would do. How do I get through this? Maybe I should just go home I don't belong here. I am not a party person; I am just along for the ride.

I decided to watch television and try to find a sad movie to explain my tears. I found one, 'Steel Magnolias'. It always got to me and Ronnie knew, it would be a good distraction too. I watched it until it was almost over. I would think about things tomorrow with a clear head.

When the girls came in, they found me crying. Ronnie ran to me, and I was sobbing so hard that I couldn't talk. They were all checking me over, and I pointed to the television, showing the credits for the movie. Ronnie said, "Well hell, it is that stupid movie she is watching. She always does that. Why do you even watch that movie Sam?"

"I don't know, I like it so much." I cried and sniffed a little. I asked them how their evening went and they told me all about it. I told them about ours, leaving out the end of the evening. I yawned, told them I had gotten up early, and was off to bed. I sniffed all night long, hoping Ronnie didn't hear me.

She told me everything, about her dates, growing up, when she had sex, and how she felt. I couldn't tell her about my rejection, not now, not yet. I was too upset and humiliated to talk about it. I was worried about work, how I was going to act. I slept fitfully I didn't get any rest.

I woke up when I heard the alarm and got up and showered. I dressed casual today, no makeup, I didn't care. Then I walked back into the bathroom and put make-up on. I usually didn't work on Thursdays, but Renee asked me to come in today. I was not going to let this guy know he hurt me. If I wanted to be a grownup, I had to act like one. I shook my head, went back to the closet, rumbled through things, and changed my clothes. Ronnie said, "You are making too much noise, what are you doing?"

"I am looking for something to wear to work. I want to go shopping tonight, will you go with me?"

"Sure, but be quiet, I am still asleep." I laughed and quieted, and left the condo without breakfast. I arrived at work and saw Edward's car, he was sitting in it waiting for me. I jumped off my scooter and ran into the building before he could get out of his car. He entered right after me. He called out to me just before I entered the building.

I watched him through the morning from the corner of my eye. He started to walk over to me several times, and I would get up and go to the files or to the bathroom. I filed slowly, going back to my desk, checking messages. I completed the tasks required of me, and by the time I was finished, it was lunchtime. I saw Edward again coming my way, jumped up, and asked the girl next to me if she wanted to go to lunch. She said sure, so we left, Edward was watching me.

I hurt so badly, I liked him so much, but I wasn't going to let him know it. Pat and I came back from lunch laughing when we entered, and I looked around but didn't see Edward. I took the long way around to my desk trying to find him. Well, maybe he went to lunch and wasn't back yet. I sighed, and went to my desk and sat down. I checked messages but didn't have any. I went to the files, and there were none there. I needed something to do. I didn't want to just sit here, all I would do is think about 'him'. I would be going home in about an hour or so anyway.

"Hi Sam." I turned around and Edward was standing behind me. I gasped.

"What do you want Edward?" I asked him gruffly.

"I wanted to talk to you. Why did you run away?"

"Remember we can't talk about this here. This is a business, and we can only have a business relationship here. Don't you remember?"

"Yes, I remember, but I can't seem to catch you any other way. I am sorry if I hurt you. I don't understand what happened to make you run from me. Please talk to me-if not now, then later. I knocked on your door last night. I have called you several times. You wouldn't answer."

"Edward, I think you said enough last night. What is there to talk about?"

"What did I say? All I can remember is saying I didn't want to hurt you and you needed to be careful. I said it for your benefit, not mine."

"I took your words as if you were telling me, you didn't feel . . . about me . . . the same way . . . I . . . I mean you don't want that kind of relationship with me. I know I should have handled it better, but it hurt at the moment, but I will be okay. I won't bother you with my adolescence and stupid reactions about what boys and girls do together. Oh hell, Edward that didn't even make since. I humiliated myself last night. I should have never made a pass at you, I have never done that before, and will never do it again, I promise."

I waived my hand at him to go, "Please go away. I am afraid I might cry, and I don't want to do that here. I don't want to have to explain anything to anyone. I don't want to cry in front of you. You probably already think low enough of me. Please not now, Edward." I then whispered, "Please, Edward, not now." He bowed his head and walked away. I watched him knowing I didn't mean a single word of what I said just now.

I felt those damn tears; I got up and went to the bathroom, fighting tears all the way. I got paper towels and dabbed my eyes, trying so hard to cover up, but it was impossible. Anyone who looked at me could tell I had been crying. What was I to do now? I was ashamed; Edward would see I had cried, and I didn't want him to know.

I am such a fool. When will I ever learn? I kept walking in the bathroom, sobbing, and washing my face, and trying to settle down, but I couldn't. I couldn't stay in there, or someone would get curious, I had to come up with something to say, something to do. I was angry now and the tears had stopped, so I took deep breaths, washed my face, turned the hand dryer up on my face to help, but it only made it redder and look worse.

I walked back to my desk; I turned and saw Edward watching me. He saw my face. He started to come toward me, but I held up my hand and shook my head, and he backed off. I went to Renee's office and told her I must have eaten something bad at lunch, because. I was sick to my stomach, and throwing up. I needed to go home.

She looked at me and said, "You poor thing. You can't ride home on that scooter; I will have Edward take you home".

I panicked, "No please! I can make it, it is not that far."

"No" she called Edward into her office, I was sure he was wondering what was going on. "Edward, will you please take Sam home? She ate something at lunch, which disagreed with her. I don't want her to ride that scooter home." I rolled my eyes.

"I would be happy to take her home and make sure she gets in okay, before I came back, if that is okay."

She told him, "Yes absolutely. Make sure she is comfortable and doing okay, before you return."

I asked, "How will I get my scooter home?"

Edward said, "I will find a way." Damn, what now? There is no way out of this.

Edward walked me outside; he opened the door for me to get in. I looked at my scooter, and he said, "Renee will know." I got in his car and looked out the window when he got in, not looking at him.

"Sam, now please tell me what happened."

"Edward, I over reacted to what happened last night. I was drunk, you know and just went too far. Forget it, okay."

"No, I refuse to forget it. I hurt your feelings and I didn't mean to. I was drinking too, I had too much too. Please say everything will be okay with us."

"Edward, I don't think it is a good idea that we go out anymore."

"Why?" He screamed at me. "We have gotten along wonderfully. I like you, you know that, and you like me too. You have to admit the truth. You like me, Sam." He pulled out on the road, heading for my apartment.

"Edward, I just didn't act proper last night. I know . . . I was moving . . . too fast. I didn't know what I was doing. You pulled away from me and told me about older guys, using yourself as one of those older guys, knew how to get what they wanted from girls. I assumed you didn't was those things from me." I felt tears slid down my checks, I turned facing the window.

I lost control crying again. I cried big sobbing ugly tears, snot running out my nose. He pulled his car over to the side of the road. He pulled me into his arms, holding me and, rubbing his hand up and down my back.

"Sam, I didn't mean I didn't want those things with you, I want you to be sure. You are younger than I am, yeah. You told me you are eighteen years old, I am twenty-four. I have been with girls before and not liked myself the next day for using them. Sam, I know you aren't ready for that yet. I know you are a virgin, I can tell by your innocence and the way you act. I do like you very much, and I do not want to hurt you. I know you came to Florida for your first fling, but I don't want to be just your fling. Do you understand what I mean, Sam?"

I looked up at him and sniffed, "I think so."

"Good, I am taking you home." He put me back in the passenger seat, and then pulled back on the road driving to my place. He parked the car, and then walked upstairs with me, and I opened the door. No one was home, so he came in, and we sat on the couch. He went to the kitchen, looked in the refrigerator for water, and brought back two bottles. He opened mine and handed it to me.

"Drink!"

I looked at him. Maybe I was too young to handle a real relationship. How does Ronnie, who is younger than me, do it? She has been having sex since she was fifteen years old. I thought Kat has too. Men were complicated, life was complicated.

"Sam, do you feel better?"

"Yes, but stupid." He hugged me.

"Please, don't. Now listen to me, carefully, okay." I nodded. "Sam, I . . . Edward . . . like . . . you . . . that is for sure. I have done things I am not proud of, with girls who were young, and I used them. I didn't care about their feelings, only my good time, what I wanted, and another notch on my belt, I guess you can say."

He held my arms looking in my eyes, "I am not telling you this for you to get angry with me and not want to see me again, and all this happened before I met you, I was a different guy then. I'm not saying I don't to see you again. I differently don't want you not see me again. You have to remember that, okay. I have experienced more things in life. I can't change what I did in the past, only how I act in the future, understand?"

I nodded again.

"Remember this though. I like you. 'You', for who 'You' are, I like talking to 'you', I like kissing 'You', I like how I feel when I am with 'You'. Yes, I have thought about having sex with 'You', I wouldn't be normal if I hadn't. I want to, man up, but I won't have sex with you until you are really ready. I want you, not me, to make the right choice. Please, for one time in my miserable life, let me do the right thing, Sam. I beg you."

I leaned into him, and cried again. He held me.

"May I kiss you now?"

"Yes."

He kissed me. It was so nice, I still felt those stupid tears falling down my face, and I tasted them, so I know he did too. He laughed when he pulled back.

"Please, no more tears, I can't take it. I thought I had done something so awful last night that I might lose you. I don't want to lose you, ever."

"Okay, I acted like a child, but I want to be treated like an adult. How can expect you to treat me like an adult if I can't act like one?"

"Maybe it was PMS?"

I was stunned; the look on my face had to be awful. I know I was bright red.

He laughed and said, "You know, 'Pissed at Men Syndrome'."

I thought I was going to lose it then, I laughed so hard I fell over. He was laughing with me and was hugging me, and I felt better.

"I have to get back to work. I will figure out a way to get your scooter here. Can I see you this evening? Maybe with your friends, not just us, okay."

"Okay."

He kissed me again, left me sitting on the couch, and closed the door behind him. What an awful way I acted. I can't believe I acted so childishly. I shook my head, laying down on the couch until I fell asleep.

# CHAPTER SEVEN

Abby and Kat came in arguing about something that woke me with a start. They saw me on the couch, and came over to see what was wrong. I told them I went to lunch and ate something bad at lunch. I came home to rest. They were satisfied with my story and went on with their arguing. From what I could gather, they were arguing about a tip someone left one of them.

"Okay, guys, what is going on?

Kat yelled out, "Abby stole my tip from a table I was handling."

Abby yelled back, "I helped with the table too and offered her half of the tip. And she wouldn't take just half, she wants it all. The man walked over to me and handed me a twenty dollar bill. He said I was pleasant and he appreciated me. He said it was for me, not the other waitress." Kat was furious.

"Well, then why did you offer me half? I waited on that table for over an hour, bringing drinks, and catering to every request, they made. I was so pissed they were taking up my table for so long. It wasn't fair. Other people were coming and going, and you were making tips left and right. I was stuck with this one table, and they wouldn't leave."

"Well that is the problem, Kat. If you had been nicer they would have given you the tip, but you showed your anger, and they didn't like it."

"I was nice to them. I brought them everything they asked for."

"Yeah, but with that attitude you are using right now. They noticed, Kat.

"Kat went to the bedroom, slamming the door.

"Sam, she was a brute to those guys. I would check on them occasionally to see if they needed anything because Kat was so rude to them. I felt sorry

52

for them. I believe the reason they stayed so long was the way she was acting. If the boss had been there, she would have lost her job."

"What is wrong with her, why is she so angry? She has been like this for a couple of days."

"I think it is a guy she likes, she Ah . . . I mean. Yeah."

"What, Abby?"

"She slept with him, and then he dumped her. He was laughing at her on the beach the other night, calling, her names, pointing at her, and telling everyone who would listen what a slut she was. That was why she found those other jerks she brought back to the condo."

"Oh, she is hurt, Abby."

"I know, that is why I offered her half the tip. I didn't mean to make her mad, but when she wanted it all, something just kicked inside me and I wasn't bowing down to her as usual. I give in to her all the time, and it is enough, Sam."

"I know Abby. But we need to talk to her."

"I tried, but she is so angry, she won't listen to me."

"Maybe we should give her some space and let her get over it. We just need to let her know we love her and are here when she is ready to talk."

"You're right, Sam. I'll bow back down and give her the twenty."

"No Abby that is not what I mean. You need to stand up for yourself with her. We just need to be there for each other always. We are friends and have been for most of our lives. We are sisters. Remember, that 'Ya-Ya Sisterhood' movie, that is what we are."

"Okay, I am going to the beach, I want some sun. And I am going to run, and try to lose some weight or tone up. I'll see you later." She went to her room where Kat was. I didn't hear anything, no arguing. Abby came out a few minutes later in her swim-suite, waved, said 'Bye' and left.

I lay back on the couch and was thought of my own fiasco. If Edward had taken me up on my offer last night, and then he walked away from me afterwards, how I would feel now. I would feel like dirt. I was lucky. I was lying there, thinking about what I should do next, when Ronnie came in the door. She ran over to me, feeling my forehead, and asking me if I was okay.

"Ronnie, you are not my mother, and are not responsible for me. Back off."

"I was just concerned. You lying on the couch, you never do that. I know something is wrong, Damn, Sam, I just wanted to help."

"Ronnie, I know you know me better than anyone else, but. I am okay. I had some bad food at lunch and had to come home early. I am fine now. I was just lying here thinking."

"Okay, you don't have to be so snippy with me."

I smiled at her, and she hugged me. She went to the kitchen and fixed herself a drink, getting me one too. She came back to the couch, setting the drinks on the table.

"Do you want to talk?"

I hesitated. I really wanted to ask her so much, but Kat was in the other room, and I didn't want anyone else hearing me. Besides, Kat needed attention right now more than I did.

"Ronnie, I am fine really."

"Okay, but you know when you are ready, I am here for you."

Damn she knew something else was bothering me, she always did. I nodded. She sat back and flipped on the television, surfing channels. Kat walked back in the room with her head down.

"Hey guys, can I talk to you?"

I scooted over on the couch, patting the seat between us. She walked over and sat down. She sighed, waiting; I guess thinking about how she was going to start or what she was going to say. She was always the strong one, never showing her weakness.

"You both know what happened. I heard Abby tell you Sam. I was angry today and poured all my frustration out on Abby. I didn't have the jerk around to yell at, so I blamed her. I feel bad about it. I did something stupid, and now everyone thinks I am nothing but a slut, I hate myself, my reputation. I don't know what to do. I believe it when boys say they like me. I like them and mean it, but I am stupid and believe every lie they tell me."

Ronnie hugged her, "Kat, listen you know I do the same thing sometimes. We just want someone to love us." She had her head up against Kat's head, hugging her. I just listened. "We both have made bad choices in our lives. Maybe we use sex as a way to show love or get love, but it hasn't worked yet for me either. I don't know why I think it will, when I don't know the guy and I give myself to him. I feel dirty afterwards and just want to cry.

Men get pats on the back when they bed tons of girls, but girls are called names, and it's not fair. Kat you know we are so much alike even though we do what we do for different reasons. You know what I mean?"

"Yeah, I understand. I had, no, I mean *have good mom*, most of the time. She loves me, she tries, but I feel so different from anyone else. I feel rejected by my father. He knows I exist. He sends my mom money sometimes but has never bothered to get in contact with me. Why doesn't he want me, Ronnie? Am I so awful, I I can't be loved? I am in this life as I am and will never change, and it will never get any better.

I hate myself. I hate the attitude I have sometimes. I wish I was like Sam, she is nice and tries to fix everything, for everyone." She began to cry, I had never seen Kat cry before in all the years we have know each other.

I joined in the hug, and we all cried. Each for our own reason but crying together was such a relief. It took so much off my shoulders and I felt closer to Kat at this moment than I ever have before, I wish Abby had been here. Kat calmed down and sat up on her own.

"I shamed all of us by jumping in the sack with that guy. I have been with too many boys since I've been here, just to have fun."

"You didn't shame anyone. You trusted the guy. Don't worry about it Kat. You thought you liked him and you believed he liked you. He is the one who lied, it is his loss. Hold your damn head up high, and don't let some jerk rule your life. If you decide to have sex, with every guy on the beach, that is your choice, don't let some scum bag belittle you.

We love you, and we are here for you no matter what, Kat. Do you hear me?" I was so angry, when I finished I was shaking. They both were looking at me, and then they looked at each other and laughed. I tilted my head. What did I say that was so funny? I was serious.

Ronnie said, "Sam you just surprised the heck out of us." We all laughed.

Kat chimed in, "Thanks, Sam, that was the nicest thing you have ever said to me. I love you. I don't think I have time for every guy on the beach, but I get as many as I can." We all hugged laughing.

We all felt so much better. I was happy Kat felt better about herself. We sat on the couch until we heard the knocking at the door. None of us wanted to move, we were comfortable and all snug sitting there. Ronnie rolled her eyes and went to the door. It was Edward; he had come to see how I was. Ronnie led him in. He saw me and Kat, huddled together on the couch, making Kat sit up straight.

Kat said, "Hey man, you here to see our girl?" She stood up and started to leave. He smiled at her and nodded.

I said, "Come on guys, you don't have to leave. Stay, and talk with us. You don't mind, do you Edward?"

"No, I would like to get to know your friends or let them get to know me. I brought Sam's scooter back. Here are the keys." They both came back and sat on the other chair. I motioned Edward to sit. N me. He sat right up next to me. I sat up straighter. I was thinking, *now where do we start. Someone say something. Should it be me?*

"Thank you for bringing the scooter. So how was work the rest of the afternoon?"

"It was fine, nothing big happened, Renee went to court and didn't come back, so I just did research."

Ronnie asked, "Edward, Sam said you are in law school. How do you like it?"

"I like it. I didn't always want to be in law, but both my parents were lawyers, so I guess I was kind of destined to follow in their footsteps."

"Sam said you are from Florida, can you tell us some places to go? Sites to see, you know?"

"Sure, I can even take you all where ever you would like. First, you have to go on an air-boat ride in the Everglades. It is a blast. There is a nice zoo close by, if you like stuff like that. There are some awesome museums in the area, plantations, the aquarium is great."

Kat said, "How far to where we can go on an air-boat ride?"

"Not far, in Ft Myers they have a good one. Can I take you guys there this weekend?"

"All of us? I mean the four of us?" Ronnie remarked.

"Yes, I would love to. My treat."

Kat beamed. She was so excited that he offered to take us and pay.

I said, "That sounds like fun. We will have to ask Abby, but I think we can convince her."

"Abby doesn't like me."

"Abby, can change her mind. She just needs to see that smile."

He smiled big, his dimples showing. Kat laughed, and Ronnie smiled. "Well, I don't want to keep you guys from what you were doing, I just wanted to make sure Sam was okay, I could have called, but I wanted to see for myself. You understand don't you Sam?"

"Yes, thank you Edward."

He stood up to leave. I grabbed his hand. Kat and Ronnie both stiffened.

"Hey wait." I stood up and walked him to the door.

"I guess we should maybe give tonight a rest. You spend the evening with your girls; and I will find something to do. Okay?"

"Okay, but you could join us."

"No, Sam, spend time with them. We will all go to Ft Myers this weekend, and I'll try hard to get along with Abby and have her eating out of my hand before you know it, using the dimples and all."

"I am sure you will."

He kissed me.

"I'll call you later, if that is okay."

"Yes, it is always okay. I am so sorry for the trouble I have put you through today. I really am, Edward."

"Hey don't mention it again. It's done."

"I acted really bad."

He put his fingers over my lips and shook his head.

"I said don't mention it again. I'll talk to you later. Have a great evening Sam." He kissed me again, opened the door, and left. I waved to him and he waved back.

I turned around and Kat and Ronnie were staring at me. They had watched the whole time we were standing at the door. I now was going to have to talk and tell them more about Edward. I just wanted to share with Ronnie but I had no choice now.

"Okay, I know you both have a million questions. I don't even know where to start, but Abby isn't here, and she will want to know too, so we should wait so I don't have to repeat it."

"You will not wait, you will start right now, and I will repeat it to Abby if necessary."

"Okay, what do you want to know?"

"How well do you know this guy?"

"I know him well enough, and we are getting to know each other better every time we see each other. He is the son of a well-know attorney in Ft Lauderdale. He is going to Harvard, I already told you that. He will be starting his final year of law School, and he is a nice guy."

"What . . . Ah . . . have you all done?"

"We haven't had sex, if that is what you mean. He is a nice guy and is giving me time. He is not pushy. He is gentle and kind. He likes to talk and he listens to what I have to say. He likes all the things I like. We like the same food, we both read every chance we get. He had a, well, not rough life, but he was alone. His father had young women around and didn't give him much attention growing up. We understand that. He feels like we do, you know."

"Really is he a rich kid?" Kat asked.

"Yes, but what does that matter." Ronnie looked down at her lap. "It doesn't make any difference at all whether he has money or not." Kat looked at Ronnie.

"Sorry, I forgot. You have never acted like some rich bitch, so I forget you have money."

"I don't have money, my father does, Kat. Money isn't what makes life better. Damn, are you so selfish that you don't see everyone else's life isn't perfect either? You make me so mad, I want to hit you sometimes. I don't know why I even try to be friends with you. You are a bitch, do you know that?" Ronnie got up to walk away.

"Ronnie, I am sorry, I know I am a bitch. I don't know how else to act. I didn't mean it the way it sounded. Come on, sit back down, and let's listen to Sam."

Ronnie sat back down, crossing her arms over her chest. Kat poked her, and then shook her to make her smile.

"Edward took me to that great pizza place, you ate the pizza, you remember. We had a picnic on the beach, it was nice, and we watched the sunset. I came home early last night remember, I was watching 'Steel Magnolia's'." I didn't want to tell all yet. "I like him, I like him a lot."

Kat said, "I think I am going to go find Abby and try to talk to her. I will tell her what went on today so you don't have to repeat your horrible story, Sam." She laughed as she went to her room to change. Ronnie was looking at me, not saying anything. I didn't know if she was still angry with Kat or wondering what I wasn't telling them.

Kat came out in her tiny bikini and left with a towel and two bottles of water, not saying anything else as she went out the door. She was different from us in so many ways, I didn't understand her, but I guess I do, it was the way her mother taught her. It boggled the mind, to think we were all so different but so alike.

Ronnie said, "Well?"

"What?"

"You know what?"

I lowered my head, and knew I had to tell it all now.

"I wasn't sick today, I had been crying."

"What did that jerk do to you? I knew something was wrong. I will kill that stupid son of a b..."

"Stop, Ronnie! It wasn't what he did, it was what I did."

"Did you go all the way with him?"

"No, I told you we weren't having sex. Didn't you listen to me?"

"Well, you didn't tell me the truth earlier about being sick."

"Listen." I said. She sat back, and waited. "I like him. Last night I got drunk on the beach and kind of, well, ah . . . I pulled him on top of me and was kissing him and making moves on him, and he stopped and jumped up and started lecturing me about men and protecting myself against guys, older guys especially. You know, like you tell me all the time, 'Mom'."

She smiled.

"He pulled back?"

"Yes, and it hurt my feelings. I took what he was saying all wrong and ran away from him, literally. I ran home and wouldn't talk to him. At work this morning, I ignored him and avoided him until he finally trapped me this afternoon, and I cried then apologized to him, that is all. I couldn't keep it inside. I was hurt. He brought me home and told me why he did what he did. He wanted to do right by me because he likes me too, really likes me."

"Well, I have to like this guy now. He really did that? Wow! I have never known a guy to back off once he started, wow! Wow! I am amazed, to protect the girl. Wow! I don't know what to say Sam."

"I want you all to like him. I didn't mean to come here and fall for some guy and ignore you all. I wanted this time for us as friends, but yes, I hoped to meet guys. I like him so much Ronnie, I don't know how to act. I was offering myself to him last night, and I wanted him. I did. But now he makes me want to rethink, and I don't know. I wanted so badly to talk to you, and I just haven't had the chance."

"Sam, I think you are doing okay on your own. I hope Edward will help you and do what is right. I hope anyway."

"Ronnie, how does it feel to have sex the first time? I mean, I know it hurts, but do you feel a bond with them?" What?

She was laughing at me.

"Sam, I have had sex with many guys, and after the first time it gets good, but I have never been in love. I do it for all the wrong reasons, just like Kat. That is why I felt her pain. I hate myself most of the time. I don't want to be the easy girl, but I am. I just want to be loved, but haven't found it yet. Yeah, there have been guys I have stayed with for months at a time. Some I really liked, and they liked me too, but it is not the same as being in love. I don't know what that is like, not yet anyway."

Abby and Kat came in, talking with their arms around each other.

"We made up, I was the villain, and I admitted it. Hey, what's going on here?"

"Nothing, we were just talking."

"Yeah, and leaving us out. You two have been crying."

"Ronnie and I were just agreeing about being needed and wanted, about being the outcasts. What keeps us all together, what are our common goals? We want to be loved for who we are and not what others want us to be. We need to be happy and loved. We need it, don't you agree? We need not to make judgments on people either. We don't want to be judged so quickly. We want people to get to know us first."

"Yes, you are right. That is why we stay together."

I looked at Abby. "Abby, did Kat tell you about this weekend, the airboat ride with Edward?"

"Yes, she told me, I don't like him, Sam."

"Fine, Abby, you don't have to like him. You can try to get along. It could be fun."

"Sam, I don't trust him, and you shouldn't either."

"You are kidding, right Abby? He wants to take us out so you can have the chance to get to know him. He wants to get to know you. We have a chance to do something together that we haven't done before. He offered to treat as well."

"No, I am not kidding, why should you change? You and I stick together always. We agreed to wait for Mr. Right."

"I don't know if he is Mr. Right yet. When do we find Mr. Right, Abby? How will we know? Are you to find him first, then it will be okay for me to find one afterwards?"

"No, of course, that was not what I meant, you are twisting my words. This guy could be trouble. His kind is always trouble."

"First Abby, what is his kind any way? What makes you think like that? What has he done to make you feel that way? Do you mean trouble for whom, Abby, me, or you?"

"All of us, Sam. He is a rich kid here for the summer to get girls, nothing else. We talked about this before we left home. Some boys will say anything, and do anything to get what they want, and I think Edward is that kind."

"Abby, you are afraid I won't be there to sit by you side when everyone else has a date or is talking to someone and you are alone. Edward is kind, and very polite to me. He genuinely likes me too. I am tired of babysitting you. Do what you want, I am going with Edward."

"Sam, think about it. He and his friend on the beach, he didn't want anything to do with us at the party in public. Do you remember that?"

"Abby, after we talked to them you liked his friend. We enjoyed ourselves on the beach."

"Sam, really, we barely talked to them. They didn't want anything to do with us at the party."

"You forget, you were the one at the party who pushed them away."

"Because freak boy was acting rude, how was I to respond to that? You agreed with me at the time."

"Talking to them on the beach was fun, and I changed my mind. We hate it when people judge us on first impressions, and you are judging him on your first impression. I gave him a second chance."

"Sam, we protect each other. Sometimes our first impressions are right. Sometimes our intuitions know something is not like it should be."

"Abby, you are being ridiculous. We have been friends long enough to know what each other feels. I like him, Abby. Please try and give him a chance."

"No, Sam. You need to trust me on this one."

"Okay, Abby, done. I told you to stand up for yourself with Kat, now I am doing the same, and finally standing up for myself with you. I have tried Abby, to talk to you about my feelings. I like Edward, and that is that. Do you understand me? I don't want to hear another word from you. I don't need your approval on whomever I date." I went to my room. I paced a few minutes, and then I got my bike keys, putting my wallet in my back pocket. I headed for the front door.

Abby yelled for me to stop. "Don't be childish about this, Sam, stay and talk."

I yelled at her, "Abby, I don't want your opinion or need it. Do what you want. I will take care of myself. Spend the summer alone. I won't be by your side." I walked out the door.

I was shaking I was so upset, I shouldn't have said that, it was mean of me to go that far. Ronnie followed me out on the stoop, and grabbed my arm, but I pulled away from her.

"Sam, you know that was not a nice thing you just said to Abby."

"I don't care anymore. I have been the peacemaker in this group since we got together, and I am tired of it. Abby is never happy, she wants to be miserable, and she wants me to be miserable too. I know it was wrong, but I am tired of her whining around, aren't you?"

"Yes, but that is her way, you know that. We are sad, and depressed, and with each other, we can be ourselves, and not judge. You just judged her."

"I am out of here. I need some space right now to think."

Abby came running down the stairs, "Wait Sam, let's talk." I kept going, I didn't even turn around, I was angry, and I was ashamed at the same time.

I yelled over my shoulder, "I need some air." She kept following me, and called out to me, but I got on my scooter and took off.

# CHAPTER EIGHT

I was riding fast, letting the wind hit me in the face, and blow my hair. I rode across the river and kept going as fast and as far as I could. I ended up hours later in Tampa, lost. I didn't know where I was at, what area of town. I didn't recognize any of the streets. I was cold and scared.

I was only wearing shorts and a tank top. The temperature had dropped, and I needed a jacket, I was shivering. People were standing on the sides of the road; I think they were selling drugs. I pulled into a Fast Stop store.

I asked for directions back to Hwy 93, to Clearwater. The man didn't speak much English, and had no idea how to tell me to get back. There were bars on the windows and doors, and bulletproof glass between him and the customers. This was creepy. I asked another guy who came in for cigarettes, but he started hitting on me. He was asking me to go for a ride with him. He told me I looked cold and he could warm me up real fast. I was getting nervous. I just wanted to go back to the area I knew so I could walk on the beach, get something to eat and feel safe again.

I went outside, and he followed me. He had another guy with him in his car. I was scared. I went back in the store and waited for them to leave. I sat there for half an hour. I got a bottle of water and went back to my scooter. I looked around, got on it, and started driving.

I finally found Hwy 93 on my own. I was so happy. I headed back to Clearwater, and all of a sudden, I found I was going the wrong way. I had to find a place to turn around. I was getting more and more pissed at myself for what an idiot I was, for going off on a rampage, and getting lost on the wrong side of town.

I lost my temper, and this was what I got. I could have been killed. Who cares anyway? I could call Edward, but that would just cause worry or more lecturing. I left my cell phone at home; all I had with me was my wallet and keys. I was so cold. I was shaking, and my thinking was all mixed up. I was ashamed, of how I talked to Abby.

I finally drove back across the bridge, to Clearwater. It was after one o'clock in the morning. I recognized the area, thank goodness. I knew they would be worried, but I really didn't care. If I had a place to sleep, I wouldn't even go back there. If I had a blanket, I would sleep at the pool in one of those lounge chairs.

I stopped at the Fast Stop near our condo, and bought a six-pack of beer and a blanket that had 'Florida' on it in the touristy items. I pulled to the back of the parking lot of our condo and parked. I saw the lights on upstairs. I went to the pool and started getting smashed. I was drinking the beer while wrapped warmly in my new blanket, all snug and comfortable.

I still hadn't eaten, so I got drunk fast. I was singing to myself, laughing, and having a great time. I was tired, I drunk the whole six-pack, and I thought of going for more. Nay, this wasn't a bad place to sleep; I was having a hard time thinking straight, I wasn't used to drinking six bottles of beer at once. Whoa, I was buzzed, I felt good. Maybe I should do this more often. Before I knew what was going on, I was asleep.

All of a sudden, I heard yelling. They were calling me by name. I couldn't open my eyes to see who it was. It was close to me. Should I worry? I didn't seem to have any bones in me, I couldn't move, "Ha!" I don't have to be afraid of anything, or anyone. I am invincible.

"Sam, where the hell have you been? I have been worried sick, so have your friends, since you didn't come home, they called me to see if you were with me. You have been gone for hours."

I finally got one of my eyes to open, and I looked up to see who was yelling at me. It was Edward; he was so handsome looking down at me. I smiled at him and asked him if he wanted a beer, giggling all the while, but my words didn't sound right coming out of my mouth, I must have looked confused, and he was looking at me strangely. I didn't have any more beer to offer him, I had drunk them all. I was thinking and laughing. Things messed up in my mind.

"Sam, did you hear a word I said?"

"Yeah . . . damn, thit . . . I hears . . . you . . ., don't shell shat me. Yous don't own mines. I can does what's I want to do. . . . Do." I was slurring every word." If I I's . . . wants someone to tells my every damn movie . . . I shah . . . should have be . . . home . . . Now if yous wants to shell to me . . . lower you's damn voices."

He was just standing there now. I guessed I told hems what to do. Ha! I was laughing and giggling.

"Sam, are you drunk?"

"Me's is what I wants to be. Goes a sway and leave me be."

He bent down by me, touching my forehead, and shaking his head at me. He tried to pick me up, and I was so limber he almost dropped me on the cement. My arms went up over my head. That was so funny. I heard him cussing, and he tried to pick me up again, but I just melted to the ground. I giggled. He was cussing a lot, and stood with his hands on his hips.

"Sam, you are going to have to help me, or I can't get you up."

I giggled some more. I felt so loose and free. I spread my arms wide, looking up at the stars and giggling.

"I don't want . . . to ah. . . . gets sup."

"Sam, I will have to stay with you all night out here if you don't let me help you. I want to take you to bed."

"You's said no, no, no, to me already bouts that one's boys, member?"

"I mean, to your bed, alone, in your condo, so you will be comfortable and safe."

"NO!" I shouted at him.

"Sam, please."

"NO! I is not going to see Abs, she pissed did me up."

"Sam."

I looked up at him and patted the chair where I was laying down. He sat down on the chair beside me.

"Holds me." He struggled trying to pull me into his lap; my arms were so limber and were going everywhere. I was wiggling and he had a hard time getting a good hold on me, but finally he got me lying across his lap. He turned me over on my stomach and pulled me up so my head was on his chest. He put my legs on top of his; he pulled the blanket across both of us and fell backwards, holding me so tight. I was so warm and comfortable. I liked him holding me. I snuggled into his chest and smelled his cologne. He smelled so good. I wanted to bite him, so I did, right on the chest.

"Ouch, damn it, Sam that hurt." He jumped, almost knocking me off him, but he held on tight.

"Um, I likes you too . . . too much." I snuggled back into his arms. He held me tighter, put the side of his face on the top of my head, and held me. It was the nicest feeling I had ever had. I fell asleep. He tried to get up holding me, but it was too hard with me being so drunk. He wrapped the blanket around us tighter, got as comfortable as he could, turned slightly on his side, and pulled me up next to him. We were face to face; with me laying on him part-way. I snuggled further into him as close as I could get. We slept there until morning.

The sun was bright, and my head hurt so badly. I wanted to cover my eyes. I felt Edward move and knew he was not in a good position. He tried to sit up, and I fell off him onto the hard ground.

"Oh . . . My heads. Damn, my butts." I hurt all over.

"I'm so sorry, Sam, did I hurt you?"

"You knocked me on the ground. I think I broke my butt. It hurts so badly." He stood up and kind of stretched a bit, trying to help me up, but I could not get my feet to hold me up, so, he bent down telling me to put my arms around his neck. He lifted me into his arms. He was struggling; he was sore and having a hard time lifting me. I held his neck and snuggled back into him. He felt so nice and warm. He carried me upstairs and knocked on my door with his elbow. Ronnie opened the door and stood there looking at us.

"Where can I put her?" He shuffled me around because I was falling out of his arms.

"Follow me." She walked into our room, and pulled the covers back, and allowed him to lay me in the bed and covered me up. I tried to pull him down to join me, but he pulled away, looking at Ronnie.

"I don't care if you want to lie, beside her. Keep her quiet. I'll sleep on the couch." He lay down beside me, and Ronnie closed the door and went into the living room. He pulled the covers over himself and pulled me up against him. We both slept until I heard the alarm, but I could not get up.

Edward stretched and I felt him behind me. Why was he in my bed? I would have awful breath, and I bet I looked a mess. How did he get there anyway? Where is Ronnie? This was my bed, and my room, I figured as I looked toward the bathroom. I felt his hardness, I was stunned. I snuggled into him, and he bolted from the bed. I turned over and looked at him. He was so handsome. He was swollen below the belly; a huge bulge was sticking out of his pants. It was very noticeable. He pulled his shirt out of his jeans to cover himself. I looked up at his face, he was smiling, but he wanted to run away. He saw me looking at him.

"Good morning, Edward. My head hurts so badly. Why are you here?"

"Do you remember anything about last night?"

"Oh shit, did we do it?" I couldn't remember. That was not the way I wanted it to happen. I was looking at him as if I was about to cry.

"No, no, Sam. You were drunk. You and Abby had a fight."

I started recalling my drive into Tampa, getting lost, the beer, and lying on the chair by the pool.

"I remember parts, I remember you talking to me, but I thought it was a dream. Oh, my butt hurts, and my head is pounding." I looked up at him again.

He sat on the side of the bed.

"Sam, I can't walk in the other room just yet, I need to calm down. Do you want to get up?"

"No, I want to sleep."

"My butt hurts so badly, Edward, what happened?"

"I dropped you this morning."

"What? You dropped me! Why?"

"We were on the chair by the pool, and you rolled over and fell on the ground,. I didn't hold on to you well enough, I am sorry. Do you think you are hurt seriously? Let me see if you have a bruise."

"No, I am okay. What did we do?"

"Nothing, Sam, you are still intact."

What was that supposed to mean? I didn't understand that, I was still intact. I looked at him confused.

"Oh, okay. Did I hurt you? You said you had to calm down. Did I say the wrong thing? Are you mad at me?"

Laughing, he said, "No, Sam, I am not hurt A little sore sleeping on that chair out there most of the night, but other than that, I am fine. My back won't be at its best for a while."

"You don't have to have an excuse to stay, you are welcome here as long as you like."

He went to the bathroom, and I heard him flush the toilet. I heard the water running, good guy, he washes his hands. He came back into the bedroom with a wet washcloth.

"Put this over your eyes now. You are going to have a hell of a hangover, I am afraid."

"Oh, yeah, I know I am. I already do."

"At least you are off work till Monday."

"Thank you, Edward."

He bent down to kiss me, and I covered my mouth. He looked hurt.

"Morning breath, I bet it is awful."

"I don't care, I want to kiss you. I was so worried about you last night, so were your friends. Don't ever do that again. I know you don't need a boss or a protector, but at least have the common courtesy to tell us where you are so we don't worry ourselves sick, please, Sam. Damn."

"I'm sorry Edward. I won't go off on my own like that again. If I do, I will tell someone where I am going."

"Thank you." He kissed me. I liked it so much. He had morning breath too. He kissed me again.

"I will see you later, get some rest." He opened the door, waved bye to me, and shut it. I heard him talking to Ronnie, and then the front door opened, and he left. I felt bad, he was so tired, and it was because of me. He was going to work, and he would be miserable all day. I heard the door open, and Ronnie came in.

"Sam, are you okay?"

"I hurt all over, my head is killing me, and my butt hurts. Edward said he dropped me, or I fell or something, I am not sure. But I hurt."

"Here, I brought you some Tylenol and water. Take this and just sleep." She waited for me to take the pills and sat the glass on the table by the bed. I am getting ready to go to work. It will be quiet shortly for you to sleep, but you deserve some loud noise to bother you for what you put us through."

She slammed the bathroom door. I cringed, grabbing both sides of my head because it hurt so much. My ears were ringing. I heard her laughing, the water running in the shower. She was paying me back for worrying them. I did deserve it. I slept until Ronnie started banging things around again.

"Okay, I know, you are paying me back. I'm sorry. I was angry. I don't know why I acted as I did. I even got lost cold, and scared last night. I ended up in Tampa on the wrong side of town on my little scooter, and some guy tried to pick me up, and some foreign guy couldn't speak English to tell me how to get back on the right highway. I finally found Hwy 93 but was going the wrong way, and had to turn around. I was so scared, Ronnie. I promise I won't do it again. Forgive me."

She jumped on the bed, and I cringed again, she grabbed me and hugged me.

"I love you Sam, I was so worried, and I can't help myself. I want to protect you. I feel responsible for you, and I know you don't want me to, but I do. I have made bad choices all my life, and I don't want you to make the same ones. I have always wanted to protect you. It is my goal in life to take care of you, whether you like it or not."

I shook my head then covered it up so I could cry. She heard me, said good-bye, and left for work. I heard Kat and Abby shuffling around in the other room, but they did not come in my room. I heard them leave around ten-thirty. I slept.

# CHAPTER NINE

I heard Kat and Abby come in from work, so it must have been after three o'clock. I still had a headache and didn't want to get out of bed. I lay there. I heard someone tap on the door. I didn't say anything, just turned over. I heard them open the door and look inside.

It was Kat saying, "Sam, are you okay?" I didn't move or answer her, so she shut the door quietly. I heard them talking in the living room. I couldn't understand what they were saying, but they were talking. I couldn't go back to sleep, listening to them. It was driving me crazy; I tossed and turned for an hour. Finally, I sat up and shook my head slightly. It still hurt but I felt alive.

I got up and went into the bathroom. I washed my face and brushed my teeth, looking at myself in the mirror I was such a looser. I was so cruel to Abby, because of a boy. We have been friends for years. I was in the shower and let the hot water hit me for a long time. I heard someone at the bathroom door, knocking. It was stupid to not respond, they knew I am in here.

"Who is it?"

"It's Abby." Oh, man, now I had to face her and, tell her I'm sorry. I turned the water off and dried off.

"I'll be out in a minute." I wrapped the towel around me and opened the door.

"Hey, Abby."

"Hey, Sam. How are you?"

"I'm fine. How are you?"

"I'm okay. We worried last night."

I hung my head, "I am sorry for making you worry, but more than that. Abby I am sorry for what I said to you. I didn't mean it. I felt protective of Edward. You have the right not to like him. It's okay. It doesn't mean, I am going to stop seeing him, but I won't force you to like him. You will have to get used to having him around though. You are my sister, and you know we have been together a long time. I like him, and maybe more than that." I paused, "Abby, Why don't you like Edward?"

"He scares me, Sam. I don't know, he is so tough-looking and serious, I am not sure."

"He is not tough though. He is so kind and sweet to me. When I am with him, I feel so happy, nothing I have ever felt before. I sometimes feel I can't bear to be away from him. It is like my heart aches, when he leaves."

"I have never had those feelings." She hung her head.

"I know. Abby, there are so many nice guys out there, but you never seem to like any of them. Why?"

"Because, I know they will dump me and hurt me, so I push them away before they can hurt me. To protect myself, I guess."

"By doing that, not giving yourself the chance to love, you may never find the guy who could make you happy. This was an accident, remember? I have always been your ally. I have missed out and rejected others because you wanted to. I can't do that now. I think I love him."

"I don't like myself much, Sam. I never have. I am the ugly one of the Quad. I am the fat one. I am the hypocritical one. You have always been at my side, when Kat and Ronnie were off with some boy, doing whatever they do. You and I were the ones who held out. You were my crutch. Now you have gone over to their side and left me alone. That is how I feel, alone."

"Ronnie and I were talking about being alone earlier, I mean yesterday. We have always felt lonely, out of sorts, searching for love, and wanting to be loved and accepted for who we are. Abby, it is okay to like someone and give them a chance. What about Sam, Edward's friend, you liked him. Why? Edward said Sam liked you."

"I guess because Edward scared me so much. I laughed, and talked to him more to piss you off than I cared for him. There has never been a time when some guy was talking to Ronnie, Kat or even you while some other guy was in the least bit interested in me, but Sam was interested that night. I felt different, and I felt like I was making you be me for once, settling for second best. But it got turned around on me. You liked freaky guy better anyway."

"Abby, I didn't know you felt like that. I would never intentionally hurt you. You wanted to hurt, me?" I felt tears fall down my face. I never let her be by herself when she acted out at parties or group functions. She wanted me to be left out so I would be with her. She wanted me to hurt because she was hurting. She hung her head. I felt anger and sorrow as well.

"Abby, I am sorry, you feel that way."

"Sam, me too. I don't know how to change, I love you all and want you to be happy, but I want to be happy too. I just never am. I am sad and feel unimportant, useless. My parents only talk to me when they are telling me what to do. I don't think I have ever heard them say, 'I love you' to me. My dad is an awful man, he yells all the time. Did you ever wonder why I never asked you all to stay at my house? My dad was mean and selfish, and I am just like him. I hate myself for it."

I hugged her.

"Abby, we will all work harder to be better to each other. I want us to spend more time together and less at parties, and I will spend less with Edward too. You are not mean and selfish."

"Sam, you are the first one of us to maybe be falling in love. I don't want to ruin that for you. I would like to spend more time together doing things and less at parties. I never liked that kind of stuff."

"Then we have to talk to Ronnie and Kat and tell them. We are going to do those things we wanted to do while we are here in Florida together, the four of us. I will tell Edward," I paused, "We will go on the air boat rides, just the four of us, okay."

"No, Sam. This weekend, we will go with Edward to Ft. Myers."

"Really?"

"Really."

"We all need to set some time to spend just us the four of us then. When Ronnie gets home tonight, let's sit down and talk."

Abby left the room so I could get dressed. I brushed my hair and pinched my cheeks I looked pale. I put on a pair of shorts and a tank top. I was starving, I went toward the kitchen, noticing Kat, and Abby weren't in the living room or in their bedroom. I wondered where they had gone. I fixed myself some toast, along with a bowl of cereal. I still felt hungry, and then sudden, my stomach started rumbling, and I knew I was going to throw up.

I ran for the bathroom and barely made it before I puked. My stomach didn't like all that food I just ate. I still felt hungry, but I wasn't going to try that again. I decided to go outside on the balcony, and the sun killed my eyes. I ran back in, found a pair of sunglasses, and went back out on the balcony. I wanted to sit in the warm sun. I needed my stomach to settle. I thought of going to the pool, but I didn't know how that would work. I was bored, so I went back in and put on a swim suit. I gathered up a towel, a wet wash cloth, a couple of bottles of water, a book and a pillow.

I headed down to the pool. I moved a chair, maybe the one I slept in last night, close to the pool so I might be splashed occasionally. I centered myself in the chair, facing away from the sun. I was lying on the towel with the washcloth over my face, and then slept.

I woke up and checked to see how long I had been out here and turned on my stomach, shading my eyes, I slept again. I heard lots of laughing and playing around. I figured there were kids in the pool. I took a peek, seeing the two guys from the first floor, Steve and Trent. I laid back and let them play and have fun. They would splash me once in awhile, which felt nice.

Trent called out, "Ronnie, Sam, which one are you? We can't tell from the side sticking up".

I giggled.

"Sam!" I yelled at them. I heard them laughing.

"You got a nice back side."

"Is it covered or uncovered? I still have my bottoms on, right?" They were he hawing.

"Yeah, you got them on, but we don't mind if you take them off."

"I am not moving then."

Trent came over by me and was trying to talk to me, I peeked at him. "What?"

"Would you like to join us in the pool?"

"My head hurts, I have a hang-over, and I just want some sun, peace, and quiet. Guess that isn't going to happen." I said. He laughed again.

"Come on join us."

I sat up and turned over; the sun was way over to the west. I checked the time. I had been out here for three hours. I checked for sunburn. I looked a little red. I still had the sunglasses on. I waved him away, and he laughed as he dove in, splashing me. It felt nice and cool. He thought he would piss me off, but I enjoyed the cool water hitting me.

I knew Abby should be home soon, or maybe already was upstairs. I didn't leave a note telling them I came down, but they should see my scooter was here and my stuff upstairs. I only brought the key with me. I should have brought my phone. What if someone called? But who cared if someone called?

I was leaning back and relaxing, enjoying the sun. It felt so good. I guessed Steve said something very dirty, because I heard a mother tell him he should not talk like that, as there were children in the pool. Steve had a nasty mouth, but he was harmless as far as I could tell.

I watched the two little boys playing at the shallow end with their mom, and finally she packed them up and headed inside. They must be new here, because I hadn't seen them before. Trent and Steve were here almost every day about this time. They had already started drinking. Trent offered me a beer. I waved it away. I already had a hangover from last night; I was not starting another one.

"Hey beautiful, it will help the old one go away. Come on, just one." I took it and took a swig; it did taste cool and refreshing. I sat up straddling the chair and watching the two of them play in the water. They were having fun all by themselves. They didn't need anyone to entertain them, they entertained themselves. They were quite funny most of the time. I laughed at them too.

I decided a cool dip in the pool would make me feel better. I stood up and jumped in. Trent and Steve were all over me in a minute. Tossing me around, Trent yelled Camel fights! But there were only three of us in the pool. I was laughing and feeling good for the first time all day. They were throwing me back and forth from one to the other.

I looked up, and Edward was standing at the edge of the pool, looking mad and ready to fight. I thought, Uh oh. I tried to get out, but Trent pulled me by the bottoms of my bathing suit, almost removing them. Edward jumped in the pool and slugged Trent in the mouth. Steve headed for him. I was afraid the two of them would get the best of Edward. Boy was I wrong. Edward threw Steve off his back and then dove for Trent with malice on his face. I was yelling for him to stop. Steve jumped back on Edward. I had jumped on Steve, trying to get him to stop, when someone slugged me in the mouth. The next thing I remember, I was lying on the ground with Edward over me, slapping my face.

"Cut it out, that hurts." I yelled at him.

"Oh baby, are you okay, I am so sorry." He hugged me and rocked me back and forth. Trent and Steve were sitting on the edge of the pool, watching. I sat up.

"Yeah, I am fine. My mouth hurts a little. Who hit me?" My lip was bloody. I could taste the metal in my mouth. I felt it, and my mouth felt swollen. My whole jaw ached. I pressed my hand to it and moaned with pain.

"I did, Trent said." Edward started toward him, but I grabbed his shirt and held him near me.

Edward said to Trent, "I should kill you, jerk.".

I said, "He didn't mean to hit me, I am sure. He was aiming for you. They are friends, Edward, that's all."

"Well hell, we are just friends. We thought we had a chance to make out with you." Steve yelled. Edward started toward him. I had a strong grip on him.

"They are joking, Edward."

"Yeah, we were just kidding around, having fun with Sam. We didn't mean to hurt her."

"Edward, I am okay. I started to get up, and Edward helped me. He was looking at the guys as if he wanted to kill them. I shook my finger at the two of them.

"See what you caused."

"Us? We were just having fun. Are you okay Sam?"

"Yeah, I'm fine." I wrapped my towel around me; Edward was gathering my stuff to help me to my apartment.

Trent called out, "Sam, I am sorry. I didn't mean to hurt you."

I yelled back, "I know Trent. It was an accident."

When we went in, he went to the kitchen to get some ice for my lip; I got him a towel to dry himself with. He removed his shirt but kept his shorts on. I sat on the couch as he put a towel filled with ice on the side of my face and lip, and I screamed. It hurt. He tried again, gentler. I took a hold of it then. I sat on the couch then patted the couch beside me, and he tried to dry himself somewhat and the sat next to me.

"Edward, those two guys are gay, or they could be bi-sexual, I am not sure. They were just playing around. They do that all the time. Don't worry about them."

"Then it is my fault you're hurt. I didn't bother to ask questions, I just saw those two men manhandling you and got angry. I don't want any other man to touch you. You are mine."

I was smiling at him.

"Oh, what makes you think I belong to you?

"Well, I didn't mean, ah . . . You know I like you. We are going out. I can't stand to see guys looking at you, let alone touch you, Sam. I've got it bad for you." He hung his head, and I ran my fingers through his hair.

"I am so sorry, you got hurt. I will try harder to control my temper. That is the reason I think your friend doesn't like me. She knew I would hurt you."

"You didn't hurt me. Trent hit me, not you."

"But it was my fault."

"I got in the middle, it was my fault." He laid his head on my lap, facing away from me, and I kept brushing my fingers through his hair and, touching his face. I felt his whiskers, and I giggled a little. I felt a smile on his face. I kept touching his face, feeling those dimples I loved so much, and I touched his neck. I felt him stiffen.

"Sam, I really like what you are doing, but it is making me Ah . . . not feel so gentleman-like. Do you understand?"

"No, what do you mean?" That was horrible of me. I knew exactly what he meant, and I kept touching him. I ran my fingers down his arm, and across his chest. I turned his face up to look at me. He had this stern look on his face. He was concentrating so hard, trying so hard to keep control, and I wasn't helping matters at all. I finally moved my hand to his shoulder and stopped. I sighed.

"Okay, Edward, I'll quite." I felt him relax. I scooted down to the end of the couch and told him to follow me. He put his head back in my lap and rested his legs up on the couch.

"How about if I just run my fingers through your hair? Does that bother you too much?"

"No, that felt good."

Therefore, I started running my fingers through his hair and brushing it back. He fell asleep. I knew he was so tired. He was soaking wet, and so was I. I was afraid he might get sick lying there in wet clothes, but I didn't have anything that would fit him. I pulled the blanket off the back of the couch and covered him up. I leaned my head back and fell asleep too.

# Chapter Ten

All three of my friends came in and saw us on the couch. They tried to be quiet to not disturb us, but Ronnie noticed my face. There was a bruise starting around my mouth going up my jaw and ending close to my eye, and she saw the split lip. She came closer and started removing the towel I was holding to see more of my face, causing the melted ice to fall into my lap, dripping cold water on Edwards's neck and shoulder. I screamed and jumped forward, trying to get up, shocked. Edward felt the cold water and ice hit him. He, had been in a deep sleep, and he rose up, forcing his head back as I was moving forward, hitting me in the nose and face so hard it knocked me up and back against the wall above the couch with a loud bang.

I knew something was broken, I felt it. I screamed with pain as I grabbed my face. He jumped off the couch and was in attack mode with my three friends. He was standing in front of me with his feet apart. He had one arm straight out in front of him with his hand up like trying to tell someone to stop, and the other arm bent and closer to his body, his hand was in a fist ready to fight.

Ronnie jumped back; Kat and Abby just watched and didn't move. Blood was pouring out of my nose and mouth, causing so much pain; I thought I was going to pass out. I grabbed my already swollen face and yelled again. Edward jumped, and looked back at me, still in attack mode. Edward threatened them, "if anyone comes close, I'll kill you." Then he recognized who they were and calmed just a bit. He kept looking back at me, and then he saw the blood running down my face and onto my shirt. He picked up the wet towel, holding it under my bleeding nose. He pushed too hard and I screamed again.

He yelled, "Someone to get another towel." Everyone was frozen in place. He screamed at Ronnie, "GO GET A DAMN TOWEL." He was still protecting me from an invasion, it seemed like. If it hadn't of hurt you, I would have laughed at the way he was looking and standing there in front of me. The look on his face was priceless. He pulled me into his arms, checking my face and nose. He told me to move my hand and I did.

He yelled again, "We need to get her to the hospital." He yelled at Ronnie, "Where is the damn ice, Ronnie?"

She handed him the ice in a plastic bag and a dry clean towel, and he gently placed it on the side of my nose. It was starting to swell. It was throbbing, and I was moaning. He stood and picked me up in his massive arms, heading for the door.

I heard Ronnie screaming, "Where are you going?"

"I am taking her to the hospital, her nose is broken."

"Not without me. She needs her ID and insurance card."

"I'll pay."

"No, you wait for me."

He carried me down the stairs, and Ronnie caught up with us. She had my bag and she was going through my wallet to make sure my driver's license and insurance card were in there.

Edward put me in the front seat, and Ronnie crawled in beside me as I leaned my head on her shoulders. She kept saying, "Sam I am so sorry." Edward got in, started the car, and pulled out onto the main street. He was driving very fast. "Slow down and be careful." I was hurting, but still listening to them bickering about his driving.

"Stop telling me what to do, and shut up."

"You had better listen to what I say, be careful jerk."

I was watching the scene, I would have laughed and not believed it. We arrived at the hospital, Edward pulled into the emergency area. He jumped out of the car and opened my door.

Edward told Ronnie, "Go park the car, I am taking her inside."

Ronnie told him, "You go park your own damn car; I am going in with her."

He said, "Can you carry her in?"

She said, "No, but I am smart enough to get a wheel chair, or you carry her in and then go park your car because I am not about to leave her side".

They were still arguing and I yelled out, "Oh... nu nies dis urts." They both stopped and looked at me. Edward picked me up and carried me inside, Ronnie following with my bag in tow.

Edward was yelling at the nurses, and they went to get a wheel-chair. I was holding onto Edward's neck for dear life. I wasn't sure what would happen next. The nurse came back with a wheel-chair, Edward placed me in it, and then she took me to a room.

Ronnie yelled at Edward, "The car." Edward shook his head but ran out of the hospital. I wanted him to stay with me too, but he had to park his car somewhere.

They placed me in a room on a gurney with my head propped up but leaning forward. They gave me a new ice bag and a container for the blood to drip. They asked me about insurance and Ronnie was doing all the answering. She told them she could fill out the paper work; she had my information and insurance card. The nurse lightly removed the ice bag, and told Ronnie it was smart to put the ice on there, it helped keep the swelling down some. She replaced the ice pack, started an IV, and told me the doctor would be right in. Ronnie looked at me and shook her head. About that time, I heard Edward yelling again outside the room. They didn't want to let him in; I heard them say, "Immediate family only."

Edward was yelling at the nurse, "I am her husband." using several choice cuss words. They showed him where I was. He ran up to me and, started talking so softly and gently as if he was two different people. He was asking me, how I was and telling me how sorry he was. I just looked at him, grabbed his hand, and tried to smile, but it hurt so much. He had put his wet shirt back on and was bare foot standing beside me. I loved this man and appreciated him so much.

A doctor came in and looked at me. I was looking back and forth at the doctor, Ronnie and Edward.

"Well, looks like a broken nose. Does it hurt much?"

Edward yelled, "Hell yeah it hurts her. Do something for her, now."

The doctor told him to, "Calm down", I hoped he was going to take care of me soon. The nurse was giving me something now, telling me it will only take a minute.

The doctor said "Hold on" then patted me on the arm.

He ordered X-rays and told Edward I needed surgery and would be taken upstairs shortly. I heard him yell again. He was so worried. The doctor had his hand on Edward's shoulder and told him I would be fine. It looked like a clean break. He also asked him how it happened.

Edward lowered his head and said, "I hit her with the back of my head." The doctor removed his hand from Edwards shoulder. The expression on his face wasn't as soft and kind as it was before. He wasn't joking around anymore. I couldn't say anything. I was squeezing Edwards's hand.

Ronnie spoke up, "it was my fault. They were asleep on the couch, and I saw her lip and face. She had an ice bag on her swollen lip, and I moved it, and the ice fell on them, it startled them, causing Sam to jump forward and Edward to jump straight up and back and they collided. It was an accident. He didn't do it on purpose." The doctor softened his look again, and asked about the lip.

Edward told him, hanging his head in shame again, "It happened in the pool, when I walked up, there were these two guys pushing her under water, and she saw me and tried to get out of the pool, but one of them grabbed her, almost pulled her bottoms off her, and then threw her back in the pool. I jumped him to kill him. His friend jumped on my back, and then Sam jumped on the one that was on my back, and the one in front punched her, knocking her out. I pulled her from the pool and brought her back around. I threatened to kill those bastards, but she told me they were just playing." He paused, "I didn't know, they looked rough with her, it scared me, and I thought I was protecting her."

I looked at Ronnie and she was smiling. The doctor laughed, shaking his head. He looked at me and patted me on the arm again; I was starting to feel woozy. "You have had a bad day." I just looked at the doc, and that is the last thing I remembered.

"Ronnie, I didn't mean to hurt her, I promise, I love her."

"Edward, I saw that in there. I know it was my fault. I dropped the ice and water on you."

"You saw her lip and just wanted to protect her, as well." He hung his head, rubbing his hands through his hair. "I think I am just bad for her, this is too much. I mean, the night before last, with the beach thing. Did she tell you?"

"A little."

"I hurt her feelings, but I didn't mean to do that either. I was trying to do what I thought was best for her. I think I should leave her alone."

"You can't mean that! That would hurt her even more."

"I need to before something worse happens to her, Ronnie. I ah . . . care for her so much, I couldn't stand to do more harm to her." He hung his head. The tears were building in his eyes, and he didn't want Ronnie to see him cry.

Ronnie put her arm around his shoulder. "Edward, I don't know what Sam has told you about our little group, but we are the misfits. We have bonded together because we felt alone, unloved, and unwanted. For Sam to feel about you the way she does, I would never do anything to take that away from her. She . . . Ah . . . cares about you too Edward. I am afraid it would kill her to lose you."

"I don't know if I could bear to lose her either, I just can't stand to see her in pain." He paused again, "Besides your friends hate me. There is no changing that."

"Ha," Ronnie said, "Abby is the only one who hates you, and she hates everyone. That is her take on life and men. If I didn't know her better, I would think she didn't like men at all, that maybe she preferred girls, you know what I mean. But I don't really think so."

The doctor walked toward them. They both stood up.

"Is she okay?" Edward pleaded.

The doctor smiled, "She is fine. I don't think there will even be any scaring or evidence she ever had a broken nose. She will have bruises that look pretty bad for a while; she has a couple of stitches across her nose. I have a prescription here for pain medication." He handed it to Edward. "She is going to be really be sore for several days, keep her down as much as possible. And sleep is good for healing. No alcohol, no other drugs, okay."

"She doesn't do drugs."

"Okay, she will be out for a while. Maybe an hour, she will be confused, unable to remember things, and be unable to walk, so take her home and put her to bed. No sex for a few days. Let her rest."

Edward blushed, he actually blushed, "Yes doctor." He finally said in a low voice.

"If there is a lot of bleeding or too much discomfort, bring her back in. Here is my card, call if you need too." He paused shaking his head, "Are you newlyweds?"

"Yes, we are." Edward said, and Ronnie just watched. The doctor left, and Ronnie was looking at Edward strangely.

"We haven't had sex, I wouldn't do that yet. I mean, I want her to make sure."

Ronnie smiled, "I know, she told me that." Ronnie smiled bigger at Edward, "I think you are all right, I think I like you."

Edward smiled at her and knew things would get better between them at least. Now, he had to win over the other two, and with the circumstances, it might be difficult.

After a couple of hours, Ronnie and Edward took me home, and I remember part of the trip and some of their conversation. It was different from when we were coming to the hospital. If was funny like they were friends. I thought wow, *Ronnie likes him, I am so happy.* Edward carried me upstairs, and Ronnie opened the door. Kat and Abby were there with a thousand questions. They gasped when they saw my face. Edward sighed but didn't say anything; he carried me to the bedroom and laid me on the bed.

"I am going to get your prescription filled, and I will be right back." I nodded.

Ronnie, Kat, and Abby all followed us in. They were asking Ronnie everything about what happened and any long-term damage, why my eyes bugged out, and if I was going to have a huge hump on my nose. What if it looked crooked and ugly? I was so tired, I fell asleep.

I heard Edward come back, and they were talking in the living room. At least they were calm. I was happy about that. I dozed off and on and didn't know what they were saying or what was happening. I slept fitfully, worrying about things I couldn't do anything about. Edward came in at one point, kissed me on the head, and told me he was leaving. He said he would check in with Ronnie on how I was doing. He would see me tomorrow.

"Hey, Sam, I am sorry."

I tried to say something, and he put his finger on my lips. "Sam don't talk, everything is cool with me and your friends. You need rest baby. I'll be back. If you want me to come anytime, day or night, just have Ronnie call me. I love you."

My eyes were huge; he smiled and rubbed my arm.

"Bye Baby." He walked out the door. He said he loved me. Edward said he loved me, 'Me'. I slept well after that; and I didn't wake until early in the morning. I had to go pee, went right back to bed, and slept the rest of the night.

# Chapter Eleven

I woke up the next day, in a lot of pain. I should have taken a pill when I got up, but I didn't think about it. Now it had been several hours past the time, and the drug seems to have worn off. I guessed Ronnie heard me because she came into the bedroom with a glass of water and a pill.

"Here take this. How are you feeling?"

I grabbed the pill and didn't say a word, pulling the pillow over my face with a yell; it hurt so badly to touch my face with that pillow. Kat and Abby ran into the room. They took one look at me and looked like they would be sick. I knew I must have looked really bad. I only remember bits and pieces of what happened yesterday.

Ronnie said, "Edward called to see how you were already." I started to cry, and Ronnie sat beside me and tried to comfort me, telling me the pain meds would take effect soon.

"It's not the pain, Ronnie. I love him. I am going to be so ugly now. He won't want me anymore." I cried, and it was making my nose and face hurt even more, but I couldn't stop.

"Oh, Hunny, the doctor said you won't even have a mark or scar to ever suggest you had a broken nose. He said you were lucky. Don't worry. Edward loves you too."

I sniffed, moaning with pain. She started to the bathroom; I guessed for toilet paper or Kleenex to blow my nose, but she remembered I couldn't do that, so she turned around and looked sympathetic. She gave me a bag of ice to put on my face for the swelling.

"Sam it is going to be all right. We have all talked; and we approve of Edward. He is a good man. I talked to him and listened to him at the hospital. He really cares about you and wants to be with you forever, he said."

I sniffed some more, which hurt like hell.

"The doctor said to try not to do that. Be still."

"I want to get up."

"You need to rest.

I can't lie here any longer." I sounded so funny, like I was all stopped up, which I was stuffed with my nose stuffed with cotton. I had bandages across my nose and cheeks. I looked horrible. My face was black and blue from above my eyebrows to my lower lip on one side and all the way across my eyes.

"Do you have trouble understanding what I am saying?"

"Just a little." She smiled at me. I guessed Kat and Abby had backed away without me noticing.

"Please let me go in the other room for a while, I can't stand to lie here any longer, my back hurts just lying on this damn bed.

"Okay, I'll fix you a place on the couch."

I walked to the other room with Ronnie at my side. She was holding me, but I didn't I need help. But then stumbled, and if she hadn't been there, I would have fallen on my luck breaking something else. I finally sat on the couch, and she told me to lie back and put my feet up, but I shook my head.

"Not yet."

Abby was sitting with her head down, and I knew she wanted to say something. I was afraid it was more bad remarks about Edward, and I couldn't defend him right now. Kat was gawking at me, smiling. I felt she wanted to laugh but held it back.

"Go ahead, say what you want. Tell me how you feel now that I can't fight back."

Kat burst out laughing. "You look awful, Sam. I am so sorry, but you look like you have been hit by a Mac truck."

I shook my head.

Abby raised her head, "Sam, I am so sorry you have had to go through this. Can I do anything for you? Get you anything?"

I shook my head, "I'm okay. I feel like I was hit by that Mac truck."

Ronnie brought me a glass of juice and plopped on the couch beside me. "Can I get you something to eat, some soup?" I shook my head. I hadn't had anything to eat for two days, but I didn't feel like anything would stay down, and I couldn't imagine puking now.

Kat turned on the television and surfed the channels. Not finding anything she liked, and not asking us if we wanted to watch, she just clicked it off.

"So, Sam, you and Edward are serious, I guess."

I looked up at Kat.

"Well, we like each other, and yeah, maybe headed that way."

"Sam, we all will give him a fair chance, don't worry about us treating him badly. We just want you to be happy, you know that."

"I know. Edward and I have talked, and we have decided it is best we don't spend every day together, or try not to anyway. He, no, we agreed, I do need to spend time with the three of you. Just do some things together, just us. Not all the time, but at least once or twice a week, like we planned."

"That sounds great." Kat said. Ronnie and Abby agreed.

"How about we all have lunch together one day, and then have dinner together another day, or go sightseeing or to the zoo and all the other places on your list one day, and maybe, maybe add some other times in there too, just the four of us." We all agreed, that sounded perfect. We sat down and started a schedule of when we were all off work at the same time. We wrote down on the calendar several lunch dates. a few dinner dates, and a few cheep nights at home playing cards or watching television. We decided to even go to a few parties together, and each one of us picked something we liked. We all agreed to be even and fair about the choices we made. I told them they were all free this weekend or until my face wasn't in so much pain and maybe I looked a little better. They agreed.

We agreed also that it was cool for Edward to come here to see me, especially while I was recuperating, and other times too. They told me they would also like to include him in a few things we all did, making it a five-person night so they could get to know him better. I almost cried, I felt tears, but I knew how badly it would hurt to cry, because of my nose.

Ronnie then announced, "We are all going out tonight to a 'Rave'. Some people call it; it is not like a drug party, but a dance on the beach. It's put on by two of the big hotels up the strip. Edward is coming over to stay with you, in case you need something. Actually just to hang out, is that okay with you, Sam?"

"Look at me Ronnie; I don't know if I want him to see me like this."

"Too late, he already has, remember?" She stood up, putting her hands on her hips, "Too bad also, he is on his way. Deal with it." She smiled, and they all went to get ready for the 'Rave'.

Ronnie came out and looked very nice as usual. She smiled, heading toward Kat and Abby's room with makeup and a curling iron. I heard them laughing and telling Abby to shut up, they weren't going to stop. I heard the door, but I guessed they didn't, so I wiggled to get up, walked to the door, and peeked out the best I could.

I opened it, and it was Edward. He was smiling, and then he frowned. "What the hell? You are to be resting. Why can't those girls answer the damn door for you is beyond me. Damn it, Sam, let me help you back to bed."

"No I was on the couch. They are in Kat and Abby's room."

"Well, they shouldn't make you answer the door. I should give them a piece of my mind. If they can't do better than this, you are coming home with me until your recover." He was still gripping when Ronnie came in.

"Okay Mr. Mom, I can hear you complaining in the bedroom. She's not an invalid. And she has a broken nose, not feet or legs. Give us a break." She was smiling the whole time she was yelling at him. I saw the look on his face, he grinned. I guessed he had met his match with Ronnie. She didn't put up with anyone bossing her around.

Kat came out smiling also, "Yeah, and whatever she said."

Then Abby came out, saying, "I agree." If I had been standing up, I would have fallen over. Oh my gosh, Abby looked unbelievable.

"Abby, you are beautiful." I gasped.

Edward sighed, "Wow, Abby, you look nice, I mean beautiful. Turn around." She blushed and turned around slowly. Edward got down on his knees and said, "Will you marry me?" I frowned, and Abby laughed. She was amazing.

"Abby, why haven't you ever dressed like this before? You look so pretty, wow!" I told her.

"I don't know, I figured if I put makeup on my ugly, fat face it would just look like a clown."

"Abby, you are not fat or ugly, why do you say that?" Edward told her. I was so proud of him.

"Do you think I am pretty, you guys?"

In unison, we all replied, "Yes!" She giggled. We all kept watching her, and her attitude changed. She felt pretty, I do believe. The three of them got their ID's, and bid us goodbye, and told us to be good and have no funny business. Edward held up both of his hands in surrender. They left, and he sat beside me, hugging me gently like if he hugged me too hard I might break.

"I won't break."

"You might. I have already hurt you too many times."

"You have not, it was an accident."

"But I did that to you. Have you seen your face? You are a mess. Your poor, beautiful face. You are black and blue all over, even around your eyes."

"Yes. Thanks a lot."

"I hurt you, and I can hardly stand it. I would die for you, Sam. I feel my heart breaking looking at your bruised face and swollen eyes and lip. It is my entire fault."

"Shut up. It is not. Do not say that again, or I will punch you in the gut."

"I won't move if you want to do it several times. If it makes you feel better. Here" He stood up and raised his shirt, and I saw his ripped muscles across his stomach. I stared at him. He was so hard and tanned, and I reached up, touching him. I ran my fingers across his abs, and they were so firm. He flinched and pulled his shirt down.

"You shouldn't do that. Hit me."

"I don't want to hit you. I wanted to touch you."

He sat back down, sitting close and looking me in the eye. I loved his eyes. They were bright and big, even though they were dark. He ran his fingers around my hairline. The corner of his mouth turned up, not actually a smile but a sexy grin. I leaned toward him and kissed him gently on his lips. He parted them slightly, but I did not dare try anything else. It was nice, and he smelled so good. He didn't remove his eyes from mine. I leaned in again and kissed him; my eyes open, and so were his. I hurt only a little. He kissed back, pressing firmly but not too hard to hurt me. I wanted so much from him. We sat there looking at each other. He ran his fingers around my face, my swollen eyes. He leaned in with a gentle kiss on one eyelid, and then moved to the other one. He kissed my cheek, and then my chin, and then my bottom lip, and then top lip, sucking it into his mouth. I felt the heat in my belly rise. I wanted to hold on to him, but I didn't move. I knew he heard the catch of my breath. My chest rose and fell, letting out a breath through my mouth with a swooshing sound.

He ran his fingers down my neck and across my collarbone. I leaned my head back slightly. He kissed my neck, in that sunken place in the middle. I leaned my head to one side, and he kissed my neck there, and then I leaned to the other, and he kissed the other side. He moved to my shoulder, pulled my strap to the side, and kissed my shoulder, and then the top of my arm. I was breathing very hard. He pulled the strap back into place and moved back just a little, not too far.

"Sam, not yet. You need to heal. I don't want to hurt you more."

I bent my head down until it rested on his chest, placing both hands on his chest beside my head. I felt the curves of his Pecs, the firm, and hard form of his body. I moved them ever so slightly. He took a deep breath. I raised my head back up.

"I know Edward, I know."

Sighing, he wrapped his arms around me. We didn't talk for some time. We leaned back and sat there. His head was resting on top of mine. I had my arms as far around him as I could reach, and I was snuggled up against him. I felt happy, a feeling I had yearned for. I felt loved, something I had missed for so long. I wondered if he felt like I did. I looked up into his face and he looked down at me.

"Is there something you want to tell me? Do you want me to tell you something? I will tell you anything you want to know."

"No, I like looking at you. I feel safe in your arms, Edward. I have wanted to know what it was like, this feeling, this tenderness you are showing me, all my life. I have craved to be desired, wanted, and more. I guess, needed. I can't imagine my life now without this."

"Me either."

"I want to tell you something. I guess, it is really our pact, mine and my friends. Don't judge me, please."

"I would never judge you."

"You might when you hear me out." I said. He sat quietly. "When Kat, Ronnie, Abby and I made a pact, we were in middle school. We all felt, you know, unloved, and just didn't really fit in anywhere. Anyway, we agreed that, if our lives didn't get better, or if we were, ah . . . if we kept being picked on by bully's and the 'In Crowd", we would do something about it. Together, all four of us at the same time, we decided to be together forever." I looked at him. "We have talked about it at different times throughout our lives, when one of us was down or really depressed, but we all had to agree and do it together.

"Do what?"

"Kill ourselves."

He gasped loudly.

"You wouldn't would you?"

"I have considered it lots of times," I said. He held me tighter. "I'm lonely, Edward. I cry myself to sleep. I hurt deep in my gut. I feel no one would care or miss me. It would actually make my brother, sister and parents lives easier, not to have to deal with my outburst. Money would be better for them. Everything would be easier if I were gone."

"Oh my, please never say it again. I can't deal with that." I saw tears in his eyes.

"I was afraid you would judge me and think I was crazy. I see it on your face, Edward."

"I don't think you are crazy. I am not judging you. I want you, don't you understand. You are not alone anymore. I am with you. We are one." He cried, he openly cried, and I didn't know what to say or do. I leaned my head back into his chest. He kept crying for a long time. I felt ashamed of myself.

"Sam, I love you." He kissed me ever so lightly, I felt his tears on my lips, and I tasted the salt in my mouth.

"That's just it, Edward, now I want to live. I have a reason."

"Please, Sam, I love you. Don't ever do that, please, I would have to follow you." He kissed me again. I leaned into him, and we didn't say another word until Abby walked in. She was smiling and happy, Ronnie and Kat followed her. It was after midnight.

I rose up, "I guess you had a good time."

"We had a blast." Abby said.

Edward pulled away from me, and I tried to keep him close but I was unable to do so. "So, tell me what happened."

"Oh my, Sam, I had so much fun. I danced, guys actually asked, 'Me, me' to dance."

"And why wouldn't they? You look gorgeous." Edward stood up and walked to the door, "I guess I can leave now. You guys are back to take care of her." He looked at me with tear-stained eyes. I couldn't say anything.

"Sam, I'll call you later. See you all tomorrow. Bye." He turned and walked out the door.

I sat there. I didn't move. I didn't want to say anything. I didn't want to make the girls think we had a fight or anything, I didn't frown, and I had a silly grin on my face.

"So tell me more, Abby."

"Oh, Sam, I didn't drink much, but I had the best time. I felt like one of the crowd. Boys spoke to me, I was asked questions. I laughed and answered anything they asked of me. I talked to people I didn't know. It was so much fun. I wish you could have been there."

"Me too, Abby."

Kat said, "You should have seen her. She put us to shame, taking all the attention. I have never seen her so outgoing and having so much fun. It was great. We all had a nice time, Sam."

Ronnie chimed in, "We all danced together at one point. We were laughing, and it was great, Sam." I was so happy for my friends. They had a nice time. I was so sad. Why did I tell Edward about our pact? I should never have done that. It was our secret. I kept the shitty little grin on my face. I yawned and told them I was so sorry, but I was so tired. Ronnie ran to the kitchen, getting me some water and a pill. I took them and went to the bedroom.

"Will you guys, tell me more tomorrow, please?"

"You bet Sam. Get some rest. How are you feeling?"

"Actually, my nose feels better. I feel drained and exhausted from so much that happened over the past few days, but I do feel better. Good night." I went to the bathroom. I wanted to cry, but I held it. It hurt my throat anyway; I couldn't let them know anything was wrong. Why did I tell him? I was such an idiot. I hurt him. I wonder if he had thought the same thing or if he just thought I was a loser. What if Edward didn't call me or want me anymore? I had to go to sleep. I had to get rid of this pain, this deep guilt I held inside me. Why do I want to die so badly? I just wanted to hurt my parents. I always thought if I died, then they would feel bad for not loving me, not talking to me, and not including me in their wonderful lives. How would they feel then, knowing, especially if I wrote a note, that I did it because of them? Because I felt sad and hated, so I hated myself. I couldn't even tell Ronnie sometimes the pain I carried. I knew she felt the same way. We didn't share some of the pain because it would just make it hurt more. I thought Kat and Abby had the same pain. I knew they did or we wouldn't have made that pact together. I pulled back the covers and crawled in. I heard Ronnie come in.

"Sam, are you all right? Did something happen between you and Edward?"

"No, Ronnie I am just tired, and sore. My head hurts, and I think I made Edward miserable being here with me, reminding him of the pain I have. He blames himself, you know, just by looking at my bruised face."

"Sam, I think there is something you are not telling me."

"Ron, I promise there is nothing more. Edward has the same unhappy home life as we do. He feels hurt and sorrow as much as we do. He never had anyone to talk to, to tell those things too. We have each other. I feel I make him unhappy more than happy by being with me. I don't know why our lives can't be like everyone else. Why we can't just be happy and glad we are alive and looking forward to a bright future, but I don't feel that way, and I never have." I whispered, "I don't think I ever will either, Ronnie. I'll never be truly happy, I won't let myself."

"Sam, please, you are beautiful. Edward loves you."

"I know he loves me, but we are two sad people in this sad world, and we can't make each other happy if we can't be happy with ourselves."

"Oh Hun, I am sorry, Sam I understand, you know that."

"Yeah, I do. I need to sleep Ronnie. Good night."

"Sam?' She waited. I turned over and didn't say another word. The pain pills were kicking in. I finally slept most of the night. I had a hard time not thinking about Edward and what I might have done, pushing him over the edge. Oh my, what if Edward did something to harm himself because of what I said. Oh my gosh, I jumped up. I reached for my phone and called him.

He answered on the first ring, "Sam, are you okay?"

"Edward, I am sorry. Please forgive me. I was just feeling sorry for myself. Tell me you don't hate me or think awfully of me."

"Sam, I told you I love you. I mean it. I will never feel awful things about you. I couldn't hate you if I tried. Sam, please don't hurt yourself. Don't take my one chance at a happy life away from me."

"I won't, Edward. I think that is why I told you. I don't feel like I did before. I am not saying it is your responsibility to make me happy. Because of you, the time we have been together has changed me. I think no, I believe I can have all those things I want, be normal, be happy. You know."

"I love you, Sam. I will never leave you, ever. We are soul mates and will be together for the rest of our lives. I love you. Do you want me to come over?"

"I love you too, Edward, more than you know. I am fine, get some rest. I will see you tomorrow."

"I know, trust me. I know."

"I am really tired, but I had to talk to you. I love you. Good night."

"Good-night, Sam. I love you too. I will call you tomorrow. Bye."

We hung up. I felt somewhat relieved. I think I must have fallen asleep soon after that. I heard nothing else until the sun came up.

I woke up feeling so much better than yesterday. Of course, I still had that bandage across my face, and I was sore, but the ache was lessening in intensity. I looked awful, looking in the mirror at myself. The bruises were dark. It looked like I had been beat with a baseball bat. I was ashamed to leave the house. .

I went back to work on the Monday. I was very bruised still. The bandage was across my nose now, but I still looked awful. Renee was great about doctor's appointments and everything else. Which was great just working three days a week, but she needed Edward more, and he worked four days a week, and sometimes Friday mornings too. We ate lunch together often, but I didn't go out, we eat in. Edward would sometimes go get us something, or I would bring things from home. We spent time together at work now, we didn't avoid each other. Renee hasn't said anything, so we didn't know if she just thought we were just friends or more. I didn't think she cared. We had been making good progress with my friends, spending time with them. We had our nights where it was just the four of us, at least once a week. Abby had talked to Sam, Edwards's roommate, twice now that I knew of.

We went to the rocks on the beach, as a double date. We drank wine, and watched the sunset. Abby hadn't gone out on a date with him that I know, but they talked at a party last night, and Abby seemed very pleased when she came home.

Edward and I were getting better every day, closer, more in love. We couldn't seem to stay apart or keep our hands off each other either, even though we still hadn't had sex. He wanted to take me to Ft Lauderdale to meet his father sometime over the summer. As soon, as I got this awful thing off my nose, we would plan a trip to Ft Myers for an airboat ride. I hoped I wouldn't fall in the water or get eaten by an alligator. With my luck, who knew, it could happen. Abby had a few dates with Sam that I know about. She didn't talk about them though. She didn't mention Sam as she had before. I thought, more hoped, that she would get on well with him, but he wasn't the one, I suppose.

Our time started passing so quickly. We had been in Florida now for over a month. Kat didn't do much with us anymore. She was gone most evenings. She was still working, but she and Abby seemed to have a barrier between them. Ronnie and I didn't know what happened. Abby stayed home most evenings, she went to the pool and spent time with Trent and Steve. She actually baby-sat for some of the residents here in the apartments. She was making lots of extra money. All the young parents seemed to like her. She was good to their kids, and each time a new family moved in, they found references left by previous families at the office encouraging them to use Abby if they needed a sitter. The guy in the office and Abby seemed to have become friends a well. Our nights together were just the three of us. It was sad to not have Kat around. She wouldn't even talk to us, but we were giving her time and space until she came back to us.

# Chapter Twelve

I had a checkup today on my nose. It was healing nicely. You could barely see the bruises anymore if I wore makeup, and the tape across the bridge of my nose had been removed. It is the second week in July; we had been here over six weeks. Half of our time was gone. I hadn't seen Kat in a week, not even at night. I had heard her come in, but she was asleep when I left in the morning and didn't come home until after I was in bed at night.

Ronnie was talking to one of the guys she met early on when we first got here. His name was Mick. He seemed all right, so now we included him in our group when we did stuff together. Sam and Abby seemed to have parted ways completely. Edward said Sam didn't talk about it and was going back to school early. Abby wouldn't say anything and didn't want to join us anymore if the guys were with us. Abby was babysitting almost every night. She seemed more and more withdrawn from us. She smiled at us, she was kind, and she talked to us when she was around, but we felt a change in her. She was so happy for a while, going to parties, having fun. The change in her was so brief.

Abby stopped wearing makeup and stopped dressing cute. She wore baggy clothes, and usually the top and bottom didn't go together. We noticed this when she and Sam had just started dating, and now, he was gone and Abby was troubled. She told us nothing was wrong. You can see it in her face sometimes, she was depressed and quiet.

Edward, Ronnie, Mick, and I were going to Ft Myers on Saturday. Abby would not go with us. We begged and pleaded for her to go. She said that she was sitting for a couple up the beach and they were paying her Two-hundred dollars to spend the night with their two kids, while the parents were going to Miami. She liked kids and liked being around them. She said, children made her feel good, she was happy around them. They liked her too. She tried to interact with them on their level and made them feel important. She hugged them and made them feel loved and special.

We left Saturday morning at nine-o'clock. We went to the 'Everglades Day Safari'. The captain of our air-boat was in his late forties or early fifties, balding with a pouch of a belly. He was hilarious. He told us jokes and showed us all around the park. He weaved the boat and scared me to death most of the time. I screamed a lot, and that made him chuckle, and every time he did, his belly bounced. I just knew I was going to fall in that dirty, stinky alligator water and be eaten by one. Ole Captain Henry kept us laughing the whole trip. I learned to keep my mouth shut when we were riding though because I swallowed a bug, a big bug, with wings, and I choked. Everyone else thought it was funny, except me. Henry took us to an area where he put out food for the deer. They came close to him. I was so surprised to see them do that. They were beautiful and graceful animals.

We paid for an hour ride, but he kept us out for at least two hours. He took us to another open area near a waterfall, he held out a piece of raw meat with his gloved arm, and a hawk flew down and took it out of his hand. Unbelievable, we were stunned. Edward wanted to try it, but Henry said he was afraid to take the chance because the hawk might claw him. He showed us some bears; we saw so many alligators and snakes. We even saw cows on the banks of the Everglades, standing in the water. I asked Henry what kept the alligators away from the cows. He told us that gators went more for small animals and crocks, which were much further south, went for the larger animals and humans. He told us the difference in crocks and gators around their snouts. He had this awesome Southern twang, and we had so much fun listening to his stories. I loved all of it, even being scared to death watching the birds and the gators. It was exciting and new. Edward loved being my protector also; I clung to him like skin, which I seemed to do even when I wasn't scared. I just liked touching him.

Edward took us to a few interesting spots. We saw a plantation. We saw some cool art and ate lunch in Ft Myers. We talked about spending the night since Abby would be gone all night. We had left a note for Kat. We didn't think she cared one way or the other. Edward said we could drive on down to Ft Lauderdale or Miami if we wanted. He said the point was a good place to go. It was the southernmost point of the United States, at Key West. We decided yeah, that sounded great. So we headed south. Edward said if his father wasn't home, we could stay there tonight, and then drive to Key West in the morning and drive back to Clearwater by night. He said he didn't want to stay at his Dad's house if, he was there.

We told him we could pay for hotels, but he said no. This trip, either way we did it, was on him. We drove up to his house, where he had grown up as a little boy. It was huge, with beautiful gables, wrought iron decoration, and two story pillars on the front porch. It was a mansion. My gosh, it must have had thirty rooms or more. It was nicer than the plantation, we visited. He went up to the door and hugged the person who opened it. He pointed to us and ran back to the car.

My dad has gone out of the country and won't be back for a few weeks. We can stay in the big house, but I prefer the boat house on the water, behind the big house. It has several bedrooms and a kitchen; there is a bathroom for each bedroom, so no problems. We can each have our own room, and we can come up to the main house to eat. How about it? Does it sound okay with you all?

We drove to the boathouse. My gosh, it was bigger than my house I grew up in. It had four bedrooms and five bathrooms, a kitchen, an office, a living room, and a huge outdoor deck with grills. There was also a diving board and a couple of boats. Ronnie's house was huge, but it was small compared to Edward's main house.

"Dang, Edward, I could live here forever."

"It's all right; I stayed here a lot, growing up. My friends and I were here every weekend, no adults, and no one to tell us what to do."

"Edward, we don't have any clothes, toothbrushes, nothing. Is there somewhere we can go now to get some stuff?"

"Yeah, the main house."

"You have clothes to fit Ronnie and me?"

"Sure, my Dad's girl friends stuff is everywhere."

Ronnie spoke up, "I am not wearing someone else's underwear."

"Me neither, Edward."

"Okay, let me tell cook, and I will be right back."

We drove to Wal-Mart, and Ronnie and I bought, underwear, toothbrushes, mascara, hair brushes, lotion and shampoo. She bought a box of surprises; and I told her I needed a few too. She laughed at me.

Edward walked up, she covered the box with a shirt she was buying. "We have all that stuff in the boat house. We have lots of extras; unused toothbrushes, shampoo, and girls' things and so on."

"That's okay, Edward, I will buy my own." Ronnie said. I picked out a shorts set and a dress I liked, and Ronnie bought several things. Mick had a pair of boxers, and a pair of shorts, and a shirt.

He looked at Ronnie, "What," Edward said they had toothbrushes." She shook her head, but smiled at him. She walked to a different register so they would not see her purchases.

Edward looked over the items I purchased, seeming to approve. He paid for them, not letting me buy anything. He tried to pay for Ronnie and Mick's but Ronnie wouldn't go for it. Mick purchased his own items as well.

"Edward, I don't want your money, please let me pay my own way."

"I told you this trip was on me."

"Edward, you make me feel shallow by letting you buy me so much. I need to pay my own way. Do you understand?"

"Yes, I am sorry. Give me Twenty dollars."

"This was more than Twenty dollars."

"I'm talking gas money, pay up your share."

I grinned at him, and punched him in the arm. We got back to the boathouse, and Cook was there with pots of food. The table was set, and there was wine and a bottle of champagne in a bucket. She was smiling at Edward. She handed Edward a small box that he put in his pocket. We sat at the table and started opening the covers of the dishes. There was a beautiful roast, boiled potatoes, and green beans with bacon, boiled turnips, fresh bread and chocolate cake.

"How did you do this so quickly?"

"I had this made for our dinner tonight. When we saw Mr. Edward, I could not tell you how happy I was to see him. I brought everything we had here."

"Who else was going to eat this with you?"

"My husband, we will have left over's."

"No, I can't do that. You come eat with us, or I am not eating anything."

"It's okay, Sam. Cook, please go get Granger and come eat with us."

"Edward?" Cook questioned him.

"Go, now."

She ran off and was back in a few minutes with a tall, slim man, in dirty overalls. She curtsied to us.

"Mr. Granger, these are my friends, Ronnie and Mick. This lovely lady here is going to be my wife."

I smiled, blushing, because he had not asked me to marry him, but we talked about being together forever. "Hello, it is nice to meet you." I said, with hesitation in my voice. Ronnie and Mick said hi. We all sat down and began spooning food onto our plates.

Cook and Mr. Granger watched us. Edward motioned for them to start, and they did. Cook kept smiling at Edward and patting his arm. Mr. Granger shook his head and started eating. We all chowed down for over half an hour. We devoured this delicious food.

"Oh, Mrs. Granger this was wonderful." I told her.

"Cook, I am called Cook."

"Okay, Cook, this was the best meal I have had all summer and maybe ever. Thank you."

"It was my pleasure and thank you for inviting us to join you."

Mr. Granger stood up, saying, "I wish you all a nice time in Ft Lauderdale, and have a safe trip back to Clearwater. Thank you for the company, but I must get back to work. I only have an hour of daylight left, and I have been preparing something special for Mr. Anderson. Edward, as always, it is wonderful to see you. We miss you around here."

"Thank you, Granger; I will try to visit at least one more time before the summer is over. I would like to speak with my father before I go back to school."

He nodded toward Edward and left the house. Cook started cleaning up our dishes and Ronnie and I helped her. Startled, she paused and she looked at Edward. I looked at Edward, and he smiled at me and blew me a kiss. I kept picking up dishes and so did Ronnie. We carried them to the sink and started rinsing them and filling the dishwasher. Cook tried to push us out of the way. We grinned at each other and kept doing what we were doing.

"Listen, Cook, I know you are paid to take care of this household. I am a guest here, and I understand your duties, but I was taught to clean up after myself. You gave us your lovely cooked dinner, and I am not used to someone else cleaning up my messes. I would really appreciate it if you let me do this for you. Please." I said to her. She looked at Edward, and he held his hands out as if saying sorry. She hugged Ronnie and me and put the food in the refrigerator.

"If you don't eat what is left, I will come get it tomorrow. Thank you, Sam, Ronnie, Mick, and dear Edward; I bid you all a good evening. Edward please come see us more often, we miss you here." She kissed Edward on the cheek and she left. I started the dishwasher, and we all went to the deck out back and sat with our wine. Ronnie sat on Mick's lap. They looked content. I sat near the water's edge, and Edward walked over by me. He put his hand on my shoulder.

"You should have let Cook do her job."

"I couldn't do that after hearing she gave us her and her husband's dinner."

"She is a wonderful lady, and she was happy to do so. She would not have done that for my father, only me. She raised me, you know. She taught me what was proper and what was not. She made me listen and play my part. She knew my father would have a fit if he knew I ate in the kitchen with them or even took my own dishes to the sink. I helped Granger in the garden when my father was gone. They don't have any children of their own, so actually, they seemed more my parents than my own father did."

"I love them, but I knew my place, Sam, I wasn't welcome in their world as I grew older. I ate meals alone in the dining room with Cook serving me. I had to learn not to hug them and show emotions toward them. It was the way they knew, and I had to learn." He squatted down beside me. He was holding my hand now.

"Sam, now back to us. I love you. I can't wait any longer to ask you. I want to spend the rest of my life with you. Will you marry me?"

I gasped.

"Edward!"

"Sam, I am serious. Marry me now, this summer, or whenever you decide, but say you will."

"Edward, I love you, and yes I will marry you."

He kissed me, lifted me up, and swung me around.

"She said yes," he yelled. Ronnie jumped off Mick's lap.

"What?" Ronnie yelled.

"She said yes, Ronnie. She is going to be my wife."

Ronnie looked at me, and looked irritated. Why? Edward saw her face too. He put me down, and we stared at her.

"Ronnie, what's wrong?"

She shook her head.

"Sam, you did it."

"Did what?"

"You have love, you have a reason. You made it. Remember?"

I bowed my head, turned, and looked at Edward. He knew we were talking about the pact. He started toward us, but stopped. He looked worried.

"Ronnie, I love him, and I know he loves me. Are you happy for me?"

"Oh, my, yes, Sam. I am so happy for you I could scream." She screamed. I laughed, and I saw Edward release the tension in his stature. "Sam, this is the most wonderful news I have ever heard. Wait, are you going to get married now, this summer? Or have a big wedding or what?"

"I don't know, Ronnie, he just asked me."

"Yes, talk, talk this evening. Oh my. I am thrilled. I love you, Sam. I love you too, Edward. I feel like you have made me just as happy as you have Sam."

I was grinning, and turned to look at Edward, and then at Mick. Mick was smiling too. Edward was so relieved; I ran to him and grabbed him. He held me and swung me around again. Ronnie was running so many things by us about weddings. Then she was thinking aloud about just eloping now or tomorrow here in Ft Lauderdale, or when we get back to Clearwater so Kat and Abby can be with us too. She was weighing out all the ideas of waiting to have a big wedding. If it was her, she would do it now, not wait.

Mick pulled her away and said, let's go to bed. She followed him, but she was still planning and talking. I heard her giggle; I knew he had done something provocative to make her giggle. She was quiet now, and then I heard them running up the stairs. I looked at my guy my Edward. I snuggled into him.

I told him, "Let's get that bottle of champagne and go upstairs, Edward. I think we need to celebrate alone. He picked me up and took off toward the stairs; I yelled, wait the champagne. He went back to the bar, and I grabbed the bottle. "What about glasses?"

"We don't need any." He was taking the stairs two at a time. He opened his bedroom door, carrying me inside. He kissed me, I parted my lips, and he kissed me deeper, deeper than he ever had before. I felt those pangs in my belly, I felt things lower, uneasiness, no, it was yearnings. I felt wetness between my legs. I wanted him, and I was going to have him finally, this night.

"Edward, do you have protection?"

"No?"

"I do, in my room."

"What?"

"I got it from Ronnie, today."

"Oh, you were going to seduce me tonight, were you?"

"Yes."

He let me go, I ran to my room and I retrieved the condoms Ronnie had given me. I brought them back, shutting the door. I opened my hand and held it out to Edward. He laughed.

"Three of them? You do have plans to seduce me."

I shrugged.

"I didn't know."

"What did Ronnie say when you took three of them?"

"She laughed."

He grabbed me. He was kissing me again. He was pulling at my clothes, I felt tingles and urges deep inside me. He laid me on his bed while he was removing my shirt and my shorts and kissing me. He had too many hands, it seemed. He was giving me deep, smothering kisses, kisses that made me want to devour him. I kicked my shoes off. He was rubbing his hands up my body, touching my bare skin. I felt the heat. I pulled his shirt over his head and moved to his shorts. He shook all over and grabbed my hands. "Wait. I can't handle that just now." I didn't understand, but I waited. He undid his shorts, letting them fall to the floor. He was kissing my belly. He undid the clasp on my bra. He had been searching in the back, and the clasp was in the front, but he finally found it and snickered. He was kissing my breasts, running his hands down my sides; I felt his tongue on my nipple. I arched my body, pushing my head back and my chest forward. "Edward, I love you." He was so busy moving all over me. He was trying to get his boxers off and not having an easy time of it. He kept his hands on me, rubbing me. I reached down and began pulling them at the waistband on one side, trying to help. He shuddered all over again. He stopped for a moment. He wiggled his hips, and his boxers fell to the floor. He was naked now, and I wanted to see him, all of him. I pushed him up. He obeyed my command. I raised myself up and looked at him. I looked at the full length of his body. I was smiling; He was beautiful, I saw him harden more, and he was increasing in size. I was stunned. My eyes bugged out of my head. He touched me between my legs, but I still had my panties on. I moaned, but I was afraid of the size of him. I looked up into his eyes.

"Edward, I don't think so."

He grinned; those beautiful dimples were deep and sexy.

"Yeah, I think so, I know so."

I was shaking my head and looking at him. He seemed to be still growing. He had to stop.

"I can't take that inside me, Edward. It won't fit."

"Baby, it will, I promise." He laid me back on the bed. He pulled my little black panties down, looking at me now as stunned as I was looking at him. His face was white, and he had a look on his face that I couldn't describe. What was he thinking? He touched me, and I groaned. He looked in my eyes. He finally gave me a half smile. I thought maybe he was sick or going to pass out, but he didn't, he kept busily touching me, caressing me all over my body.

"I love you."

I still was staring. This couldn't work, it just couldn't. He will kill me.

"Don't worry." As he was kissing my belly and moving lower. I tried to stop him; Ronnie never told me things like this. She told me about their rod and about what they did with it, but not that is was so big. His tongue was moving over me, and I fell back onto the bed in absolute pleasure. He told me to relax, but his tongue and lips never stopped. It was going in and out of my part. I moaned, and pleaded for him to. What, stop? No! Go on, yes. "More"

He obliged me. I felt arousal; I spread my legs naturally not even thinking about it. I let him take me; I wanted to pull him inside me now. I was aching for something. Oh what can happen next? Oh . . . "Edward?"

I yelled with pleasure, "How . . . ? Oh my . . . What? Edward!" I screamed my release, it flooded my senses, and it swept through me like nothing ever known to me before. I had my hands on his head, encouraging him to continue; I couldn't believe I pulled his hair to me, to fill me with this desire. I seemed to feel the pains, the aching glory subsiding in me, I relaxed on the bed, and he started moving upward, kissing me. He reached my breast again. He suckled my nipples, one, and then the other.

He moved up further, and he was panting with an urge I didn't understand. He touched me with his self; his hard sex was on me. It felt hot and wet, and he moved his hand down and placed the end, the engorged head, inside me. It felt warm and soft. I was very tight, and I wanted him to come in further. I arched my hips toward him. He pushed; he entered further. I felt full now with him, and he was only part way inside me. He pushed, and I felt a pain, a sharp, cutting pain. He pushed again, I watched his beautiful, strong face, and he didn't seem to be able to say anything to me either. His eyes were glassy and shining. He was watched me with his mouth open, panting. I arched up again, and I felt he was in me as far as he could go, but he was hovering above me, it seemed between life and death. He was looking in my eyes. He had lust and power all over his face. I saw the hardness that scared Abby; I saw the kindness that pulled me toward him. He drove into me fast and hard, and I felt pain, like no other before. He filled me up so much, and I felt his body touching mine now, he could go no further. I felt the tears in my eyes. He kissed the tears away. I felt love between all the pain and horror and excitement of this moment. I didn't think I could bare another moment like this. This was wonderful and grand. I rubbed my hands on his back, and he watched me.

"Are . . . you okay . . . Sam?" He was so out of breath, his voice so raspy.

"Edward, yes, yes, yes. I want it all, Edward." He pushed inside me until I felt he could go no further. I wrapped my legs around him, and then he started moving in and out. He had his hands on my hips, pulling me with him, showing me the way. In and out, up and down. It was wonderful, and I felt building inside me again, this agony, and explosion. I would die if I squeezed, and he thrust into me once, twice, and a third time, calling out a sweet moaning sound. Then I felt his fingers touching me and felt like I was rising off the bed. I exploded with pleasure for several moments and then collapsed on the bed, him lying on top of me, breathing and sweating. I smelled the sex and the aroma of sweet lust and love in the room. I knew this was what a man and woman are supposed to be for each other. I knew this is what I waited for, to be with Edward forever. It was painful, so painful; at a couple of times, I thought I couldn't bare it. Ah, but the pleasure, the explosion in my belly seemed to be electricity flowing through my veins. I could still feel the after effects. My body twitched with excitement.

He tried to catch his breath, but he still could barely talk. "Sam, are you all right?"

I squeezed, and I felt him shudder and I loved that feeling. He gasped and smiled at me. "I love you, Edward; I am the most wonderful happy person on earth. No one could feel like this. I can't imagine feeling like this ever again. I love you so much."

He kissed me and laid his head beside mine on the pillow. He lay there a moment and rolled off me. I tried to hold him on top of me, inside me, but I was unable to. He lay on his back and pulled me next to him.

"Sam, my darling wife to be, I forgot the condom."

I laughed.

"We have three, so we can try it again, when you are ready."

He moaned and shut his eyes. He held me tightly, and I heard him say, "I'll be ready in just a while." I wondered if that was true.

# CHAPTER THIRTEEN

We slept all night in each other's arms. I felt his hot flesh next to mine when I woke up. He was rubbing my side lightly, up and down to my hips. He was looking at me. I knew my breath had to be bad. What were you supposed to do the morning after? I thought. Do you talk? Ronnie was so vague with her stories. I held him; I pulled him tight to me. He moaned a sweet, deep sound that rumbled in his chest. I looked up at him.

"Good morning."

"Good morning, Edward."

"How do you feel?"

"I'm, Ah, okay."

He laughed.

"Ready to try those condoms?"

I blushed, why was I blushing now?"

Edward?"

"Yes, dear?"

"Edward, I Ah . . . Love you."

He squeezed me so hard, so tight, that I couldn't breathe, I was afraid he was going to break my ribs. He eased up a bit finally.

"Sam, I love you too. Do you remember you said yes to my proposal?"

"Uh huh."

"I have something for you. Wait right here." He got out of bed and walked to where his shorts lay. His butt was tight and white, but the muscles were so firm when he walked, it was the most magnificent thing I had ever seen. Edward was gorgeous from head to toe. His body was hard, and you could define every single muscle. When he turned around, he saw me propped up, and watching at him. He smiled and shook his thing at me. I fell back on the bed and covered my face with my hands, I was so shocked. I felt my face flush, it was hot. I heard him laughing and felt him get back in bed. I couldn't remove my hands, I was so embarrassed. He removed my hands from my face, and I saw he was covered. I let out a whooshing sound of relief. He laughed at me again.

"Sit up; I want to give you something."

I sat up, holding the sheet under my arms to keep it from falling down.

"Sam, I forgot to give you this last night along, along with using the condom. Let me do this again, do it right." He turned and faced me. The sheet slipped away from his groin, and I could see the hair above his thing, and I couldn't take my eyes away. He flashed me and then covered himself again. I gasped and looked up at his face. He was going to tease me a lot, I knew. It would take me a while to get used to all this.

"Sam, I love you with all my heart." He started saying. "I wish to spend the rest of my life loving you and taking care of you. I promise to do everything in my power to make you happy and make you love me back. Will you be my wife, Sam? Will you marry me?"

I grinned at him.

"Yes, Edward. I love you, and I would be so honored to be your wife." I leaned forward to kiss him, but he pulled back. I frowned. He opened his hand, holding a small box, the box Cook had handed him last night. He opened the box, and a beautiful Ruby ring was inside it. I gasped.

"Oh. My."

He placed it on my third finger. It fit me. It was a large stone on a silver band. It was beautiful. I just stared at it.

"Sam, this was my mother's ring. I don't know what happened to her engagement ring, but I know this was hers, I remember her wearing it. My father said I could have it and do what I wanted with it. I want to give it to you."

"Oh . . . Edward. It is so pretty."

He grinned and flashed me those beautiful dimples. He leaned forward and kissed me. We kissed deep, sensuous kisses. I felt arousal again in my belly. He was breathing fast, and he pulled back.

"I think a shower might be appropriate right now. How about it?"

I nodded. He picked me up and carried me to the bathroom. He turned the water on and got in, still holding me. It was warm and felt good. He stood me up and let the water flow over his face. He ran his hands over his hair, letting the water run down his beautiful muscled back. I touched him, and he turned around, smiling at me. He moved aside and picked up the soap and started soaping up. I stood under the water, letting it pound down on my head. I leaned my head back while it hit me in the face, running my hands up and down my face. Man, this was what I needed. It was so relaxing. I opened my eyes, and he was watching me. He handed me the soap. I started washing myself. It was a little uncomfortable, but I turned my back to him and washed quickly. I felt his hands on my shoulders, gently rubbing down to my waist. I moaned. I started rinsing the soap off as he washed his hair. I moved aside so he could rinse. He picked up the shampoo rubbing a handful in his palm, and turned me around so my back was to him. He rubbed the shampoo on my hair, scrubbing, and washing to the ends of my hair. I shut my eyes and let him do what he pleased. He pulled me back under the running water and rinsed it out. He asked about conditioner, and I told him it wasn't necessary.

He turned the water off and grabbed a towel, rubbing it on my head and drying the water and then rubbing down my body. He wrapped it around me, and I stepped out of the shower. He got another towel and dried himself, and then wrapped it around his waist and got out.

Edward opened the drawer beside the sink, and pulled out a toothbrush in a package, and opened it for me, put toothpaste on it, and handed it to me. I started brushing my teeth. He got another one, doing the same, and began brushing his. I rinsed and stood there until he finished. We hadn't said anything except him asking me about the conditioner. He turned me around, and we started back to the bedroom. He sat in a chair and pulled me into his lap.

"Sam, can we do this every day of our lives from now on?"

"Yes, Edward this was nice. The best shower I ever had." We both laughed, and he hugged me close to him.

"Sam, I guess if we are going to the Keys, we had better leave soon so we can get back to Clearwater this evening."

"Sure, I can be ready in ten minutes."

He held on tight, not letting me get up.

"No, I want to hold you just a minute." I settled into his lap, resting my head next to his. This was a nice feeling. I heard Ronnie and Mick laughing in the hall. I thought they were going downstairs. I hope they didn't hear us last night. I didn't hear them. I knew Ronnie will know what happened by looking at me. I felt different and I probably looked different. I didn't want to say anything in front of Mick though. Edward sighed, so I got up, but all my clothes were in the other bedroom. I walked to the door. I didn't want to go out there with just a towel on. What if they saw me? Edward came over to the door.

"I'll go get your clothes for you, wait."

I turned around, and he dropped his towel. My eyes lit up. He opened a drawer and pulled out clean boxers and shorts. He turned and saw me watching him. He danced across the floor to the closet and found a shirt. I was laughing now. He was laughing too. He pulled the shirt on and told me he would be right back. He came back with my stuff, everything I had.

"Here, now you can get dressed." He sat on the foot of the bed and said, go-ahead. He wanted me to drop my towel and dress in front of him. I shook my head and headed for the bathroom, but he jumped off the bed, catching me.

"Nope, you watched me, I watch you."

"But Edward, you, Ah . . . you have done this before."

"Never with the woman I love, he said. I blushed. "Please."

I bowed my head "and walked over to the bed, putting my bag down. I pulled all my clothes out, removing the tags. I held up the shorts, and then the dress. He pointed to the dress. I shook my head. I dropped my towel. Oh my, I was so embarrassed, but I did it. I put my panties on, then my bra I wore yesterday, and then I pulled the dress over my head, and straightened it. He watched me very closely. I picked up my dirty clothes and stuffed them in the bag. I started to brush my hair; but he jumped up and grabbed the brush.

"Let me."

I handed him the brush, turning my back to him and letting him brush my hair. I found my shoes and slipped them on. I had everything in the bag and was ready to go. My hair was wet, but it didn't matter. He grabbed his wallet and left his dirty clothes there.

"What about the bed?"

"Cook will take care of it."

I gasped again.

"She will know, there is blood on the sheets and, ah . . . and ah, you know."

"It's okay, it is her job."

I took a deep breath as we walked out of the bedroom and, down the stairs Cook was there with bacon, eggs, pancakes, toast, jelly, butter, and syrup all out on the counter.

She said, "If you want an omelet or anything I haven't made, I will make it for you fresh."

"Oh Cook, this looks great. We are cereal girls usually." Ronnie laughed as she shoveled food onto a plate. Mick already had a plate piled high with food and was eating like it was his last meal. Cook just laughed. Edward grabbed a plate and started filling it up. He walked by Cook and kissed her on the cheek. I got a plate and put scrambled eggs and a piece of toast on it. I lathered the toast with butter and fig jam.

Cook said, "You have to eat more than that to keep your strength up." I blushed.

"I'll start with this then and come back for seconds."

Ronnie burst out laughing at me. She saw my face and just knew, just like she always knew, what I was thinking or what I had done. I glared at her, and she shut up. I sat next to Edward and ate slowly, watching everyone. They were talking and laughing. Edward asked Cook if she had already eaten, and she said she had with Mr. Granger. Edward nodded. Cook stood behind him, rubbing his shoulders. She hugged him and went back to her cleaning and arranging plates.

"Well, are we still headed for the Keys?" Edward asked.

"Sure, it sounds great. We won't be able to stay long, but it would be nice to say we were there." Mick remarked. Ronnie and I agreed. We finished our food, gathered up our stuff, and packed it in the trunk. Edward hugged Cook and waved to Mr. Granger, and we were off to the Key West. It was a three-hour drive. It was scary driving across so much water. What if the bridge broke?

It was cool outside, with the sea breeze moving through the car with our windows down. I relaxed sometime into the trip. The salt air was brisk, and you could taste the salt on your tongue. We looked at all the amazing things we passed. We went to the Ft Zachary Taylor Historic State Park. We took pictures and had a great time. We spent a couple of hours there.

Edward took us to a Cuban restaurant that was great. It was spicy and good. We knew we had to start back or we would be late getting into Clearwater. It took us about nine hours to get back home. It was a long trip. It was after ten-o'clock when we arrived. Ronnie kissed Mick good-bye, and he went home. Edward came upstairs with us.

We opened the door, and Kat was there waiting for us.

"Where have you been?"

"We went to Ft Lauderdale then down to Key West. Why? We haven't seen you in days. Where have you been?"

"It doesn't matter, Abby is in the hospital."

"What?" I inquired.

"She tried to kill herself."

Ronnie and I looked at each other.

"Kat, is she alright?"

"She isn't dead if that's what you mean. Her parents are there. Her dad is such a jerk."

"What happened?" Ronnie asked.

"Well, I am not sure. I know something happened between her and Edward's friend, Sam. She wouldn't tell me any details. Has he said anything to you Edward?"

"No he went back to school. He wouldn't talk to me."

"Well, Abby won't say anything now that she is better. We were to be together. We had to agree together." Kat hung her head. I felt cold chills all over my body. I glanced up at Edward, and he was watching me intently.

"Kat, did she leave a note?" I asked.

"I have looked all over the apartment for a note or something. I couldn't find anything." She paused, looking around at us. "I knew she felt down and was depressed, but I didn't want to be depressed. I thought if I stayed away, I could find something, anything, you know. I couldn't take her whining and bossing me around anymore. You two found boyfriends that have stuck with you. I am with a different guy almost every night."

"We begged her to go with us." I told Kat.

"Yeah, that is great, the fifth wheel that is a lot of fun. You know better than that." Kat said with cruelty in her voice.

"No, I don't, I was always with Abby. Neither one of us ended up with the guy. You and Ronnie always dumped us for your own pleasure. Remember Kat?"

Kat hung her head and Ronnie looked ashamed. I didn't mean to hurt Ronnie but I did.

I spoke again, "Look, I am sorry, but we need to go to the hospital and see Abby. I am sorry Kat; I didn't mean what I said."

"Yes you did. And it is the truth," Kat said. Edward wasn't' moving or saying anything.

Ronnie said, "Come on, let's go." Kat got in Ronnie's car. I told Edward I would go with them, and he could go home. I would call him and let him know what was going on.

He nodded and kissed me.

"Sam, you aren't going to do anything, are you?" He looked terrified.

"No, Edward, I have you, and we have happy plans. I swear I will never do anything like that. I love you." He kissed me again. I got in Ronnie's car and we drove to the hospital.

# CHAPTER FOURTEEN

We parked at the hospital and went in, straight to the floor where Abby's room was. We couldn't just go into the area where they had Abby. The doors were locked, and they buzzed us in after they checked our bags and stuff. I guessed she was on a suicide watch on a restricted floor. We went to a waiting area Abby's parents were there and her little sister. Her father was sitting by the windows with his arms crossed over his chest. He glanced at us and then turned away. Her mother was crying. Her little sister was reading a book, but when she saw us she ran to us. She asked us about Florida and how much fun we were having, what the beaches were like, the boys, and so on. She didn't have a care in the world about her sister.

I just blew her off and I went over to Abby's mother and asked her how Abby was. She just cried. Abby's little sister, Ashley told us her mother was embarrassed at what Abby had done to the family. It was wrong of her to try to get attention this way. It caused her father grief and he was losing a lot of money, missing work and having to fly to Florida to sit in a hospital. I glared at Ashley; she was such a little bitch. I shook my head at her and went to the nurses' station. I asked the nurse about Abby, and she asked if I was a relative. I told her I was her sister. Ashley smarted off, "No you are not. I am her sister." I frowned at her and told her to ask the nurse then about Abby please. Ashley asked the nurse, she said that Abby was alert and conscious, but she wouldn't talk to the psychiatrist. I asked if we could go see her. The nurse said she would ask, but it was up to Abby if she wanted visitors.

The nurse called me over and said she agreed to see a Samantha Lord only. I told her I was Samantha Lord, and she asked for identification. I showed her my driver's license, and she took me through another set of locked doors to Abby's room. She unlocked the door to Abby's room and led me in. She said I had fifteen minutes, and she would return. Abby was facing the wall. I ran to the side of the bed, touching her. She didn't move.

"Abby, it's Sam, are you alright? Please look at me."

She slowly turned over; I saw the bandages around her wrists. She had sunken-in eyes and was pale. I sat down beside her. She looked at me and then looked away.

"Abby?"

"Hello Sam"

"Why Abby? Why did you do this? You didn't give us any kind of warning. You didn't try talking to us first. Please, Abby, I love you, I don't want to lose you."

"Sam, you are different now. You have a boyfriend. I am alone. I did try to talk to you, but you were too happy and not interested in what I wanted to talk about."

"I am sorry I didn't listen. Why did you do this? Please, Abby, what happened with Sam? I thought you liked him. Was he the reason for this?"

"Sam, I am sorry . . . Give me a minute." She asked. I held her hand and brushed her hair out of her face. "I liked Sam . . . I thought we were getting along good. He seemed . . . to like me too." She paused. "He kissed me. I felt happy being with him, getting to know him. I was trying to do like you said and give people a chance and it was working." Pausing, almost every other word, she started again. "He . . . he took me out to dinner one night." She was crying and sniffling, "We were having a" sobbing, "Ah good time I thought. He made me laugh about things." She sniffed, again. "We went back to their place." She turned her head away from me, looking back at the wall. "We were drinking beer and listening to music. He was kissing me, and he got a little touchy-feely. He was putting his hand up my shirt. He grabbed one of my breasts. I told him to stop." She looked back at me a moment, and then looked up at the ceiling. "He . . . ., wouldn't stop. I was kicking and yelling." She took a deep breath. "He then . . . ripped my shirt. He was too strong. I tried to stop him. He was laughing as he kissed me. He, ah grabbed me between my legs hard." Tears were forming in her eyes. She was snubbing.

"Oh Abby, I'm sorry." I gasped,

She shook her head, "He, Ah, was tearing at my clothes again. I was yelling at him to stop it. He held me down on the couch . . . I was fighting him; I swear I was fighting as hard as I could, but I couldn't make him, make him stop. We slid onto the floor. He was laughing and touching me all over. My arm was pinned under, under the couch somehow, so now, I, ah, only had one to fight with. I was kicking him, and screaming. I tried so hard. He punched me in the stomach, and I had a hard time catching my breath. By the time I did . . ., he had me striped down. My clothes were in shreds." She was crying, and it was hard to understand her words, but I knew what he had done.

"He touched me . . . in my private area and told me I was pretty . . . I calmed . . ., I tried to anyway, to avoid him hitting me again. I thought maybe, maybe I could talk him out of . . . what he was doing. I told him I liked him, but I needed some time to think . . . just a little time to think about having sex. He called me a tease." She cried uncontrollably, for a moment, and then continued. She was hiccupping. "He . . . unzipped his pants; he stuck himself inside me. It hurt. It hurt so badly. He had one hand over my mouth and threatened me . . . to hit me, if I didn't shut up. I was crying, sobbing, trying not to yell. I was in so much pain. I just wanted him to finish so I could go home at that point."

She looked back at the wall. "He yelled out a loud moan, and fell on me. He tried to kiss me, but I turned away. He slapped me across the face." She took another deep breath. "He sat up and smiled down at me. He said I did well, for my first time." She let out a short hurtful sound. "He said he thought, we were all sluts like Kat. He didn't know I was a virgin. He said he was sorry for hurting me, but he was sure I knew what it was all about."

I was just lying there, looking under the couch. He got off me, and I scooted away getting up, from the floor. I gathered my clothes what was left of them. There was blood on the floor. He left the room and came back with a T-shirt, handing it to me. I took it and pulled it over my head. It was long, so it covered me, half way to my knees. I stood there because I was afraid." She put her hands over her face as she cried. She needed a break before she continued. "He had the nerve to ask me . . . ask, if I wanted to use his bathroom to clean up. I shook my head, picked up my purse, and went to the door. I was so afraid he was going to stop me, but he didn't. I opened the door, ran down the stairs, and ran home crying; I stumbled and fell a couple of times. I kept looking behind me. Afraid he was following me. When I got home none of you were there."

She was so out of breath as if she was still running away, she didn't say anything for a while. I knew the nurse would be back soon. She was trying to start talking again but was having difficulty getting her words out. "I got in the shower with the shirt on, and turned the water on full blast, as hot as I could get it. I stood there for an hour and cried. I removed the shirt and washed myself. I got out and heard you and Edward, so I couldn't face you with him there. I hid the shirt and then I went to bed. There was nothing else I could do."

"Oh, Abby! This is horrible. Why didn't you call the authorities? We should press charges and send his ass to jail." I tried to hug her, and she turned over and pushed me away. I hadn't been there for her when she needed me the most.

"When did this happen?" I said emotionless.

"Two weekends ago, on a Saturday night."

I gasped.

"I remember the weekend you were withdrawn and sad. I am sorry I didn't help you. I was so involved in my own world and happiness, I failed you, Abby."

"Sam, I told you I didn't trust Edward but it was Sam who was the one to hurt me. I make such bad choices. I just felt I couldn't live anymore. No one would ever love me as Edward loves you. I see it Sam, how can you not? Everyone sees it. He loves you so much; I think he would die for you."

"I feel the same about him, Abby."

"I know. I am glad for you. I hate my parents being here. They don't want to be here. They are ashamed. I have no one but you to talk to. I am a burden on everyone."

"You are not a burden. I love you. Did you tell them what happened? Maybe they will understand?"

"NO!"

"Why not?"

"I don't want them to know. I don't want anyone to know."

"Why not? The jerk needs to be punished for what he did."

"It is his word against mine, you know that. I have no evidence, I cut the shirt to shreds when I was alone and threw it away."

"Abby, did you know he went home?"

She sat up and looked me in the face, "Yes. He cornered me on the beach the other day. I was terrified. He told me he was sorry. I told him I hated him and hoped he died. He was crying, trying to get me to forgive him, and forget it happened. He said . . . maybe we could start over. He said he liked me. He said it was the alcohol that made him lose control. Can you believe that? I screamed as loud as I could, and there were people close by me. He ran away. I didn't leave the house except to baby sit."

"We knew something was wrong. I am so sorry Abby."

"It is not your fault. I don't want to go home, but when they let me out of here, my choices are to go home or stay for psychiatric evaluation."

"Oh Abby, what can I do?"

"I don't want to see Ronnie or Kat. You can tell them what happened. I don't want to see my parents either. Don't tell them anything."

"I won't Abby."

"I know you want to tell Edward, so I don't object. Sam probably will tell him anyway, but he said he hadn't talked to Edward yet about it. He said Edward might kill him. Ha! HA! You don't think he would do that, do you?"

"I don't know, maybe."

She smiled. The nurse opened the door.

She said, "Times up, I even gave you extra, so come on." I didn't want to leave her.

"Sam, thank you, for always being at my side, I love you." I hugged her and she hugged back.

The nurse was anxious, "Girls, come on." I let her go, and she watched me walk to the door. I turned and looked back at her before walking out. I left, and the nurse shut and locked the door. I went back to the waiting room, and everyone jumped when I walked in, asking what she said and what happened.

"She wouldn't talk to me. She's closed up and won't say anything." I looked at Ronnie, who knew when I was lying, so she elbowed Kat, and they didn't ask anything else. Abby's mother wanted to know if they could come get Abby's stuff. We told them we would pack it up and bring it to them. Abby's father asked if she had any money. I told him I didn't know, but we would bring everything back. What an ass. We left, and when we got in the car, I repeated Abby's story almost word-for-word to Kat and Ronnie. Kat cried and Ronnie was stunned, and not saying anything. Cold chills ran up my arms again. My cell phone had been on silent, but when we reached our place, I pulled it out of my pocket; I had missed a call from Edward. I told Kat and Ronnie I needed to call him.

I walked over by the pool, dialing Edward's number. He answered on the first ring.

"Sam, is everything alright?"

"Edward I am fine. I know what happened but I want to see you to tell you in person. I can't do this over the phone."

"Sam, I have some bad news for you. Something bad happened between my roommate Sam and Abby. Sam shot himself in the head yesterday." I had cold chills all over my body. I sat down in a chair, stunned by his words.

"Sam, are you still there? Are you okay?"

"Edward, is Sam dead?"

"Yes."

"Good."

"Sam?"

"He raped Abby." There was silence on the phone.

"Can I come see you?"

"We have to pack up Abby's stuff and take it to her parents. Can you wait a while?"

"Yeah, just call me when you are ready."

"I love you, Edward."

"I love you too, Baby." We hung up. I went up stairs to helped pack.

# CHAPTER FIFTEEN

We hauled all of Abby's things downstairs. We discussed her money that we found and decided to put it in her account at the bank the next day. That way, if her parents got to it, it would have to be a court order. We weren't just handing it over. I went into the hospital and told the Halls that Ronnie was down stairs, with Abby's stuff, so they needed to go down. Luckily, all three of them went down stairs to the car. I asked the nurse if I could talk to Abby for one minute. She said she would ask her. When she started back to the desk she waved me to follow her she was holding the doors open. She let me in Abby's room, telling me it was past visiting hours, but I had two minutes, unless someone caught us. I thanked her and went in; she locked the door behind me.

"Abby, we packed your things and brought them to your parents as they requested. They are down stairs putting them in their car."

"Thank you, Sam."

"I found your money; it is over Six hundred dollas. I was going to put it in your account tomorrow instead of giving it directly to them."

"That's a great idea, that way they can't take it unless I am committed or something."

"They won't be able to get to it unless it is court ordered. It will be waiting for you when you are released. I found your check book, so I kept a deposit slip."

"Sam, there is a check register in there."

"I took it out, and I have it in my stuff. I hope that it is safe. Can I do anything for you?"

"Call me, still be my friend."

"Always, Abby. We are the Quad Misfits. We will always be together. Edward told me to hug you and tell you he is wishing you the best. He doesn't know the details yet, Abs." I paused; I didn't know whether to tell her about Sam. "Abby, I have news regarding Sam. Do you want me to tell you?"

"Is he dead?"

I looked at her stunned. She saw the look on my face. She was jesting when she asked the question. She put her hand up to her mouth and gasped. "Sam, no. Really?"

I was waited; I didn't want to hurt her more.

"Abby, are you okay?" She shook her head.

She shook her head, yes.

"I didn't want that to happen really. I don't think he thought what he did to me when he was doing it was a bad thing. I didn't understand his attitude or the things he said to me. Then when he asked me to forgive him on the beach, I said no, and hoped he died. Oh my gosh, Sam, I told him I hoped he died. He killed himself."

"Yes, Abby." I said. She cried. I heard the nurse at the door. The nurse saw Abby crying and was angry with me. She motioned for me to leave. "Abby, please take care of yourself. I love you. I will call you soon."

"Thank you, Sam, for everything. I love you too. Bye." She sniffed, raised her hand, and waved as I walked out the door.

The nurse had a hold of my arm, asking me what I said to her.

I told the nurse, "I told her I gave her personal effects to her parents and I told her I would always be her friend. She will be all right, won't she?" The nurse calmed.

"I hope so, Hun, she is a sweet girl. I hate to see her go home with her parents. They are not nice people, and that other daughter of theirs is driving me crazy."

I smiled at her. "I wish I could do something for her."

"Pray Hun, just pray."

I thanked her again and left. Down stairs, the Halls were yelling at Ronnie about Abby's money. I butted in and told them Abby puts her money in the bank. They asked if we had access. I told them, of course, we didn't. Mr. Hall wasn't happy about it. They had Abby's belongings, and Ashley was unzipping bags and looking inside. I couldn't believe these people. They had no care or concern about their daughter. I shook my head, crying for my friend, and we drove away.

When we arrived back home, Edward was waiting in the parking lot. I jumped out of the car and hugged him. He hugged me tight. I told the girls I would be up soon. We had all cried on the way back from the hospital.

We couldn't believe what was happening to our friend. We depended on each other for most of our lives, and now we were split up for the first time.

"Will you stay with me tonight?" he asked.

"Are you sure you want me to?"

"Is there a reason, I don't know about, why I wouldn't?"

"I can't think of one."

"Then get what you need and let's go."

"Come up with me?"

"Sure." We ran up the stairs and opened the door. I yelled Edward was coming in so they wouldn't walk out in their underwear or something. I went to our room and told Ronnie I was going to Edward's place tonight, and not to worry about me. I would ride with him to work tomorrow. She nodded. I hugged her.

"Ronnie, are you all right? Don't make me worry about you."

"Oh Sam, I just can't believe what has happened. Kat is in her room. I wish I could go to Mick's place, but I don't want to leave Kat."

I hung my head. Now what do I do? "Call Mick and ask him to come over here."

She raised her head and smiled.

"Did you want me to say I would stay home so you could go to Mick's? Ronnie, did you? If you did, that hurts my feelings bad. I have always been the responsible one. Ronnie?"

"Sam, I am sorry. I am selfish, I know it. I am spoiled, and I am sorry. Go on, I will call Mick after I talk to Kat. You know, to make sure it is cool with her. She might be going somewhere too."

I looked at Ronnie. "Fine, Ronnie. If you need me, you know where I am." I got my clothes and things and left the bedroom. This is not the way to behave especially, when I have one friend in the hospital. I am being selfish, because I want to stay with my boyfriend. I am mad at Ronnie, because she did too. I am awful. I held up my hand to Edward, signaling that I would be just a minute. I ran back to, Ronnie hugging her.

"Ronnie, I am sorry." I hugged her tighter, and she had tears in her eyes. "I will stay if you want to go, or maybe we should talk to Kat before either of us decides what we are doing. We are all sad because of Abby, not just me. I was being selfish."

"Edward doesn't want to be alone tonight either. He found out his friend died today. Let's go talk to Kat, including Edward. Come on." I came out and pulled Edward to the couch. We have to have a talk first. We can't just leave Kat alone. We have to agree on something." Ronnie brought Kat out to the living room.

Ronnie started the conversation, "Kat, what are your plans for tonight? We want to know what you want before we tell you what we planned."

"I was just going ready to go to bed."

"Sam wants to go to Edward's place to stay. I wanted to go to Mick's, but I don't want to leave you alone. Is it alright for Mick to come stay here tonight?"

"I would rather Mick come here than you leave too."

"Are you sure, Kat?"

"Yes, I am going to bed, I don't want to talk about anything yet, but I don't want to be alone."

"Okay, I will call Mick to see if he can come over, if not it is okay. You go with Edward, Sam, we will be fine. We'll talk tomorrow."

I took Edward's hand and we left.

I had never stayed at Edward's place before. I had only been there a couple of times. I was anxious and very nervous. I was hungry too. I wondered if I should tell him, to feed me. He was carrying my bag in when my stomach growled. It was loud. He looked at me and laughed. I shrugged.

"I'm hungry."

"Me too. I'll fix us something okay?"

"That sounds good." We walked in. It was very clean, and it was only him there now. He put my bag in his room and went to the kitchen. He opened the refrigerator and frowned. He shuffled around a bit, and then went to the cabinets, He looked and moved can's and was still frowning. He shut the door and turned to me.

"Sam, I don't have any eggs or anything in the cabinets that looks good to me."

"How about peanut butter and jelly?"

"I am not feeding you peanut butter and jelly on your first night at my place." He rubbed his chin. "Well actually, instead of bread, I could rub it all over you and lick it off, and then you can do the same to me."

I was shocked turning bright red.

"You are kidding, right?"

"I was, but it sounds good." He picked up the phone, called the local delivery, and ordered a pizza. "Well it won't be Guido's but it is kind of late to be calling him. He grabbed me, pulled me toward the couch, sat, and pulled me to his lap. I sat there very still.

"Are you afraid you will hurt me?"

I shook my head no.

"Are you afraid you will arouse me?"

I nodded. He laughed, grabbed my hips, and started shaking me, moving me all over his lap. I was giggling and screaming for him to stop. When he did, I felt something moving under me. It was getting bigger. I blushed and put my head down. He laid me back on the couch, kissing me. He ran his hands all over me, moaning, and then growling, and then barking, I didn't know what to do but laugh.

"I am starving; I hoped the pizza gets here soon. You go sit on the other chair and don't try anything." He said.

I got up and moved. "This, okay?"

"Maybe that is far enough. Don't do anything sexy." We both laughed. He adjusted himself in his pants. I was watching him move his hand on himself, and he told me to stop that, or he wouldn't be able to control himself. I snickered. He lowered his head and frowned at me again. He went to the kitchen, found a bottle of wine opening it. He offered me a glass, and took a glass and sat on the far end of the couch. He adjusted himself a few times, I snickered each time.

Twenty minutes later, the pizza was at our door. He ran to the door, gave the boy a Twenty dollar bill, and told him thanks. He shut the door and put the pizza on the table. I followed, smelling the air, the aroma of the pizza. He opened the box, and then heading to the kitchen, and got a couple of plates and turned. He looked at me. I already had a piece in my hands, eating away. He laughed at me, and I shrugged. With my mouth full I said, "I am hungry." Slurring my words, I chewed the big bite of pizza I had in my mouth. He told me to sit and I did. We ate almost the whole pizza. It was good. Now though I felt too full. My belly was hard, and it pouched out. He jumped up yelling.

"Exercise time."

I reared back in my chair and looked at him.

"What?"

"Bedroom exercises follow me." He put the left over pizza in the icebox, and then ran, and dove onto the bed. He was on his back, holding his arms out for me to jump. I crawled up from the foot of the bed between his legs, lay down on him, and moved myself around, touching him, his private area, knowing now I was going to try a few seduction techniques, and maybe learn something. He was grinning and growling at me. I giggled, and he pulled me up and kissed me until I was dizzy. He turned me over and got on top of me, kissing me all over my neck and arms and face. He then raised my dress and kissed my belly, trying to move my panties down with his teeth. I couldn't help myself, I was laughing at him. He had both hands on my breasts, so he couldn't get my panties off with just his teeth. He was pleading with his eyes, and all I could do was laugh.

The look on his face changed from jolly to serious. He slid his hands off my breasts slowly, moving down my belly, still pulling my panties with his teeth, and he was getting them off now. I felt his breath on me, and I wanted so to part my legs, but he had me pinned in place with his arms and legs, as he was moving down my body. I felt his tongue touch me, and I raised my hips and moaned. He took my panties and tore them off me; He spread my legs, kissing me. His tongue was probing inside me, and I was beyond control. Oh my, Edward was a great lover. I wanted to do this to him. He was rubbing my legs and up my sides, killing me with his mouth and the warmth of his breath entering my body. I lifted my hips as far as I could to encourage him for more. I was about to explode when he pulled away.

"Edward, don't stop." I heard him snicker.

"Ah, my dear, do you want more?"

"Yes . . ." My breath was catching, and I was rolling my hips. He held my hips, moving me around, I followed him as he wished, and then It' hit me. It was like a bomb had detonated inside me, and wave after wave was hitting me with pleasure. I fell in exhaustion, but he still had his mouth on me, and I still had bursts or explosions going off low in my belly and down to my toes. He moved up, smirking. He had a scary look on his face. He crawled slowly over me, like a sleek cat coming in for his kill. He sat up with his knees between my legs and sat back on his haunches. He was looking at me. I could see he was firm and big, bigger than I remembered, and I wanted him, all of him. He touched me with one finger and slowly pushed it inside me, watching my face, and then looking at what he was doing. He slid his finger out and pushed two finger inside me, I moaned, and he stopped I moved with his motion, I moaned, and he stopped part way. He pulled them out and slid the two back in.

"You are tight, and hot, Sam. I like watching you." I watched him watch me, which was sexy and arousing me again. He slid those fingers out and then quickly back in, as far as, he could get them. I pushed on his hand to get them deep. He smiled, a twisted smile, pulling them out and pushing them back again. I reared up and pushed hard against his hand, aching for him to go deeper. He looked at my face snickering then back at what he was doing. I spread my legs further; I was so wet, warm, and hurting for him to come inside me. He knew I wanted him and he was tormenting me. He looked up at me with his fingers still deep in me, he was shaking them and moving them around, and I felt an ache so deep in my belly. I wanted to pull his damn hand all the way in. He was teasing me, and it was driving me crazy. He pulled his fingers out again.

"OH my Gosh, Edward, I am going to die, literally die, if you don't stop that and come inside me now." I was reaching for him, I tried to sit up, but his fingers were still deep in me, moving and teasing. I finally sat, and I grabbed his cock and pulled him. He moaned and came up off his butt. He held his head back, and a cry of a wolf or something came out of his mouth. Did I hurt him, or did it feel good? His head was back, but he brought it forward, and a sneer was on his lips, so I knew it was good. He pulled his fingers out part way and slammed them back in hard, and I cried out. He had that sneer still on his face, so I pulled his cock. I felt the end, and it was soft like velvet. I looked at him as, I started moving my hand up and down him, squeezing. The sneer on his face was gone, and it was a hard look in its place. I wanted to lick him as he did me, but I couldn't get there with the position we were in.

He pulled his fingers out, and I pulled him closer to me. He tried to pull back, but I had a firm grip, and I pumped his cock a couple of times and pulled him closer. He moaned and touched ne. I placed the soft head inside me and scooted down to push it further in. He was moving up now, breathing rapid, I think I had his full attention. No more wasting time, he was coming further and further inside. I lay back on the bed and pulled his shoulders down, and he entered me in one swoop, hard and full. I moaned, rolled my hips, and squeezed myself until I felt it was so tight I might teat. He pushed harder and came down on my body, moving in and out. I joined him, every thrust he made I was riding along with him, until he sounded like he couldn't breathe any longer. He jutted in one time hard, and then again and again. About the fourth or fifth time, he yelled out my name and I felt him shudder and quiver all over his body.

He was shaking, sweating, and I needed just a little more. I was so close; I needed him to do it again. He was losing it, and then he found some strength and thrust inside me hard. I felt his finger touching me and slipping inside with his cock. I screamed my climax, pulling him deep, holding him to me as if I couldn't bear him to pull out. I wrapped my legs tight around him and held him there. He didn't try to move. He didn't try to pull out. He lay on me. I felt his heavy sweat, soaked body next to mine, and I loved this man. He lay there for some time. I was kneading the muscles in his back; I didn't want him to leave me.

"Am I smashing you or hurting you?"

"NO, don't leave me?"

"I won't Sam. Tell me when it is too much." He relaxed and lay there. I felt him lightly push, and I pulled at him. He turned his face toward mine, smiling at me. I could feel his body relaxing.

"Sam, I really don't want to hurt you."

"Edward, you are not hurting me. I want you right where you are. Please don't pull out, don't move."

"Okay, I will stay as long as you want as long as I can." I felt him getting smaller, and I knew he wasn't comfortable, but I didn't want him to leave my body yet. I felt my hip going numb, so I knew I would have to move soon. I felt him shift his weight, and I felt him slipping out. I sighed and then moaned loudly. He rolled over on his back beside me.

"Sorry, Baby, It happens that way."

I turned over on my side and rubbed his chest. He was exhausted and sated. I rubbed down his body, looking at him. I laid my head down on his shoulder.

"I forgot the condom again. We can't keep taking this chance you know."

"Edward, I love you. Does it just get better and better?"

"If you work at it, sure it does."

"Will you teach me other things too?"

He had a deep growl and laugh coming from deep in his chest.

"Oh hell yeah. I will teach you lots of things."

"I want to please you, and I want to learn everything."

I sighed, "Edward, I am on the pill, I got on it right after I met you."

"You please me immensely. Thank God for the pill. But someday I hope you want a family."

"Maybe, even three or four." I snuggled into him and fell asleep.

"Four?"

# Chapter Sixteen

The next couple of weeks went by like a flash. They were working on a hectic case at the firm, and everyone was pumped about it. Edward did research and was doing some investigative work with a private investigator. I rarely saw him at work; he was gone all the time, back and forth from the courthouse and whatever he was doing. He loved what he was doing. I hadn't seen him this excited about anything before, except sex. Oh, and the sex was going great. I stayed at his place most of the time.

Kat was dating a guy who was from Texas, and she seemed to like this one for more than a couple of days. His name was Joe. Ronnie and Mick were together most of the time. They were talking about getting together over the holidays and springs breaks. I had called Abby's parents, but she was at a rehabilitation center, and they told me I couldn't call her there. I called my mom asking her about it. She told me where Abby was and got the address for me, so I wrote her a couple of letters, but I hadn't heard anything back yet.

Kat, Ronnie, and I talked when we could. We worried for Abby. We lived each day the best we could. We were happy, and at times, it made me feel guilty, knowing where Abby was. I had so much confusion in my head. I felt happy being with Edward, but I felt shame for ignoring my friends. I couldn't bear to be apart from Edward for very long. I knew Ronnie and Kat liked sex and wanted it often.

Edward wanted to go see his father since he was back in Florida, but with the trial now, he couldn't leave just yet, or didn't want to. Edward spoke to him on the phone a couple of times, both of those times ended in not-so-good terms. My mom had called me twice since Abby's incident to see how I was doing. Ronnie hadn't heard from one time since we left. He had to know about Abby, but he didn't call to check on Ron. She never hears from her mom. Her mom lives very to where we were, if she knew we were in Clearwater, she might show up, and Ronnie didn't want that. Kat talked to her mom often.

I had a great tan and lost a few pounds. While Edward was working so much, I had been running and exercising, and toning up. I looked much better in swimsuit now. I had Edward eating better foods, not so much junk food. I cooked at our place and his almost every day. Ronnie, Kat, and their guys all enjoyed eating home cooked meals, instead of eating out so much too. Some evenings we played cards, sometimes drinking and always laughing.

Ronnie, Kat, and I went to the zoo one day, just the three of us; it was nice strolling around the park looking at the animals and, making faces at the monkeys. The bears were inside, and so were the big cats, and we didn't see a one. They had an elephant out working, but we didn't watch long. We walked through all the buildings, stinky buildings. We saw gators and crocs and snakes. We watched the monkeys mostly walking and talking, it was nice and relaxing being together. I thought it brought us back close a bit. We had been distant from each other all summer, arguing over stupid stuff and then Abby. This was a reconciliation between us. We talked about our guys, and our future. Kat really liked the guy she was dating, and she talked about him all day long.

Our time was getting shorter before we had to leave. I was terrified about leaving Edward even for one day. The trial was going well, and I thought it would end this week, so Edward planned a trip back to Ft Lauderdale to see his father. I was worried about the meeting; I knew he wouldn't like me or approve of our marriage.

We left early on Friday morning for Ft Lauderdale. Edward was so uneasy about seeing his father, he was quiet during the trip, and I was just plain scared. I feared this man was going to hate me and think I was some lowlife after son's money. I bought new clothes from a dress shop in Clearwater, new underwear, bras, the whole works. I wanted to impress him. Why I wasn't sure. I told Edward I just wanted him to be proud of me, and I wanted to look good on his arm. He told me I always looked good on his arm. I was going to be his trophy wife.

We stopped before we got to his dad's house. Edward wanted to calm down. We went to a couple of stores; I encouraged him to take his dad something, a gift of some kind. We looked and hadn't a clue what to buy a man who could buy yachts and cars with cash. Edward said he smoked cigars. I found a lighter that was supposed to be good even in the wind, and wouldn't blow out on the golf course. I bought it and had them wrap it for me. It was only twenty-five dollars but it was a gift, I hoped he didn't think I was cheap. Edward was having fits; he was talking to himself and shaking. He couldn't keep his mind straight on what we were looking for. We ended up at the liquor store and he bought him a bottle of vodka, which was over one hundred dollars, and a bottle of Brandy. I didn't know any liquors cost that much, but they had wines for two to three hundred dollars. We walked back to the car; he sat behind the wheel and didn't start it. I touched his shoulder, and he jumped a foot off the seat.

"Edward, calm down. It will be fine. We are trying, that is what is important. Give him a chance."

"Baby, it's not you I am worried about, it is what he thinks of me. How he treats me. That is what it is, the disappointment, I hate it." I kept rubbing his shoulder and I leaned over to him as he leaned to me. We kissed. He smiled and tilted his head. "Babe, you made it better, I don't care what he thinks, I have your encourage me and you boost my ego."

"Yes, you do, and I think you are the most handsome, smartest, sexiest man in the whole world. You can conquer anything you put your mind to. I love you and am so proud of you. You are kind, gentle, and loving, and my best friend and a fantastic lover."

"I love you, Sam. You had better stop before my head gets too big and explodes."

I smiled, and he sat back and started the car. He pulled out, and we were on our way. We were only about ten minutes from the house. We pulled into the long driveway and pulled up to the front. He had both hands on the steering wheel and looked at the front of the house.

"Edward?"

"Yeah, we are going in!" He opened his door, and then came around for mine. I had learned to wait for him to open my door, or he yelled at me. He put his arm around my shoulder, and then moved it down and took my hand. He moved his arm to my waist. I looked at him. "Edward, relax." I took his hand in mine again, and he nodded. He inhaled deeply then let it out. Before we got to the door, Cook opened it, ran to Edward, hugging him. I saw his father standing in the door. He looked like an older version of Edward, graying temples, a little pudgy in the belly, but not a bad looking man. He was, almost as tall as Edward. He had the same eyes and nose. His mouth was set like Edwards, when he doesn't want anyone to know what a nice man he was. I guessed Edward learned that from his dad. He crossed his arms across his chest. Oh shit, it had just begun. I saw the look, I glanced and Edward, and he took a quick look at me, squeezing my hand. We walked up the steps into the house.

"Hello son."

"Hello, Dad. I would like you to meet Sam, Samantha Lord. Sam, Dad."

He shook my hand and turned back to his son. Edward was waiting for something to me I guessed, as he looked at me and then back at his dad.

"Edward, would you and your friend please come in." The house was magnificent. I mean, Ronnie's stepmom, decorated their house beautifully, but this was out of a magazine or should be on the front cover. They're ate Nights at armors standing in the entryway. The chandelier was crystal, and it would light the whole house it looked like if turned on. The staircase was winding and ornamental. Edward's father led us into a sitting room. It was pretty, with pleasant fabrics and, delicate curtains. The furniture looked like it wasn't to be sat on, old—fashioned, but Edward's put his hand out for me to sit down on a lovely, dainty chair. I looked at Edward, and nodded. I sat slowly to make sure I wasn't going to break the chair.

Edward's father sat in a big, heavy chair that looked sturdy and capable of holding a man. Edward sat in a similar chair beside him. They were talking, in a friendly manner, about school and what he had been doing all summer and when he was going back. I didn't move for fear of the chair breaking. Edward was trying to get my attention. I hadn't noticed, but Edward's father had asked me if I wanted something.

"Sam? Sam? Are you okay?" He raised his voice, getting my attention

"Yes, sure. I am sorry, what did you say?"

"Sam, my father asked if you would like something to drink."

"Oh, no, thank you, sir, I am fine."

Edward smiled at me. His father didn't. They talked some more, I was listening now because I didn't want to miss being asked something again. That was embarrassing.

Edward's father asked me, "Sam, is that what most people call you? You don't look like a boy, and that is a boy's name."

"Yes Sir."

"Please don't call me sir. Well, since Edward is here, you can call me Ed or Edward Sr. Please don't be so formal, I don't care for 'sir'."

I nodded and swallowed hard.

"Sir, I'm sorry. Ed, Edward Sr., my parents called us by nick names when we were young, my brother, and sister too. Samantha seemed too grown up, but now I don't mind being called by my given name. Sam just seems easy for everyone, once they get to know me."

"Then Samantha, I will call you by your given name. It is much nicer than 'Sam'."

"Thank you Edward Sr."

He grinned, but I don't think he meant it.

"Just Ed, I think it will be easier for everyone for now." I nodded.

"Are you hungry? Cook has prepared a late lunch for us." He called her, and she came running. He asked her if luncheon was ready, and she answered 'Yes Sir'. I felt confused, I guessed his employees called him 'Sir', and he was trying to be less reserved.

My Edward said, "I have been looking forward to some of Cook's food." I was sitting there like a lump, not trying to join in the conversation. I was being standoffish and felt like an idiot.

Cook came back in and told us luncheon was set up and ready, and asked us to please follow her. Ed and, Edward both stood up, and Edward held out his hand to me, I took it, smiling up at him, and stood.

We walked into the dining room, and Ed prepared to sit at the far end, assuming the head of the table. Edward looked at me, and I followed him. He pulled out the chair next to his father's and I sat. He sat across from me to his father's right, and then his father took his chair. Cook had all the food prepared on a side buffet. She brought over a soup tureen and spooned soup into our bowls. I noticed it was a chicken broth with tiny noodles or rice, mushrooms, and green onions. I watched Ed eat the soup, so I began to eat it. It tasted like chicken broth and mushrooms, nothing out of the ordinary. It was like a clean freshness to awaken the taste buds, I assumed. She then brought over a large platter with prime rib. I could not eat that. It was blood raw. My eyes bugged, and I looked at Edward.

"Dad, Sam is kind of vegetarian, or doesn't eat red meat."

"You told me, I remember. We have vegetables and salad of her choice." He said. I felt relieved. Ed and Edward each accepted the prime rib. Next, Cook brought around a mixed vegetable dish. I nodded, and she placed a couple of spoonfuls on my plate as she did to Ed and Edward. Then she started around with raw vegetables, lettuce, radicchio, green onion, radishes, cucumbers, and cherry tomatoes. I nodded to it all. Ed took none, but Edward took a couple of the items. Cook offered me dressings; I accepted some Caesar dressing and told her I was satisfied. She backed away. I ate most of the food on my plate, and Ed watched me carefully. I was careful with my forks and knife to be polite, using the proper item the proper way. I didn't think he expected that, neither did Edward. I had eaten at Ronnie's house enough times to know what was what.

Ed said, "Your plate looks like rabbit food, what do you eat for protein?"

"I eat lots of nuts and grains. I eat chicken occasionally, I ate the chicken broth, I eat soups, even beef broth soups, just not too much red meat. I eat meats on pizza and pasta. I try to eat it, but it has to be well done, I seem to a problem with meats. It tends to hurt my stomach. I didn't mean to offend you, Ed, I am sorry."

"Oh, you haven't offended me. I would just worry about protein, that's all."

After dinner, Cook offered us dessert. I declined, but Edward ate his and mine as well. His father laughed. "I remember as a child, I had to watch you to make sure you didn't eat only your dessert."

Edward beamed with the remark his father made. That was the first time I had seen actual contentment between the two of them, other than that, you would think them strangers. I then almost immediately saw the smile on Ed's face go grim. Edward saw it, and his expression also changed to bleakness. Wow, that reaction was brief. They both finished their desserts in silence.

Cook returned and cleared the table. Ed asked us to the sitting room for a brandy. Edward said he didn't want any, and I declined as well. He called for Cook and told her to show us to our rooms. My ears perked up, 'rooms?' I knew how it would be at my parent's house as well. They would not allow us to sleep together, besides there was no place to put us in like that. Edward, I was sure, knew where his room was. This man acted as if we were merely a guest for the evening. I saw a hurt look on Edwards face. He rose, and I followed. He took both of our bags, and we went up the winding stairs.

There were huge framed family portraits on the walls in the hallway upstairs. There were beautiful, ornate antique tables and lamps I heard a grandfather clock's chimes from below, but I didn't see it when we entered. There were exquisite works of art on the walls, some famous artist. Van Gogh, I recognized.

"Edward, is that real?" I asked stunned. He nodded. Wow. Cook patted Edward on the back, and he went to his room. Cook paused and started to take me to a room down the hall, and I looked at Edward. He said, "Cook, she is staying in here." Cook nodded in acceptance.

I followed Edward into his room. It was large, with a large bed in the center of the room. It was all simple colors, nothing fancy on the walls. The tops of the dresser and chest were clean of clutter. He placed our bags in the closet. He walked to the bed and sat with an exhale of breath, hanging his head low. I walked to him and placed my hand on his shoulder.

"Edward, how are you?"

"It is just as I expected, Sam." He pulled me down beside him.

"Edward, I don't care what he intend. You are mine, and as long as you want to stay here with me, you will."

I smiled and wrapped my arms around his arm, and leaned on his shoulder. I heard heavy steps coming toward Edwards's room. I was sure it was Ed, and he was coming to talk to Edward or tell us he did not approve.

The door was ajar, but we heard a tap, tap, tap on the door. I quickly stood up, but Edward remained sitting on the bed.

Edward called, "Come in." His father stepped into the room.

"Sorry to bother you, but I had informed Cook to offer you two rooms but failed to tell her it was fine for you to be together. I wasn't aware of your sleeping arrangements."

"We'll be together." Edward said as I hung my head in shame. "That's fine."

Edward stood up and walked toward him.

"Dad, I came here to talk to you about something. When you have a chance, I would like to spend just a moment with you privately."

His father nodded.

"How about we talk after supper, this evening? Cook has planned a light supper since we ate lunch so late. We can talk then."

Edward nodded, "That will be fine. Thank you."

"Relax and take it easy for a bit, when you are rested, we will look around the grounds or visit the boat house. We can go out on the boat, or I can invite a couple of your old friends over for dinner, it is up to you, Edward." He said. I was surprised at his offer.

"No, Dad I would be happy to spend a quiet evening with you." Edward said. Ed nodded and left the room, shutting the door. Edward walked back to the bed and sat down.

"You want to lay down a while, and rest?"

"As long as you are laying beside me." We scooted up on the bed and he lay there. I wrapped my arms around his arm again and laid my head on his shoulder. I was holding him because I was afraid he would get up and leave me. He was like a statue, no movement, no emotion. The look on his face I couldn't read.

I must have dosed off because when I woke up, Edward was gone. I knew he wouldn't wait until after dinner to talk to his father. I wanted him to be patient. I looked in the bathroom, and he wasn't there. I panicked. I washed my face, brushed my teeth, straightened my clothes, and went down stairs. There was no one in the sitting room, and dining room. I didn't want to prowl through the house. I walked toward the back of the house, glancing in rooms as I walked by them. I saw double glass doors, and I headed toward them, I heard talking, loud talking. I hesitated. If they were arguing, I didn't want to walk in on it. What should I do? I turned around and looked for something to do. I thought if I could find Cook, I could ask her.

I went back toward the dining room, walked through the adjoining door, and saw it was the outer area of the kitchen. I walked through another door. Ah, finally I found the kitchen, but no Cook. I went back toward the back of the house by the double doors and listened. I heard no loud voices now, so I walked closer, seeing them walking out in the yard. Ed's hands were moving up and down, he looked as if he was lecturing Edward. Edward was moving his hands too when talking. I couldn't understand and what they were saying, but sporadically their voices grew louder. I hesitated and then opened the door. I walked out on the open deck and, saw a table and chairs on the far side of the deck; I walked over and took a seat next to the table. There was a nice breeze blowing, and I heard them raising their voices again, but I did not want to retreat. I was afraid I would interrupt them if they saw me. Edward was yelling now, but they were too far away for me to understand the words.

Cook came out. She looked out toward the two men and sighed, shaking her head. I was so relieved to see her. She turned back to me, offering me something to drink. I asked for iced tea, and she said it would be her pleasure. Mr. Anderson and her drank iced tea throughout the day, she said. She also said, she had some made and she would be right back. I wanted to ask her if she thought it better for me to go back inside, but she was gone too quickly.

Cook returned with the tea. I took her hand in mine and asked if there was somewhere, I could go to be out of the way, that the tow of them were arguing and I didn't want to interrupt them. She told me they always argued, and there was no place safe in the house. I was allowed to go anywhere in the house or surrounding area that I pleased. I smiled at her and told her I was uncomfortable.

She patted me on the hand and said, "You stand your ground, Sam. My boy loves you, and I can tell you love him too. He is happier than I have ever seen him. Please do not hurt my boy, but stand by his side and 'Do Not' let Mr. Anderson intimidate you or break you. I love that boy out there, and will do anything I can to see to his happiness, even if I have to quit."

I gasped.

"Cook, I will. I will stand by Edward. I love him, I really do. I promise you, I will take care of him." She nodded.

"I have faith in you, dear. I knew it the first time I laid eyes on you." She smiled, nodded, and walked away. I raised my head, pushed my shoulders back, and sat there waiting for them to come back to the deck. I was ready for battle if need be.

I sat there watching them, and my big, bad confidence was fading. I was getting more and more nervous again because their voices were rising, and their arms were in each other's faces. I hoped there would be no hitting match, I didn't know what to expect. I so worried about Edward's words and what his father might say to hurt him. I didn't want to be the cause of their disagreement. I sat there wringing my hands, thinking I should call the marriage off. We could just be together and put the wedding off until a year or two. That way, Ed could get to know me.

# CHAPTER SEVENTEEN

Edward had an angry look on his face when he was walking toward me. I smiled, but; the muscles in his face didn't budge. He had a scowl on his face that would worry the pope. He looked straight ahead, as he walked up the steps, across the deck and into the house, it was as if he didn't even see me. He went inside, not even bothering to shut the door. Well, I guessed my having his back will be on my own. His father was walking up the steps. He wasn't looking my way either. I decided to speak.

"Good afternoon, Ed."

He looked over at me, perplexed.

"Hello, Samantha. Did Edward say anything as he walked by?"

"No, I don't believe he even saw me."

"Oh, we were having a family discussion."

"I heard raised voices. Is Edward all right? Was it about us?"

"Young lady, it was between me and my son," he said sarcastically. I stood up. I thought I should go in the house and find Edward. Their fight, whether it was about me or not, was not for me to question his father about. I should talk to Edward. I felt strong, and I wanted things to be right between them. I spoke sympathetically. I thought maybe I could make a difference, make it right with them.

"I am sorry for intruding, but if it was about me, I want to know if I can help. I don't want to cause any more animosity between the two of you, but I feel I have to say something to defend myself."

"Young lady, I'm sure Edward will tell you my feelings concerning you and these preposterous wedding plans." He was so angry that I had butted in.

"Sir . . ."

He raised his voice, saying, "Are we back to that now? I can tell you have no manners and can't seem to keep your mouth shut. A woman's place is not to question man. Dou you understand me?"

I moved toward him, tears filling my eyes, but I did not want to let this hateful man see me cry.

"Ed, please do not raise your voice at me." I sniffed but tried to act, brave. "You do not know me, and if you have a problem with me being with your son, tell me. I wish you would try to get to know me. I am not a bad person. I was not raised in the lap of luxury, but I do have manners, I know what social skills are required of me when in public or as a guest in someone's home. I have tried to be pleasant and understanding of Edward's feeling. I am in love with him. I stood taller. "I want him to be happy. I am not a floozy, as you might think that I am. I am young, but I have taken care of myself most of my life. I work hard, and I am not after Edward's money or yours, 'Ed'. I am responsible and more mature than most so-called young women my age. I am sorry to have put you out by coming here. I want the two of you to make amends. I don't want to be a cause of more distress."

"I never said you were a floozy, maybe a girl interested in being bedded with the ideas of love being something it is not. I think Edward needs to finish school and be settled before he makes a major decision about his future that could be all wrong for him. Young men have needs, I know that, he has to satisfy those need. But marriage need not be the result of those pleasures, unless you are pregnant. Are you pregnant, Samantha? We can take care of that easily enough."

"No, I am not pregnant. You married, you must have loved Edward's mother."

"Let me tell you a little story. I was twenty-four when I married. Love had nothing to do with the arrangements. It was a financial and prestigious understanding. Both of our families were prominent. Our marriage was arranged, you see, more for status. She was a sad little woman, which her father forgot or decided not to disclose. She despised me. She hated my touch, even more after she was with child with Edward. I tried to be kind to her and make her happy, but it wasn't possible. The she no longer allowed me to touch her at all before she died. She died because she drank too much and ran off the road, killing herself and my unborn child she carried. She was drunk most of the pregnancy, so it was probably for the best anyway. She left me alone to raise a spoiled son who doesn't appreciate what he has, but If he plays his cards right, he could go far in politics, even to the White House."

"I'm sorry for you loss, I mean, I am sorry it was the way it was." I hung my head and thought about if I had ever heard Edward mention politics. I remember him saying he wanted to do pro bono. Help the homeless and needy. "Edward has never mentioned politics to me."

"You, Missy, do not know what kind of future that boy has in front of him. If you want to be in politics, you have to start preparing when you are young. You can't make stupid mistakes by getting a girl pregnant and leaving her high and dry or marrying the wrong kind of girl who would shame you later on in life. You can't marry to your potential. Look at some of our past presidents and the rumors and scandals that have come out. I don't want those problems for Edward; I care where his future leads him."

"If Edward wants to be in politics, it shouldn't be a problem. I do not have a seeded background, I am from a respectable family, not a very loving one, but decent and respectful. I do not want to hurt Edward or his career."

"I love my son regardless of what you think, you don't seem to understand. I have made arrangements for him to meet the woman he is to marry, and she is suitable for his standing."

I was shocked and at a loss for a moment. I stepped back.

"Have you talked to him about this?"

"About what?"

"About this girl he is to marry and his political future. I will stand aside if that is what he wants. Why would he ask me to marry him if that was the way he was headed?" I was thinking, *did Edward know what his father had planned? I don't think so.* "Ask him, ask Edward if he wants that kind of life."

"Samantha, you are very young and have noble ideas about life and living on love, and that is not the case. It takes power and money to get ahead in this life, and Edward could be the one to go all the way to the White House. Do you really want to be the one to hold him back?"

"No, absolutely not." "I know I am not the same level in society as you and he is. I have already tried to back away from him, telling him my faults and concerns of our different backgrounds. I told him I wasn't in the same league he was." I felt the fear darken my heart. I was going to lose Edward to someone else. "I knew nothing of love before I met your son. My parents, who are quote unquote' professionals, have never told me they loved me." I paused and exhaled. "Do you feel loved? Have you ever felt wanted for yourself, not what you can do for someone? It is important to Edward and me. He wants your approval. He needs to make amends between you and him. He needs to know you care about him, who he really is. If you love your son and you truly think I am wrong for him, tell him you love him, and I will walk away, it my choice so he will not blame you. I love him enough to leave if it is better for him." I bent my head, and tears were falling down my face. I pushed them down deep inside me lifting my head higher and kept going. "Edward is a good man, an honest hard working man. He is smart. Do you know how smart he is? He has been working this summer at the law firm I work at, and he's helped the attorneys so much. They have been so amazed with him. He found cases in old files that saved the attorney's hours of work and weeks in court, winning a case that no one believed they could win."

"I know my son is educated and has done well with his grades. Life is not always a snap of the fingers. You can't always expect to get everything you want."

"I didn't say he wanted or expected anything. He researched and found old cases. He knew where to look to find precedents about every element of the case. I believe him to be brilliant. He would be an asset to any Law Firm in the country and I know many are aware of it.

I can also see where he could do so much good for this county and its people by being involved in politics. He could make a difference in so many lives. I understand your concern and dreams for him. I would never want to take that away from him. Do you hear what I am saying, he is good and honest, he's loving and kind, and he is wonderful to me."

"Then you understand my concern for the betterment of his life with a socially accepted wife at his side," he said. I hung my head, understanding and believing he was right. "You know, the so—called law firm he works for called me for my recommendations regarding Edward. I told them he was lazy, but smart enough. This is the first I know of the, actually hiring him."

"I can't believe you did that. You tried to sabotage your own son's career. He was doing it to make you proud. He was trying to show you he could make his own way." I stood looking at this man, at how ugly he was by what was in his heart. I turned and walked away. I was angry, disappointed, and so very sad for Edward's sake. I would never tell him what I had learned today. I should have not said anything to him. It was none of my business. I started to slam the door upon entering the house, and I was surprised to see Edward standing there. He had heard us, I just wasn't sure how much he had heard.

I looked in his eyes and saw sorrow. "Ah, hi. How long have you been there?" I asked, terrified.

"Long enough to hear every word you said to him," he said. I hung my head. "I am so proud of you. I started to come to your defense, but I became aware, very quickly, that you could handle him on your own."

"I am sorry I interfered, I just want you to be happy. You deserve to be happy."

"Sam, nothing you say will change his mind. I am am pissed at what you did, and you better never do it again."

"I am so sorry." Tears were now streaming down my face, and I was shaking because I was scared that he wanted what his father wanted for him.

"You told him you would leave me. That is one thing I will not listen to, do you hear me?" I looked up at him and threw my arms around his neck, hugging, felt so right, so wonderful.

"Yes, I did. If it were true, and if I am holding you back for any reason, I would walk away. I refuse to do harm to you, or your career. Do you understand my feelings on that? What about this girl, the one he is talking about, to better your future? He could be right."

"You silly girl, I love you, Sam. 'You', you will not hurt me by being with me. Politics is his dream. He didn't make it because of the scandal of my mother drinking and driving, killing herself along with an unborn child. That is the truth, as I know it. I never wanted politics, and I never will. I told you about my goals of working with the poor." He hugged me. "Let's get our stuff and go. I tried to tell him, but he doesn't care what I want." He took my hand smiling at me. We ran up the stairs hand in hand, grabbed our bags, and came back down. Ed was standing at the foot of the stairs, waiting for us.

"Edward, if you leave this house, do not expect to come back for anything."

"Dad, I am sorry you feel that way. I have done everything recently to make up for my past mistakes. I have done my best in school. I will abide by your wishes by not returning. I just feel sad for you not knowing my future wife and never knowing your grandchildren. You will die a lonely old man."

"Edward, do not walk out that door. I will not give you another cent, if you do."

"Dad, I have two trust funds, what do I need your money for? I will be working in a year. I think we will be able to make it on our own. I never wanted your money, only your love." Edward was holding my hand, squeezing so tight that he was cutting off the circulation. He pulled me, and we walked past Ed and out the front door. I turned to see if he might change his mind and come after his son, but he did not. I saw him walking up the stairs, and I saw Cook wave then hang her head before shutting the front door. We got in the car and drove away.

"Edward, I am sorry. I made it worse."

"I already made up my mind before you spoke to my father. He is no longer a part of my life. It is you and I. We will not discuss this again."

# CHAPTER EIGHTEEN

Edward started driving up the coast, heading south; I knew he wasn't going back the way we came. He pulled over, parking the car and looking out over the Atlantic Ocean. He had both hands just resting on the steering wheel.

"Sam, I really tried to convince him how good we were for each other. I told him how sad and lonely we both felt, and he to toughen up, I should act like a man." Edward sighed, "Sam, I don't think he knows what love it. I don't think he has ever know love, so why believe in something you know nothing about?" He looked over at me.

"I think you right, Edward. I am sorry; I don't know what to say. I wonder how my family will handle the news of our marriage. Will we both lose? No, it is their loss, not ours." I reached over, touching his hand on the steering wheel.

"Well, I am not ready to go back to Clearwater. We have the weekend off, and we have only been here a few hours. This is my hometown. I am going to show you a good time. We are going to get a room and go to a dinner theater, I am going to call a couple of friends, and I am going to see if I can set something exciting up. In this town, there is a lot to do and see. Is that okay with you?"

"Edward, I'm with you."

He smiled and pulled back out on the road, heading to the hustling part of the city. We drove around, and he was thinking. He pulled into a parking space in front of pool hall. He got out, coming around to get me, and we went inside. He looked around until he found who he was looking for. He walked up to him; the guys back was to us. Edward tapped him on his shoulder, "Hey man, you're in my way, move it." I was baffled, I stood still. This was a big man he tapped on the shoulder, huge with broad shoulders. He was about the same height as Edward, but outweighed Edward by a hundred pounds. The guy turned around slowly, and he was a very big man, muscular arms and, chest. He was holding a pool cue. His face was hard, and then it softened. He grabbed Edward around the neck, bending him over forward. I thought he was going to kill him, but the guy was smiling and rubbing his knuckles across the top of Edward's head.

"Dude, where have you been? I haven't seen you in over a year." He turned and looked at me.

"Damn, Edward who is this lovely vision beside you?"

"Thomas, this is my fiancée Sam. Sam, this is my best friend of all time, Thomas." We both nodded. He was looking me up and down.

"Man, I want to grab her and squeeze the little thing, until she pops."

He handed Edward his pool stick, grabbed me, and squeezed me until I thought I was going to burst. I grunted aloud, and then he planted a kiss on my cheek. "Now that is a proper, friendly Florida welcome." He smiled from ear to ear, and so did Edward. My knees were so weak. I thought I might fall down. I actually stumbled, and Thomas held me steady. I was shocked, looking back and forth from one to the other, and they both started laughing. I thought *'Well, hell; I might as well join the crowd.*

"Thomas, it's my pleasure to meet a friend of Edwards." I tried to hug him, but my arms only went part-way around his chest, and barely behind his arms, so I patted his arms and smiled."

"Damn, she's a keeper."

"Don't I know it?" Edward beamed. Thomas told one of the guys he was playing with to take his place, and he walked to the back of the room and sat in a booth, Edward and I followed.

"Have you seen your dad?"

"Yes, we just came from there. Big fight as usual. I left and swore never to go back. He told me I wasn't welcome."

"Same oh, same oh, huh dude?"

"How long you in town?"

"Well, we were going to stay at the house, but we are going to get a room and stay a couple of days. I thought of taking Sam to a dinner show, maybe Broward County. I thought about seeing if we could get some old friends together for a party."

"Now that sounds like fun. Well, since you and your dad are on the outs, that means no boathouse. How about William's place? I think his parents are on a cruise. Let me check a few things, it may take me a couple of hours, but do you want to come back or wait?"

"I want to go get us a room, and we'll be back." We stood to leave, Thomas was already dialing numbers, so Edward patted him on the shoulder, and we left.

We checked in to the Hilton. We weren't hungry yet, so we just sat and talked. His cell phone rang, and it was a friend. He talked to him for a bit, and then said, "That sounds good." As soon as he hung up, it rang again. He said a girl's name, 'Valerie'. He said he had missed her too. I didn't like the sound of that conversation, but I knew I shouldn't worry about Edward. The girls he grew up with I might need to worry about. He was a catch. As soon as he was finished with that call, another one came through. He was laughing and talking, and then he told whomever he was talking to, he had another call He hung up with that one and answered the next. By the time he had finished on the phone, I bet he had fifteen to twenty calls. He let out a deep breath.

"Well, Sam, my friends are happy I am in town."

"It sounds like it. Who is Valerie?"

He laughed.

"She is an old girlfriend." I frowned. He laughed again.

"She is married with three kids now. She and her husband want to join us, she is looking for a sitter." I eased. "Baby, I am with you, I am not a cheater, and I promise you I love you, Sam."

"I Know, I have no reason to be jealous." The phone rang again. It was Thomas calling to tell us it was all set up. There would be food, beer, wine everything you could imagine. It was at the 'Old Sully Place'. I guessed it was an old hang out, maybe a barn or shed falling down, tailgating maybe. He told me to wear something comfortable. It would be hot, so I thought shorts, shirt and tennis shoes.

When we arrived at the party, it was a huge red barn. Lights were strung up around the outside, and you could see a bright glow inside the barn. I bet there were a hundred or so people milling around outside and inside. We had stopped at the liquor store and bought tequila, vodka, whiskey, beer, and several other bottles. We carried it all inside. They had tubs filled with ice and we sat the liquor bottles. We carried it all inside. They had tubs filled with ice, and we sat the liquor bottles on the table and put the beer in a tub. Someone had brought a keg, and it was sitting in ice. People were walking by and patting Edward on the back, saying "nice to see you" and asking how he was. I think he knew everyone there. On the far wall were tables set up with dishes of food. I saw trays and trays of meat, salads, bowls of green things, and bowls of pink stuff. There were cakes and cookies at the end of the table. There were paper plates, napkins, cups, forks, spoons, and knives. There was a whole table with nothing but breads. Hamburger buns, hot dog buns, croissants, sandwich bread, and cornbread. There was enough food on these tables to feed three times as many people here.

Edward held my hand and walked by, saying hello to people. Occasionally he would introduce me to someone. I don't remember any names, it was such a blur. There was a stage, and a band was setting up to play. At the back of the room were tables and chairs. There were even chairs along the sidewall behind the beer and alcohol. I guessed that was for the serious drinkers. The music started playing, this band was good. People were dancing and moving around, and everyone was smiling and laughing. This was the first time I had been to a party that was as exciting as this. It felt good, and everyone was treating me nice, and telling me what a great guy Edward was, which I already knew.

A very pretty brown-haired woman came over to Edward. I was standing back with another girl who was talking to me. The girl I was talking to looked somewhat restless, I guess you would call it. She was biting her bottom lip and wringing her hands, and her words were slow and pausing. I saw her look around for someone, and she must have found them because she waved them over. He was tall, nice looking man. She pointed at the girl. The young man said a few cuss words as he and the girl talking to me walked across the floor toward Edward, and the brunette.

The girl walked up to Edward and put her hands on his butt. He turned around smiling; I hope he thought it was me. She kissed him on the mouth. I stood where I was for a moment. Edward's face turned white. He looked around for me and caught me looking at him. He started to move away from her toward me, but she grabbed him and kissed him again, and grabbed his package. I thought, *'okay, I am going to kill the girl.'* My face was red and hot as fire. The girl I was talking to and the guy ran to the girl, and they pushed her on her ass to the floor. I found myself moving quickly across the floor toward Edward. Edward watched the girl hit the floor. It was in slow motion, slow motion, and everyone was looking now.

I looked around the room, and people were pointing and whispering to each other. I thought, *this is an old girl-friend, definitely not Valerie, but an old girl-friend.* I didn't think I had anything to worry about. I leaned my head forward and then lifted it with a smile. Edward saw my face, and he relaxed seeing me walk up beside him. I put my hand in his hand. We both looked down at the girl.

"Sam, this was my step mother, Regina. Actually, she is one of my dad's ex-wife," he said. She looked pissed, sitting in the floor. Edward helped her up. "So you spoke with Dad already?"

"Yeah, he told me you brought a slut home with you, and I heard about the party, so I came to see for myself."

"Does Dad know you are here?"

"Sure, he knows. This little whore?" She was pointing at me.

"Regina, say one more word, and I will flatten you I don't care if you are a girl or not."

She stood up, but the pretty girl and good-looking guy stood close to Edward and me. They moved off to the side.

"So you need body guards now to protect you, Edward?" Regina said.

"No." He looked at the guy and girl. "But thanks, Net and Greg."

"You should leave, you weren't invited." Edward said to Regina.

"I just wanted to see you. I miss you Edward."

"I don't miss you, and I won't be back again."

"You always say that. Can we go outside and talk?"

"No, get the hell out of here."

"Come on, you can't talk to your 'Momma' Like that." She stood up, trying to reach out to put her arms around his neck, but Edward pulled away.

"You are nothing to me. Go away, you are ruining the party and making a fool of yourself, Regina." Greg motioned for a couple of men to come over, including Thomas. Two of the men each took one of Regina's arms and escorted her out of the barn. I didn't know what they said to her outside, but she didn't come back in. We had a blast the rest of the night. I liked Edward's friends. The food was great and the booze zonked me.

We tried to leave around 3:00 a.m., but friends kept asking us questions and wanting to talk to Edward. There were about twenty or thirty people still here. The girls were cleaning up the food, covering it, and packing it up to take away. I tried to help, but they said they had it under control. They were so nice to me. I was sitting in a chair half asleep at 4:00 a.m. Edward walked over, picked me up, and carried me to his car. "Let me tell Thomas, thanks, and I will be right back."

I relaxed against the seat, leaning my head out the open window for fresh air and dozing off and on. I heard a woman talking to a man close to the car. I rose up and saw Regina with a man. They were talking in low voices but standing close to Edward's car. They didn't see me sitting in the car. I was trying to understand what she was telling him, but I was drunk and having difficulty even staying awake. I saw her hand him a baseball bat. Oh no, damn, they were going to hurt Edward. I saw guys standing in the door of the barn, and Edward was talking to them. I knew if I yelled, Edward would come see what was wrong with me, but maybe alone. I couldn't walk, I couldn't even think straight. I was wasting time.

I pressed on the car horn with both hands. It was loud, Regina jumped, looking my way. She yelled at the man with the bat. Edward ran out toward me, and a couple of other guys followed him. They saw this dude run away, and Regina running to a car, she tripped and fell. Edward got to her, pulling her up by one arm. He was shaking her, yelling at her. One of the guys was now standing by my window, holding the bat they had dropped. Two others were going to where Edward was. He pushed Regina in her car, slammed the door, and walked away.

When he got in the car, he leaned down and waved at the guy by my door, saying thanks. We drove away.

"Sam, thank you for honking that horn. If you hadn't, and I came out alone, they might have hurt me bad or killed me."

"I know." I started crying. The adrenaline was running through me now I couldn't fight the out-of-control sobbing. When we were a couple of miles away from the party, he pulled over and hugged me. He was rubbing my back, and trying to calm me back down. I sat back in the seat, and he pulled back on the road and headed for the hotel. He went to the valet parking and told them about Regina and how, she might counter-attack.

He helped me walk to our room. He turned around and motioned for me to come to him. He threw me on the bed and had me striped down in seconds. I was drunk; I don't know how great it was. I remember I couldn't stop giggling. He was laughing too. I remember wanting him. We made love, but I hated that I was in and out of consciousness and didn't recall everything that happened. He held me and told me he loved me many times. He said he wanted to make sure I never forgot.

# CHAPTER NINETEEN

Saturday morning, we went shopping. I bought a dress to wear to dinner that evening. We met Thomas and a couple of the other guys for lunch. We ate at a little cafe out on the highway. It looked like the building could fall down around us. Thomas said it had the best food in town. They served old-fashioned burgers and fries, meatloaf dinners, chicken-fried steak dinners, fried chicken platters, beans and cornbread, things you found in the South. I ordered a burger and fries with a chocolate shake. Edward ordered the chicken fried steak with a Coke, and Thomas ordered the meatloaf dinner plus an order of fried chicken with water. One of the other guys ordered a huge breakfast platter with three eggs, bacon, sausage, pancakes, grits, biscuits and gravy. He also ordered two glasses of milk. The other guy ordered a double burger, with bacon, three kinds of cheese, cheese fries and onion rings, and a strawberry shake.

Then the food arrived out table almost wasn't big enough for all the food. They gave us huge orders of fries and onion rings. The chicken-fried steak was as big as the platter, and the fried chicken was half a chicken. The meat-loaf looked like half of a loaf pan.

I smashed my burger, pressing some of the juice from the meat onto the bread. I opened my burger and removed the meat patties. Everyone was watching me. I laid it on the side of my plate; I put my burger back together minus the meat and took a bite. It tasted good, the juice and grease from the burger soaked into the bread, with the mustard, onion, pickles, cheese, and tomatoes. It was perfect for me. The fries were fat greasy fat, fries perfect for dipping in ketchup.

Thomas laughed and said, "I thought you were going to just eat the meat, and leave the bread, not the other way around."

"I am not much of a red meat eater. Do you want the meat?"

"Maybe later, I have a lot on my plate." The guys all laughed.

"If anyone wants the meat, they can have it." I looked at Del who had the double burger. He said, "I'll take it and make a triple for me." I passed my plate over, and he forked it onto his plate. The food I had was very good and not a bad price for what we got. The shake was thick and creamy. Del's even had chunks of strawberry in his shake. I ate almost all my burger and a part of the fries. Edward ate some of my fries; Del offered me some onion rings, they were cooked perfectly, very crunchy. The other guy with the breakfast platter ate all of his. He said sorry to everyone because he didn't offer anyone anything. They all laughed. I patted my tummy and felt quite proud of myself for eating what I did. I was stuffed.

Thomas said, "Got quite a pouch there, Sam." They all laughed at that. These guys were big guys, I didn't know what they did but they must have worked out every day. Their arms were the size of tree trunks, and their legs are so huge that they walk bow-legged. I mean they were not fat; there was no fat on them at all, they were muscle-bound. We waddled out of the cafe. Thomas wanted Edward and me to go to the pool hall for a while. I told Edward it was fine with me. I would watch. Edward played a couple of games; these guys were all pretty good. Thomas asked us to come to his place this evening, but Edward told him he wanted to take me to a dinner theater. Thomas told him he could do that in Clearwater or Ft. Myers, so Edward agreed we would drop by later.

I was so full I just wanted to sleep for a while. We went back to the hotel in the late afternoon and slept for a couple of hours. I woke up about 5:00 p.m., and Edward looked so peaceful lying beside me. He was on his belly with one arm curled around his head, the other arm to his side. I touched the side of his face; he smiled, not opening his eyes. I ran my hand down his back to his belt and slipped my fingers in his pants. He turned more on his side, I thought I wasn't much at initiating sex, but I was going to try.

I pulled his shirt out of his shorts. With my palm on his hot, soft skin, I ran my hand over his belly. My finger-tips were slightly in the waistband of his shorts. He moaned and turned more on his side, his eyes were still shut, but I knew he was awake. I giggled. I pushed my hand further down the front of his shorts, touching the patch of thick hair above his groin. I played with the course, curly hairs, pulling until one, until he said "Ouch." His hand automatically went down there and rubbed, and then he moved it away. I giggled again. He was spread eagle, lying on his back, still still not opening his eyes. He was grinning from ear to ear, I watched his face, and then looked at where my hand was. I unbuttoned his shorts, very slowly pulling the zipper down one tooth at a time. He pushed his hips up and he groaned. I pushed my hand further down until I could touch his hard cock. He pushed his hips up and groaned. I pushed my hand further down until I could barely touch his shaft. I ran my fingers, pushing back against the flat area on each side of his shaft. My middle finger was down the length of him, reaching only half-way to the tip. He raised his hips again, asking for more. I pulled my fingers back up and played with the hair. He was moving his hips. I ran my hand down his shaft squeezed, he rose off the bed. I was thrilled to know he reacted this way to my touch.

I released him, running my fingers to the head of his cock and making tiny circles around the small hole. A drop of wet, warm sperm was on my finger, making it easy to slide around. I pulled my hand back out of his pants and straddled him. I pulled on his shorts, trying to get them off. I tugged and tugged, and he finally raised his hips so I could get them freed enough to come past his hips. I worked my way down to the end of the bed, pulling his shorts and boxers off.

I crawled back up his body. His eyes were still shut. I saw his shaft hard and standing up, that tip was so soft and velvety. He kissed me down there, he licked me too. I liked it, so what would it do to him? Might he enjoy my tongue running around the tip, licking and kissing? I leaned down barely touched my tongue to the tip of the bulging rod. He jumped off the bed into a sitting position, I rose up with a start, and we almost bumped heads again. His eyes were wide and glassy, looking me straight in the face. I smiled at him and tried to push him back down to the bed, but it wasn't an easy task. I bent forward and touched him again with my tongue. He groaned so loudly arched his back, bringing he cock straight up in the air. I put my hand around it to hold him still and put the head in my mouth. He reared off the bed again, moaning. I pushed him back down. He was breathing very hard, and his chest was rising and falling in quick, short breaths. I kissed the head and then licked him. He arched back up. I was pumping his shaft with my hand, squeezing and pumping him up and down. I was seducing him for the first time all by myself, using what he had taught me.

I kissed him one again and ran my tongue up the length of his rod. He was so hard and throbbing in my hand, he grabbed me by my upper arms and pulled me up on him. I was straddling him, and he positioned me over him and went inside me in one single thrust. It felt good, so good. He had his hands on my hips, moving me in slow circles while moving me up and down, so I caught on to the rhythm quickly. His hands slid up to my breast, and he pinched the nipples, squeezing my breast and rubbing them hard, making me go crazy with desire and lust.

He moved one hand back down and started touching me, pinching that nub and going round and round it. The idea, the excitement of what I had done to him, was what I was feeling now and it was too much. I went down on his cock hard and squeezed him inside me. He pushed up, and I felt him all through me. He gave another hard push as I pushed hard against him, and we came together like an atomic bomb. My insides exploded, I felt the tremors up my spine and flowing into my limbs, and finger tips. I was shaking and trembling. I felt his muscles shudder under my touch. He relaxed and I wanted him to stay inside me. This was a good way to keep him there. I was in control, I moved around on his shaft, making him moan and groan with pleasure or agony. I jerked forward, and he arched again, coming deep inside me. I fell down on his chest, unable to catch my breath now. He was rubbing his hands up and down my back. I couldn't talk; I was so exhausted and tired. I lay on him, smelling his sweat mixed with his cologne. I kissed his neck, biting him hard on his collarbone. He yelled out and panted.

"Sam . . ." He couldn't talk either, "I . . . Love . . . you."

"I . . . Love . . . you . . . too . . . Edward." I rolled over onto my back beside him and lay there feeling half-dead. I couldn't move. He looked over at me, touched my hand, and squeezed my fingers. We lay there relaxing our over-worked bodies for twenty minutes at least. He turned on his side, I still had my dress on, and it was up around my neck.

"Do you want to take that off?"

"When I have the strength to get up, I will."

He rubbed my belly, shutting his eyes and inhaling and exhaling deeply. His fingers slid down until he was touching me, moving his middle finger inside me. We both dozed off.

# Chapter Twenty

We woke up about an hour later. Edward got up, crawling over me and rubbing against me as he moved.

"Is that to make sure I am a wake?"

"Yelp."

I sat up and pulled my dress off. He was already in the bathroom when I stood up. I followed him. He had the water on and got in. I had to pee, so I sat down and cleaned myself some. I got in standing behind him, hugging him to me. The water felt good hitting me in the face full force. I pushed him out of the way, letting the water pound on my head. I moved back so he could get back under the showerhead. I soaped up, we were doing a little dance back and forth, taking turns under the faucet, laughing and shoving each other out of the way, play-fighting for water. I washed my hair and was rinsing when Edward got a towel, stepped out, and fried himself. I finished up, I opened the curtain, and he was standing there doing a little dance for me. He was shaking his thing and making it go round and round as; he had his hands behind his head. I laughed until I cried. He grabbed me and toweled me off. I held onto the towel and walked back to the bedroom, trying to find clean clothes. He was walking around naked, not a care in the world. My eyes stayed on his naked body, he was exquisite.

"Edward, why do men have no care walking around like that?"

"I do care, but not in front of you. You are my lady."

"Yeah, but I can't do that in front of you. I have bulges here and there and worry you will notice them."

"You are perfect, I love you just the way you are. You don't have any bulges; you only have curves just like a woman should have." He yanked my towel off. I covered myself with my hands the best I could, and he laughed and touched me. He tickled me, grabbing my arm or leg, and then my crotch. He slapped me on the ass.

"Edward, stop that."

He chased me all over the room.

"I like touching you." He was shaking his limp member at me again. I tripped on the corner of a chair and tumbled to the ground, he tackled me. He landed on me kissing me and licking my neck and face, moving his hands everywhere. I was trying to fight him, but I was laughing so hard I couldn't.

"Edward, you have to stop, I can't take it." I laughed and giggled. Finally he stopped. He was sitting on me, looking down at me and smiling.

"Baby, you are beautiful. Have I told you today how beautiful you are?"

"I don't believe you have told me that today." I said in a proper voice.

"Well, then, I will tell you again. I love you, and you are beautiful, the most beautiful thing I have ever seen." He was touching me gently and softly. He bent down and kissed me. Looking in my eyes, he placed his hands on each of my cheeks and kissed me again, soft and gentle. "I love you." I was so happy and felt so wonderful, and the the jerk slapped my bottom. He jumped up and ran across the room, laughing.

"That hurt," I rubbed my bare ass.

"Get dressed. We have to get going soon."

I jumped up and got dressed in a Capri set. I fixed my hair and put on mascara and lip-gloss. Edward was wearing shorts and a button-up shirt. He looked handsome. He was rubbing his hands together, demanding I hurry or we would be late.

We arrived at Thomas's house about twenty minutes later. He had about six big guys there, and Edward knew them all. I remembered a couple from the night before. One was standing by my door when Regina was going to hurt Edward. I was the only girl. I hoped it wouldn't be that way all night. I felt out of place, with no one to talk to me.

The doorbell rang, Thomas opened it and three girls arrived. Good, at least there were other girls here, but they didn't say a word to me, and walked to where the guys were standing. I was still on the couch sitting by myself. Then someone knocked a while later and it was Net and another girl. I was so glad to see her, I liked her a lot. She immediately came and sat beside me, asking me how my day was. She was very nice. She introduced me to her friend Tory, and she seemed nice too. I saw her walk over to Thomas and pull his arm. He leaned down, and she kissed him. Okay, that was his girl. She was this tiny little thing, not over 5' 2", and weighed maybe a hundred pounds. She was cute as she could be.

Net said, "They make quite a pair, don't they?" We laughed.

"Yeah, they do."

"They have been together for years. She is the same age as the rest of us. We all graduated high school together. She is very nice. Thomas adores her. He would do anything for her. Thomas is a big guy, but he is like a kitten when it comes to his friends, and especially when it comes to Tory." She said. I smiled, thinking about the two of them in bed. He would squash her.

Net told me her boyfriend was visiting his parents and wasn't due back until Wednesday. She said they were getting married next summer or fall; they hadn't set an actual date yet. She said she met him at a party; he was living in Florida going to school. She told me he was a big man like Thomas and his friends, but much better looking. She smiled, telling me Thomas and two of the guys were body-builders and the other one, Del, was a bouncer. He worked at a hot spot nightclub downtown. She guessed he was off this weekend. He was also in college, studying to be a doctor, of all things.

"Can you imagine a guy like that coming in to take care of you in an emergency or doctor's office?"

"I laughed. Well looking at him, no, but once he stars talking to you, yes, I think I would trust him."

"He is a great guy too. He has a girlfriend, who should be here soon. They usually aren't apart often unless one of them is at work. You'll like her too. She is our songbird. She sings, plays the piano, and guitar, and hilarious to be around. She is a comic and can make a dead man laugh. I can't wait for you to meet her."

The music was playing and the guys huddled in a group, Tory came back to join Net and I. She told me about her and Thomas. She said they had been engaged for four years. Thomas was holding out. The doorbell rang, and in walked a beautiful girl. Net poked me with her elbow. "That's Del's girlfriend, Silly Sal, we call her." Del ran to her and bent her over and kissed her. It looked so romantic like, 'Rhett Butler and Scarlet O'Hara' in 'Gone with the Wind'.

Net called out to her, "Sal come meet Edward's girlfriend." She ran over and hugged Net and Tory.

"Hi Sam, I have heard about you all day long. Del can't stop talking about you. I thought I was going to have to come beat me up some chick flirting with my guy." She said. I smiled at her. "Just kidding you know. It is a pleasure to meet you."

"It is nice to meet you too Sal," quite relieved. The music got louder, and the girls were bouncing around, sort of dancing, Sal began to sing.

'*Oh my Gosh*', *sing*. She sounded like an angel. She was on key, and knew every word. She should be on the radio. I told her so. I told her she had the most amazing voice I had heard. She said she had some demos and was sending them out. She actually had an agent helping her. She said she had a meeting next week with an organizer from Atlantic Records, so maybe soon she would be on the radio.

I liked these three girls a lot. The other three girls never came over to talk to me, and I didn't try to go talk to them. I was comfortable with Net, Tory, and Sal. We had a good time. We stayed until 4:00 a.m... Everyone was tired, and they all were leaving. I told everyone how great it was to meet them and would see them again sometime. The three girls I liked hugged me, along with Del and Thomas. They invited me back anytime with or without Edward.

We were driving back to town and talking about the party when a siren came up behind us. Edward said a few choice words. He hadn't been drinking much, but I had. He told me he wasn't speeding so he didn't know why he was stopped. He pulled over and got out his license, and registration, and insurance papers. He had his window rolled down by the time the cop stepped up to the window.

"Step out of the car," The cop said. I was terrified. We were out on a dark road, with no one else in sight. Edward shook his head and opened the door, handing all the papers to me. I put my hand on his arm, "Should we be worried?"

"No, sit tight. But you never can tell about these backwoods cops," he said.

I heard the officer talking to Edward, and then Edward took a swing at the officer on the arm. I couldn't imagine why. I thought he must be crazy to swing at a cop; he was going to get shot or go to jail. I jumped out of the car, running around to the other side I tripped and fell. I felt blood in my mouth, the taste of iron. I knew I busted my lip again. I jumped up, starting toward Edward and the cop, holding my mouth. Blood was running down my face on my clothes. They hadn't noticed me falling, as it was so quick.

I yelled, "What's going on? Please stop. Edward, stop."

I grabbed for Edward. He and the officer both turned around and saw the blood running down my chin onto my dress. They both were smiling, not really fighting; this was another friend of his. I was terrified, Edward was going to get hurt, and they were playing a joke on me. I stood up straight and told the officer to take Edward's ass to jail as I stomped back in the direction of the passenger side door.

Edward ran around to me, yelling. "What happened to your face?"

I pulled away from him and kept walking.

"Sam, stop now."

I turned and glared at him.

"What the hell is this about?" I was looking at the cop too. "I was scared to death, you meant to scare me, you knew when you got out of the damn car who this guy was, didn't you?"

He hung his head, "Yeah, he used to torment me when I was in high school. He is a friend of my dad's. He saw my car that was why he pulled us over. I was telling him about my dad and my disagreement today. I am sorry, Sam. Are you okay?"

"I tripped running to save you, and you didn't even notice." My lip had already swollen, but the bleeding had slowed down. The officer walked over and held out his hand.

"I am Frank Walker, I went to school with Ed, Edward and my son grew up together. You met him earlier tonight. Del, Del Walker."

I looked at him and saw the similar bone structure. Del's father was a lot thinner, but I could see the father and son in them now. He handed me his handkerchief for my lip. He looked at my lip and said it wasn't too bad.

"It's nice to meet you Sir, I am Samantha Lord." I was glaring at Edward still.

"I am sorry you got hurt. I wanted to scare Edward, but then he recognized me before I got to do anything, I am real sorry you got hurt."

"I am fine, it's not like it is the first fat lip I've had."

"Has this boy hit you? I'll kill him if he has." He said gruffly.

"No, it was nothing like that. We bumped heads, and I got a busted lip and a broken nose several weeks ago. Edward has been nothing but a perfect gentleman and very kind to me. Well, maybe he isn't all that perfect now that I see what he is capable of doing, but I love him. Did he tell you?"

Edward spoke up, "We are getting married."

"Well congratulation."

"That was part of the disagreement with Dad."

"I see. He wanted you with that girl, oh that rich girl from Miami. I can't remember her name, but with a lot of family influence."

"Yeah, that is what he wanted. I want Sam."

"You seem to have both made a good choice. I will let you go. Nice meeting you, Miss Lord, and good to see you, Edward." He got in his car and drove away. We got back on the road and finally made it back to our hotel. Exhausted again, this had been a long weekend, and we still had another day, driving back to Clearwater. He slept after a short tryst together until morning.

# Chapter Twenty-One

I woke up late in the morning stretching, and twisting around. I saw Edward on his side watching me. I giggled He smiled.

"Do you do that every morning?"

"Well, yeah I do, it's a habit. Ronnie makes fun of me."

"I think it's beautiful." He pulled me close to him and kissed me. "We need to get up and get something to eat and get on the road soon back to Clearwater." I tried to pull away, but he held me tight.

"You have to let me go so I can get up and get ready."

"I don't want to; I want to stay like this always."

"Me too, but . . ."

"There is always a 'but' . . . "He loosened his grip, and I got out of bed and ran to the bathroom, Edward right on my heels. We got in the shower. We played and satisfied each other immensely. We finally got out, brushing our teeth. I ran my fingers through my hair, shaking it and letting it do its own thing today. I donned mascara, packed my bag, and was ready to go in forty-five minutes.

We were starving when we checked out of the hotel, so we went to another of Edwards's old haunts. We ordered breakfast instead of lunch. I tried not to eat too much because I would be miserable in the car for hours. Edward stopped to get gas, and I bought some snacks and drinks to have in the car. I had a hard time just sitting for hours, so I had to eat or do something to pass the time. I was an eater.

We stopped a couple of times to stretch and use the bathroom. We arrived home before the sun went down, which was a good thing; we had time to relax before the week started. We unpacked our clothes at his place; I started washing my clothes, and then his. Everything was clean. I thought I should go to my condo and see how things were with Kat and Ronnie.

We drove over there, and I knocked on the door, which felt strange, but I was rarely there anymore, so I didn't want to barge in. Ronnie opened the door and hugged me. She pulled me inside, asking about the weekend, how it went, I looked at Edward, and he nodded. I told her about what happened at Edward's dad's house. I then told her what a great time we had with Edward's friends.

Ronnie told me Kat was with her boyfriend all weekend. Mick stayed here, or she stayed at his place. I told Ronnie I should go ahead and take all my stuff over to Edwards, that way she would have the room to herself. We packed up what clothes I had left, and I told Ronnie I would bring her clothes I borrowed to her the next evening. She told me she wasn't worried and didn't even remember what I had. Ronnie got us a beer, and we sat out on the balcony talking. I missed being around her. I missed seeing her every day. As we were leaving, she hugged me and asked if we could all go to dinner one evening this week. We thought that would be nice.

"Sam, I miss you."

"I was just thinking the same thing." We hugged, and I told her I would call her the next day. We took my stuff back to Edward's, and I fixed us some scrambled eggs for dinner. We ate and then sat on the beach, feeling the breeze blow through our hair.

"I sure do hate going back to work tomorrow."

"Me too, Sam, I had a good time despite what went down with my dad, being with you made it nice. I enjoyed seeing my friends."

"You know, we need to get out more. We spend all our time in the bedroom and don't even go to the beach much."

"Tomorrow, I want you to make a list of what you want to do with the time we have left here in Clearwater. I will make a list too. We will put them together and do as much as we can."

"Sounds good." I leaned up against him, and we sat there looking out across the Gulf, until I started to yawn. We walked back to the apartment. I cleaned up everything out of place and sorted Ronnie's clothes from mine to take back to her. Edward was already in bed, and I joined him.

The next week was my last week to work. I had given them notice so I could have what time left to just be lazy and do what I wanted to do. I worked diligently all week. I wanted everything done and caught up for Renee. She had been a good influence on me, and I appreciated her giving me the job over the summer. I was in early everyday and stayed as late as she wanted me to. Renee was in the office most of the week, and Edward was out doing research for her. I didn't see him much at work all week long.

Friday, Renee gave me a bonus and had a small party for me, which was kind of her. Everyone gave me little things that would remind me of my time here at the firm as well as being in Florida. I cried most of the day. I loved what I had done and learned from the research she let me do and all the odds and ends I helped her and Edward with.

The summer had gone by so quickly. I felt so sad that my time with Edward would end in a week and a half. We still hadn't made plans of what we were going to do about being together, getting married and me changing schools. We had no answers as of yet. I left my job and got on my scooter, leaving for the last time. I took pictures of everyone and pictures of the building; I waved to Edward and told him I would see him later, but. I still felt the end was coming for us with no clue how to fix the sorrow we would share in twelve days. We had twelve more days in our own little world. As I rode home, I wondered if we would manage the distance and stay together. So many times long distance relationships didn't work out. What if Edward found someone else? What if I did? No, that was not going to happen. I loved him and always will.

I went to the grocery store and bought stuff for dinner. I wanted to make tonight's meal special, along with every night we had left of the summer. I went home, cleaned the vegetable, and started the meat simmering in a skillet. I grated cheese and, mixed the cheese, eggs, and ricotta together. I had the noodles boiling. I removed them and laid them on a paper towel. I greased the baking dish with butter, and then placed a small amount of meat and sauce mixture on the bottom. I laid a layer of noodles on top of the meat, then a layer of ricotta mixture on the bottom. I laid a layer of noodles on top of the meant, and then a layer of ricotta mixture, and then cheeses, repeating three times. I topped it with a half a pound of grated cheese and put it in the oven to bake. I sliced bread and buttered it with garlic butter and Parmesan cheese, ready to bake when Edward came in. I opened a bottle of red wine to let it air and sat waiting for Edward to come home.

It was after 6:00 p.m... Edward hadn't made it home yet. I wondered where he was. I called his cell, and he didn't answer. I took the lasagna out of the oven and placed it on the counter to cool. I called the office, but no one answered there, they didn't answer the switchboard after 5:00 p.m., but sometimes Renee answered if she was still in. It was almost 7:00 p.m. now with no word from Edward. I kept trying his phone, and it went straight to voice mail, as if it was turned off. At first, I thought he had gone somewhere to buy me a present, but he would have called by now. I was worried. I finally called Renee's cell phone. She answered and told me Edward had left at 5:00 p.m. as usual, everyone did since it was Friday. She said he didn't say anything about other plans. She asked why I was so interested n Edward. I told her the truth about us, and she said she had no idea. I told her we didn't want to cause trouble at work, we decided not to bring any lovey-dovey stuff or arguments to work, and we kept our promises on that. I told her I was really worried. She suggested I check the police or hospital. I agreed, but it was too early to file a missing persons report.

I got my nerve up and called the police department. They told me there had been an accident on the main street, but they would not give me names. I was crying, asking if anyone was hurt, they told me there had been an injury and the injured party had been taken to the hospital in Tampa. I called Ronnie frantically, crying and trying to tell her something was wrong, but she couldn't understand a word I was saying. She jumped in her car and came to me. She was trying to get a straight answer out of me. All she could understand was the hospital. She asked me if it was 'Kat'. I shook my head, "Edward?" I nodded, yes. We found a close parking spot and went in through emergency; we had already been here twice before, so we knew our way around.

Ronnie asked the nurse at the desk for Edward Anderson. They told us he was in surgery, and then told us where the surgery waiting room was. We ran up the stairs and found the waiting area. I checked in as Edwards's wife, and they told me he was in critical condition when he brought into emergency, and he was in surgery now. The woman behind the desk told me when someone was available to advise me on his condition, she would tell him or her where I was. I was hysterical and couldn't talk or stop crying, that was bad, I needed to know what happened. I had no idea.

Two police officers walked into the waiting room, and the woman and the desk pointed to us. I panicked again, screaming, "Is Edward alright?" I stood up, and they walked toward me. What was going on? They asked if they could talk to me privately. I couldn't talk, I was crying so hard, so they took Ronnie and me into a private waiting room. They asked if I had Edward's insurance information or any other information about him.

Ronnie told them, "His auto insurance papers were in his car. His medical insurance information would be in his wallet." I gave them our address and his cell phone. I told them I didn't know his father's phone number it was programmed in Edward' cell phone.

Ronnie asked, "What happened?"

They told us, "A drunk driver had run a red light and smashed into Mr. Anderson's car. His car looks totaled. The fire department used the Jaws of Life to remove him from his car. He was unconscious, he had a serious head wound, and his legs were pinned under the steering wheel area. He was wearing a seat belt. The air bag deployed, causing lacerations on his face, neck, and chest. All the glass in the car was broken into fine pieces. Mr. Anderson's car was pushed two hundred feet from the point of impact." I gasped, tears running down my face.

The other officer added, "It was a miracle he is is alive." I screamed and fell on the floor, and the officers stood up. Ronnie was crouching beside me, rubbing my arms and trying to get me to calm down.

A doctor came, seeing my hysteria, and called a nurse, telling her I wasn't handling this well. They asked Ronnie if I was allergic to anything or had any conditions she was aware of. Ronnie told them everything there was to tell about me. I wanted to know how Edward was, but I couldn't ask.

Ronnie saw the pain on my face and asked the doctor, "How is Edward?"

The doctor replied, "Edward is strong and holding his own. He came through the surgery well. He is still sedated, but he will come out in the next hour or so, but you cannot go see him in the state you are in. He is in serious condition now, no longer critical."

I nodded.

I want to give you a mild sedative to help you cal down. It will not knock you out, only calm you down somewhat. I am worried for you, Mrs. Anderson"

"I want to be alert. I want to be here for Edward." I was still crying uncontrollably. The nurse came in with a syringe.

Ronnie said, "Yes, give it to her." I looked at her crying, sobbing, and shaking. I nodded, okay. The doctor handed me a sedative and told me to stay in this room. He would come back when Edward was conscious. I nodded.

The officers waited outside the room until the doctor left. They wrote Edward's condition in their report. I couldn't stand up. One officer helped Ronnie get me up and sat me on a small couch. The other officer left the room but came back shortly with a blanket and pillow. They covered me and moved away, talking to Ronnie. I saw Kat come in, and she ran to me and hugged me. I started up all over again. I couldn't talk. I had never been the one to lose control, but now I couldn't make any sense out of anything.

Kat rocked me and held me until Ronnie came back over. Ronnie sat on the floor in front of me and told me the rest of the story. I seemed to be leaving my body, I so didn't want to go to sleep, and I needed to be alert when I could go see Edward. They must have noticed the calming effect the drug had on me. I felt I was falling but couldn't catch myself, I didn't care either. They were talking, but I couldn't understand the words. I was looking from one person to the other, thinking of Abby. I still hadn't heard from Abby. I must have said her name aloud because Ronnie was patting my hair and telling me Abby was okay. She said we would see Abby when we got home. I felt myself fall over on the little couch. Kat put the pillow under my head, and I wasn't crying anymore I stared at the ceiling waiting for what came next. What if Edward dies, what would I do? What if Edward had some permanent damage, will it change him. I didn't care as long as he is alive. What if he had amnesia and didn't remember me? I wanted to look in his eyes. I wanted to see him smile and see those dimples that light up my world.

I thought I was over the sadness I had always felt, but it was crawling back in my skull. I felt this black shadow creeping in behind my eyes, down my spine and into my gut. Sorrow, death, pain, and loneliness always crept into me to destroy my dreams. I would die if Edward didn't make it. I will join him. I found something I didn't think I would have, and I would miss it now. I knew if he made it through this, I would follow him to the ends of the earth. I didn't need to go to school. I will manage without an education, or I will start when he was finished. I will get a job. I can do what I was doing here anywhere. Renee will give me a good reference. I was dozing off, and the doctor came back in the room. I heard him but couldn't open my eyes. I heard him speak but could not respond. It was as if he was speaking another language.

"Sam, Sam, are you okay? Wake up, Sam . . . Sam . . . Wake up Hun." Someone was shaking me and calling my name, but I felt drunk and couldn't quite understand. "Sam . . . Sam!" Ronnie and Kat both were calling my name. I heard them, why couldn't I answer?

"Sam!" someone slapped me, I opened my eyes to see the doctor standing over me. I tried to rise, he had to help me. "Looks like that sedative did the job a little too well. Stand up, Sam, we need to walk a little of this off. Come on, hold onto me."

I was holding his arm, I felt someone on the other side, and it was Ronnie. I was walking; I could see Kat ahead of me. They walked me around and around the room. I was getting my senses back. I took a deep breath, and the doctor asked me if I felt better. I nodded. He asked me my name.

"Samantha Lord." Someone handed me water, telling me to drink it.

"Good, you are coming around. You have been out for two hours." He said.

"Two hours." I screamed. "How is Edward?" The doctor told me not to get excited. He was resting well, and he would recover nicely. I exhaled and almost fell down. They both still had a hold of me and caught me.

"Can I see him?"

The doctor said, "Absolutely. That is why we are trying to get you back on your feet." I tried harder to walk and stand up straight, taking deep breaths, in through my nose and out through my mouth. I drank more water.

The doctor said, "You are doing great. I am going to get you a wheel chair and take you back to see your husband myself." He went out in the lobby and came back with a wheel chair.

"Girls, we will return shortly." He said. They both nodded. He pushed me around corners and in through doors, punching in codes. And then into a large room with several patients in small cubicles, the patients were hooked up to all kinds of machines, tubes running in their bodies. There were nurses going from one cubicle to another, I heard people crying and moaning with pain. I couldn't imagine what Edward was going to look like. I saw him. He was bruised and bandaged around his head. There were tubes in his arms and in his nose. A bag on the side of the bed looked like it was holding urine; he had a bandage around his chest and stomach area. He opened his eyes, saw me, and held out his hand. The doctor wheeled me right next to the bed. I touched him so softly, as if he might break. He squeezed my fingers.

"Edward, I love you."

"He nodded."

"Are you okay?" That was a dumb question, but he nodded.

The doctor started talking and telling Edward what his condition was. "You have some internal bleeding, but we got it under control. You have lacerations on your face, chest, neck and upper back and arms that are mostly minor. You will have scars, but you are alive, and in better shape than we thought you would be a few hours ago." Edward just nodded, listening to the doctor. Edward put his hand on the side of my face, and I leaned into it. Tears were running down my face, and he touched them and shook his hand at me, pointing his finger, as if saying, "No, No, No." I hushed the crying and held his hand with both of mine.

"How long will he be in here?" I asked the doctor.

"He will probably be here, four to ten days, depending on his recovery. He has a broken leg that will mend in six weeks, but other than that, he is doing well." He continued, "The head injury and the internal bleeding where our main concerns, but the heart and lungs are strong. Edward, being in as good a condition as he is, helped a lot. When the tubes come out, we will check his speech and know more then."

"You will come out of ICU tomorrow if all goes well tonight." He patted Edward on his arm, smiling at him.

"Can I stay with him?" I asked.

"No one can stay in ICU. When he gets a room, if it is a private room, you can stay there if you want too." I nodded in acknowledgement. Edward sighed and then made a painful sound from his chest.

"You will be sore. We worked on you for over four hours. You're bruised internally as well. You will see the signs of bruising externally, also the bruises will look bad, but they will go away within a week or so. Mrs. Anderson has to leave now, but she can return tomorrow." "I don't want to leave him."

"You need to get rest so you can handle the long recovery time he is going to need, and Edward will need you for help. You had better no come back before tomorrow." I tried to argue, but Edward nodded in agreement. I sat back in the wheel chair and knew I wasn't going to win this battle. Edward was alive and looking at me and knew who I was. We would come through this fine. I stood up and kissed him on the cheek. He put his fingers over it, patting it, and touching his fingers to his mouth.

"I love you Baby." I said. He nodded. I held his hand once more before the doctor pushed me out.

"Have you told us everything"?

"Yes".

"We are here on summer vacation. We are supposed to leave in twelve days."

"Did you drive or fly?"

"We drove, but Edward's car is totaled because of the wreck."

"He should be fine to go home, but you might need an extra day or so to stop and rest if he needs to."

"We could fly home, that might be easier." The doctor took me back to my friends, and I stood up. I walked around and had some strength back in my legs.

"I won't be able to see Edward again until tomorrow. He is doing well. He can't talk yet because of the tubes, but he is okay. He is cut all over his face, chest, arms, neck, and back, and has horrible bruises all over his face and chest." Ronnie took me home. They came in, and we ate some of the lasagna and drank the wine.

Ronnie said, "Sam, come stay back at our condo".

"I don't want to be alone. Mick could still stay there. I can sleep on the couch. I don't want to put anyone out. Ask Wayne too if you want.

Kat said, "I can be away from him one night."

"I insist, I want you all to be there with me. The couch makes out into a bed. I don't have to work. You can sleep in your rooms, and I will be fine just knowing I am not alone."

I wrapped up the rest of the food and took it with us. When we arrived at the condo, Mick was already there. We told him where we had been and what happened. He said we should have called him. Kat called Wayne, and he came over. The two guys finished off the lasagna, and we opened a couple more bottles of wine and went down to the pool. I had my phone by my side, checking to make sure I didn't miss anything. It was nice and quiet, sitting out by the pool. The breeze felt nice. Trent and Steve came out to join us. I sat mostly just thinking, worrying about Edward. I knew he was going to be okay, but I didn't know what else to worry about. We sat there by the pool until about 2:00 a.m.

We went upstairs and everyone got ready for bed. Kat and Wayne went into her room first, and then Mick disappeared into Ronnie's room. Ronnie didn't want to leave me.

"I am fine." She felt strange making me sleep on the couch. "You didn't make me do anything, I volunteered so I wouldn't be alone, and I appreciate staying here." She finally slipped off to bed.

My cell phone rang, startling me. It was a Florida number. Oh no, something went wrong, but the area code was different. I answered, "Hello, what's wrong?" There was silence on the other end of the phone.

Again, I yelled, "Hello!"

A man's voice answered, "Hello." There was a pause. "Is this Samantha?"

"Yes, who is this? Is this about Edward?"

"This is Ed. I received a message saying Edward was injured in a car accident last evening, and I have been unable to reach him." I didn't know how to talk to Ed; he was worried and needed to know about his son.

"Ed, Edward was hit by a drunk driver. He will be all right. I have been with him all evening. It happened after work today, I mean yesterday. He was injured pretty badly, they thought in the beginning, but he is conscious. He is not talking yet because of the tubes, but they are going to take them out tomorrow." I hesitated then continued, "They made me leave because he is in ICU. I, ah, got a little hysterical. I was given a mild sedative, so the doctors made me come home. Edward should be able to come home, the doctor said, in four to ten days."

"Did he say anything about me?"

"Sir, sorry, Ed, he is unable to talk yet. You are welcome to stay at our place. We have an extra room if you would like."

"I can get a hotel."

"I just meant, if you wanted to stay at our place, Edward's place, it would be fine, now or when Edward gets out of the hospital. You know that way you could see for yourself how he is doing. Ah, maybe talk some more, or, I don't know, make amends."

"Samantha, Edward left. I don't want to discuss what happened now. I may visit in a few days after he has had time to recuperate some. I will give you a call."

"Okay, do you want me to tell him you called?"

"If you think it won't upset him more, it is up to you."

"Okay."

"Thank you Samantha. Good bye."

"Bye." I wondered how to handle this with Edward. If I told him his father called, will he get angry and tell him to get lost? Or he might be encouraged by the concern and believe his father to really cares, and then be hurt again if he up and leaves or thinks he is going to dump me. Maybe his father was genuinely wanting to make amends with his son, all all of a sudden thought I was the greatest. I know that last part wouldn't happen, ever. So actually, do I take the risk in hurting Edward more than he was now mentally? On the other hand, do I take the chance that Ed was scared enough to finally admit to his son how much he loves him? I guessed there was no answer to my question until it happens. First, there was a risk. Second, there is a chance. Third, it might open the door at least half way for a fall or a reunion. Maybe I should sleep on it, but I thought I wanted to take the chance, that was the best thing. If we didn't take the chance, we could lose completely. I smiled and was glad I made the offer, and I prayed he comes to Clearwater.

# CHAPTER TWENTY-TWO

I was at the hospital by nine o'clock on Saturday morning; they hadn't moved Edward yet or removed the tubes in his nose. I was able to see him for only a minute before they hightailed me out of his cubical, but I saw he was feeling better and very alert and anxious to get that stuff out of him. I was waiting for the doctor, pacing the floor, back and forth. The woman at the desk called me over and told me they were removing the tubes and Edward would have the IV and maybe the catheter until the doctor was sure he was able to walk all right. I was so excited. They were moving him to a room as soon as one was ready on the fifth floor; it was a private room, which had a couple of chairs and a couch for me to sleep on. I could stay with him at night, until he could care for himself.

The lady at the desk called me again, telling me Edward was ready to be moved and that I should go to the floor and wait for the doctor. Once he was in his room the head nurse would come in and ask questions and answer concerns regarding his care. She gave me the room number, and I went up to the fifth floor. I went to the nurses' station and asked if Edward had been brought up yet, and they told me he was en route, and I could wait in the waiting room. I preferred to wait in in room. I wanted to see him, kiss him, and know he was really on the mend. The room was like any other hospital room, except there was no bed, but there was a couch, a recliner. It had a table that went over the bed and an end table next to where the bed would be. I was pacing the floor when they finally brought Edward in. I backed up against the wall to get out of their way. They asked if I was family or would like to step out of the room, but I told them I was his wife and they let me stay.

Edward was smiling when he saw me and heard what I said. They pushed the bed into place. He had on a hospital gown, and it bunched up. His shinning glory was out for all to see. At least it was still all intact. He saw me looking and frowned at me and the smiled. They hooked up the IV, plugging the bed into the wall, and setting his oxygen, placing it over his nose. They checked his catheter tube, which was still in him, so I knew that would be his first complaint to get it removed. A young nurse came in to check his vitals, and I stood back as the dutiful wife would do. Yeah, right. Everything was good, the young man who had brought him down left, and then I went straight to his bedside. I kissed him. I pushed his hair out of his face.

The nurse asked Edward, "Do you need anything? Are you in pain?"

Edward whispered to her in with a very horse voice, "I just want to rest."

"I'll be back with water as soon as the nurse gives the order." She said. He nodded and she left the room. We were finally alone. I kissed him again, touching his face, I saw the tears run from his eyes, and I was crying and kissing his tears away when the door opened again.

The head nurse introduced herself, "I am Paula, your RN. Are you in pain?"

He whispered, "No, just tired."

"You're status is very good now. You will be having some pain in your chest and back. Coughing will be a big issue. You have to try to cough to make sure you get all the fluid out of your lungs. She handed him a weird little contraption. She showed him how to put a hose in his mouth and suck in, and then blow out helping him to cough. You can have pain medication every four to six hours. You are on a regular diet and can have water, tea, juice, or coffee as you wish." She checked him over by pushing his feet, raising his arms, and raised the head of the bed to elevate him.

"I want the catheter to be removed."

"Not yet, maybe in the afternoon".

"It hurts." He said. She checked, and it looked raw and sore. He was embarrassed with both of us looking at him like that.

"I can get some salve to help with the slipping of the tube." When she touched the tube, he jumped and it made his side hurt, and his head. I wanted to cry with him. "I will bring your wife a pillow and a blanket if you intend to stay."

"Yes, I do intend to stay as much as I can, or as long as Edward lets me."

"A nurse will be back with ice and water shortly." Then she left the room

I bent down next to his face and laid my head next to his.

"Edward, don't try and talk yet, just nod and I will get you some paper and a pencil to write with for now. But first, are you okay?"

He nodded yes. I kissed him gently on the cheek, and pointed to his lips. I kissed him all over his mouth as each as I could. He smiled up at me. "Edward, you scared the hell out of me. I know you couldn't call or weren't able to call, and I feel guilty because I waited so long to find out where you were." I said. He tried to speak. "No I know that wasn't a question, don't speak." I laid my head back by his and had my hand on the other side of his face.

"Edward, I love you so much." I said. He nodded, and I heard him whisper.

"I love you too." Tears ran down my face. My cell phone was ringing. I rose up and answered it. It was Ronnie. I told Edward who it was, and he nodded. I spoke with her briefly and, then disconnected. I told Edward she was calling to check on him, and I had told her he was good and in a room. "Well, you heard what I told her." He nodded again.

"Do you want to sleep a while?"

He nodded. I said, "I can go sit in the lobby and let you rest. He grabbed my hand and pointed to the couch. I told him okay, I would stay and watch over him, but he had to rest.

He nodded again, and whispered. "I am tired."

I kissed him again, walked over to the couch, and sat. A nurse tech came back in the room and brought Edward ice water. He looked at her and covered his face with his right arm.

"He is trying to sleep."

"I will be right back." She left the room again and came back with a pillow and blanket.

"Thank you."

"If you need anything, I am on duty until eight o'clock.

"Thanks again." I said. She left the room, pulling the door closed.

I curled up on the couch with the pillow and blanket and slept for a while. Someone else opened the door. I jumped up, and he told me he was making rounds and just wanted to do a quick check on Edward. I told him he was tired from the move and everyone poking and prodding. He is won out. He said that was the way it was in a hospital. He told me he would be back the next day, but if Edward needed anything, I was to have the nurse call him. He was on call all evening. I thanked him, and he left. Man, so many people come into a when you are trying to rest.

I lay back down and must have slept a good hour because I felt really good when a nurse came in and said, "I have to check his vitals."

"I understand."

"I already came in and checked once. You both were asleep. Neither of you woke up." She said.

I laughed. I liked her. She checked Edward, and he didn't wake or move while she did her thing. I thanked her, and she shut the door behind her. I decided I needed to bring a couple of books up here and my laptop next time I went home.

It was so boring just sitting around when Edward was sleeping. I was getting stiff and wanted to walk, but I couldn't leave without telling Edward I was just going or a walk. It might upset him if he woke up and I wasn't here, or someone came in the room and I wasn't here to deflect them. I walked around the room, looking out the windows. I could see the Gulf from the window. There were birds flying around, and kids where playing on a playground below. I watched cars moving on the roads, wondering where they were going. I turned and looked at Edward, He was still sleeping. I walked to the door, looking down the hall and watching nurses going into rooms, nurse techs with their little carts going from room doing vitals.

People were hustling from rooms to the waiting area or vice versa. This was a busy place. There were young men and women pushing gurneys with patients on them into rooms or taking them out of rooms, probably to get tests done. I turned and looked at Edward again, and he had moved a little. I shut the door and then walked back toward the windows. Damn if I didn't trip on the handle from my bag and fall on the couch on my back with my feet and arms up in the air, causing the couch to bump into the wall with a loud bang pushing it into a little cart knocking it over, with another bang. Everything fell onto the floor. I turned to see the chain reaction, rolling over then onto the floor on my belly with a "Humph," sound knocking the breath out me.

I felt like I had fallen in slow motion; the whole incident was in slow motion. I turned to look at Edward, and he was watching me frowning, and then he smiled. He looked the other way, because if he laughed, it was going to hurt. I felt ridiculous. I tried to get myself up as fast as I could, stumbling as I was moving toward the cart. I picked up the cart, putting all the stuff back on it and straightening the couch and chair. I turned around, and he laughed. I was angry and worried at the same time. I ran to his bedside. He was holding his side and getting up, laughing. I just knew he was going to pull his stitches out. I told him in a very stern voice to lie still and stop it. He could laugh later, but he had better not do it now or I was leaving. He looked at me so pitifully, I thought I would cry. I kissed him, begging him not to do anything that would hurt himself more. He nodded, taking a deep breath and groaning with pain when he did.

I looked under his gown, seeing his glory again. I smiled. I was looking to see if there was any blood coming from the bandage. It looked clean and dry. I put his gown back down and looked up at the door. A nurse was standing there looking at me. My face turned red because she didn't see the incident of my fall, so she must be thinking I was just looking at his package. I looked down at Edward and back at her. She had a stunned look on her face, and Edward snorted, trying not to laugh; I pointed my finger at him warning him against it.

I walked over to the nurse, telling her what had happened about me falling, knocking things over, and Edward laughing, so I was worried he might have torn stitches out, blah blah blah. She laughed aloud, very loud with her hand over her mouth and then she stepped out of the room, leaving me there feeling like a complete idiot. I held my hand up to Edward and said, "Don't. Just lie there and be quiet", I will be back. If you move at all, you will be in so much trouble." I went after the nurse. She was half-way down the hall, and I was calling her, but she wouldn't stop. When she got to the waiting area, she plopped down in a chair and burst out laughing even harder with her head between her knees. I stood there looking at her with my hands on my hips. Well, at least she was able to get it out of her system, Edward couldn't, but she could.

When she half a hold of herself, she said, "Hun, that is the funniest thing I have ever heard and seen. I have to believe every word you said because it is so awful it couldn't be a fib."

"Well, I told you what happened. Of course it's not a lie. Would I tell you something to make me look so stupid when I didn't have to? But I guess I didn't want you to think I was just ogling Edward."

She was laughing again. "I know, I am sorry, I needed this laugh. This has been the best therapy I have had in a long time."

"So, I'll send you my bill." I crossed my arms over my chest.

She laughed again. "Okay, I did wonder why you were looking under his gown, but I hadn't registered yet exactly what you were doing."

"Well, hell, then I didn't have to tell you all that." I was being sarcastic now.

"I heard the bang and stuff dropping, but I didn't know where it had come from." She said. I raised both hands and pointed at myself. She laughed some more. "I am going to enjoy having you here. I might make them keep Edward even longer just so I can see what happens next."

"That is not very nice."

"Just kidding, I am sorry, please forgive me. There is so much sadness, crying, and complaining going on. I work my butt off, and all I get is someone else unhappy with something. I will go home tonight and sleep well because of the release and shit you took off my shoulders."

"Well then, I guess I am glad it happened, for your benefit anyway."

"Okay, let's go back and check the stitches and see that Edward is okay."

I nodded. "Can you keep a straight face so he doesn't laugh?"

"I don't know, but I will try."

"Thank you. He acted as if it hurt very badly."

Fortunately, Edward was fine, no rips, no pulls, and no blood seeping out. She put some more cream on the entry of the catheter area.

"Are you alright?" He asked when the nurse left.

"I am fine. I didn't get hurt at all, I fell so slowly."

"I saw the whole thing." He started to laugh, and I stopped him.

"We will talk about this later, dear." I said and he nodded.

Ronnie and Mick visited Edward that evening; they brought me some clothes and a toothbrush. They stayed quite a while. Edward was happy to see them, see someone else besides me. While they were there, I had Mick stay with Edward, and I walked around with Ronnie just to get out of the room. I told her about my little performance, and she laughed until she cried and had to run to the bathroom. I didn't see all the humor everyone else saw, but if it made them feel good. Ronnie had brought me some food and a chocolate shake to eat. I shared the shake with Edward. She said she would bring me anything I wanted. I told her I would have to go home, take a shower, and get more clothes as soon as I was sure he was improving. She told me Kat would come tomorrow. They had decided not to all come in at once and wear Edward out too much. I told her we were doing well. "Ronnie, remember to bring me a book."

Edward was worn out again by the time they left. He was still begging for the catheter to be removed, but the nurse said the doctor told them maybe tomorrow. They didn't want him out of bed yet. He didn't eat much, but he was drinking lots of fluids, and his color was good. I could tell he was better. He was cranky just lying in bed; he couldn't take just sitting around anymore than I can. We tried to watch television, but that got boring. The nurse gave him some pills at 9:20 p.m., and he was getting tired, so I hoped one was to help him rest, and it was. I lay down and tried to sleep but tossed and turned most of the night. That couch wasn't comfortable to sleep on. It creaked and made noises every time I moved or sat on it, but I was here with Edward, and that was all that mattered.

# Chapter Twenty-Three

Edward was calling me complaining how badly the catheter was hurting. He wanted to pee, and he couldn't. I called the nurse. It took them fifteen minutes to answer. I told her if they didn't take this catheter out now, he was threatening to pull it out himself. The nurse said he didn't want to do that there was a balloon in his bladder that had to be deflated, or it would hurt like hell.

Edward screamed, "It hurts like hell now. Get it out." She said she would call the doctor. She came back about ten minutes later and told him the doctor said okay. She raised his gown she noticed how inflamed the head of his penis was. She had some ointment with her she rubbed on it.

"Edward, take a deep breath and then letting it out. This is going to hurt just a little. I have to pull the tube out just a little to put the ointment on the tub to make it slip easier. There is a small amount o pain-killer in the ointment to help as well." I He took a deep breath; I was holding his was holding his hand watching, she fiddled with the tube and pulled it out. Edward came up off the bed and screamed. He squeezed my hand so tight I thought he broke my fingers. He was in excruciating pain. I could barely stand seeing him this way. He fell back on the bed; he had tears in his eyes and didn't say a word. The nurse asked him if he was okay, and he only nodded with his eyes tightly shut. She told him it would feel better soon. She rubbed more of the ointment on the end of him, and he jumped. She pulled the covers back over him, covering his. She handed me the ointment and told me I might need this again. She patted his leg and left the room.

I stood by his bed, giving him time to recover and rubbing his arm and chest. He opened his eyes. I had so much concern for him. I could tell by his reaction that was the worst pain imaginable.

"It seems to be easing some." He sighed. "That hurt, Sam. I don't want that ever again."

"I am so sorry, Edward." rubbing his arm.

"Sam, I'll be okay." He was gritting his teeth so hard his jaw was locked in place, so I could tell he was still in pain.

"I know, hate what you are going through."

"Why don't you go home so I can rest?"

"I am not leaving until I see the doctor and see you get up and walk." I said. He nodded. He dozed off as the pain eased up until the doctor came into the room.

The doctor said, "Well I heard we had a meltdown with a catheter." Edward glared at doctor. "Oh, didn't like that much, did you? Well, that is one of the most painful things a man can go through, but imagine a woman having a baby, now have some sympathy." My eyes bugged; Edward looked up at me and reached for my hand. "So you feel better Edward?"

"Yes, I feel like going home." He said. The doctor laughed.

"Not yet, son, let me check you out." He looked at his chest and removed the bandage. It looked clean and dry. The nurse came in with clean bandages, and the doctor dressed it himself. I am going to push on your belly some, it might hurt so let me know if it does." He pushed all around Edward's stomach and sides. He looked at his chest and removed the bandage and it looked clean and dry. The nurse came in with clean bandages and the doctor dressed it himself.

"So Edward how is the pain?"

"Not bad, since the catheter is gone."

"On a scale from one to ten, one is the mildest and ten being the worst pain."

"I'd say a two or three just lying in bed."

"I want you to try and walk." The doctor said. Edward tried to get up and the doctor held him back.

"Not so fast, let us help you. You have a broken leg, and you have to learn to walk with on it as well." They helped Edward sit up and then stand on his own two feet. The nurse was on one side and the doctor on the other. I had never seen a doctor do so much himself. He was a good doctor. They walked Edward to the bathroom and back.

"Okay, that is enough for now. You didn't stumble, you did very well. I want the nurse to come back in a few hours and walk you to the door and back. Then a few hours after that maybe out in the hall, until we see you walk on your own with crutches," the doctor said. Edward nodded. He was out of breath and didn't insist on going home. He knew he needed some more time to heal.

"Now, young lady," the doctor said. I stood up straight. "I want you to go home and get some rest. You can see Edward is doing quite well. We will put an alarm on his bed so the nurses will know if he tries to get up."

"I can't leave him, I can help the nurses."

"No, you need rest. You are going to have to take care of him on your own once he goes home. Now do as I say, and you can come back this evening. Leave your number at the desk, and someone will call you if you are needed before."

"But- -."

He stopped me before I even got a word out of my mouth.

"Young lady, I will put a 'No Visitor Allowed' restriction on him if you don't listen to me. Then you will have to sit in the lobby." I frowned at him and was angry. He laughed at me I raised one eyebrow.

"I see you understand my point."

"Yes doctor." I said. Edward patted me on the hand.

"I'll be fine, I'll sleep. I promise I'll be good now."

"Nurse, did you hear what I said about this young lady being in the room?"

"Yes doctor."

"Okay, tell the others my orders. Now, Little Missy, I am waiting for you to go home." H said. I looked at Edward, and he was smiling. I bent down and kissed him.

"I'll be back soon."

The doctor said, "This evening." I frowned at him. I got my bag and headed for the door. I turned and looked at Edward, and he told me he loved me, and told me to get some rest. I stepped outside the door and waited. I heard the doctor laugh and tell Edward, I was a tough one. He told Edward he thought I would do fine taking care of him, and because of attitude, he might let him leave tomorrow. I smiled. Edward told the doctor I would be by his side constantly, never giving him a minute's peace. They both laughed. I of course, I was frowning now. The doctor told him he was doing well again and to take care. He said he would be back the next evening. The nurse walked out of the room and caught me listening. She gasped because I startled her. She pointed her finger at me and then down the hall. I hung my head and walked. I heard her say; she would take care of him while I was gone. I turned around to look at her, and she was smiling. I turned back around and ran into the wall, knocking me backwards and onto my butt. The nurse ran up to me.

"Well, I guess the doctor knows what he is talking about. You must be tired. Can you drive yourself home?"

"Yes, I'm fine." I said. She helped me up and made sure I could walk and was okay.

"We will see you this evening." She snickered asking me my name.

"My name is Sam." She told me again, that her name was Paula. She took my number and, using her hands, for me to leave. I did reluctantly. I stopped and turned back again and the doctor was watching me walk away also. I knew I had been defeated.

By the time I got home, I was exhausted. I was hungry and felt dirty. I was so tired I lay on the couch and slept for hours. When I woke up, my stomach was growling. I fixed myself a cheese sandwich and drank a bottle of water, and then turned the television on. I watched a few shows and lay back on the couch. I called Edward's father and told him how well Edward was doing. I told him Edward would probably get to come home tomorrow or the next day, but he had a long recovery ahead of him. I got up and took a shower and cleaned up a bit, and then thought it would be safe to go back to the hospital.

I took another book, some snacks, and a bottle of water in my bag and headed back to the hospital. When I arrived, Edward was sitting in a chair.

"Good evening Beautiful." He smiled at me. I was so pleased he was smiling, and sitting up, and looking marvelous.

"Wow, you look ten times better than you did when I left."

"I feel better; I slept most of the afternoon, so I may be up all night. I walked in the hall with the help of two male nurses. I pushed myself hard to show them how much I was improving. They told me I would need crutches, but the doctor didn't want me on crutches yet because of the incisions in my side."

"Don't overdo it, Edward."

"I won't, I want to go home and sleep in my own bed, next to you as soon as possible. I want to be able to sleep all night without being woken up to have my blood pressure or temperature taken."

I walked up to him and kissed him. He tried to pull me down on his lap, and I resisted. "Edward, you are moving too fast."

"Sam, I missed you, but you look better too and smell much nicer." He said. I lightly hit him on the shoulder.

"Has the doctor been back yet?"

"No, I can't wait to tell him my progress." He said. I pulled a chair up close to him so I could hold his hand. He put his other hand on top of mine. "I love you, Baby. Thank you for all the care you've given me."

"Edward, I love you too, I haven't done anything but sit and do as you asked of me. I would bend over backwards or fall off a couch for you and let the world laugh at me to see you better." He laughed, and then grabbed his side. I thought, Oh, no.

He winced in pain and then saying, "I'm okay, it didn't hurt so badly now. The catheter was the worst, every time I moved or even breathed, it slipped, and I felt like I was on fire, rubbing and peeling back the skin." He chuckled, "You can rub the ointment on me

"Okay," I laughed, "I believe you. I don't know about that one," I said. "I believe you can do that yourself now." He was in such a good mood. Maybe this was the time to tell him about his father calling and how I invited him to visit.

"Edward?"

"What? Don't hesitate, just say what you want. Life is short and time is so precious, we need to say, do, and act on what we want in life before we lose it, Sam," he said. I thought, *Wow, he doesn't know what he is in for. He just led me into my speech.*

"Okay, I am glad you feel that way. Don't interrupt me until I finish, okay."

"Okay,"

"Your father called me, worried about you. The hospital called him after the accident. They found something with his cell phone number on it," I said. He turned pale.

"Don't interrupt me." I gave him a stern look. "I told him what I knew at the time and that he was welcome to stay at our place to visit you, then or after you came home." I rubbed his hands, "I told him I would keep him informed. I called him back when we knew you were okay. He was so pleased to hear you were better. He said he wanted to visit, but he wanted to know it was okay with you and didn't want to make anything worse for you, Edward."

"Was he rude to you?"

"No, he talked about you, concerned about you."

"He hasn't changed his mind."

"Edward, you don't know that. Remember what you just said, he is making an effort to reconcile. Give him a chance. This life is short, you almost died in that wreck, and your father loves you whether he tells you he does nor not. I heard him. I heard the worry and concern in his voice. He was a broken man that first night, Edward. He was terrified you were dead and he would never see you again. I think that was when it really him him. Don't you feel the same? You love him or you wouldn't try. You would have never taken me there to meet him. Edward you have to talk to your father and give him a chance. I love you. I just want what is best for you. If he doesn't approve of me, we can live with that as long as the two of you make amends, please,: I said. He was thinking.

"Sam, I can't handle anyone hurting you or treating you badly, even my father."

"I know how you feel, but we can try to work this out. This is a sign, a chance, it may not come along again. It is a chance worth taking.".

"Sam, you don't know what you are asking."

"Yes, I do, damn it. I am asking you to take a chance on me, on my opinion, that this time I know what I am saying. He doesn't like me. I can handle that. I have my whole life, remember? We can make rules. He is your Dad, Edward, please try."

"Okay, Sam, okay I will try one more time."

"Don't say that. It may take ten more tries, don't ever give up," I said. He squeezed my hand. I heard someone gasp in the hall. I thought it was the doctor, but he didn't come in. Maybe it was just someone passing by. I went and looked out the door but didn't see anyone I knew. There were nurses here and there and people milling about. Maybe a nurse heard us in a serious conversation and decided to come back later.

The next two days Edward was getting more and more bored in the hospital. He wanted to go home, but they wanted him to be careful with the broken leg and his other injuries. He needed time to heal. He didn't always listen and was cranky with the nurses. I tried to read to him, I tried to get him. I brought cards up to play with. We even went to the waiting room and worked on puzzles. I pushed him all over the hospital to get him out of his room. I was so sore after that I could hardly walk. My arms hurt, my legs hurt, and I just hurt all over.

At night he would sleep well because of the sleeping aids, they were giving him and the pain pills. The days were long, and he wanted out, out to do anything. He yelled at the nurses and me. I would leave his room for hours to give him space, trying not to yell back at him. When I would return, he would feel ashamed, hold me, and tell me he loved me. He was just bored out of his mind. I tried so hard to be patient and entertain him, but it wasn't what he wanted to do, or it was sissy stuff, or he didn't like the book I brought him. He was a lousy patient, but I loved him, and I showed him every chance I got.

Edward had several visitors. Renee and all the people from the firm visited him. Ronnie and Mick came every day, and Kat tried to do the same. He was so irritable; I couldn't make it better for him, and I worried about being at home. He would get tired of sitting around the apartment all the time as well. We only had a scoter, no car to go riding around in even. How was I to keep him entertained at home?

The police officers came to see Edward in the one afternoon and gave him the other driver's insurance information. They mostly wanted to see how he and I were doing. They brought him a get-well card. I offered them chocolates that someone had brought Edward and some homemade cookies. They liked them, they said. I thought that was so nice of them to visit and give us the information. They were very nice men, and I had forgotten the other driver was at fault. Maybe we could get a rental car.

Edward called the insurance company and they had the report, but they were still investigating. Their client had called and turned it in. They just needed his recorded statement of the incident, and then the adjuster told Edward that he could get a rental car upon his release from the hospital. He called a rental car company, and they said they could bring a car to the hospital today if we wanted it. Edward told them tomorrow morning would be great. They said they would be there by ten o'clock. That would be perfect. I could turn the scooter back in tonight, and have Ronnie bring me back up here to stay, and we would have the car to go home in whenever they Edward was released from the hospital.

The doctor came in about eight o'clock that evening.

"Wow, Doc, this is a late visit," Edward said, a little annoyed.

"Well, I was in surgery all afternoon and evening. I am sorry for being so late."

Edward felt a little ashamed of himself.

"I am sorry Doc, I feel much better. Did they tell you how I was walking and how great I was doing?"

"Yes I read the chart and saw how far you walked with assistance. You are doing well young man."

"Can I go home?" he asked. The doctor laughed.

"That is always a good sign, when someone is ready to go home. Maybe tomorrow you'll be released. You will need to use a cane to walk, and it will be difficult, so I don't want you over-doing, do you understand?"

"Yes sir."

"I want you to walk, but short distances and on flat surfaces for a week or so. You still need to heal, and I am afraid a fall could tear out the stitches, so you have to be careful. But I don't see a reason to keep you here much longer. But,. I have serious concerns about you obeying me. I insist you resting and not, I repeat 'NOT' doing more than feels comfortable. Do not push yourself until you have pain. Okay?"

"Yes sir."

"Little Lady."

"My name is Sam."

"Sam, I still like calling you Little Lady." He said. I grinned and nodded. "I want you to lay the law down on him, okay."

"You know I will."

"Yes, I believe you will be a good nurse." He said. I smiled

"Okay, Edward, I want you to stay till tomorrow so you can be monitored one more night. You did have major surgery, and complications still could occur. But I have confidence you will listen to me."

"Yes Sir, I will listen."

"I want you to make an appointment to see me next week. No over-exertion, if you know what I mean, until then." I blushed, and Edward frowned. "I know you two are newlyweds, but you have your whole lives ahead of you."

"We understand." I said.

Edward frowned again, looking from me to the doctor, "Yes sir, I understand."

"Okay, tomorrow, if all goes well tonight, you will be on your way home." We were both excited. It had been five days since the accident. This had worked out perfectly, the car would be here in the morning just in time.

# CHAPTER TWENTY-FOUR

Edward was so anxious, he couldn't stand it. He was sitting in a chair; all he was wearing was a pair of boxers, the hospital gown, and some slipper socks. His clothes were thrown away after the accident. We didn't know he was going home for sure, and I didn't think to bring him any clothes. He said he would leave naked just to get to go home. He was beside himself. I loved watching him; he was so excited and happy. He wanted me to come kiss him, every five minutes, and I eagerly obliged. The nurse came in several times checking on him. She brought his breakfast. He had a hard time getting it down, but I kept encouraging him to eat to get his strength back.

They notified us the rental car was downstairs, I went down, and it was an SUV as we had requested, for Edward's broken leg. I signed the papers for acceptance and parked the car in the parking lot. I went back upstairs, and Edward still hadn't seen the doctor. He was angry because they had called him about lunch, and he wanted to go home. I told him to calm down, or they wouldn't let him leave. He was acting like a crazy man. He told me he was a crazy man. I reminded him that the staff that brings his lunch had nothing to do with him being released, so he should not have gotten upset with them. I told him he should not have gotten upset with them. He said he was sorry. Eleven o'clock in the morning before the doctor came in and told him he had signed his paperwork. As soon as a wheel chair was available, we could leave. Edward was ecstatic.

"Can't Sam just push me down?"

"No, it is hospital policy just to prevent further injuries. It has to do with insurance liability."

Edward accepted that and said, "Okay." He had me calling down to the nurses' station repeatedly to see if the wheel-chair was here yet.

Finally, I walked down to the nurses' station, telling them, "I'm sorry, Edward is so excited; he just wants to go home."

They had been very kind to us, and I appreciated them very much.

The nurse at the station told me, "We understand. We go through this often, but the transport people also are the ones who transport patients to and from tests, as well as to rooms from emergency and check out."

"I will tell him and we won't bother you again".

I went back and told Edward if he didn't cool his heels, I was going to leave him here another day. He sat all sulked up, not talking to me. I told him when we got home I would have to go to the store for groceries and to the drug store. What was I to do with him? He needed a baby-sitter, because I couldn't trust him. He looked at me all huffed up and said he didn't need anyone to watch him; he could take care of himself. I told him that was what I was afraid of, him trying to take care of himself. He had to stay put, or I would have to wait until our friends got home to go to the store.

"I had no idea you were such a baby."

"Sam, don't insult me."

"You are acting like a child, and you are going to have a temper tantrum if you don't get your way. I won't have it," I said. He looked at me again, my arms crossed across my chest. I was serious; he was going to do things my way.

"Sam, I just want to go home," he answered me civilly with a sigh.

"You are going home, but you can't just do the things you used to doing, ear. You have to be careful. You had major surgery. You have a broken leg and cannot get around as you did before. You had internal bleeding. You had a head injury. You have to have patience and I didn't know you had none."

"I have patience's, I waited for you."

"That was different."

"How?"

"I don't know, but you are not showing any right now, and I am getting pissed. Do you hear me?"

"Yes, Sam, I will be good. I promise." He was calming down, and he held his arms out to me. I walked over, bent down, and kissed him. "Thank you, Sam." I grinned I couldn't help it. He was so like a little boy, and I loved him so much. I could just see our son acting just like he was now, that cute little grin and his dimples making me forgive anything and kiss him all over his face.

A guy with a wheel-chair came through the door just then. Edward tried to stand and fell forward. I jumped to grab him, pushing him back into the chair, losing my balance, I fell forward hitting my head on the wheel-chair and almost knocking myself out.

"Edward!" I screamed. I told you to be patient. Oh damn, my head hurt, there was blood running down my face.

Edward tried to get up again, and the transport guy very sternly said, "Sit down." He did. The guy tried to help me up and leaned me against the bed. He pushed the nurse button and told them over the intercom that he needed help, stat. The nurse tech came running and saw me sitting on the floor bleeding. She ran to get stuff, I guessed to clean me up. I felt like an idiot again. I glared at Edward. He was sulking no; I thought he felt bad at being in such a hurry.

"I am so sorry, Sam, are you alright?" Edward said.

"I am fine," I said very angrily.

The young man told me, "Lean your head back," so I did.

"Just get me some paper towels, and let's get out of here."

"We have to wait for the nurse to come back." A nurse aid entered the room with a RN, of course, the RN was Paula, who saw me looking under Edwards's gown. She leaned down to examine my injury.

She snickered first, and then she pushed on the cut. She cleaned it with some stuff that stung like hell. She said, "It doesn't need stitches. Head wounds seem to bleed a lot." She cleaned all the blood off my face and put a bandage over the cut. She told me to be careful; she didn't want to see me back in here. I thanked her for what she had done. She told me to take care and helped me up. "Do you feel okay to walk?"

"Yes, I will be fine."

The transport guy helped Edward into the wheel chair, and we walked away. The nurse followed us for a while, to see if I was going to do something else stupid, I thought. The young man with Edward waited at the door, while I went for the truck. I pulled up next to them. The young man helped Edward into the car and told him to be patient and do as I asked him to do. He looked at me sympathetically with the white bandage on my head. The young man told us bye, and I pulled away. Glancing in the rear view mirror, I saw him laughing.

"Edward, you have to do as I tell you. Please."

"I will, Sam, I am sorry. I didn't mean for you to get hurt. I keep doing that though, don't I? Does it hurt badly?"

"No, I just felt like an idiot again."

"It was my fault, you tried to help me. I promise I will do as you say."

"Okay, I am going to stop at the drug store on our way home, and then I will come back later for groceries." I didn't trust the man as far as I could throw him. I went into the local drug store, gave them his prescription, and then walked back to the front of the building to watch Edward. He sat in the car and didn't try to get out. I heard them call his name over the loud speaker, so I headed back to the pharmacy section, paying for his pain pills and leaving the store.

I pulled into our lot. We got the first parking place next to our apartment. I made Edward wait until I opened the door and came back, and he did this time. I helped him out. He used his cane, and I held the other side. We made it inside and got him on the couch. He was worn out completely. He was out of breath and he couldn't have walked any further if his life had depended on it. I turned on the television and propped his foot up on the table. I went out and got my bag and stuff out of the car. I carried in flowers, cards, and gifts. I got him a bottle of water and asked if he wanted anything else. He said he had to go to the bathroom. I thought, *well great*. I helped him stand, and we made it to the bathroom. I told him he would have to sit down, he laughed and said I could hold it for him while he held the cane. I blushed.

"Edward!"

"Well," he said. I made him sit down and stood there waiting.

"I can't go with you standing there looking at me."

"You said you were not shy? Go ahead, pee."

"It is different now, I can't."

"Oh hell, Edward. You have never acted shy before." I walked out of the bathroom, leaving the door ajar because I still didn't trust the man. I heard him use the bathroom and then fart. I giggled and he heard me.

"Damn it, Sam, you weren't supposed to be standing there," he said. I was bent over laughing. "Sam, you are hurting my feelings."

I couldn't stop laughing. "Well, at least you are not mad at me anymore."

"No, I am not mad at you I am worried about you." I walked back in, and he flushed the stool. I helped him to the sink. He washed his hands, and we went back to the couch. I got him a T-shirt and removed the gown, putting it in the dirty clothes. I was as exhausted as he was. I plopped down beside him, looking over at him.

I blew out a breath, "Whew. That was rough." We both laughed. I bent and put his foot back on the table with a pillow under it.

"Are you comfortable?"

"Yes," he said. I leaned back and held his hand with both of mine.

"I am glad you are home. I missed sleeping beside you."

"Me too." I was relaxing, and it felt good being home sitting by Edward. Someone was at the door, I couldn't believe it; I had just settled down and didn't want to move.

Edward said, "Ignore it".

"I can't". I stood halfhearted but went to the door and opened it.

"Oh my Gosh." I gasped It was Edward's father. "Hello, Sir, sorry, Ed. Please come in." I turned and looked at Edward. He raised some and then leaned back against the couch.

"Are you sure I am welcome?" Ed asked.

"Yes, I asked you to come. You are welcome. Please come inside. I need to run some errands and buy groceries. I need someone to watch this brute so that he doesn't get up and hurt himself while I am gone, can you do that?"

"Yes." He said. I motioned for him to enter again. "Hello, Edward."

"Hello, Dad." Edward said coolly.

"How are you feeling?"

"Much better, I just got home ten or fifteen minutes ago."

"I saw you pull in the parking lot, and come inside. I was giving you a chance to settle before I barged in."

"Thank you. Sam had a time with me." Edward said. Ed looked up at my bandaged head and back at Edward.

"Did you do that?"

"Well, I caused it, sort of."

I remarked, "I fell." I smiled at them both. "I am going to give you some privacy. I can be ready to leave in a few minutes." I ran to the bedroom, changed my clothes, fixed my hair, brushed my teeth, grabbed my bag, and was ready. I heard them talking while I was rushing around, so it was going okay so far. "Okay, I am ready to go. Ed, is there anything you don't like to eat?"

"I am not picky. Oh, let me change that a bit. Like you, I don't care for a lot of fried food, but I am a meat kind of guy."

"Okay, so is Edward, I know what he likes, so I will cook for him. I hope it will be okay for you. I will be back in an hour." I kissed Edward good-bye.

He said, "Bye." I looked back as I was shutting the door, hoping for the best.

# CHAPTER TWENTY-FIVE

I called Ronnie to tell her Edward was at home and that his father showed up at our door. I told her I left so they could talk. She didn't think that wise of me but I thought it was for the best. I called Kat and talked to her a bit, and she said her and Wayne were doing well. I was happy to hear it. I asked if she had heard from Abby, and she said she hadn't. I told her I had written her twice but had no response. She told me she had called and talked to Abby's mom, but they wouldn't tell her anything. I told her as soon as we got home; we had to make the effort to visit her.

I went to the dress shop I liked and bought myself a nice plan outfit to wear around Ed. I bought a pantsuit, a skirt, and a blouse. I felt very good about my purchases. They were mature clothes for school or work. At the grocery store, I bought lots fresh vegetables, fruits, milk, cheese, meats, breakfast stuff, snacks, and so on. I spent over a hundred dollars, and we were only going to be here another week. I guess we will have a party. I went to the liquor store, buying beer, wine and brandy for Ed. I bought the stuff Edward had bought in Ft. Lauderdale.

I started carrying groceries and stuff inside, putting them on the counter. It took, trip after trip, back and forth to the car and house.

Edward asked, "Dad would you mind helping Sam carry stuff in?" Ed came out and helped me carry in the last two loads. I appreciated it."

"Thank you, Ed, I appreciate the help."

He sat back on the couch next to Edward.

"How are you two?" .

Edward said, "we are fine, but I need to go to the bathroom again." I went to help him up.

Ed said, "I will do it."

"I don't mind."

Edward said, "Dad, Sam can help me." I walked him to the bathroom.

"How is it really going?" I whispered when we got to the bathroom door.

"It is cool." I stepped out of the room and shut the door. When I heard him flush, I went back in. I helped him stand and watched him put himself back in his boxers; we had never put any shorts on him. He was as he was when we came home from the hospital. I smiled, and he asked me to help. I nodded. I got him back to the couch and put his foot back on the table. I grinned shyly at him and winked. His face was flushed. I went to the kitchen.

I decided to make steaks tonight, so I put salt and pepper on them wrapped them up in plastic wrap and put them back in the refrigerator. I cleaned the fruit and vegetables, putting them in air tight containers that went in the refrigerator. I put all the groceries up and took my clothes to the bedroom. I hung them in the closet and sat on the bed. I was tired. I felt as if I had worked a whole day nonstop. I didn't want to bother Edward and his dad, so I lay back on the bed to rest. Just as I settled, Edward called out to me. I got up, went to the door, and asked what he needed.

"Sam, what is for dinner?"

"I am making filets, scalloped potatoes, green beans, and salad. Do you want something to drink now? Ed, I have brandy."

They both said, "Not right now." I was happy they were getting along well.

Edward asked, "Join us Sam."

"I have things to do in the bedroom."

"Please, Sam." He said. I went over and sat on a stool next Edward.

Ed started by saying, "I want to thank you first for caring for my son. I was terrified when I got the call regarding Edward and the accident. I was in Kenya when I got the call, which is why I wasn't here right away."

"Oh, I didn't know, you didn't tell me that. I would do anything for him, anything."

"I've have seen that. But I want you to know I appreciate it anyway."

"You are welcome."

Edward laughed and started by saying, "She took such good care of me, and they almost had to move another bed in the room for her." I frowned at him. Ed was eyeing the bandage on my head. I was so afraid Edward was going to tell about me falling on the couch and then on the floor and eventually looking under his gown. However, he didn't add anything else to his comment yet. "Dad, she is in my life. You have to accept that. We have discussed things, Sam and I."

"I will not . . ."

Edward interrupted him, "We will make the rules regarding our relationship, Sam and I will, not you Dad." He took my hand in his. "It is okay if you cannot find it in your heart to see how wonderful she she is and what a great catch she is for me and how lucky I am to have her. You will not disrespect her by any gesture or comment ever. I mean it, Dad. I want you in my life, our lives Dad. I love you and wish we had a relationship like normal fathers and sons, but we don't'. I don't' know if you can say those words to me. I believe you feel them for me. It was Sam's desire that you and I make amends, trying to be adult and be friends."

"Edward, I would like that."

"Good, me too. You agree about Sam?"

"I don't dislike her, she seem to be a caring young girl." Then facing Edward, "I wanted what was best for you, Edward, and I thought she might not be."

Edward interrupted him again, "Dad, be careful with your words."

"Let me finish, Son." He had his hands up in the air like he was surrendering, "I have seen how she cares for you, and I will not cause trouble between the two of you again. I will not say or do anything to hurt Samantha, Edward, I promise." He said.

Edward smiled, and so did I. I rubbed Edward's leg. It was time for a pain pill, so I got up, got him another, and handed him the pain pill. He took it without any arguments. Ed watched us as I took the empty bottles to the kitchen and brought Ed a new bottle of water as well.

"Edward, you can't have beer, you are on pain pills and antibiotics. But, Ed I would be happy to get you something if you would like."

"No, water is fine."

The two men talked more, I excused myself to the kitchen and started preparing the potatoes, green beans, and salad. I broke the beans and put them on to cook first. I slow cooked the potatoes so they would be very tender. I got out the cheeses, made a simple sauce, to pour it over the potatoes with some herbs and spices, and put it on a low heat. The green beans were cooking down good. I fried some bacon and onions chopped fine for the green beans. I made a salad with lettuce, grapes, tomatoes, and pecans. I had radishes and green onions on the side. I made my special Caesar dressing and put it all back in the refrigerator to stay cool.

I took the steaks out and sat them on the counter. I asked Edward if he would, rather I make the steaks on the grill or in a skillet. Edward said grill, so I went outside and fired up the grill. Ed watched without saying anything about what I was doing. I set the table for three. I made a pitcher of iced tea. I didn't have any fancy dishes or glasses for the table, so Ed would have to deal with our plain stuff, well, Edwards condo stuff actually. I kept checking the green beans and potatoes. The potatoes were cooked, so I turned the fire off so that maybe they would thicken up some. I tasted the sauce, and it tasted good to me. The green beans needed just a bit more time. I went to the living room and sat by Edward. I told them it would be about twenty minutes or so.

Edward said that was fine. He put his hand on my hand and told me it smelled good. He told his dad I was a good cook and kept him working out every night so he wouldn't get fat. Ed just sat there smiling. I was afraid of what he was thinking. Was he thinking his son would have to live with a woman who cooked and cleaned like a maid? I didn't care. It was what mattered to Edward anyway. I gasped, thinking what his working out statement could be about. What if Ed thought I kept him busy in the bedroom all the time? I was going to hurt Edward for that statement.

I excused myself again to check the green beans, and they were tender. I drained them, putting them in the skillet with the bacon grease, bacon, and friend onions and I turned the fire on to simmer for a few minutes. I checked the grill, and it was ready, so I came back in and took out to the grill. I put them on and came back in. I washed my hands and turned to ask how Ed liked his steak, and he said medium. I said, "Just like Edward?" he said "Yes." So I could take them off at the same time that made it easy. The beans were looking good, tender and smelled good with the onions and, bacon. I snuck garlic n them and the potatoes and green beans on the table. I filled the glasses with ice and asked the men if they wanted iced tea or water. I told them we had milk, juice, and beer. Edward said beer, and I said, "I remember now, sorry." Ed said he would drink the tea. I told them it was unsweetened, so I put the sugar bowl on the table. Edward took the tea also, which he usually did not. I went outside, turning the steaks. I ran back to the kitchen, getting a clean plate and then back to the porch, to take the steaks off. I turned the grill off and went back inside. I told the men the steaks needed to rest, and dinner was ready.

I helped Edward get up and walk to the table. Ed asked to use the facilities. I pointed to the bathroom. Edward whispered, "Dad wants to wash his hands." I nodded. Edward said it looked great and smelled wonderful. I told him I had my fingers crossed. Ed came out and sat at the table across from Edward. I sat between them. I told Ed I hoped he enjoyed the meal and to help himself and have as much as he would like. I held the platter of steaks over to Ed first and he took one, then I held it toward Edward first, and he took one, and then held it toward Ed, and he took one. I sat the platter down. I then offered the potatoes to one and then the other, the same with the beans and salad. Edward took some of everything. Ed did not take the salad. Of course, I took everything except the steak. Ed asked why three were steaks if I didn't eat it. I told him sometimes I did eat filet. I liked it well done, however, or almost. He nodded. We all ate our food, not talking a lot but for some conversation between Ed and Edward.

Ed said surprisingly, "Samantha, this is very good. This is the best steak I have ever eaten, I do believe. What did you put on it?"

"Just salt and pepper."

"You're kidding."

"No. I put salt and pepper on each side and rubbed it in, and the. I covered it with plastic wrap and let it set in the refrigerator. I took it out to get to room temperature before I grilled it. That is it."

"I can't believe how good this tastes. The potatoes and beans are good too."

"You should try my salad dressing." I said. He kind of flinched.

"Okay, I'll try a little." He said. I handed him the bowl of salad, and he took a small amount. I handed him the radishes and onions, but he declined them. I handed him the bowl of dressing, and he put a generous amount on the salad and took a bite. He made a face, raising one eye and eyebrow and doing something weird with his mouth.

"Samantha, this is good. I've never had pecans in a salad well, I don't eat salad. There are grapes in here too?"

"Yes, there are, and usually I put dried cranberries or strawberries in it too, but I didn't have any. I forgot to buy them today."

"My hat comes off to the chef. This was a great dinner. Thank you, Samantha."

"You are welcome." I hesitated. "I am sorry about dessert. I forgot all about dessert, but I have fresh fruit and ice cream if you would like."

"No thank you. I would like half of that steak though, if you don't mind."

I held out the platter, "It is my pleasure to cook for you, Ed."

"Edward, do you want anything else?"

"No, Babe, I am stuffed, thank you."

Ed ate the other steak and rubbed his belly just as I had seen Edward do. I felt good, very good for what I had accomplished today. I helped Edward up and started to the couch, but he said he needed to go to the bathroom, so we made a turn that way, and I took him in and helped him sit down. I walked out and shut the door, waiting for him to flush. I opened the door and went back in to help him up. He said, "I would shake it for you, but I am afraid I might fall down.

"Please don't try that just yet." I said. He laughed. He washed his hands. He kissed me told me I had won his dad over with my cooking and charm. I smiled and said, "I hope so. What happened to your shyness? It seems to have disappeared since your Dad arrived." I took Edward back to the couch. I knew he was getting tired and needed to go to bed, but they were getting along so well that I didn't want to interrupt them. I let them talk a while longer, finally seeing the tiredness on Edward's face. I knew he had to go to bed.

"I am sorry, Ed but Edward really needs to get some rest."

"You are right; I shouldn't have stayed so long. I'm sorry."

"On no, we have a room for you to stay in. I washed the sheets, it's clean, please stay."

"Are you sure, Samantha?"

"Yes, absolutely, I invited you, remember. Do you have a in your car?"

"Yes." He went outside, and Edward rather frowned at me. I gave him a stern look, and he nodded okay. His father came back in with a bag and a couple of shirts on hangers. I showed him to the other bedroom, and he said it would be fine. I told him to make himself at home. If he wanted anything during the night, I said he should just get it. There's bottled water in the icebox along with tea. I told him we had a coffee pot and the coffee was in the pantry. He said he would be fine.

"Please make yourself at home." I left him and he shut the door.

I went to Edward and helped him up. We stood a minute to get balanced well, and then we hobbled to the bedroom. On our way, Ed opened the door and walked out, heading for the bathroom. He asked if we were going that way. I told him we had one in our room. This one was just closer while we were in the living room. I took Edward into our room and sat him on the side of the bed.

"I need to get your pain pills and antibiotics. Is there anything else you want?"

"No, I just want you lying next to me." I went to the kitchen and getting the pills and water heading back to the bedroom. Ed stopped me.

"Samantha, you are doing a great job taking care of my son. I have to thank you again."

"Ed, just you lying beside me," he said. I told him I would be right back. I went to the Kitchen and got the pills and water and headed back to the bedroom. Ed stopped me.

"Samantha, you are doing a great job, taking care of my son. I have to thank you again."

"Ed, it is my pleasure, believe me. Good night."

"Good night, Samantha." He said. I went back into our room and shut the door. I gave Edward his pills and asked if he wanted to to the bathroom. He did. He brushed his teeth and I brushed mine. I needed a shower. I knew I smelled like smoke from the grill and sweat, but I was so tired. I helped Edward to bed and got his T-shirt off. I helped him lie down. I was exhausted

"I need a shower. I feel awful, but I am so tired I think I can sleep for a week."

"Come here, baby, shower in the morning." He said. I turned the lights off, fell into bed, and scooted over next to Edward. I felt his hot skin, and I knew he was all right.

"I love you Edward."

"I love you too Sam." We fell asleep. He only woke me up once during the night having to go to the bathroom.

# CHAPTER TWENTY-SIX

I woke up before Edward; I looked to see Ed was not in the living room. I jumped in the shower and let the water pound on my sore, tired body. This was so much harder than I expected it to be. I heard Edward in the bedroom, so I got out and dried off, wrapping the towel around me.

"Good morning, Baby. Need to go to the bathroom?"

"Yes, I need to hurry."

"Okay" I helped him up. We moved quickly to the bathroom, barely getting his boxers down on time. And he sat down. I said, "Sorry, I was in the shower too long."

"No, I'm sorry you didn't get to stay longer, I know how tired you are."

"Don't worry about me."

"I sure would like a shower, can we do that?"

"Yeah, I'll figure something out." I left him on the toilet, going to the front door to grab one of the plastic chairs. I turned around, and Ed was standing in the kitchen, making coffee. I stopped cold in my tracks.

Ed said, "Hi, I was trying to make coffee, and I can't figure out how. Can you help me?" I looked down at my towel and the chair. I walked over to the kitchen and started the coffee. I got out the bread, I told him how to use the toaster and told him the butter, and jelly was in the icebox. I grabbed the chair, heading back to the bedroom shutting the door and then leaning against it with a sigh, my God why can't I get a break.

"Edward your dad was in the kitchen and saw me like this." He laughed but not long because of the pain. "You need a pill." I ran to the bedside and got him a pain pill and a bottle of water. "Okay, this is what we are going to do. I am putting the chair in the tub. You have to prop your broken leg on the side of the tub and not get it wet. Wait, we need a trash bag. I grabbed a robe this time and went back to the kitchen. I got a trash bag telling Ed what I was trying to do. He asked if I needed help. I arched an eyebrow, but told him I could handle it. I hoped I could anyway. I told him I would be out as soon as I could to make him a real breakfast. He said he was fine.

I put the trash bag on Edwards's leg and tied a belt around it so water couldn't go inside it. I got him in the chair, turned the shower on low, and detached the head. I had him hold his head back, wetting down his head and back. He said it felt wonderful. I wet the side that wasn't operated on. I got a washcloth and started wiping the other side down to moisten his skin. I got soap, and he watched me smiling. I knew this felt good after a week. They had bathed him in bed, but no actual shower. I soaped him up under his arm on the left side, and then rinsed with the cloth; a couple of times to make sure all the soap was gone. I washed around the bandage, trying to get as much of the red iodine off him as possible. I moved to his left leg, doing the same as before. I soaped up his other side, his back, and down his leg, and then with the sprayer I rinsed him off. I washed his hair and face. I was a little hesitant, wondering how this would make him feel, but I soaped up his genitals and washed inside his legs. I rinsed him off. He was getting aroused, and I didn't know how to stop it. "I need to wash your back side."

"Hell no, you are not washing my ass." He yelled at me.

"Edward, can you do it?" He wasn't around anymore, and he did the best he could. I washed his toes between each one on the broken leg and tried to do the same to the other one, but he was pissed now, not letting me. I turned the water off and toweled him dry. I helped him up and back to the bed. He yanked my towel off.

"Edward, stop it."

"You just did the most humiliating thing to me, and you tell me to stop it."

"Edward, I was trying to help. Can you do it on your own, next time? I won't help then."

"I'm sorry, Sam. It was embarrassing to have you wash me like a child."

"Get over it. This is the way it is for a while. When you are well, you can do it to me." I smiled at him.

I got him some boxers, stretchy shorts, and a T-shirt. He said forget the boxers, it is too much trouble pulling down one thing, let alone two." I got dressed and helped him to the living room. I fell onto the couch when I finally got him situated. I looked over at him.

"Edward, that is hard work." I said. He leaned his head forward and looked pitiful.

"I need to rest just a minute, and I will fix you some breakfast."

"I'm not hungry."

"Oh, yes you are. You have to eat with your medication and to keep your strength up. I can't do this if you aren't able to help me." I said. His Dad was sitting at the table, watching us. I leaned forward, asking Edward what he would like to eat. Eggs, pancakes, and toast. He only wanted toast for now. I pulled myself up, waling to the kitchen. I got out the sausage and eggs. I made sausage patties, scrambled eggs, and toast and put it all on the table. It took about thirty minutes. I got the juice out and coffee cups just in case. I set the table for three. Ed said he ate toast, he was okay. I told him there was plenty I he decided he wanted more. I set the third place anyway.

I helped Edward to the table and sat him down.

"I just want toast."

"Fine, eat just toast, I am hungry." I sat and put sausage and eggs on my plate knowing I wouldn't eat the sausage. I ate all the eggs and dished more on my plate. They were watching me. I got a piece of toast, buttered it up good, and took a big bite out of it. I cut the sausage up in tiny little pieces, playing with it on my plate. I ate a few bites of eggs and another big bite of toast. I drank some juice. No one was saying a word.

Ed put some sausage and eggs on his plate and ate it all. Then I saw Edward put some on his plate, a small about, but at least it was a start. He ate it all and then got some more. He ate a piece of toast and drank his juice.

Edward said to me, "Aren't you going to eat your sausage?" I looked down at it and stuck a piece in my mouth. I chewed it up and swallowed it. I drank some juice, ate a bite of toast, took another bite of the sausage, and drank the rest of my juice.

"I'm full. Can I get anyone else anything?" They both shook their heads. I gathered up the dirty dished and took them to the sink. I washed the pans I had used to cook, and then went back for their plates and the leftover food. I put everything away. I had the dishwasher full and washed all the other stuff, stacking it in the drainer. I went to Edward to help him back to the living room, but Ed said he would do it, so I let him. I was exhausted. I went to the bathroom. I thought I would throw up, but I didn't. I kept my food down. I surprised them and myself as well.

I went back to the living room and asked what they would like to do today. Did they want to go anywhere or sit outside for a while? Edward wanted to sit outside. I thought that would be good for him. I took the chair back outside and dried it off real good. I set it up so they could prop Edwards foot on the railing. Ed helped Edward outside, and they sat and talked. I went back inside and fell on the couch, I was drained. I just lay there relaxing every muscle in my body, taking deep breaths until I felt normal again, but I didn't get up. It felt so nice to lie on that couch and do nothing. I heard the men were laughing and laughed to myself, feeling proud and happy for what had come about from this terrible accident

Edward's cell phone was ringing, so I answered it and took it out to him. It was the insurance company, wanting to come by and see him. He told them today would be fine. They asked if he had the title to the car. He said it was back at school. They said that would be fine for now. The adjuster was a woman, and she came just before noon. Edward and his dad were on the porch, still talking. I got a chair from one of the neighbors and pulled it up for her. I stood behind Edward. She said their client had accepted responsibility for the incident, and from the police reports, he was at fault in the accident. She asked about Edward's medical bills. He said he didn't have any yet. She told him she would give him a certain amount for his totaled vehicle. He told her no it was worth a lot more than she was offering. Looking at cars like his in the area, she said her offer was satisfactory. Ed didn't say anything but I knew she was in for a ride. Edward just said "No. I don't live in this area, my car was a fifty-thousand-dollar car, and you won't give me less than what it will take to replace said car with another of the, same year, make, and model." She said she would inquire about a higher amount, but it would not reach the fifty-thousand.

He crossed his arm and listened to what else she had to say. She told him they would pay for his medical bill up to the insured's limits. Edward asked what that was, and she said she wasn't at liberty to answer that. He told her his medical bills would be in the hundreds of thousands. She just nodded. "I also require pain and suffering. As you can see, I am unable to walk or do anything by myself, and I almost died in that accident because your client's drunk driving.

She nodded. You are free to get an attorney if you are so inclined.

Edward looked at his father, and his father nodded.

"This is my attorney, Ed Anderson."

The woman was shocked.

"You should have told me sooner. This is not the way things are done."

"I didn't have an attorney until your offer was too low, and you said I was free to get one, so here he is."

"But he was here the whole time."

"He is my father." He said.

She didn't say anything. She asked him to sign some paper work, but he refused. She picked up her belongings.

"May I have your card?" She said to Ed.

He walked to his car, got one, came back, and handed it to her.

"Now may I have yours?" Ed asked. She handed Ed a card. "I will be contacting you soon, thank you." She nodded and walked away. Ed and Edward both laughed. I didn't see anything to be laughing at. She had offered him much less than he thought he should get. Could they make a case in court? I got it then, they had done it together. They were father and son, and I was going to be part of this family. I went back inside, letting them discuss their tactics and strategies. I flopped back down on the couch and fell over. Ed came in, asking for paper, and I gave him a spiral notebook. They wrote down everything. Ed patted Edward on the shoulder, and they laughed and talked for hours.

Ed helped Edward to the bathroom several times that day. I fixed them lunch, and they ate outside. They enjoyed sitting outside, feeling the warmth of the sun. The breeze was nice. I watched them, happy to know they were working together, not that a fight might occur again about something else. Both of these men were stubborn and wanted to be the boss. Ed was holding back, I could tell. Several times he disagreed with Edward but held his tongue.

The men came in to eat supper. I fixed chicken-fried steaks and even ate a small amount of the meat. I ate mostly salad and potatoes. Everything was going well in our household. My friends came by to see Edward and meet Ed. Ronnie especially got along well with him. Kat was more standoffish, but she was with older father figures. She had a lot of resentment since she didn't have one.

I got a letter back finally from Abby. She was improving and happy. She was at St. Simian Clinic and wanted to stay for a while. She would not allow her parents to visit, so she didn't know I had written her. She said she wanted me to visit when I got home. She said she was talking to other people in a group discussing her depression and was on an antidepressant and genuinely felt batter. She said she actually was begging to like herself.

Ed seemed satisfied staying in our humble apartment. I made an appointment for Edward to see the doctor on Monday. I needed to go shopping again. He was beginning to walk on his own with the cane, just short distances. I worried he would fall, but he moved slowly Still, showers were a problem; it took us an hour every time he took one, so most days he just took a sponge bath by himself. He was getting more amorous though, I had to fight him off at night. He was playful and touchy-feely. I wanted him as badly as he wanted me though, so it was hard to deal with. I giggled a lot at night, and I knew Ed might hear us, because I would have to get stern and loud to make Edward settle down. I tried to release his tension, but he said no, not unless he did the same for me. Edward hugged me every chance he got. H demanded kisses and would touch me when his father was out of the room. I knew he was going crazy. I was, so he had to be, he was a man.

Sunday night I played with him. I kissed him, running my tongue around him. I tried to give him some release, but he wouldn't let me take it all the way. I felt his pain. Touching him made my belly tense, aching for him. He grabbed my hand, held it to him, and pumped himself hard, up and down until he exploded with a moan. I watched the look on his ace and so wanted that sweet desire and warmth, but I didn't say anything. I tried to kiss him, but he turned over on his side away from me. I go him a washcloth. He took it but wouldn't look at me. I had my hands on his back, trying to see why he was angry with me. He wouldn't talk to me. I lay down and snuggled up against him, rubbing his arms and back He fell asleep, and I wrapped my arms around him and held him.

# CHAPTER TWENTY-SEVEN

The next morning we had to go to the doctor, Ed came with us. Edward wouldn't talk to me, and it was noticeable that he was angry with me. The doctor said he was healing well. He told Edward to take it easy for another week and keep his incision dry. He told Edward he could get a smaller cast on his foot to make it easier to walk and shower in a week or so. Edward looked forward to taking a shower on his own.

Edward told the doctor that the pain was minimal, and he wanted to do more exercise and stuff. The Doc told him it was fine to do light exercise and some walking, as long as it didn't cause too much pain. And sex was okay to try, but not too rambunctious. I flushed, Ed was in the room with us, and I had to walk out. The doctor laughed, but Edward didn't say a word a I was leaving.

I was waiting out in the lobby when they came out. Ed was smiling, but Edward was not. He walked out of the office without saying a word to me, as if I was nobody. What had I done? Ed held the door for me. Ed helped Edward into the car, and I drove us back toward the condominium.

"Would you guys like to eat out today, maybe Guido's?"

Ed said, "That would be nice, celebrate Edwards's fast recovery." Edward still didn't say anything. I drove to Tampa and parked. Edward got out of the car on his own, and Ed and I walked behind him. I held the door, and Guido came running up to Edward, asking what had happened. He sat us at the back, where we had sat before. He brought us out bread and oil, and glasses of water. Guido was happy to meet Edward's father. Guido brought out mushrooms, artichoke dip, and cheese sticks. He asked us what we wanted. Ed said he would try Edwards's favorite pizza. He had heard about it all the way here from me. Guido nodded and went to the kitchen.

I didn't want to confront Edward now at Guido's with his dad sitting here, but it was all I could do not to cry or run out. Ed could be enjoying the trouble between Edward and me; thinking Edwards tired of me, constantly hovering over him. The summer was over. Maybe that was exactly what it was, but Edward told me to trust him. He said he loved me, and we would be together forever, so he was just mad at me. But why? Guido brought out the pizza, and I ate half a piece and a couple of mushrooms. Ed loved the pizza and all the appetizers. Edward ate almost half the pizza and Ed the other half. They were stuffed and both stretched their long legs out and rubbed their bellies. I looked over at Edward and he was glaring at me. He was so angry. I couldn't remember what I had said or done to make him feel this way. I tried to touch his hand, and he jerked it away. I wanted to cry. I knew Ed saw his reaction and the angry look on his face.

I excused myself and went to the bathroom. I slapped my face to perk myself up and make me look more cheery. When I returned to the table, Ed and Edward were arguing. I thought. *Well great, I am gone two minutes, and they are arguing.* I asked Guido for the bill, and Ed tried to take it away from me, but I paid the bill. I gave Guido a fifty dollar bill and headed for the door. Edward tried to say something, but I kept walking. They followed me out the door.

I got in and started the car, Ed helped Edward, and then Ed jumped in the back. I pulled out on the street and headed back to Clearwater. I knew we needed some distance from each other. Edward had a temper and needed space. I would give him some time away and maybe he would calm down.

"Ed, I would like to spend some time with my friends this afternoon. Can you drive the two of you back to the apartment?"

"Sure, Samantha, but are you positive you want to do that?" Ed said. Edward looked at me still angry.

"I'm absolutely sure I want to spend time with my friends and let the two of you spend some quality time together as well." I drove to my old condo and got out, leaving the car running. "I will see you later." I waved to them, and then I walked up the stairs. I sat on the second flight of steps and cried. I heard them drive away. I didn't know if anyone was home or not. I sat on those steps for maybe an hour. I went on up and knocked on the door, but no one answered. I left my phone in the car, in my bag. Damn, I didn't have any money, no keys, no phone, nothing. I walked over to the pool and sat in a chair. I thought I would get some sun, since it was my last week and I had spent the last two weeks inside.

We had three days, and we were going home. Do I worry about it being the end? I was never going to be secure and happy. Edward wouldn't talk to me, so I couldn't even guess why he was so angry. Maybe Ed was right, love was not enough. You have to have communication, and I couldn't seem to talk about my depression, and I believed Ed was right about me bringing Edward down. I didn't see it before because I loved Edward so much, but now I understood what he meant. I was a loner and always will be. I was just like Abby and fought to act as if I wasn't. I had always thought of dying, and every time I was sad, it comes forward again. How miserable would I make Edward in the end? I was a sad little girl, I couldn't be fixed. I would always think that it was my fault, that I did something wrong, making my loved ones unhappy. The Quad . . . the four of us unhappy and unlucky in love, and always will be. The misfits that, no one loved, no one can love. We were not worth the waste of time; we couldn't be loved because we didn't think we deserved it. I lay there alone and cried.

Trent walked up and put his hand on my shoulder, "Sam, are you all right?"

I sniffled and tried to wipe the tears away, "Yeah, I'm fine. I'm the way I am." I turned back over. "I just need some time alone, that's all."

"Are you sure?" he asked. I nodded, and he left. I didn't hear them playing in the water, so I guessed he or both of them went away to let me be. I took a deep breath and decided to walk up the beach toward our rocks. I carried my shoes, stepping in the water, and let the water run over my feet and sand run between my toes. It felt cool and refreshing. I walked to the rocks and sat on one. I pulled my knees up to my chest, resting my chin on my knees, and hugging myself. I looked out over the Gulf. I watched the seagulls flying overhead and then dive down to catch a fish.

The sun was bright and hot on my face, but the ocean breeze felt cool. I could taste the salt in the air, and the sand was blowing against my skin. This was what we had planned for the summer, sitting in the sun, being together with friends, laying on the beach, and just having fun. Well, I didn't feel like I was having fun right now, but I liked this place. This was a happy place for me. I could walk out in the water here, and no one would ever know. I took off my shorts and shirt and jumped in the deep Gulf waters. It was cool, and I let it wash over my face. I swam out and dove down. The bottom was only about ten feet deep where I was. I played and swam, diving down and swimming farther out. The water was getting deeper and deeper and colder. I was forgetting my pain. I was so tired before I knew it. My arms were aching, but I didn't head back in.

I floated on my back, trying to rest my arms, and then I would swim out some more. I dove down and couldn't even find the gulf floor now. I was out very far. I floated and thought maybe I could swim all the way to Cuba. I laughed. Well, not in this direction. It was South, I was going west. Maybe I could swim to Mexico. I heard the birds above me. I floated on my back, feeling so. I was getting cold I started to shiver. I started to swim back; the waves were pushing me farther from the shore. That was why it was so easy to swim out, I guessed. That was why no one swam in this area. I was struggling to swim toward the beach but the waves were pushing and pulling me further from the shore. That is why it was so easy to swim out I guessed. That is why no one swam in this area. I floated on my back, I was so tired. I thought this could be the way I went, the way to die. Just swimming and having a good time on my last day in Florida.

Why try to get back? There was no reason. Edward was angry with me. Maybe he didn't know how to tell me he was tired of me, so he was just pissed at me so I would leave on my own. Sam and Kat had their lives ahead of them. I was just in the way. I floated until I felt myself sinking in the water, going deeper, and I needed a breath. I struggled and pushed myself back to the surface. I chocked and spit out the salty water, struggling to hold my head above the waves. My legs were so tired, I could barely move them. I gasped for air when I hit the surface. There was no way I could make it back now. I could never tell Edward I loved him again. I would never see his smile or those dimples in his cheeks. He would blame himself. I didn't want that, I couldn't let him live with that guilt. I had to do this some other way. I couldn't have him blaming himself for my death. That would hurt him too much.

What was I to do now? I couldn't get back to shore. I was too tired to swim. I was scared. There was no one around, for me to yell for help. I was alone in the Gulf of Mexico, and I was going to die. I laughed. Wasn't that funny? I was worried about being alone and dying. I felt myself giving up, I was sinking again, and I didn't have the strength to go back to the surface. My arms couldn't seem to pull me up; my legs had no strength left at all. I needed air, but I couldn't fight any longer. I gulped in water, I was drowning, and I was giving up. The fight was gone. The cold dark water filled my lungs, I saw Edward's face. I saw his beautiful eyes; his gorgeous smile with those dimples, he was looking at me smiling. I reached out to touch his face but it shimmered and moved away, then it was gone. What have I done? I love you Edward. I always will.

# CHAPTER TWENTY-EIGHT

Edward and his father looked for hours along the beach. Trent had told them he had seen me near the pool crying hours before. Ronnie, Kat and their friends were all searching everywhere they could think of. They asked everyone that might know me where I could be. However, they couldn't find me. Abby was the only one who had been to the rocks with us, so Ronnie and Kat didn't considered looking there. I wasn't there now either, only my shorts, shoes, and shirt left lying on the beach. A friend of Edward's found my things near the rocks, shortly before dusk. Edward screamed out in pain, hugging my passions to his body. He cried, his father father trying to home him and comfort him. He knew I had in the water. He knew I thought he was angry with me, not at himself.

He cried as his father held him, but he wasn't able to be consoled. Edward knew about the pact we had made. Ronnie and Kat also thought about the pact, and they cried. Abby had failed in her attempt, but they were all afraid I had not failed in mine. They called the Coast Guard and they searched for hours not finding a body. They had to suspend the search until daylight. The Coast Guard, and they searched for hours, not finding a body. The Coast Guard informed them that sometimes the currents carried bodies out to sea; they warned them that it was possible my body might not be found. He fought everyone who came near him until they sedated him because he was hysterical, wanting to follow me into the ocean. His father was worried and terrified what his son would do next, so they admitted him into the hospital.

Edward's father didn't leave his son's side for a minute. He stayed with him, talking to him and comforting him the best he could. Ed cried with his son. When he cried, he hurt with his son. Surprisingly he had grown fond of me in the short time he had been with us. He held his son, as he hurt. Father and son reconciled under bad circumstances. The loved each other, supporting each other in the saddest time of their lives.

My friends waited until the next day to call my parents. Ronnie was the one who called my mother. She hated what she had to do. She spoke with my mother. She told my mother they looked all night. She cried with my mother, hearing the hurt in her voice. My mom was beside herself with pain and sorrow. My dad was numb to the news and didn't or couldn't respond. Ronnie told Mom she would let her know if they heard anything else, but at this time, it didn't look good. My parents didn't fly to Florida; they waited at home for news.

I awoke in a dirty, smelly room. It smelled like dead fish, and I was so thirsty. An old woman was sitting near me. She offered me a drink. I gulped it, and choked, she pulled it back waving her hands at me. I wanted more so badly of that cool water, "Poco . . . lento." I nodded taking smaller sips but I didn't think I would ever get enough water down to satisfy my thirst. She said, "Dos Dias." Holding up two fingers, "two" she repeated, nodding her head. She was Cuban or Mexican. She had a strong accent. "Mi hijo," pointing to her chest, "Son. Yes, son." She was rambling in Spanish, and I couldn't understand every word. "Hijo, son encontrado... agua, water." She shook her head. She spoke more Spanish, and seemed to be calling someone, "Eduardo" She used her arms trying to get me to understand. "Son bring you here."

"Have you called anyone to tell them I am alive?" I asked her.

"No, no call." She was waiving her hands in front of her face, and then called out "Eduardo" again.

A nice looking young man walked into the room. He held his head down. "I will take you to a phone." He started telling me, "You have been unconscious for almost two days."

He hesitated, "We are not legal. We not know your name; you only wore a little." He turned his head in puzzlement. "You left in the water to die? Smugglers? Bad man?"

Confused, I was having a hard time remembering what happened. "No . . . I swam out in the water . . . too far. I . . . couldn't get back to shore. The waves and currents pushed me farther out . . . I was so tired. I tried, I really tried. I thought I was dead."

"You almost were dead. I only see you in a flash."

The woman gave me a bowl of soup. She pointed for me to eat pointing her fingers to her mouth.

"Where is home?" the boy asked me.

"I am staying in Clearwater." I was gulping down the soup. I was starving and it was delicious.

"Here, Redington Beach, about twenty-five miles from Tampa."

"Do you have a phone?"

"No. No phone"

"Will take me to a phone so I can call my family? I won't say anything about you or your mom?"

"Yes," he said," He hesitated; I thought maybe he was changing his mind. "You say you washed up on beach or no remember, okay?"

"Okay, that sounds good."

The woman gave me an old dress to wear. It was too big but it covered me up.

He helped me to his pickup, and we drove up the coast. He dropped me off at a place in Indian Shores. I thanked him and promised I would not mention anything about him. He nodded and left. I had a blanket wrapped around me. I went into a store and asked them to call the police for me. An officer drove up, and I told him I woke up on the beach. I didn't know how I got here, but I was spending the summer in Clearwater and needed to get in touch with my friends. He took me to the station and they called Edward's phone, but no one answered. I thought about his car wreck. He didn't have a phone any longer. I could have them call my cell phone, but I didn't know where it was. I couldn't remember Ed's number, it was in my phone. I had them call Ronnie, no answer, I then had them dial Kat, and she answered.

"May I speak to Kat? Katherine Patterson?" The officer looked at me then handed me the phone.

"Kat, this is Sam." She screamed then started crying. She tried to talk but I couldn't understand what she was saying. Finally she calmed some, "Sam is this you? Is it really you?"

"Yes Kat, I am at a place called Indian Shores. Is Edward okay?"

"Oh Sam, I can't believe you are alive. Where are you? How fast can you get here?"

"Kat you didn't answer me, how is Edward? Where is he?"

"Hun! He is in the hospital, he had a breakdown. His father is with him. Oh my, Sam. What happened? Where did you go? Sam, are you all right? You have to get back here as soon as possible."

"I have no money, no phone, nothing."

"We all thought you were dead. Edward will be so happy. I'm happy. I will find Ronnie and we will come get you right now."

The officer said, "I'll take you home miss." I cried.

"My boyfriend and friends thought I was dead." I kept crying. He took the phone away from me and talked to Kat. He told her that he would take me to the hospital in Tampa, that they could all meet me there. He told her I needed to be examined by a physician. He helped me to his car and asked if I was hungry or thirsty. I told him I wanted water, I hadn't eaten except for the bowl of soup since the day I went missing, but I wanted water. He gave me a cold bottle of water and took me to the hospital in Tampa. I fell asleep on the way there. Ronnie was standing in the doorway when the officer pulled up. I started to climb out of the car when the officer came around to help me inside. Ronnie ran out, grabbing me and holding me while crying. I checked in, and the officer took information and told me how lucky I was. I thanked him, and they took me back to an examination room, Ronnie never let me go.

"I have to see Edward, where is he?" I was trying to tell everyone.

"He is upstairs, he will never believe this. We all thought you died, Sam."

I told Ronnie about my swim. I told her what I went through, about how I tried to get back to shore, how the waves pushed me, how I was sinking. She hugged me; the doctor came in and examined me. He said I was dehydrated. He ran X-rays, blood tests, and ultra sounds. They started an IV. The tests were taking forever. It had been hours since I had come too. I wanted to see Edward, and hoped he wanted to see me too, but they were checking me over. I was sunburned from floating in the water so long, but it would heal fine. I heard noise in the hallway and arguing. I knew it was Edward and he was close.

I yelled out his name, "Edward!" He opened the door and he jumped out of a wheel chair, stumbling to my side.

"I am so sorry, Sam. I hurt you again. I can't believe you are really here." He was yelling and sobbing as he spoke.

"I'm sorry Edward, you didn't hurt me. I didn't mean to worry everyone. I swam out to cool off and couldn't get back to shore."

"I love you, I love you, please don't leave me again." His father was standing behind him, tears in his eyes. Where they happy tears or sad tears that I was still alive?

Ed walked over to me and said, "I think you two need me living close by. You can't take care of yourselves, and you need me."

"Yes we do." I agreed.

"I am sorry too, Samantha. My son wanted to die because you were gone. Please stay with him." I smiled, not letting go of Edward.

They asked me questions, after question. They let the police came in asking more questions. I could tell they didn't believe me. They asked the same questions but in different ways, I caught on to their tactics. I kept saying I just wanted to go home and finally when the second IV was empty then released me. Edward was released in his father's care. Ed drove and Edward held me close hugging me not letting anyone or anything come between us.

We arrived at our apartment and went inside; the place was torn to bits. I gasped, "What happened here? Did someone break in?"

"No, I thought you were dead." Edward said.

"Oh. I'm sorry. You were angry with me. I just wanted a little time to myself, to figure out why"

"I was angry at me, for the night before, not you, Sam."

"Why?"

"Now is not the time to discuss this."

"Okay." I said. His father said he would go outside for a short walk. "Why then did you act like you did when we woke up? You were so pissed at me. You didn't talk to me all day. At the doctor's office, you gave me a very upset look. At lunch, you wouldn't say anything to me. I don't get it."

"I was upset at myself because I forced you to . . . ah . . . you know . . . jack me off."

"What? That's your reason for all of it"

"Yes, I was embarrassed and humiliated. You bathed me. You took me to the bathroom." shaking his head. "You were so concerned about my pleasure, and I couldn't do anything for you. I forced you to please me."

"Edward! Doing things for you and, taking care of you has been the most pleasurable thing I have ever done. Don't you understand, I would do anything for you? Wouldn't you do it for me?"

"Yes." He hung his head, cried, and leaned into me. I held him.

His Dad walked back in. "Everything okay?"

"Yes, everything will be fine now. We can't seem to have misunderstandings between us often. We can't seem to tell each other exactly how we feel. We need to change that right now. Ed, will you join us please for a while?" I said. He sat down.

"Edward, Monday I was so upset, I thought about the pact, I have to admit. Ronnie and Kat weren't home, so I sat in the chairs at the pool, but Trent came out, and I wanted to be alone, so I walked up the beach to our spot. I walked up the beach to our spot. I sat there for a long time watching the waves, the birds, and smelling the salt water in the air. Calming myself down, trying to push through the darkness in my soul away. I was hot, so I thought I would take a swim. I left my clothes on the beach, and got in the water. It was cool and refreshing. I swam out and dove under to touch the bottom, not too deep. I kept dong that until I was out too far. I thought of not trying to go back to shore, thinking Ed was right about me ruining your life, and making you unhappy."

"Dad I could hate you for this. Sam, promise me . . ."

"Let me finish. I'm depressed Edward, and it's a problem, and it is always going to be a problem unless I get help. "I need help." They both listened quietly, knowing I was being totally honest. I hung my head then continued, "I decided I wanted to live, to really live." I looked up at Edward, touching his face, "I wanted to see your face, see your smile with those beautiful dimples. I wanted to kiss you and I wanted to live, I had a reason for the first time in my life. But I remember you said you didn't want to be my reason to live. I had to want it for myself. I was confused."

"Sam! Come here." He held me.

"I tried to get back, but the waves kept pushing me farther out in the open water. No one was around to help me. I floated until I was exhausted. I sank in the water, swallowing the water, and couldn't help myself. I saw your face under the water and knew my life was over."

"I love you Sam. I thought I would never see you again. I wanted to join you. What if I had done that too?"

"Then how did you get out?" Ed asked.

"I didn't know what happened until I woke in a shack. A Spanish woman was standing over me. The boy that saved me is an illegal, he and his mother. He didn't want to get in trouble so he took me to his home in Redington Beach. I didn't have any identification and they didn't know what to do with me."

"His mother tried to talk to me but she didn't speak English. The boy drove me to Indian Shores to call for help. I was brought back here by a police officer."

"I will do everything I can to help them, Sam."

"I'm so sorry, Edward. I'm so sorry I worried you all."

"It's over now; I have you in my arms where you will stay forever. I will get you help. You will never feel unloved or unwanted again."

"What if I can't be helped? What if I cause you too much grief? What if I . . . embarrass you or your Dad?"

Ed added, "I was at the hospital. I heard you talking in your room."

I asked, "Today?"

"No! When Edward was still in the hospital."

"When?"

"You were telling Edward to give me a chance."

"I thought I heard someone at the door, that day. I even looked out."

"It was me; I hid so you wouldn't see me. I felt ashamed, I hurt my son intentionally, my only child. I hurt the woman he loves intentionally, also.

I hurt because I felt alone as you both felt, so I used my pain to inflict it on you and other. I heard the words Edward said also, about this life being short, and we need to take advantage of what we have. Because what we have could be gone in a day, or in an hour, or even a minute. Son, I love you. I haven't said that to you since you were a little boy. I need you in my life, I want you in my life, and I want Samantha in my life."

"Then it must be a family trait. Dad, I'm sorry, I wasn't a better son. I love you too Dad."

"Edward you must be kidding. I was ashamed when your mother died. I knew she never loved me and I knew she was pregnant with another man's child. I didn't care whether she lived or died. It wasn't the first time she had an affair. I believed you weren't my son any more. I did love her Edward, I tried my hardest."

"Dad the past is the past." Ed shook his head

"Maybe some family counseling is needed for us all."

"Yeah, it couldn't hurt." Ed placed his hand on his dad's shoulder.

"Dad, I love you and I am proud to be your son." They stood hugging each other.

"I love you both." I blubbered.

Edward and I sat on the couch hugging each other until I feel asleep.

Ed must have carried me to the bedroom because Edward wouldn't have been able to. I woke in Edward's arms lying in our bed.

"I have to call my parents."

"Dad called them, and spoke with your mom."

"How did they take it?"

"They were beside themselves. Your mom said she couldn't wait to hold you and see you for herself that you are all right."

"Really?"

"Really, Sam."

"Where is Ed now?"

"Dad cleaned the apartment all by himself. He then went driving around town to see the sights. He said he would bring back something for dinner. He wanted to give us some time alone, just a couple of hours." He kissed me repeatedly, telling me he loved me. I felt so much guilt for the pain I caused.

"Edward, I don't know why I feel like I do, but when things are good with us, I'm so happy I could bust. But when I feel I am losing you, or you are tiring of me, I feel sorry for myself."

"I will never tire of you, believe me. We will have lots of arguments about things, politics, kids, household things, but I will always love you. Believe me."

"I want to believe that. Why do you love me? I cause trouble."

"You fixed Dad and me. Yes, you do things that make me laugh and I love it, and what better medicine than laughing is there?"

"I didn't fix anything; I just invited him to stay."

"You made us agree to talk, and we did."

"From this moment on, we have to talk. We have to tell each other our true feelings and concerns."

"Yes, I agree."

"Okay, now this is our a pact, all other pacts ever made are now null and void. Got it?"

"Got it."

# CHAPTER TWENTY-NINE

Edward had to go back to school. He had an appointment with a doctor that was pre-set by the doctor here in Florida. Ed was flying home with Edward to help him. I was going home to face my family and tell them about moving to Cambridge, Massachusetts.

Edward had planned to go with me, but because of circumstances, that wasn't going to happen. I contacted the University of Tulsa and informed them I would not be attending this fall. I sent an application to Harvard, but it was too late to hear anything regarding this term. I applied a a community college for nursing. I also applied at the University of Boston, knowing it was a shot in the dark.

We had stayed two days longer than expected. We had all our bags packed as Kat, Ronnie and I were heading home. They didn't want to leave their guys any more than I did. After a while, we talked about the guys and what we planned to do about seeing them. Ronnie was still planning on going to OU. Mick was graduating from a college in Denver next year, so they were taking about him checking out Oklahoma or her checking out Colorado. Kat still wanted to be close to her mom. Wayne was from Texas. He said he hadn't been many places around the country and couldn't wait to visit her. He had two more years of college.

We stopped at noon and ate. We drove into the night until we were too tired to drive anymore and found a place to stay the night. We were back on the road early the next morning. We made it home before dark. Ronnie stopped the car on the outskirts of town.

"Well, here we are, back home. It doesn't seem to be the same place we left just a few months ago. We are not the same girls just out of high school.

I mean, our lives have changed, we have grown up, we have learned life's lessons, some very hard lessons. We three have hopes for our future and Sam, yours looks the brightest right now, but Kat and I have something good to look forward to. I want us to promise to stay close friends always. I love you both and need you in my life. I would not be here today if it weren't for our 'Quad'. Thank you for loving me." Ronnie sighed leaning her head on the stirring wheel.

Kat said softly, "I agree, we need to keep in touch even though we may not see each other often. We have a bond. We survived our childhood together, because we had each other. I love you both, and I can't wait to see Abby. I wish you both the best in life and please be happy."

I sighed, "I can't imagine the next step. Did we live a dream the past three months? God, I hope it was real? I love you both more than I can every tell you. I look forward to moving away from here for good. I learned the truth about love and who is important in my life. I will never forget who stood by me, who was there for me, when I needed someone the most. You two know me, the real me, and love me anyway just as I do you. I don't want to dwell on our past, but it was our past, and we can't forget it. We can look to our future, hope, and dream of a good life. We have the opportunity to be happy, normal young adults. I hope you both always keep your spirits high and remember how much you mean to me. Thank you. I love you. I will always love you."

We all cried and knew we had to go home. Kat had no problem going home. Her mom was anxious to see her. Ronnie hasn't spoke with her father all summer, so she didn't know if he even knew what happened in Florida with Abby or me. My parents didn't come to Florida when they thought I was dead or missing, but I talked to my mom since then, but I was reluctant to go home.

Ronnie dropped Kat off first. We unloaded her stuff and hugged each other and promised to stay in touch. Kat's mother wasn't at home so Kat had to crawl through a window to get in her house. She told us she would be fine and to go one home. Ronnie drove me toward my house. She stopped at the end of my street. "Are you ready for this?"

"I think so." She drove to my house pulling in the driveway. My mother ran out, along with my sister and brother. We unloaded my stuff after a few tears from my mom. My dad stood back watching us. Ronnie now would have to face the inevitable alone and haul her tings in by herself. I hugged her and told her again how much I loved her. We cried a little, and she drove away. I watched her until I couldn't see her car anymore. I turned, looked at my family, and walked toward them. My dad said, "Welcome

Linda Gee

home," and walked into the house. My mom had her arm around me, asking me how I was, and telling me she was glad I was okay.

Alex and Ray wanted to know what we did, where we went, and what I brought home for them. I told them the places we visited and about the beach and the sand. I told them about our jobs and the boys we met. I then paused, and told them about Edward. I showed them my ring, and my mother gasped. I told her we were getting married. I told them about the injuries, my father already knew about the medical bills, as he had received them in the mail. The insurance paid for everything except the co pay, and I paid those, but he got the bills showing what was done, except for the last one, which he hadn't received it yet. I wondered if that was why he was pissed. He thought I might cot hm. I shook my head.

I continued tell them about Edward. I told them I was moving to Cambridge, Massachusetts. And I had already contacted TU and informed them of my decision. I told them about the community college I applied to and how I was changing my degree to nursing. My dad wasn't very happy about that, but what could he do? I opened my bags and gave them all the gifts I brought from Florida. Alex and Ray were happy with all the things I got them. My Mom said she loved her shells, and wind chimes. My dad looked at the shirt and put it aside. My phone rang, and I saw it was Edward. I ran upstairs and saying hello. I told him things were okay and I had told them everything. He snickered and said 'Everything'?

"No not the things I want to keep to myself. I love you and miss you."

"I love and miss you too. I am going to the doctor today. I have my place set up for you to join me. Sam's parents came and took all his belongings away. They had questions but I didn't know how to answer them. I didn't want to tell them about the rape. I feel it would hurt them more. It is up to Abby if she wants that told or not anyway."

"I agree." We talked for a while, and he had to leave. I told him I needed to get my stuff put away and finish talking to my parents. We said our love--yous and hung up.

I went back down stairs and told everyone it was Edward on the phone. He was sorry he couldn't come with me, but he was still under a doctor's care and he wasn't able to right now. I told them we would make plans for Thanksgiving or Christmas. My mom cried. My Dad asked me if I was pregnant. I told him no. I loved Edward. He loves me, and I was moving in with him. I met his father, and he was a lawyer, a big-to-do guy in Florida. His name was Edward Anderson II. He lives in a mansion in Ft. Lauderdale. He was with Edward now helping him until I can get there. My dad asked me how I was going to pay for all this. I told him I saved money over the summer, and Edward would help me until I could get a job. I told my dad he should be happy, he was going to have to pay for part of my education, but now he didn't have to put out a single penny. I grabbed my bags and went up stairs. I was so angry with him. He didn't give a damn about me. I thought of unpacking, and then, I thought I would just have to pack it again.

I pulled out another suitcase and packed it with clothes until it was full. There were many things I wanted to keep but I wouldn't be able to take with me to Cambridge. I walked to the store and got a couple of boxes and then packed my stuff in them, things I wanted to keep but I couldn't take with me right now. I went down stairs to ask my mom if I could put them in the attic. I had to ask for permission to leave my stuff in the house I had grown up in. I didn't feel at home here. I was feeling depressed, feeling the black cloud crawling into my soul again. Mom said I could leave it here, leave it in my room where it belonged. It would always be there for me. I told her by packing it away, it would be better for Alex. She could have the room all to herself and not feel like he still had to share. I told Alex if she found things that were mine, she should put them in a box and put them in the attic. She said she would. I gave her tons of stuff she said she wanted. I had my stuff I wanted to take with me ready. I could leave right now if I so desired. My plane ticket wasn't for two more days thought.

I called Ronnie, and she said it was about the same at her house. She was washing clothes and packing stuff for school. She said her dad wasn't home yet, and her stepwitch was being a bitch. I asked about her siblings, and she said she gave them the junk she brought them, and they took off and she hadn't seen them since. I told her this was harder than expected. I wanted to leave now. She said she did too. I asked her if we could spend the next couple of days together to get away from them. Go to a movie or go shopping, anything. She wanted to do that too, but she wanted to see her dad today before she left. I understood she still had hope. I told her I talked to Edward, and he was ready for me to come. She said she had spoken with Mick a couple of times and missed him so much. I knew the feeling. I heard my mom calling me; I had to let Ronnie go. I told her to call me later.

Mom was asking me to help her with dinner. I set the table and did all the stuff I used to do. I didn't even get one day off before she was putting me to work again. Something's never changed; she was trying to talk to me. She asked me if Edward was a nice man. I told her he was wonderful to me. He was kind and caring. He loved me, he showed me in so many ways every day we were together. She was trying to talk about sex. I interrupted her.

"Mom, Edward shows me he loves me in ways that have nothing to do with sex. He hugs me or reaches out and touches me when I am near him.

He smiles at me, and he has the most beautiful smile in the world, with white straight teeth and dimples that pull me to him."

"Does he go out with his friends and drink a lot?"

"Oh no Mom; we do almost everything together. We shop for groceries. He likes to go dress shopping with me. He buys me cute little things, he brings me flowers he has picked. He brings me sea shells that he thinks are pretty and reminds him of me. He listens to me when I want to tell him something, even if it is boring to him. He cries when I cry, he laughs when I laugh."

"Does he complain, you know about how you feel?"

"When I feel sad, he listens and tries to encourage me to feel better, about myself, but he doesn't judge me or tell me I am stupid for feeling that way. He is proud of me when we go places. He took me to meet his dad. I met all his friends, they were great. They are happy people and love being together. They talk to each other. They stand up for each other; they don't fight or argue all the time. Those are things I didn't know, Mom. I am a sad little girl, and no one has ever noticed me or loved me for being me."

"Sam that's not true. I love you. Your dad loves you."

"Mom, do you really love me? Does Dad? I don't remember you saying that to me before today, Mom. Did you know how depressed I've been most of my life? I wanted to die, and we had a pact to kill ourselves together, Ronnie, Kat Abby, and me. I received love from them, unconditional love, and understanding. We held each other together when times were bad."

"Are you gay?"

"No, Mom! Why would you ask that after what I just told you about Edward? My friends and I loved each other like family. We were the family we needed. I got compassion from them I didn't get any at home. I got encouragement from them; I had someone who showed me they cared for me even when I made mistakes." I had raised my voice; my father came into the room.

"What's going on in here?" he asked. Mom hung her head and was crying.

"Dad, we were talking, I was trying to tell her who I am. Dad, do you know me?"

"Well, that is about the stupidest thing I ever heard. Of course, I know you."

I hung my head, feeling defeated, "Dad" I lowered my voice, "Did you love me?"

"Well of course we love you, you are our daughter."

"But, Dad, do you love 'Me'? Do you know what I like? Do you know I feel sad? Have you hugged me when I cried and then told me it would be all right?" I just looked at him, and he said nothing more. My mom was crying. I shook my head. "Well, I will be leaving in two days. Edward loves me. I had hoped things would be different, but I see they are not. I'm sorry for being such a burden to you. I am mostly sorry for disappointing you."

I walked out of the room and back upstairs. I called Edward, but he didn't answer. I called Kat, and she was all involved telling her mom about Wayne and our vacation and wanted to call me back. I grabbed by bag, I wanted to see Abby, but I was afraid it was too late to see her. I called the clinic Abby was at, and asked for visiting hours. They told me they were Monday, Wednesday, and Friday. It was Wednesday. I had one hour to get there. I ran out, got in my car, and drove to the clinic. I had to leave everything in a locker, and they let me in to see her.

When I saw her, I ran to her, hugging her and crying. She was crying, and the nurse came over and told us if I upset her, I would have to leave. I told the nurse we were just so happy to see each other. TI didn't mean to upset anyone. The nurse took us to a room and spoke to us briefly to make sure Abby was okay, and then she left us. I hugged her again, asking how she was, what she had been doing.

"I am in a group, we meet every day. I enjoy the kids in the group. Did you know there are a lot of kids like us?"

"No, I didn't know that."

"Well, they talk and tell their stories, similar to mine and yours. I do arts and crafts. I really like it here. I read lots of books, self-help book, funny books; I only do things I like. We watch movies together, happy movies. We go outside at least once a day. It is nice to get out in the sun. It reminds me of the good times we had in Florida. Sometimes when I am out there, I pretend I am lying on the beach in Clearwater, soaking up the rays. You can see I have lost all my tan." She giggled.

"I think you look great, I have missed you more than you can know."

"I missed you too." She really sounded good. She was happy, this group stuff must work. I have never seen Abby so excited about crafts and talking to people about her problems. She seemed so normal. I was so proud of her and happy for her.

"How are Edward, Kat and Ronnie?"

"They are all doing well. Edward was going to come with me, but because of a car accident he was involved in, he had to go to a doctor in Cambridge and wasn't able to come with me. He sent his love and best wishes." Pausing, "When will you get out?"

She said, "I will miss the first semester of school. I really am feeling better. I am on medication, and the depression isn't as bad now as it was."

"I had a little swim in the ocean, and almost died, but a young man saw me and saved me. I wanted to end it, but once I was out, too far, I wanted to live. I tried so hard to get back in, but I couldn't. It changed something in me. I feel I have a reason to live now, and want the future and look forward to it. We need help so many years ago. I think we may have done as much harm to each other as we did well. We leaned on each other, and we were only kids. We needed someone to help us, not encourage our sadness and our bond." I paused. "I love you Abby."

"I love you too. You should ask for that help now, it works."

"I have already talked to Edward and his father, but I don't know how to ask for help or whom to ask."

"You could ask here." She added.

I paused.

"I am leaving in two days, Abby." She grew sad. I continued, "I wanted to stay in touch, and Ronnie and Kat will be here to see you in a few days." We got quiet, and I felt out of place, as if they might keep me here if I stayed any longer. Abby, I have to go. I am sorry, but I will come back before I leave town." She walked me to the door, and we hugged and cried a little. We said good-bye.

Driving home, I thought about the times I told Edward he had to give his dad another chance on my drive home. I was walking away from my Mom and Dad. I wasn't giving them a chance. I was walking away from my mom and dad, not giving them a chance, but I feared it wouldn't make a difference. But, I had to try again and keep trying. That was what life was about too, never giving up. I went home. I found my mom and apologized to her for raising my voice.

"I love you, Mom; I will never talk to you like that again." I said. She hugged me and cried, telling me she loved me. I felt it for all it was worth. That moment, with my Mom, was one of the happiest I could remember with her. We talked some more, and I told her I really wanted her to meet Edward, she would like him. I thought Dad would like him too. He was smart and kind. He had a hardness about him that was scary, but he was good. He was honest, and he will never intentionally hurt me. She said she was going to miss me and wanted me to make sure we came home for Thanksgiving. I told her we would. I told her about Ed, and it depended on him too about holidays, but Thanksgiving for sure we would be here.

"I'll try to come as often as I can."

"Do you think Edward will come with you? Is he gentle with you when you want to do things like that?"

"Oh, yes Momma. He is wonderful to me. I don't feel I deserve him."

"Invite Ed to join us."

I laughed, "Three attorneys in one house, what an argument."

Ronnie called, she said she and her dad talked, and things were pleasant but still uncertain. He hugged her and told her he had missed her. She said she cried and saw tears in his eyes as well. I told her about Mom and me, and she was happy for me. I told her I visited Abby, and she couldn't wait for Ronnie and Kat to come see her. Ronnie said she would go the next visiting time. She said her stepwitch was calling her, so she had to go but would talk to me later.

I tried to spend time with Alex and tell her happy stories and get her to laugh with me, and she did some. We talked about boys, what she liked to do for fun, and her girl friends. She told me they were prissy and fake sometimes. They were all boy crazy. I laughed at her. She told me about things she did over the summer. She went to the pool a lot with her best friend. They met some new boys from another school. She said she went to several slumber parties and had a good time. She told me, that Mom even let her have five girls over one night when Ray was at a friend's house. She said they had a blast. I hugged her, and she hugged me back. I felt something I had never felt for my sister. I cared about her, I genuinely cared about my sister.

I went to see Ray, to see how he was and if he was looking forward to school. He said yeah, he couldn't wait to get back in school, to play soccer and basketball. I told him I would miss watching him this year and hoped he did well. I told him to call me whenever he wanted. I asked him to write me letters or send me e-mails, and he said he would. He hugged me and I felt tears falling down my cheeks. That was the first time I made an effort to be friends with my brother, so how did I ever expect him to make an effort, being the youngest? He was just a little boy. I had done him an injustice. I wanted him to know I cared for him and was interested in what he wanted to do. I felt closeness with my brother and sister I had never felt before.

# CHAPTER THIRTY

My dad seemed to avoid me. It hurt but I kept trying to talk to him again. Finally, I cornered him outside on the patio. He was smoking a cigar, trying to relax. He told me he didn't want to talk now, it was his quiet time. I told him I was leaving tomorrow and it had to be now or never.

"Dad, just listen to me. I love you. and have just wanted our approval and love my whole life."

"Is that why you tried to kill yourself in Florida?" he said. I gasped.

"Why do you think I tried to kill myself?" I said helplessly.

"Did you, or didn't you?"

I hesitated, "Dad, it didn't start that way, but when I was out in the water, yes, I felt pain, and what good did it do, being on this earth? It felt good in that cold, dark water. I dove into the water and came back up to the surface repeatedly until I was exhausted. That is kind of, what my life has been like, the ups and downs. It seemed as if going down in the deep, dark, cold water was like my sorrow, the sadness I felt, the black cloud that hangs over my head most of the time. And then coming back up to catch a breath was like those good times, when I felt happy and loved, not alone. I was sad and lonely, because Edward and I had a kind of a disagreement. I didn't want him to blame himself if I died, and I decided I wanted to live, but I couldn't get back to shore then. I was too far out, the waves and currents were strong and pushed me out farther and farther. Dad, I tried, I really tried to swim back, but I was worn out by then."

I looked out across the yard then continued, lowering my voice. "I felt tired but happy. I'm not sure why I felt so at peace for once." I glanced at my dad, and he was looking at me, so I looked away. "It's like I never please you or Mom, no matter what I do right. I always did something else wrong to disappoint you."

Letting out a breath sighing. I looked away hanging my head then whispered, "Dad, I am sorry."

My dad said, "You thought of Edward, not us, not your family who has cared for you your whole life?"

"Have you cared for me? "I thought of Edward, because I know he loved me. I don't know if you love me, or just take care of me, out of obligation. I've asked you more than once and you haven't answered me."

"You had had a roof over your head, clothes on your back, food in your belly, you have never gone without. I have worked long, hard hours to give my family what they wanted."

"Things are not everything. We needed you too, Dad." I hung my head. "Dad that is the reason I asked you, if you loved me now. I felt unloved and just a fixture in this house for as long as I can remember. I was just a thing, not a person. I depended on my friends for love. My friends looked love in other ways, even. I did not look to sex and boys for their love." I paused, giving him a chance to respond, watching his face. "I don't mean to disappoint you, I love you, Dad. I will always love you and be your daughter."

He turned his head away. I sighed again and stood up, "Dad, I leave in the morning. I'll be back for Thanksgiving. I love you." I waited, but he didn't move. I walked away. He wasn't ready, but I felt he heard me for the first time.

I didn't make it back to see Abby. I felt bad about that, but I was so busy getting things ready and spending quality time with my brother and sister. My mom was so happy in the time we spent together. I took Alex and Ray everywhere I went. I hugged them often and told them I loved them. I told them I would miss them. They said they would e-mail and call me. I even noticed a difference in how Mom treated them. She made the extra effort to show them love and caring.

It was time to leave for the airport. Mom took me, and Alex and Ray went with us. We all hugged and cried, and they waved until I got on the plane. I was excited and anxious to see Edward. I had spoken with him every day while we were apart; he was excited for me to come be with him as well. His Dad had to go back to Florida, so Edward had been alone for a whole day, and I worried about him. He said he was getting around good. He had a smaller cast on and it was easier to walk in. He said he was slow and being very careful. He was going to be waiting for me when I arrived. I was sitting there so excited to hold him, to see his face. It had only been five days since I last saw him, but it seemed so much longer. We were landing and I was looking around. The airport was huge.

I hurried off the plane and rushed down the hallway toward the baggage claim, knowing Edward would be there waiting for me. I scanned the people, and then I could see him. I yelled out his name. There he was, standing with a cane waiting for me.

Tears flooded my eyes, and I ran to him, cried, and kissed his face as he kissed mine. It seemed like such a long time to be apart. We tried to walk toward the baggage claim, but there were so many people, and his cane and broken leg made it difficult. We stayed back and let the crowd go first. He was look at me smiling. The turn-style started, and bags came up. I stood close and grabbed my first bad, and then I saw the second one. I got it and then moved back toward Edward. I pulled the handles so they would roll. We started for the doors. He had a taxi waiting. The driver loaded my bags, and we got in the back seat. We hugged all the way to his place. I didn't even know which direction we had gone in. We got out, and he had an upstairs apartment.

"I will have to take the bags up one at a time up."

The driver said, "I will help you." He carried the heaviest one, and I carried the other. We got to Edward's door, and he opened it. It was clean and nice inside. Edward gave the driver a fifty dollar bill and thanked him. He shut the door and started kissing me, stumbling. He almost fell over.

"Edward, show me to your room, now." He hobbled toward a door, and I followed. I started undressing and so did he. We made love; we kissed, and held each other. Feeling his skin next to mine brought back happy memories of the beach and Florida. "I love you," I told him over and over, and he told me the same. We lay there for the longest time, snuggling into each other. His scent made me remember the love and happiness we shared. We got up. He covered his leg with a plastic bag, and we showered, kissing and holding each other.

Later, he said, "I would like to show you around town." I just wanted to be next to him all day. He told me he had food in the refrigerator that was ready, it only needed to be warmed up. I got it out and put it in the oven. I was starving. I sat on the couch beside him, holding his arm and leaning on him. This was where I belong by his side.

I told him about Abby, about how; she seemed happy where she was. She had friends who felt the same way she did and it, but it was in positive atmosphere. I told him about the time I spent with my mom, brother, and sister. I told him I tried with my dad, but he didn't respond the way I had wanted. But I tried and I told him I would not give up. Edward was happy for me; he couldn't believe what I had accomplished on my own. We ate and sat back on the couch. I looked over at my bags. "Those aren't going to get put away if I just sit here." He told me to look through the apartment. I went in every room. I asked if he was going to get another roommate, and he said he already did, 'me'.

I pulled my bags into Edwards's room. I looked in his closet. He had so many clothes, and I didn't think mine would fit. I hung as much as I could. I asked about a drawer. He said I had three. I put what I could in the three drawers. I put my personal items in the bathroom. I had some books, and stuff he said I could put in the living room. He said I could use the other bedroom closet, and we would move winter and summer stuff around later. I got everything put away. I put the bags in the other bedroom closet. He asked me if I wanted to see the town now.

We went for a walk, arm in arm. He showed me the campus; we lived close, so he didn't have to walk too far to most of his classes.

"I have to leave early and get out of classes ahead of everyone to make it to the next one. I have it all worked out so far, I believe".

"I applied at a community college for nursing." He wasn't surprised. He nodded.

He said, "After what you did for me, I thought nursing was a better career for you, but that had to be your choice, not mine." We went back to his apartment."

He had the use of another rental car, but he couldn't drive because his right foot was broken. He got it though so I could get us around, and he would be the navigator. I told him I needed to get on his insurance and get them my driving record. I told Edward I didn't have and tickets or accidents. I had good grades and got good rates before, but on a sport car I didn't know if that could hurt him or not. He said his father spoke with the insurance company, and he only had four more days with the rental car and then he was responsible. He said his dad got the offer up to where he could find a similar car of the same value. He was waiting for medical bills. He said his doctor bills would be more than the driver of the other car had coverage for, so he wouldn't get anything extra. He said he had already hit the max. He said he was using his uninsured motorist coverage and would get all his bills paid. His dad had looked at some cars, and he had decided he might want an SUV instead of a fancy sports car. He didn't need to attract women anymore, so an SUV might be better, seeing as how we might have kids eventually. He was grinning at me as he spoke. He laughed agreeing to wait until we both finish school. He looked at me. "I would prefer to wait just awhile on that, Edward." He said, "Okay, I could finish school first." I thanked him for that kind gesture. He laughed a deep, sexy laugh.

Edward would start school on Monday. We had Friday and the weekend to do what we wanted. I looked for jobs in the paper but couldn't find much I was qualified for. I couldn't live off him. I had to have my own income, and my father wasn't willing to help me at all. I had a couple thousand dollars to my name, and that was it. Edward told me not to worry about money, but I worried. He took me to some of his favorite spots. I met some of his friends and some he studied with. He said this year would be tough, and he would be gone a lot studying. I told him I understood. He said he would do as much as he could at home. I told him it would be fine. This would all work itself out; we would be fine as long as we had each other. I hoped it did anyway. I hoped I his grades stayed up. I didn't want to be responsible for him failing or not doing as well as he had before. The things Ed said still stuck in my mind.

I loved lying in Edward's arms at night; it was wonderful being with him. We felt like old souls together. His skin was hot, firm, and soft at the same time. I loved touching his naked body, kissing him everywhere. There were places on a man's body they were so soft, that the simple touch of it made me hot wanting him. He made me tremble and respond with a touch or a word, or even a single breath. We would be naked lying on his bed; I would look down at him and shiver every time. I couldn't seem to keep my hands of him. This was a mutual feel. He touched me too, in a special way that would make me moan, groan, and beg for more. I was open with him about my feelings, and I felt comfortable about my desires and even my naked body around him now. When he walked into a room, he had to touch me, always with a smile. Those dimples drove me crazy, but I tried to resist him. Sometimes it worked and sometimes it did not. We were so happy together, loving, and living life.

Ed called us every day to see how we were. "Dad is coming for a visit in a few weeks. I have a professor that I like a lot. She seemed to be my dad's age and would be perfect for him."

"If you want to matchmaker, you need to remember your father tried that with you."

"Yeah, I remember, but this professor is nice, and she agrees with Dad's philosophy. This is different, Sam, I am not trying to manipulate him, just help him be happy."

"Well, invite her to dinner when Ed comes, but do it carefully. Edward, Ed just wanted you to be happy too. He believed he was doing what was best for you, for your future. Don't do anything to hurt your relationship with him, okay?"

"I don't mean to try to force them, just introduce them. The rest is up to them." He smiled, loving the idea. He looked like a little boy who had done something wrong.

I spoke to my mother, and they were all fine. Alex and Ray were happy heading back in school. Ray was already playing soccer and excited about it. Alex saw a new boy was in her class this year, he was cute, and she hoped he liked her. She said every time she would look up, he would be staring at her. She would smile at him, and he would sometimes blush turning away, sometimes smiled back. It was good hearing from them. It was so nice to hear Alex laugh and tell me her secrets. I didn't speak with my dad. My Mom said he was busy and working a lot, but he missed me. I knew he hadn't said it himself, Mom was saying it for him.

Edward started to school on Monday. I drove him to the front door. I kissed him good-bye and told him I loved him and to have a great day. He laughed and said it felt like kindergarten all over again, so I patted him on his head and told him to have fun and learn a lot. I had plans for the day and didn't have to pick Edward up until three o'clock in the afternoon. I applied for jobs in law firms. The second one I applied at told me they had so many kids went to a couple of places and applied for jobs in law firms, but second one told me they had so many kids applying that they only took second year law students. Most area law firms worked the same way. I thought, *Well I had better go a different route.* If I wanted nursing; I needed to check into it seriously. I went to the community college and asked about classes.

They sent me to a counselor, and she said I could still start and get my basics. I would not be able to file for scholarships until the second semester because it was too late to apply but I could start at least. They received my grades and application. I asked about books and grants. My counselor, Ms Jacobs, told me there was little I could get at this late date, but she would check for me. I told her I only had so much in the bank, and my partial scholarship and all my grant money had gone to TU, but it would be it would be put back in an account for me when I decided which college I wanted to attend. But it would be spring classes before it would apply. She said she would pull all the records and see if she could get anything at all early. I enrolled in classes. I paid my entry fees, parking fees, and what I had to pay to get started. I bought used books in the classes I could and still spent over three-hundred dollars. I spent almost eight-hundred dollars today just to get started. I didn't know what I was going to live on. I was doing this on faith.

I went back to the counselor in the early afternoon, and she said she found a financial aid program that would accept my application now. It would pay what remained of my first semester at least, and then the other things would help next semester. I told her now all I need is a job. She said great, she had an opening right here in her department. If I worked for them, I also got a discount on my classes and books. How fantastic. It was going to work out. I filled out the application, and she looked over it. I told her she could call Renee at my last position in Florida, and she would give me a great recommendation. I also had several employers from home that agreed to give me the best recommendation for employment, but it was grocery store work and waitress stuff. They agreed to give me the best recommendation for employment, but it was a grocery store work and waitress stuff but it showed I was always on time and didn't call in sick.

She hired me as soon as she got off the phone with Renee. I shook her hand and promised to be a hard worker and be on time. She said I could start tomorrow if I wanted. I told her yes. I looked over my class schedule and gave her the times, and she said she would work me in and call me this evening. She said she would put everything in the computer, and I would get a refund on the excess I paid on the books, classes, and fees. I thanked her again and went to pick up Edward.

I was so excited telling Edward I found a job and enrolled in classes at the community college. He was thrilled for me. He reminded me that next summer, we might be moving again. I told him I would follow him anywhere, and I could go to school anywhere as well. We had a wonderful evening. He studied and I read in the bedroom to stay out of his way. I looked over all my books and went online to get a syllabus I was excited about school. I had done it on my own. Now I just had to worry about the second semester. Edward kept coming in to kiss me.

"Edward, if you don't learn to stick to the books, with me living here, I might have to find someplace else to live."

"Over my dead body."

"Then I will have to leave in the evenings so you can do what you need to do. We have to make it work for both of our sakes."

"Okay, but right now it is new, and I want to make love, and then I'll get back to the books." He looked so pitiful and sincere. He had this puppy dog look on his face. I was shaking my head no, and he stuck his lip out and frowned. I was still shaking my head. "Just this once time?" I couldn't take it. I smiled by accident, and he tackled me, knocking me back on the bed. . His hands were roaming and finding just the right spots to make me moan and groan. He won this time, but I enjoyed the loss.

By the end of the week, we were working little problems out, about getting in each other's way and little disagreements over time and space. We were learning our routine and getting to know each other well. We were learning to give and take, which was harder than I expected. I had always shared a room with my sister, but I didn't have to share every aspect of her life. I wanted Edward to be happy and not be sorry for his choice in having me move in with him so soon. He tried hard to make things work, worrying about my depression, so I contacted a doctor and made an appointment.

I told the doctor about my past and about my depression. He recommended an antidepressant, and told me to consider talking to a counselor about it.

I told him, "I have a full schedule, but I know I need help. I'm aware, now that if I don't get some kind of help, I might have this problem always and hurt others around me as well as myself."

He told me, "You are a brave girl, going through this all these years with your friends. But, sometimes, friends' helping each other with depression is not good; it's like operating on yourself. You wouldn't want to do that would you?"

"I have reconnected with my family, but my dad is still holding out. I knew we would never be the family I dreamed of having, but we have a beginning, and it is because of Edward and his father. Their problems showed me my own and opened doors that I had closed off to protect myself I am learning to share my feelings. I want to share a life with Edward. We work hard together, making things right, getting along well, sharing our time and space, and learning to be apart when we need to be. There are so many reasons I still need profession help, and I look forward to a happy future."

He set an appointment up with a psychologist for the next week.

Edward seemed happy with the decisions I was making about doctors, school, and life in general. I kept the appointment with the psychologist, Dr. Margaret Dean, and she seemed wonderful. She let me talk and say what I wanted. She told me I had feelings, I had value, and that I was on the road to recovery with the progress I had initiated on my own with my family. She asked if I could visit her weekly, and I agreed. She set it up so I was her last appointment each week, not interrupting my school or work. She never told me I was wrong or shouldn't feel a certain way, only that I needed to do what was best for me. My option, my worth, my life was mine, and no one else had power over me. The very first meeting with Dr. Dean made me feel so much better. She told me to keep a journal and write down my fears and my sorrow. Write down what made me happy, anxious or anything I needed to work on. It was for me personally not for her to read or critique. I had value; I felt it for the first time in my life. She told me to keep a journal and write down my fears, my sorrow, what made me happy – everything I wanted to write down. It was for my purposes only; no one need ever read it but me. She told me to be honest with myself and to learn to depend on myself for happiness and self-gratification.

During the weeks after, life seemed to work out for us. We were getting along great Edward's father came for a visit as he had promised. Edward set up a dinner at a nice restaurant and invited his professor. I told him he should really tell his dad, not just spring it on him. Edward finally broke down and told his dad there would be a fourth for dinner that evening. He told him a little about her and how helpful she had been to him during his attendance at Harvard. Ed wasn't thrilled with the situation of a blind date, but he accepted the consequences, although he told Edward not to do it again.

We met at the restaurant with Ms. Ingerheart. Ed stood up and said, "Vivian?" As if, he knew her. Ms. Ingerheart said, "Ed, how are you?" Edward and I looked at each other. They hugged each other, and we all sat down. They talked and asked questions of each other. Edward told the waiter that we wanted water and that we would look over the menu, give us a few minutes. Ed and Vivian couldn't stop talking and laughing about old times. Finally, Edward got a word in.

"Okay, you two tell us what is going on here."

Ed started, "I knew Vivian in school, high school. We were close but we didn't see each other after we graduated. We went our separate ways.

Vivian said, "I thought about Ed early on in my career, but I got married, and this happened and that happened, and I didn't think about him anymore. Edward, your name stuck out to me, but I never bothered to ask about who your father was. You didn't tell me about him coming tonight."

"I know, I'm sorry. I liked you and thought the two of you seemed right for each other. Sam made me tell Dad before we came, so he knew about you, but I guess Ingerheart is your married name."

"Yes, it is. I was Vivian Jones back then. When I divorced, I kept the name."

Ed butted in, "Vivian, you are just as pretty today as you were then. Maybe I should have had my son fix me up on dates before. He did a great job this time."

Edward laughed, punching me lightly on the shoulder.

"Can I have your phone number, Vivian?, I would love to talk to you further about careers, and life in general, you know."

Edward and I smiled. They liked each other and had a past, a good past. We ordered and ate; Vivian and Ed talked all evening. It was charming to listen to them talk. We went home and Ed and Vivian said they would get together the next day and reminisce some more. Edward was so pleased with himself; I would have a beast to put up with tonight. I liked the beast; he was a lot of fun. The beast growled, scratched, and pawed my body for hours. I love the beast.

# CHAPTER THIRTY-ONE

Ed had to go back home, but Vivian promised to visit him, and he said he would be back, of course, to visit Edward and me. As time passed, they started visiting each other often, and we saw less and less of Ed. He called often, but he was this or that with Vivian. Ed asked us to his home for Thanksgiving. He had invited Vivian and wanted us to come as well. We told him we were going to my parents, because they had not met Edward yet. He said then he may ask Vivian to go on a cruise with him instead. He said he would miss us, but he would visit us the week after. He made sure Edward was okay with not being together the first holiday that they would actually be a family. Edward told him he would miss him and the next week would be fine. We would make a big deal out it with Vivian and all of us.

Thanksgiving week was here before we knew it. We were flying in on Tuesday evening, to spend as much time as possible with my family. I wanted to spend time with Abby as well. We checked at a hotel near my home and drove over that evening to meet my parents. Edward was nervous, and his hands were shaking. It was cold but at least no snow yet. He kept looking at me and reaching over to hold my hand. I would squeeze his hand and tell him it would be fine.

I missed my family. Being away from them was hard now that I felt close to them. When we pulled into the driveway, Alex ran to me and hugged me, and Ray was right behind her. My mom was so excited, and so were Alex and Ray. I hugged them all, telling them I had presents for them and how much I missed and loved them. My mother hugged me tightly and then turned to Edward hugged him.

"Son, you are welcome in our home, and we are so happy to finally meet you."

"Thank you, I am happy to finally meet you too."

My brother and sister were all over him, asking him questions. Alex thought he was so cute, she ogled him all evening. He watched her making her feel important, and listened to her every word.

I gave them the gifts I brought them. I asked where Dad was. Mom said he would be home soon. She told me, "Ronnie is in town and has already called to see if you are here. She brought her boyfriend home with her too."

"What about Kat?"

"I haven't heard from her."

We made a promise none of us had kept about keeping in touch. I called Kat's cell, but it had been disconnected.

I called Ronnie, "I am so happy. Mick and I are getting married next summer. My dad likes him, and we will be in town until Sunday."

"We will be too. Have you heard anything about Abby?"

"I haven't had time to get in touch with her. I saw her before I left, and that was the last time we spoke."

"Have you heard from Kat?"

"I talked to Kat, but it has been a while. She said she and Wayne were doing fine. She was thinking about moving to Texas, and I don't know anything else."

I wanted to go see Abby the next day. Edward was going with me. Ronnie said she would like to come also. Mom had told me Abby came home so I called her parents, and they let me talk to her. She seemed calm and cool, maybe too cool. She sounded somewhat drugged. I asked if we could come see her. She told us it would be fine tomorrow afternoon. I told her it would be Ronnie, Edward, Mick and me. We can send the boys to do something else so we can spend time with her. She said she would prefer that we come without the guys. I asked her if she had spoken to Kat. She said she hadn't heard from Kat since Florida. I was a little surprised to hear that. Kat was supposed to visit her last summer.

My father finally came home and met Edward. They talked law mostly. Edward tried to talk personal stuff.

Edward asked my Dad, "May I speak to you privately when you have a moment, Sir?"

My Dad replied, "Sure, now is fine." They went out on the patio, where Dad always smoked his cigars and had a drink. He offered Edward a drink, but he declined. "Have a seat and we can talk. What do you want to discuss?"

"Well, Sir, I would like to ask for your daughter's hand in marriage."

"I see. Well, I have nothing to do with it, that choice is up to Sam."

"Sir, I just wanted your approval. I fell in love with her the moment I saw her."

"I really have nothing to say about the choices Sam makes, and it's up to her."

"I know Sir, I already asked her and she said yes. I just want you and your wife's approval, Sir." Edward hung his head.

"Well as far as I am concerned, it has already happened. She lives with you; she already sleeps in your bed doesn't she?"

Edward tried to talk civilly with my dad about it, just wanting Dad to like him. "I promise to take care of her and treat her with respect."

"Well I hope so."

Dad informed Edward how arrangements would be in his house. They came back inside and Dad went into his office shutting the door leaving Edward behind.

Edward told me about the conversation. "Your dad did not approve, or disapprove our engagement."

"It's okay."

"He informed me about our sleeping arrangements this evening. I hesitated, asking what he meant. Your dad said they don't have an extra room, so they could put the kids together, or I could sleep with Ray and you can sleep with Alex. I told him we had a room at a nearby hotel so we wouldn't put them out. Your dad shook his head, and then walked away."

I thought my dad had been very rude to Edward, and I wanted to punch him. If it hadn't been for my mom, brother, and sister, I would have just left right then. No, I had to remind myself to give him all the chances he needed to show his love for me. I will get it, one-way or the other.

We visited for a while. It was getting late, so we wanted to head back to our hotel. I knew my mom wanted punch my dad as much as I did. She was irritated with him, and we could tell it. Dad was embarrassed by mom's attitude toward him. He excused himself and went to bed, so we told Mom we would see them tomorrow and left. Edward and I talked about my anger toward my dad and how he acted with Edward. Edward held me and told me, to remember what I had once told him. I said I would do my best. I wrote in my journal for some time that evening before retiring to bed. I wanted to make sure I didn't let that cloud creep in on me.

The next morning, Edward and I went to pick up Ronnie and Mick. They looked so happy with each other. I saw the stepwitch at the door, waving good-bye to us. First thing, I asked was how it was going, being home. She said, "Stepwitch is being very nice. I am afraid of what was up, maybe because Mick was here. She likes him, I think she wants him."

Mick laughed saying, 'Yuck'. We all laughed. We had lunch together and saw a few people we knew from high school, none of them were our friends. When they saw the handsome men we were with though, two of the girls came over to talk. Ronnie and I just rolled our eyes. It was two of the cheerleaders. One of them had a baby on her hip, and the other one was pregnant and huge. We asked if they were married. They giggled saying, of course they both married football players. One was working as a bricklayer, and the other was a carpenter. They were so proud of their lives now. They asked us how our summer was, what school we were attending, and so on, just like they had been best friends with us instead of the group who tormented us most of our lives. We told them it was good seeing them, and was happy to see how well they were doing, but we had things to do and told them bye. They rolled their eyes at us as we left. We both laughed.

We went by Kat's house. It didn't look like anyone lived there anymore. We knocked on the door, and no one answered. We peeked in the windows and no furniture was in the house. I knocked on a neighbor's door, but they didn't answer either. We drove to the place where Kat's mom worked days, asking for her, but we were told she didn't work there any longer. One girl told us she believed she moved, they thought to Texas, with her daughter. We didn't know anyone else to check with about Kat. She had no other family we knew about, and we didn't even know Wayne's last name.

We went to Abby's house at three o'clock. Our guys said they would drive around and find something to do, so we could visit with Abby. Edward told me to tell Abby hello, and he hoped to see her when they came back. I told them to be back in about an hour. We walked up to the door, hoping Mr. Hall was at the store. Abby opened the door. She looked horrible. Her eyes were sunken in. She had lost weight, too much weight. You could see the bones in her face, and her clothes hung on her. Ashley, thank goodness, was gone to a friend's house.

Abby asked us in, offering us drinks or snacks. We both declined. We asked her if she intended to go to college next semester. She said no, she didn't feel well and stayed inside most of the time. She was pale, and she looked, and acted weak.

"Abby, are you okay?" I asked her.

"Sure, Sam, I am fine. How are you?"

"I'm fine. Are you on medication?

She spoke slow and defined. She had to think about each word she said. Her eyes were glassy. She looked at me, but there was nothing inside those eyes.

"Yes, I am on several medications. They keep me calm and happy, everyone tells me. No more suicide watches. I don't leave the house though. My dad wants me to go back to work but I can't seem to stand up for long periods, I fall down. I need to sleep every few hours too. I am afraid of people, germs, and someone might touch me. I clean house and cook for Mom."

"Abby, why are you on so much meds?"

"So no one has to worry, and watch over me." She looked away.

"Abby, I am on an antidepressant too, but I don't feel that way. I can function and do normal things; I just don't feel so sad all the time."

"They tried different things, and I cut myself again. My dad told them to fix me or else. They gave me enough drugs to make me mild and meek. I always was weak minded, now weak bodied too." She laughed; she seemed to be looking off into nothing. Her eyes were empty.

"Abby, can we help you?"

"No, no, I'm fine." Ronnie couldn't seem to say anything, so I did all the talking.

"Abby, we will be here till Sunday. Can we come get you and take you out with us maybe Friday for lunch?"

"Oh no, I don't leave the house, Sam. I can't go, sorry. You can visit me here, but I can't leave. I haven't since I quit therapy." she exclaimed.

"Why did you quit therapy? You said, you loved being with those friends, talking with them, doing positive things together."

"My father thought it was too expensive and not worthwhile." Ronnie and I looked at each other, knowing he was a selfish, evil old man.

"Abby, we love you. We just want to spend some time with you while we are in town, like old times."

"That's nice; you are welcome to come back." She said. I hung my head feeling tears run down my face, Ronnie patted me on the back.

"Abby, Edward told me to tell you hello, and he wished he could spend time with you, with us all together on Friday."

"NO! I'm sorry, Sam but no I cannot leave this house." She said. My heart was breaking. What could I do? I couldn't just kidnap her, take her out of here, and get her off the drugs. I could force her parents to see what they were doing to her, it wasn't right, but I had no say in the matter. I cried again. Abby's mother came home and saw me crying.

"Now listen here, young lady, don't be putting any ideas in her head. She is doing fine now."

"I just wanted to see her. I wanted her to go with us Friday, on just a day thing, a few hours, all of us together."

"Abby doesn't leave the house. She doesn't like to be around many people anymore. She is fine, here at home, safe, where no one can hurt her ever again."

"We don't want to hurt her, we love her."

"Your idea of love and mine are two different things. She is our daughter, and we want her safe at home." She said. We stood up to go.

I looked at Abby. I took her hand in mine. "I will keep in touch, I promise. I will write. Do you have e-mail?"

"We don't allow that filth in our house. You can write her letters."

"Okay." We walked outside and down the road a ways. I sat on the curb and cried and Ronnie held me.

"Ronnie, how are you doing? Are you, sad? Do you feel loved? Loved enough now?"

"Sam, I am not the same as I was before. I have Mick. He is good for me. I have friends at school. I am liked. I get along well with classmates. I think I am happy. As me tomorrow, though. We laughed.

"Ronnie, I hurt deep inside for Abby. I don't want you to feel neglected by me ever. I love you like a sister. I am depressed, but I am seeing a counselor, and she is helping me. Edward and I are getting on well, and I am in school. Oh, by the way, I changed majors. I'm going into nursing. I am working part-time, and I am happy. I love Edward and being with him. If we were to part ways now, I thing I would be very sad, but able to make it on my own. I wouldn't want to die, at least truly die. I feel happy and secure. I keep my journal. It helps me know who I am inside. I depend on me to be happy now, and not someone else. I have a ways to go to be healed, and I am really not sure if I can be healed. It feels like an alcoholic, once you are, you always will be, but I am making it. Edward helps me. We are doing it together."

"Sam, I am really happy for you. I feel better too, really I do. I think that is why I don't stay in touch. I didn't want to be reminded of the way it was before."

"Me too."

"I want to be close to you, but I can't go back to that life. I don't want it. I am not lonely, even when I am alone now. I try to keep the negative away from me. Do you understand what I mean?"

"Yeah, I do."

"I wonder about Kat. I hope she's okay."

"So do I, Ron." We saw our car and stood up, they stopped, asking what happened, and we told them. We decided to go to a movie together. We went to the funniest one we could find. It was great to be out together, with these beautiful men, laughing and being happy.

We had dinner with my folks, and my dad seemed so alone even with us all there. I patted him on the back, hugging him from behind as I walked by him, telling him I loved him. He didn't say anything, but I was still trying. Mom had tears in her eyes when she saw what I did. Alex went to her room. Ray didn't even notice.

Thanksgiving was great. I spend it mostly in Mom's kitchen. It was fun making pies, stuffing the turkey, cooking, and preparing all the traditional stuff, together; even Alex helped or sat in the kitchen with us. Ray and Edward would come see what we were doing, stealing bites of food here and there and then running away. They played football in the yard, Edward wrestled with Ray. They ran and played all day. Dad sat in the living room, watching football on TV.

We called all the men in to eat at the table. Dad said a prayer, thanking the Lord for the food and the family around the table. It was not too sappy, short and sweet. Ray had an idea he saw on some program that we all tell what we were thankful for this year. We all agreed it was a great idea, except Dad.

My Mom started, "I am thankful for my family, for the love I feel around this table today. I am thankful God blessed me with three beautiful children, and they are healthy and safe."

Alex was next. "I am thankful for that turkey I am about to eat and that chocolate cream pie for dessert." We all laughed.

Ray said, "I am thankful I had someone to play with today. It was fun. Thanks Edward." Dad looked up; I thought his feelings were hurt. He looked hurt anyway.

Edward was next, "I am thankful for my new family, and I am most thankful that Sam came into my life, I love her, I need her, and I never want to lose her."

I had tears in my eyes, "I am thankful, of course, for Edward, I love you too. I am thankful for my mom, who has given me memories today that will be with me the rest of my life. I am thankful for Alex, for spending time together, laughing, and loving one another. I am thankful for Ray, my sweet baby brother, you are such an ornery little snit, but I love you. I am thankful for my Dad. He works hard for the family to give us all that we need." He looked up again with tears in his eyes. I continued, "I am thankful for being alive and spending this day with the most important people in my life, except Ed, and I am thankful for him too. Amen." Everyone looked at me and said, Amen.

My dad didn't want to do this, but he said, "I am thankful for my family." I believed he meant it.

We had a wonderful meal and spent the afternoon afternoon lying around the living room watching football with my dad, and making too much noise. He would give us all dirty looks. I saw him smile a couple of times. It was the first holiday I had ever had that was a family affair. It felt like I was at home, my home, I held Edward's hand; this was what a family felt like. I knew he felt it too and wished so much for Ed to have been with us. Ed did call us to tell us, "Happy Thanksgiving," and we wished him the same. They were having a good time together on the cruise.

I spent Friday morning with Alex. We hit several good sales and bought Christmas presents for Mom and Dad. We ate lunch together and had a real sister time. In the afternoon Edward and I took Alex and Ray to the park. It was cold but Ray enjoyed himself. Edward ran after him yelling like a banshee and Ray screamed and laughed the whole time. We spent Friday late afternoon and evening with Ronnie and Mick. We drove out to the lake and drank a couple of beers. We laughed all day long. It was nice being with Ronnie. We didn't stay late it was so cold and we didn't prepare for the freezing temperature when we left the house. We went back to Ronnie's house and watched TV and ate snacks. Ronnie's stepwitch was uncommonly nice making us snacks of all kinds. She even made the step siblings leave us alone.

We spent the rest of the time, as much as we could with my family. Saturday morning my Mom and I cooked together, laughing, and talking during the preparation. I helped her clean, just anything to be by her side. Alex started trying to join in and help cook and clean. She enjoyed it too and didn't want to miss the fun. I didn't know Mom was so funny. We laughed so much, I would cry. Mom would hug Alex, and thank her. Alex would smile. We spent a lot of time in the kitchen the three of us. I loved it for a change.

Edward played with Ray most of the time. He and Dad would talk somewhat, but not anything regarding the heart, only about work. They did talk some about the wedding, and Dad wanted to know a date, but Edward told him we didn't have one yet. My Dad seemed to like Edward and he treated him with respect.

We were preparing to leave my parents house on Sunday afternoon when my Dad shocked the hell out of me. He patted Edward on the back, and gave him a hug, telling him to take care of me. Edward told him he would always take care of me, and love me. I was crying and could hardly talk as we got in the car. I hugged everyone especially my Dad, and he hugged me back. It was hard to tell them bye, but I looked forward to going home, back to our everyday life.

# CHAPTER THIRTY-TWO

Christmas came and went so fast. Mom and Alex came to visit us for two days before Christmas. We cooked and had a dinner celebrating together; we opened presents and had a wonderful time. Ray stayed with Dad, Mom called them several times to see how they were doing. Ray told Mom he was enjoying being with Dad. He said Dad didn't work one time while Mom and Alex were gone so far. Dad played with him, went to the movies, and took him to the park. They played catch and worked on the car. Mom cried after talking to them. I wished they could have stayed longer, but they had to get back home.

On Christmas Day, it was just Edward and me. We had a special gift for each other and spent the day in each other's arms. We talked and made plans for New Years Eve and spring break. We wanted to start the year off good. We decided to go to Florida for a couple of days. We would be close to Edward's friends and his dad and Vivian. We went to parties but spent New Year's Eve with Ed and Vivian alone at Ed's house. We celebrated with Cook and Granger.

During the next semester, I was still working on basics and seeing my psychologist, Dr Dean. I was getting better every day. I wondered if nursing was where I wanted to be. I had a depression problem, and like so many other kids, I wanted to die because I felt left out, unloved, and unwanted. There were so many reasons why kids did things to hurt themselves; I saw it on television every day. Kid's lives were hard enough without the pressures of helplessness. I wanted to make a change. My friend Abby finally, committed suicide in February of that year. Her parents had her so drugged up that she had a hard time thinking, lee alone trying to have a conversation with someone. Abby took pills, too many, more than her weak body could handle, and ended her life alone, as she always felt. Her father was the one who found her. He tried so hard to keep her safe and away from harm, but he didn't think about destroying her from the inside out. It hurt, so bad when I found out. It hurt, really badly when I found out. It was after the funeral. My parents didn't even know until Dad read the obituary, looking for something else in the newspaper. I didn't get to tell her good bye. I still wondered about Kat. Was she okay? How could I find her?

I talked to Ronnie often. We called each other about every week or so. We e-mailed junk jokes and short messages back and forth. We would say "Hey" on Facebook. I studied more and more about depression online and asked my therapist about it. She told me how many teenagers died by their own hands, usually leaving notes, will still a hope of being saved, maybe given what they felt they lacked in life. She told me about the websites on-line where kids could talk to other kids about killing themselves, about how they felt, about abuse in so many ways, and about just being the different kid. There were Christian groups trying to save these kids lives. Kids hurt other kids because they are afraid of being like them. Being singled out; being made fun of, it hurts, and sometimes causes kids to take their own lives, especially kids that are already partially broken. High school kids are the most at risk.

There was a movie we rented and watched called, 'To Save a Life'." It was touching, and very close to home. Kids are not adults; they haven't learned yet how to handle failure or success. Kids need love and protection. They need to be held, and they need to know they are of value, real 'Value' that is what Dr. Dean keeps telling me. It is important to feel you are normal. I mean, so many kids want to look different. They are considered as those, 'Goth Kids, and thought of as bad, vampires who drink blood, kill themselves. Goth is just a way to be them self, to find where they belong, a way to, just fit in somewhere. They are a group for support, not like everyone else out there on the planet. It is important to be accepted for who you are inside, not by your looks. I mean the same thing with tattoos. People are afraid of people with tattoos or big, bulky guys. I have seen some people cross the street just to not to walk by a Goth or a huge tattooed man. Those people have feelings, they want to be loved. They are not different inside. They don't do what they do to make you fear them, they are just trying to live in a 'world that is made up by a few, not the all.

I found what I believe I want to do with my life. I want to help kids. Edward can do the law and help the injustice for those less fortunate. I can help or be a part of those who feel left out and unloved. I talked to my counselor, and she informed me about what I needed to take to become a psychologist, but she told me nursing was somewhere I could use it too. I could help in so many ways. Every profession has the ability to make a difference. She said teachers were the front-line to many of those kids. Home life can be painful and dangerous, and everyone should be aware of something that that. Parent's wanted usually what was best for their child and didn't always see the hurt inside them. We all need some education on how to see depression, to know if a kid might be in danger of hurting himself or herself. She also told me to find where and how I wanted to help, and then make my choice. First, I had to be happy in the field I worked in, and then find a way to help. I told her I would think about it. Really think deeply about what I wanted. I went home to talk to Edward about it. He helped look online. He said he would do research and told me not to make a decision just yet.

We finally set a date to get married. I, of course wanted to go to the courthouse, but Edward wanted the big 'Ta Dah' thing. We were getting married in Ft. Lauderdale, FL on his father's estate. I would have a somewhat traditional dress. Cook was doing the food. My family would be there, of course. Ronnie and Mick too, I invited Ronnie's dad but didn't expect him. I looked for Kat on community networks, along with a few other places. I checked Dallas and Houston phone books for her mother, but found nothing.

Most of Edwards's friends were coming to the wedding, and of course, Vivian would be there, since she and Ed were engaged now to be married themselves. Our wedding was to be outdoors. We were, hoping the weather went our way. I invited Renee and some of the others from the firm in Clearwater. Edward and Ed found the young man who had saved me and was trying to get them green cards do they would be legal without making it obvious who and where they were. He gave them money to improve their way of living, and they were appreciative. I invited them to the wedding too, but they said they didn't want to be around that many lawyers and politicians. We completely understood.

Ronnie was to be my maid of honor, and Kat would have been included too, but I couldn't find her. Thomas was standing up for Edward. I talked to Net, and she volunteered to help with plans, since she lived near Ed. She said she would get with Vivian and keep in touch. I asked my dad to walk me down the aisle. He said sure, not showing any enthusiasm. I was still trying with him. I called home and told him I loved him every time I talked to him.

Ed had really changed since the accident last summer and even more so after meeting up with Vivian again. They were trying to make plans so they could spend more time together. Vivian loved Harvard Law, and Ed loved Florida, so it was a bit of a problem. Neither wanted to give up what they had built, which was understandable. Finally, Vivian decided to take an extended sabbatical and move to Florida. She had tenure and was willing to teach in area schools of Ft Lauderdale and still would make trips to Harvard for special seminars and speeches she would give.

Time passed so fast now. When I was younger, it seemed to take forever to reach a certain age, but now it was in high speed. We had two months until the wedding, and I was still trying to figure out what I wanted to do. I prayed, and we did research; I talked to teachers in public schools. I talked to teachers in elementary, middle and high school, along with some of the colleges. I volunteered to make a speech at one of the local schools regarding depression and suicide. The kids accepted me easily. I looked young anyway. I was nine-teen but looked younger, especially without makeup on. I talked and answered questions. I received requests to visit other schools with good references from the past program I had done. It was moving fast, and I couldn't keep up with it, work, school, Edward, and trying to plan a wedding. I was getting less and less sleep, but Edward, was gone so much now studying for finals, and then his Bar. I did every program I could before the end of the school year. Dr. Dean helped me with what to say and how to say it. She attended as several of the programs. She encouraged me to do all I could. She believed in me and what I was saying to these kids. It felt good and important, what I was doing.

I wanted to reach those kids who might not have another chance. I was told I gave them hope and encouragement. I received letters of thanks, and more request across the country to speak at other schools. There was no way I could do it all. I knew there was a reason, but I couldn't quite get which way to go with this. My counselor advised me to finish school whatever else I decided to do. If I wanted to do the programs, work them around my school on Fridays, and ask for traveling room, and board expenses. I thought, *yeah, I could do that, not every day but on Fridays only.* I could travel on Thursday night to get to my destination, whether flying or driving. Edward encouraged me to do it too. He said it sounded like a worthwhile plan. If I saved one life because of these seminars, just one life, it was worth the time. I agreed wholeheartedly. I visited schools every week. I got letters from parents saying they saw a difference in their kids and thanked me. It made me feel good, really good.

Over the summer, I could write speeches and set up trips for the next school year, and. contact those who had already contacted me by e-mail. I would get on- line and make a webpage. Edward said he would help when he could. I talked to Ronnie, and she said she would love to join me, but it depended on her fall classes. She would like to attend at least one time with me. I told her I would love it. I talked to my psychologist and my counselor, and they helped me set up a web page and got information to help with speeches and what not to say that might cause legal problems. Dr. Dean said she would like to travel with me more when she could, along with Ms. Jacobs. The two women had become friends through me and enjoyed what we were doing. They encouraged me to do what was best for me, along with reaching out to others.

I worked on the web page every chance I had to make it attractive and interesting to look at and easy to get around. I set up pages for kids to look at, and then for teachers and places to request my attendance and so on. I had an open forum for kids to talk, and it was already being used. I was amazed to see kids talking to other kids, all positive attitudes. It was looking great. I had already many teens looking over the site, asking me questions about how they could find out more. I had to get my psychologist involved in this part of it. She helped answering their questions, letting me put her name on the site as contact, a professional therapist. She even included an emergency number for those in serious need. Kids were talking to her already too, asking for help or advice. It was amazing. I kept learning and working on the site, it was growing faster than I could keep up. Dr. Dean contacted other psychologists to get them involved across the country, and many responded, since it was online, and it was an outreach program to help our country's youth.

People of all ages, who felt as I did, commented. Others wanted to know how they could help in their communities doing programs. I told them how I started by speaking with counselors and psychiatrists. I pointed them in the right direction.

Edward and I were happy and spent what time we had together loving each other and making the time special. He was so busy now and would be until graduation. I had to work extra hours at work, helping with summer class schedules, books, online classes, workshops, classes over the summer, and so on. I even had to work a couple of Saturdays to get things done. My counselor told me I was the best investment she had ever made; hiring me had been great for the college, and the community. I kept working on my web site and had some times arranged at schools, mostly close by, but a few out of state. They were willing to pay expenses as I requested. They checked with Ms. Jacobs and Dr. Dean as well for references. Both of them gave me high recommendations.

It was one week until school was out. The kids were having wild parties because finals week was almost over. The fraternities and sororities at Harvard were up all night, roaming the streets, drinking, shouting and having fun. There were parties every night. It was so loud at night that we couldn't sleep, and Edward still had finals. We switched to the back bedroom because it was away from the street, and shutting the door, it was quieter. Edward and I hadn't had much sex recently because of his study schedule and my work schedule. He was cranky and complaining, so, I knew he needed some 'Me' time. On Friday, I told him we were having a party. It was his last final, and he should be in a better mood. He didn't want a party, but I told him not to invite anyone. The guests on the list were all mine.

Friday, I took off work early. I made appetizers, light foods, finger foods. I had wine and champagne in a bucket of ice. He walked in the door, "Not a lot of food for a party. You only have one bottle of champagne and enough appetizers for just me."

I smiled, "It is just us."

"Really?" He said, with a grin from ear to ear.

"Yes, but it is a celebration for us". His finals were through; he was a graduate of Harvard University, Harvard Law School. I was proud of him.

"I still have to get my scores back. Oh my gosh! Are you pregnant?"

"No, I am not pregnant. How do you think you did?"

"I feel like I did well."

"That's enough for me." I kissed him, "I have to get ready for our party."

He looked puzzled. "I thought it was just us."

"I still have a special outfit to wear to celebrate in."

"Do I have to change?"

"Not yet." I said. He grinned and sat on the bar stool, waiting for me to return.

I came back in the room wearing a big red bow tied around me and nothing else on.

"Is that my present".

"It sure is."

"I want to unwrap it right now."

"Like all good things, it has to wait." We drank champagne, and I noticed he had a little bulge in his pants, so my plan was working well. He tried to touch me, but I pulled away.

"Not yet", I said. He moaned. I fed him finger foods, and he ate asking what each was. He liked them, and I let him feed me some, but only at a distance, I sucked on his finger. I drank more champagne and filled his glass again.

"Do you plan on getting drunk?"

"No, but I am giggly and happy, and will do anything you wish soon." I said. His face went blank, and the front of his pants was tighter than before. I saw him try to move himself around.

"Remove those uncomfortable pants."

He dropped them where he stood.

"Boxers too?"

"Uh huh."

He dropped them and 'Bong' straight out in front. He tried to grab me. I moved away. He peeled his shirt off and threw it across the room. He was completely naked and looked fine.

"I can't wait, I need you."

"It has been days since we were together, and this is going to last a while and be worth the wait." I said. He moaned again, knowing now how things seemed to play out between us. I was stronger and more knowledgeable than I was in the beginning.

I danced away from him, and when I turned around, he groaned as if he was in pain because my bare bottom was so close to him. He brushed his hand across it as I went by. I turned, reach out, and ran my fingers down his long hard shaft. He jumped and grabbed me. this time not missing. He pulled me close and kissed me, and he ripped the bow off and carried me to the bedroom. We spent hours in there. I made him go slow and take his time. I made him seduce me with kisses, and he was begging and pleading for me to let him touch me. I pulled away and then let him catch me and pull me back close. Then I would run from him, making him chase me again. He touched places that made me wild; I licked and kissed him in places that made him come up off the bed. We played until we couldn't stand any more. We came together feeling thunder and lightning going through our veins. It was, dare I say, a Good Friday night. We burst with happiness and gratitude of just being together. We were so tired when we finished we could hardly move let alone breathe.

Hours later, showered and back in the kitchen we finish off the champagne, he helped me put the snack foods away. He ate most of it, but we got the kitchen clean and were ready for sleep. I took the bottle of champagne with us. I would offer him a drink and then spilling some on him so I would have to lick it off. He did the same, spilling and licking until it was gone. I promised him giggles, and he got what I promised. I touched him and he moaned. He kissed me until exhausted. We feel asleep.

# CHAPTER THIRTY-THREE

I woke up with a start. Our wedding was three days away. Edward was not in bed. I crawled out of bed and went to find him. He was looking over those lists again. We were leaving for Florida today, but he worried about our future. Edward had passed all his finals with excellence. I passed my finals and did much better than I had expected. I didn't do perfect, but I had a 'B' average. A 'B' would hold my scholarships and grants in place for the next year. I just had to know where next year would be. Edward had offers from several firms, but he was having difficulty deciding where he wanted to go. He made lists of all his pros and cons but wasn't working it down, as he had hoped. It was all he could think about, trying to make the best decision possible for my benefit, more than his own. With him worrying, so much, it made me worry about those lists as well, until I couldn't sleep. I thought it kept him from worrying about the wedding. I stood behind him, putting my arms around his neck and telling him he had until we were back from our honeymoon to decide. We would find the answer together. He said he wasn't worried about the wedding; he was ready to spend his life with me. We had the past year and it would only get better. He said he knew the day would be grand with Vivian and his dad taking care of plans and such. I also had Net calling me daily with new ideas and making the guest seating arrangements. She was great; I couldn't have done it without her.

Edward spun the chair around and held me, burying his face in my chest. "I have the best woman in the world who has agreed to be my wife and I have so much to look forward to. I am blessed, with everything I do and wish for is for her, more than me."

I hugged him and rested the side of my face on top of his head.

"I love you Edward."

He squeezed me.

"I love you too." We stood there a moment.

He raised his head up looking up at me, "We have to get ready to go, don't we?"

"Yes, we do. Are you all packed?"

"Yes, you did most of it for me. I added a couple of things."

"I'm packed, I have new toothbrushes, toothpaste, and shampoo and soap so we don't have to bother with what we use today. Come on, join me in the shower." I said. He rose and followed me. We were ready to leave. We looked around the room; we made sure we had phone chargers, laptops, cell phones, passports, driver's licenses but I was under twenty-one, so I was not sure how that would help me much. We had everything. We locked the door behind us and were on our way. The taxi was waiting. We made it to the airport just in time. We checked in and, checked our bags. We each had a carry-on with laptops and miscellaneous stuff. We were called as we reached the boarding area. We really cut it close getting here getting here.

We arrived in Ft. Lauderdale on time, and Ed and Vivian picked us up. There were hugs and kisses all around. Ed asked if we needed anything before we went home, and we told him we were ready. My dress was already here. Edward would get his tuxedo and stuff tomorrow. Ronnie should be in this evening. My parents would be here tomorrow, and everything was going as planned. It felt good to be back in Florida. I wanted to go to the beach and lie in the sun. Net was at Ed's house when we got there, waiting on the porch with Cook and Mr. Granger. Cook hugged us both and welcomed us. She was talking a mile a minute as we walked up the stairs to Edwards's room. Net was telling me about everything new she had done and about how cool Granger had fixed up the back yard where the wedding was to be held. The reception would be on the deck and surrounding area. She told me about the champagne fountain, how cool it looked, and they had already tried it out. She said Cook was preparing some of the greatest dishes she had ever tasted. We were in Edward's room, and Cook was still talking to Edward and Net to me. Ed said, "Hey you two, let them put their stuff down at least. I know you are excited, but give them a minute." We dropped our bags on the floor and then we were hustled out of the room flanked by Net, Cook and Ed. Vivian had the decency to wait for us downstairs. Net was great, but she never stopped talking. I think she and Ronnie should hit it off well.

I spoke with Ronnie and learned that she passed all her finals, with a 4.0 grade point average. She said she and Mick were kind of on the outs, the long distance wasn't working well for them. She was dating and so was he. They still talked but didn't visit each other often as they used to. I told her Edward had lots of friends and some single guys, I would make sure she had a good time. She said she wasn't worried about having a good time with boys, she knew she would be seeing me again. I loved her and was so looking forward to seeing her. We all ate lunch together on the back deck. It was a simple lunch, sandwiches, but not like, I was used to having. We had three different kinds of breads, all kinds of condiments, every vegetable possible, at least ten different meats, and cheeses. We all ate sitting around casually, something Ed was not real used to doing, but he was a wonderful host today. He was kind and talked to all the young people and they talked to him. I was so excited, I couldn't sit still, and I was ready to pick up Ronnie. Her plane would be here, in about an hour. Everyone was so relaxed and comfortable, Net volunteered to take me to pick her up. Edward kissed me good-bye and told me not to get lost. I told him Net was driving. He said that was what he was talking about. She was the one who got lost in her own neighborhood. Net hit him; I was six years old then, Edward.

"I am so happy for you the two of you, Sam. Edward is a lucky guy."

"Thank you Net. Where is your boyfriend?"

"He will be here this evening. There will be a few single men, as you requested. I picked them out myself. Two of them I would have chosen for myself, but I was treated like the little sis or just one of the boys growing up. Most of them didn't look at me, as a girl."

"I can't imagine that, looking at you. You are gorgeous."

"Thank you, but I am not. I don't see myself that way."

"I think you and Ronnie will like each other. She is pretty, nice little body. She is out going and funny. Not like me."

"What do you mean not like you? You are beautiful and have a very cute little body."

"I have bulges here and there. I have a pouch for my tummy. My butt is too big, and my boobs are too small and I have freckles all over my face."

"I don't agree, has Edward ever complained?"

Laughing, I said, "No, but he loves me."

She put her finger up against her chin, tapping and looking up and said, "I wonder why!"

"Hey that's not nice." We laughed and talked all the way back to the airport. We were early, of course. We sat in the car and waited until it was close for the plane to land. We saw one go over our head, and I said, "That has to be it." Net and I ran to the terminal and saw it was on time. We went to the gate to wait, and the board said it had arrived. I was jumping up and down. I seemed to take forever to unload the plane. I waited and waited.

"What if she didn't come? What if she missed her flight?" I kept shaking and looking around, jumping up and down. Net was laughing at me.

"She would have called you," Net said, trying to calm me down.

"Yeah, I guess so." Then I saw her, I ran toward her and the buzzer went off because I had gone under the sensor. I backed up, and a guard come over and watched me. Ronnie was running and kept dropping her bag. She finally got to me, and I hugged her, crying, and didn't want to let her go.

"Ronnie, I am so happy to see you. I can't believe we have been apart for so long. I missed you so much." I said. Net walked over, and I introduced them to each other. They said hello, and I hugged Ronnie again. Net took her bag, and we walked to the baggage claim area to get the rest. We both were asking how we were and what we had been doing. We talked and held each other as we did as little girls. Net let us go on and on to one another and would laugh occasionally at something we said. I told her I was sorry, but I missed Ronnie so much I couldn't ask enough. We spent our whole lives seeing each other almost every day until we went off to college. She said it wasn't a problem, and we should get it all out now and enjoy each other. I started trying to include Net in our conversation. Ronnie asked Net about Florida and what she liked to do and about college and other things. They were getting along just as I thought they would.

I told Ronnie about the party tonight at Ed's boathouse. All Edward's friends would be there, as well as Ed and Vivian. My parents wouldn't arrive until the next day. They would be party poopers anyway. I asked about her dad if he was coming. She told me he sent his congratulations with her. He sent me a gift but he and the family weren't able to make it. I told her I didn't expect him. She said things were on and off with him again, but they spoke.

We drove up to the house. We saw Edward come out front to greet us. He ran to Ronnie and hugged her, picking her up and swinging her around. He took all her bags into the house and told us to go out back. I asked her if she was tired or wanted to rest, and she said no way, she didn't want to miss a moment of fun this weekend. We walked through the house, and Ronnie said, "Nice." We went out on the deck; I asked her if she was hungry. She said, "Starving." I walked beside her as she fixed herself a sandwich; and then, we walked over to sit by Net. The three of us talked and laughed. Edward came out and asked if anyone wanted beer or anything to drink.

Friends of Edward started showing up. Thomas came and walked up to me smiling. He squeezed me, and bent me backwards, and kissed me on the cheek. Edward threatened his life. Ronnie didn't know whether or not they were serious. I told her they were best friends, and Thomas was the 'Best man'. She nodded. Others started arriving, and they headed down to the boathouse. Ed walked with Del, and a couple of other guys. Del turned and waved at me, I waved back. I asked Net again when her guy would get here. She said it would be later, as he was at work. I told her I was anxious to meet him. She told me to wait, and her fiancé was the most magnificent man of all of them.

I saw Silly Sal and some other girls show up, I saw Tory. I pointed out who was who to Ronnie. I told her as much as I could remember. Net said if she didn't remember names, it was cool. There are a lot who will show up tonight, not all will stay all evening, but most will. She told Ronnie the guys all loved Sam, so they will love her too, and she needn't worry. Net told us she would stay at our sides to help us remember who was who, until her boy friend arrived. Then she might spend time with him. I told her she didn't have to baby-sit us, she said she wasn't babysitting she liked us. I hugged her and Ronnie did too.

I heard Sal singing, I told Ronnie we needed to go down to the boathouse and hear this girl, because she was great. Net told us Sal had a contract with a label and was doing an album. We walked down and everyone said hello as we walked by, asking how we were. Of course the men were asking about Ronnie. She smiled and was friendly, but not the same flirty girl I knew in high school. She was all grown up.

Net introduced Ronnie to a couple of guys. One was Bebop, and the other was Sly. She poked me, telling me these were her favorite two. They were nice guys, she said, and looked good too. Ronnie laughed and talked to them. They talked to me too, Edward came over and told Sly to keep his hands off me, that I was his. Sly and Bebop were huge men too. Edward almost looked small compared to this muscle bound friends. Del came over and said hi with Sal. I asked her to sing some more, and she started back up. I told Del he must be proud of her, and he said yes, he was. He told me they had gotten married in April. I congratulated them. He said he was a lucky guy. I told him I thought so as well. Ronnie seemed to be having fun talking with Sly and Bebop, so I wandered over to Edward again. Net stayed with Ronnie.

A guy came walking up to Edward, and they bumped chests. The guy almost knocked Edward over. Edward introduced him to me. "Sam this is Terry". He was gorgeous, every muscle defined perfectly that I could see through his tight knit shirt. I looked at him from head to toe.

His pants rounded his lean waist down to his hips. I wanted to ask him to turn around so I could check out his butt, but I didn't. The muscles in his legs were huge. He had the biggest neck I had ever seen. His hair was thick and straight, a dirty blonde against his nicely tanned skin. His face was beautiful, that square jaw and those beautiful deep blue eyes were to die for. He walked with his arm curled around his sides. He was hot. I can't imagine being in bed with this guy, I wondered if he was as good as he looked. I guessed my mouth was open, as Edward told me to shut it. I just said "Uh huh". They were laughing at me, both of them. Net ran over to this hunk of a guy, and he bent down and kissed her, lifting her with one arm.

I looked at Net, "I see what you mean now, Net." She burst out laughing.

Edward gave me a dirty look. I blushed, walked over to him and kissed him. "I am going to be married, not dead. He is worth looking at," I whispered in Edwards's ear.

Edward squeezed me hard, "You are mine, don't forget it."

"I won't ever forget that, I was just checking him out." He frowned profusely. I walked back over to Ronnie and joined in their conversation. Edward brought us beers, and Ronnie and I both accepted them. Net and Terry came over and joined us. Ronnie ogled Terry just as I did. He was one good-looking man.

The guys were talking about body-building. Bebop said he was going to school at BYU. He was a wrestler when he started but, he got into bodybuilding and couldn't keep his weight down. He was going into business but wanted now more in a medical field. She told him she wanted to be a veterinarian, and he thought that was cool. He said he loved animals; here at home he had dogs and cats. He has a boxer named Muscles, he adored. Ronnie said she loved dogs especially. He said while she was here, he would bring Muscles over, or she could go see him. Sly was trying to talk to Ronnie too. He said he liked dogs and had a couple. He was going to school in California and was majoring in Engineering. He liked California and was considering staying there. It depended on the job situation when he graduated. Ronnie told them she wanted to go anywhere but Minnesota.

Both guys were super nice and Ronnie liked them. She was really enjoying both of them wanting to get to know them. Another guy came over later in the evening. He was the third guy Net had picked out for Ronnie. He was tall and lean. His was built similar to Edward. He was nice looking but had a simple look to him, or maybe it was just being next to these two brutes. Well, including standing next to Terry anyone would look plain. Net introduced us to him as J.T. He was friendly but quiet. I watched him; he didn't interact as the other guys did. Ronnie kept looking at him and smiling. Bebop did most of the talking; he was funny and nice to look at. He was considerate; when he got up to get himself something, he asked all the rest of us if we wanted anything. I liked him. but I liked Sly too. He was even funnier than Bebop, but he seemed to be a jokester and happy-go-lucky all the time.

J.T. asked a question here and there. Edward said he liked T.J. He didn't know him as well as he did the other two, but he was an okay guy. Born and raised in Florida like the rest of them. He was more a loaner in school. He said you can tell looking at him he wasn't like Thomas, Bebop or Sly. Edward added, neither was he. Sly wandered off sometime later. Sal was singing and everyone was having fun. Vivian and Ed were dancing with the kids. They looked so happy. Cook and even Mr. Granger came out for a while. All the young people seemed to love Cook and Granger and she hugged several and told them to come around and visit. She hugged Edward and me and said she missed these times. Edward put his arm around her and said he did too, but he missed her more than anything else round this place. I saw tears in her eyes. She kind of punched him on the arm and said, "Ah Mr. Edward, cut it out." He squeezed her and she went back to the house with Granger following her.

The party kept building. There was always something going on, someone doing something funny, or acting up. Sal and Del were doing a skit or play-acting, they were hilarious. This big guy was afraid of Sal's character, and it was just so funny watching them run around and Del screaming like a girl, with his arms up in the air. Everyone was laughing at them. They bowed and then it was back to music for a while. I noticed Ronnie was talking to J.T. I wondered where Bebop had gotten off to. I looked around for Net, and she was hugging her guy and swaying to the music near the water. I couldn't find Bebop or Sly anywhere. Edward was holding me, and we were talking about the next day. We had so much to do. He had to go get his tuxedo and Net, Ronnie, Vivian, and I were going to get pedicures and do some girly stuff together.

My Mom and Dad should be in around five o'clock tomorrow, so Mom and Alex weren't included in the girl thing. I wished they were coming earlier, but Dad couldn't get away any earlier, he said. When Alex got here though, I was going to make sure; she had the time of her life. I was excited to see them all, I hadn't seen them since Christmas. I saw Bebop talking with another girl, one of the three I saw at Thomas's house. He had his arms around her so I guessed Ronnie got tired of him.

I watched Ronnie; she was laughing, and talking with J.T. It seemed they were hitting it off well. I asked Edward to go over that way so I could talk to her a minute. We joined them. She told me a bit about J.T. and told me that she liked him. She said he graduated last semester. He was a Marine Biologist. She said he was going to Hawaii next week to check on a job. He said it was nice there, and he was hoping for this opportunity. I told her that sounded great. I told her I didn't want to interrupt long; I just wanted to make sure she was all right. She said she was having fun, she liked Bebop and Sly, but they wandered away. I told her to have fun and took hold of Edward's arm. He told J.T. he would see him later.

We walked back toward the group, singing with the music. We sat down on the deck, and I sat on his lap, leaning back into Edward. People started leaving, little by little, some had to work the next day, and some were just tired. It had dwindled down to about fifteen or so left. Net and Terry left along with the crowd. I was exhausted. This had been a very long day, with flying in, I wanted to spend time with Ronnie, but we didn't get much time together. Edward was wrestling with Thomas, and I was afraid he would get hurt, but they were having fun. J.T. and Ronnie joined the small group and sat close to each other near me. J.T. asked about where we were going on our honeymoon. I told him we were just going to spend a few days in Jamaica because Edward had to get back to take the Bar examine.

Vivian and Ed retired to the house, Ronnie and J.T. decided to stay at the boathouse and talk. Edward said they used to all stay here, but now they had work, families, kids and lives to take care of. No more 'care free sleep until noon days'. We will have some next week. "I told him. He hugged me as we walked to the house. We were in bed talking and playing.

"Edward, tomorrow night you have to sleep in the boat house."

"Why?"

"Because you can't see me on Saturday until the wedding, bad luck."

"No, I don't want to sleep alone the night before we get married."

"You can have your friends stay with you. I don't know Ronnie's plans, but I will be here in this bed alone, or well, you won't be here."

"Then I'll just make up for it now." Boy did he ever make up for it. When he was ready for number three, I couldn't do it. I was about to pass out. He begged and pleaded, but I whined and persuaded him that the early morning time would be nice. We finally fell asleep.

# CHAPTER THIRTY-FOUR

The morning was beautiful. The sun was shining brightly; there were no clouds in the sky. I ran down the stairs to find Edward. He was in the dining room eating breakfast. He said he found J.T. and Ronnie asleep on the couch in the boathouse. They must have talked until they passed out. He told me Ronnie went up stairs to shower and change, and J.T. went to his parents. Vivian and Dad are already up, and Vivian is ready for the pedicures.

"Wow, when did she get up?"

"Before I did."

"Okay, as soon as Ronnie is ready and has had something to eat, we will go."

We are hitting the liquor store today and getting tuxedos. Dad couldn't eat this morning, he was so nervous."

"Wow, Ed was?"

"Yes, I think he is anxious to have a daughter in the family."

"I like the sound of that."

"Me too. Next, grand-kids."

"Slow down, there just a little." Ed and Vivian walked into the room, hearing us laughing.

Ed asked, "What is so funny?"

Edward remarked, "I was telling Sam next comes grand-kids, she told me to slow down."

"I am ready anytime, Samantha."

"Thanks, Ed, take his side."

"He is my son, I love him, and I always have his back."

"Thanks Dad." They took a long look at each other.

Vivian asked, "What time does your parents get in?"

"At five o'clock."

"Where is Ronnie?"

"She is in the shower. Hopefully today she will be quick. What about Net?" Knowing Ronnie she could take an hour or longer in the shower. I was afraid Vivian might go get her herself if she didn't hurry.

"Net will meet us in town."

"Okay. I will check on Ronnie." I ran up the stairs and went to Ronnie's room. I knocked lightly, she said, "Come in." She was dressed and fluffing her hair. She looked lovely today as usual.

"Are you ready to eat something?"

"I am starving. What do they have downstairs?"

"There are scrambled eggs, bacon. Toast, pancakes, sausage, rolls, or something, I am not sure. They have biscuits and gravy. Anything Southern you can mention, it is prepared in the dining room."

"Let's go then." She said. I grabbed her hand, and we were down the stairs, swinging arms as we did as kids.

"Thank you so much, Ronnie for being here."

"Sam, it is my pleasure. I love you, remember, friends forever."

"BFF's."

I handed her a plate, and she started getting what she wanted as everyone was telling her good morning and, asking her if she had a good time last night, if she liked the guys, if she slept well, and so on. She tried to keep up with all the questions but missed a couple. She particularly liked Ed though. She hung on to his every word. Ed asked her about her father. He told her he wished her father had been able to come. Ronnie made his excuses for him and tried to get out of that conversation. She finished eating, and we ladies got in one car and the guys in the other, and headed for town.

We went our separate ways, us going to the shop to have our feet massaged, the guys off to do their things. They gave me the deluxe manicure, along with a pedicure. They rubbed my feet and legs, and I felt silky and smooth from the tips of my toes to above my knees. It was so relaxing. I had them paint my toenails, bright red like my flowers. They did my fingernails too. I told everyone I was wearing red lipstick also and everything else was white.

Net took us to a Chinese restaurant for lunch. It was a lot of fun. We ordered all the appetizers and shared. We had sake, laughed, and spent two hours talking about this evening. Ronnie finally got me alone in the bathroom and told me she liked J.T., more than a lot. She said he as a kind and soft-spoken person. He was smart and was the valedictorian in his class in college. Can you imagine being valedictorian in college? That is amazing. Out of that many kids. She said they talked until the sun started coming up. Everything was easy, no pretense, or forcing the conversation, just laughing and whatever came out, came out. I was so happy for her. She leaned her head down.

"Ronnie, he asked me to go to Hawaii with him. Should I go?"

"Do you want to go?"

"Yes, I do."

"Then why not? Ronnie, why would you question now something you would have jumped at last summer?"

"Because, Sam, I have changed, I told you I was different. I haven't slept with a guy since Mick and I broke up. I don't want to be that girl anymore. I'm living a respectable lifestyle. I am truly happy with the choices I have been making. But if I go with him, I know I will end up sleeping with him."

"Ronnie, then take it slow. Wait and see how it goes today, tonight, and tomorrow. The right answer will come to you." I patted her on the arm. She hugged me.

"You are right." We went back into the restaurant and everyone was ready to go.

Net was taking me to the airport from town. The others headed home, to get things ready for the party tonight. Net asked if I was excited about seeing my family. I told her we had our difficulties, but for the most part, I was looking forward to seeing them. My little sister, Alex, I wanted her to have fun, especially. Ray didn't care about parties or girl things; he will enjoy being with those guys when he sees the size of them. "It would have been good for your sister to have been with us today." She said. I told her I wished she had been.

We sat talking so long we were late getting to the airport this time. My parent's plane had already landed. I ran in to find them, and Net stayed with the car. I found Mom, and she showed me where everyone else was waiting. Dad wasn't happy waiting even a few minutes. I helped them out to the car with bags and things. We loaded it and headed for Ed's house. I let my sister sit in the front so I could talk to Mom. She said they had a nice trip. It was comfortable and had no delays, a real smooth ride.

Alex was asking Net about everything she saw. She was so excited being in Florida. I tried to talk to Dad, but he was complaining about the heat and all the traffic. I told him that Ed's house was out of town and about five or more miles. It was quiet and peaceful there. I hoped he would like it. We pulled up to the house, and Mom cried out, "Good Lord. This place is huge. Just one man lives in this house?"

"Well, kind of, basically. Vivian, his fiancée is here most of the time now." There is a house behind the main house, called the boathouse. It has four bedrooms, each room has a full bath, and there is a huge living room, kitchen and dining room and a deck on the back that leads to the boats and the water. It is super nice. It is bigger than our house."

"Wow, does the inside look as nice as the outside?"

"Better, Mom, unbelievably better." I said. Net pulled up to the front of the house. Edward came out to greet us. Alex jumped out and hugged Edward. Mom, Dad, Ray and I followed. Net said she would give us some alone time to get situated and she would go out back. I told her she was welcome to stay with us. She was the main reason everything had gone so well. She said she would wait for us on the deck behind the house; she would try to find Ronnie. I told her we would be there shortly.

I took Mom and Dad inside, and Mom loved the place, just as I did. "Now this is a mansion."

I laughed, "Yes, I agree."

Dad, "Humphed." Edward led us upstairs and showed, showed Mom and Dad which room was theirs, and took Alex to her room and Ray to his. Alex said, "We get our own rooms?" Edward said, "Yep, and if you don't like it, I will find you a better one. She couldn't believe the size of her room. She said she wanted to stay here always. Dad told her to be quiet. Ray was okay with his room. That's a boy for you. He wanted to go see people and play.

Mom and Dad wanted to rest a bit, so we left them, telling them how to get to the deck when they came down stairs. Alex and Ray came with Edward and me. I asked if they wanted to eat, but they both said no. They wanted to see the place and see Edward's friends.

We walked out on the deck, and Ronnie and Net were talking. Ronnie came over and hugged Alex and Ray. Alex hugged her back a little reluctantly. She hadn't been treated like that before by Ronnie. Ronnie asked her to join her and Net and Alex beamed and followed Ronnie. They included her in what they were doing. I heard them telling her about the good-looking boys that would be here later. See beamed with anticipation. Ray was off chasing a squirrel. Edward was chasing Ray, and laughing with him. Ed and Vivian came out and laughed at Edward playing with Ray. I told them my parents would be down soon, they were resting and getting situated. Ed said sure, no problem. I told Ed, "You know the relationship I have with Dad was like is less than yours and Edwards's was." He said he remembered what I told him.

"Ed, my dad can be rude, I want to apologize now."

"Sam, don't worry about it."

"You called me Sam." I was smiling from ear to ear.

"Samantha, this weekend is about you and Edward, and spending the rest of your lives together, not my feelings, not anyone else's, but yours and Edward's. I want you to have the best day of your life tomorrow. Please don't worry, I will behave myself too." He said. I hugged him and he hugged me back. I looked out over the lawn and saw Edward watching us. He smiled and waved to me, and I waved back. I went to sit with Net, Ronnie, and Alex. They were still telling her about boys. I told them to take it easy. She was only fifteen years old, and these 'boys' were men. They told me not to be a ninny and all laughed. I smiled at them.

I turned around and saw Mom and Dad walking out on the deck. I went over to greet them, and to introduce them to Ed and Vivian. They were cordial, and Dad even smiled. Ed asked them if they would like drinks, and they accepted. Ed called Cook and she brought out tea, lemonade and asked if they would like a drink. They both accepted the tea. Ed asked them to sit.

My Mom told Ed what a beautiful house he had, and he thanked her. Ed talked to Dad about law, and then during the conversation, he started talking about Edward and me. He said he was overjoyed with me as his new daughter-in-law and Edward was happier than he had ever been. Ed was trying to get Dad to comment, but Mom was the one who always answered.

Ed said he had some cigars; maybe he and Dad would have a brandy and cigar in his office later. Dad said he would like that. I caught Dad looking at me several times. I was relaxing some. J.T. came walking around the back of the house. Ronnie lit up when she saw him. She waited for him to come to the deck. She told him, Alex was my little sister, and he said she was beautiful and talked to her just as he did with the other girls.

I heard Thomas before I saw him. He was loud and you knew he was here, whooping and hollering as he drove around to the back and parked. Ed waved to him. Del and Sly were in the car and when they got out, Alex's eyes bugged out of her head. She said, "I didn't know boys got that big." Net told her to wait until she saw her boy friend, Terry. Alex asked, "Should I be afraid?" Net and Ronnie laughed. I was listening to them off a ways. Net told her no they were all big 'Teddy Bears' and if she let them, they would hug her until they squashed her. Alex giggled.

Thomas stopped just as he was nearing the deck, "Oh my, who is this vision of loveliness? I didn't think it was possible for any woman to be more beautiful than Sam, but this lovely vision has stolen my heart." He bowed down to Alex. She had her eyes open wide, and her mouth was open as well, and Ronnie pushed up her chin to close her mouth, and she obeyed. "My lady what is your name?" Thomas asked, Alex giggled.

"Alex." She said shyly. He kissed her hand, and she swooned, and placed the back of her hand on her forehead. I thought I was going to fall off the deck laughing so hard. She was playing right along with him.

"My lady, Alexandra tonight I must have the first dance. May I?" He asked. She was grinning so big you could see her gums.

"Why yes, you may, kind sir." She said. He bowed again. Sly and Del both told her hello, but she could not take her eyes off Thomas. I wondered how Tory will react about this, smiling to myself. Edward walked up beside me and said, "Thomas has a little brother Alex's age. He is coming over later this evening."

"Oh my, I don't know how Dad will handle that." I remarked

"Net has a couple of younger brothers as well, one is close to Ray's age, the other is older, maybe fifteen, but I am not positive."

"That will make her day, if two cute boys were around. We will need pictures for her to take home for the stories she can tell."

"They are both charmers, I should warn you. They are cute boys." Edward went over to talk to my parents, and his dad. They seemed to be getting along well.

By dinner time, more of Edwards's friends had shown up. Del's dad came and joined Ed and my parents on the deck. The three young boys came with Thomas, and I thought Alex was going to faint. These boys were hot for their age. Even Ronnie and I were impressed. Net laughed at us. Ray hit it off with the youngest boy, Net's brother Adam.

Net's other brother, Andrew was fifteen, and Thomas's brother, Theodore was seventeen. They sat with Alex and talked while she giggled. I told Net to keep an eye on them. She nodded. J.T. and Ronnie were enjoying their time together. I knew it was a match. How far or how long would be another thing, but Ronnie was doing well; she wasn't depressed, and she was happy.

The evening progressed along too fast. I didn't want to be separated from Edward, but it was midnight, and Ronnie and Net took me upstairs. We had champagne. Mom and Vivian came to join us for a little while. We sat upstairs and watched the guys at the boat house. Dad was off with Ed and Del's dad, smoking cigars and drinking Brandy. I prayed Dad was nice. We drank our champagne until we all were drunk. I saw Tory and she was giving my sister a hard time accusing her of flirting with her boyfriend. It made me feel good they were making my sister part of the crowd. The two younger boys didn't leave her side.

Net told us she and Terry were getting married in October; they had to put their wedding off because of several different reasons. She wanted to make sure I would be there, and Ronnie too. We told her we wouldn't miss it for anything. She said she was having five bridesmaids, and five groomsmen. She considered more, but it was just getting too much. Terry had such a large family; they had invited over three hundred people. She said she loved his family and he loved hers so no problems there. There was just so many, and she couldn't leave anyone out. She told us all the details, the colors, and about the dresses. Talking about her wedding made the time pass quickly and the nerves calm down.

Alex came upstairs later, joining us, told me how much fun she had and how much she liked Thomas and Tory. She said Andrew and Theodore were wonderful. She especially liked Andrew. Net giggled. I told her that he was Net's brother. She got embarrassed. It was okay, Net wouldn't tell, but Alex wanted her to. She said Thomas danced with her. She said Mom made her come up and she wasn't ready yet. I told her we had a long day tomorrow. She asked if the boys would be there, and I told her I bet Net could get them to show up. She giggled and went off to bed. Ronnie said she wished she had a relationship like that with her sister. Ronnie and I talked most of the night about Kat, Abby, and our pasts.

# Chapter Thirty-Five

I awoke, stretching and smiling. This was my wedding day, and my moving around woke Ronnie up as always, and she watched me.

"Do you wake Edward up every morning that way?"

"No, I wake Edward up other ways." We both giggled. Net was asleep across the foot of the bed. I tried to get up without waking her. She was curled up in a little ball. I tiptoed to the shower. I turned the water on, brushed my teeth, I was smiling, and dreaming about tonight. In the shower, I sang and danced, I was so happy I was giddy. I put on lotion and put a bra and panties on. I put on my robe and walked into the bedroom. Net and Ronnie were sitting on the bed laughing. They each had a cup in their hands.

"Where's mine?" I asked. They pointed to the dresser. I got a cup of tea, adding sugar and cream.

"Did you sleep well?"

"I slept like a baby. I am getting married today, and I danced around the room with my arms out wide." They were laughing. "I am so happy I can't stand myself."

There was a knock on the door, I ran to the bathroom. Net went to the door, it was Alex, and she came into the room and jumped on the bed with Ronnie. Net went back and sat on the bed. They all looked so cute, sitting cross-legged in the middle of this big old bed. I ran out and hugged Alex, and then Ronnie, and then Net.

"It is a wonderful day."

Net said, "I think it is because it is your wedding day."

"Oh, yeah it is." We all laughed again. We talked about what we were to do until we started getting ready. Someone else knocked on the door. Net asked who it was. It was Vivian, so Net opened the door, and she joined us. She told us the guys were up and eating breakfast and Edward was singing and driving them all crazy. Ronnie said, "Same thing in this room." I pouted.

Another knock, Net and Ronnie both yelled, "Who is it?" It was my mother, she walked in and asked how I was doing, wanting to see if I needed anything. We all talked and laughed a while. Another knock on the door, everyone yelled, "Who is it?" It was Edward.

I ran to the bathroom and shut the door, leaning my back against it. Net told him to go away. He said he just wanted to talk to me and tell me good morning. He had for the past nine months, and he didn't want to stop for one minute. Net opened the door, and Edward saw Mom, Vivian, Alex and Ronnie. He said, "Oh I didn't know everyone was in here. Where is Sam?"

Net told him, "Hiding in the bathroom."

He yelled out, "Good morning, my love,"

I said, "Good morning, sweetheart." Then Net ran him out of the room. He was arguing with her and trying to hold his ground, but no use. "If I can handle a big ole boy, I can handle you. Now get out, and she will see you when she starts down the aisle." He stuck out his lip and said, "Okay." Then he walked away. All the women laughed at him. I came out and told them I wanted to open the door and give him a kiss, but I knew I had to wait. Mom said she was going back to see if Dad needed anything and she would see me later. Alex went with her, soon after Vivian left.

"I wish my dad would talk to me. He hasn't said more than 'Hi' to me since he has been here."

Ronnie hugged me, "Sam you knew this could be the way it was."

"I know, but I hoped for more." She hugged me tighter. Net got dressed in the clothes she had worn yesterday. She was going downstairs to see how things were going. "You know, setting up the tables and chairs." She said she would report back in just a while. Ronnie got dressed in shorts and a shirt. She said she would get us some food and be right back. She told me to lock the door and not let Edward in. I promised. She left me alone. I was all by myself, deserted by my friends and family. They were out there having fun, talking to each other, and I was locked up in the tower. Someone knocked on the door, and I asked who it was. It was my Dad. I went to the door and opened it slightly.

He said, "Can I come in?"

"Sure, come on in." He came in, I asked him to sit down, and he sat on the chair instead of the bed. I sat on the bed in front of him.

"What's up Dad?"

"I just wanted to see for myself that you were up and ready."

"I am up, and I've showered, but I won't get dressed until just before the music starts. I don't want to wrinkle my dress or spill anything on it."

"Sam, are you sure you are doing the right thing?"

"Yes, Dad, I love Edward." I paused and looked out the window, thinking, not wanting to say something that might hurt him. I was happy today and I didn't want a quarrel or any sadness around me. "I love Edward . . ." I said again. "He is the best thing that has ever happened to me. I can't imagine what my life would be like today without him . . . Dad do you know what I mean?"

He hung his head, "Sam, I'm sorry you felt you had a bad life."

"Dad, no, not today. This is a happy day for me. Please don't . . ."

"Sam, I wasn't going to be mean, I just wanted to say I am sorry." He said. I shook my head because I wanted to cry. "I haven't been there for you, your brother, your sister, or your mother in years. I have been a selfish, lonely man. Your depression came from me."

"Dad . . .?"

"I need to say this to you." He said. I nodded and looked at the floor. "I love you, Sam. I love your mom, Alex and Ray, but I never knew how to tell them, except to work and give you all I could." I was staring at my feet, swinging them back and forth. He stood up and walked toward me. "Sam, look at me." I looked up; my eyes filled with tears. "Sam, I love you! Will you give me a chance to make up for the past?" I sat there thinking *'oh my-gosh' finally, he told me and, I sit her, afraid and, quiet.* Did he really say what I thought I heard? I was biting my lip. I tasted blood and he pushed at my lips and told me, "Stop that, you don't want a swollen lip on your wedding day."

I was thinking, *it wouldn't be my first fat lip.* I jumped off the bed, grabbed him, and hugged him. I let out a huge breath; I didn't realize I had been holding. He hugged me back, and I heard him crying, not just tears falling, but big sobs. We fell to the floor on our knees, holding each other hugging. "I love you, Dad, I love you so much. Thank you, Dad. This is the best present I could get today. I love you." We cried, and he kept telling me he loved me, and we cried some more. This day would be ~cial to me in so many ways.

Dad finally released me, and we sat back in the floor up against ~lked for a while. He told me about his childhood and how He told me about his parents and said he didn't want to be like them. He told me that when I was born, it was the best day of his life, he held me and kissed me and told me he would never fail me, but he did in time.

When it was just me, he was there all the time, helping Mom and being a happy family. Mom was always the glue. He said when Alex came along, he loved her too, but he had to work longer hours, and she didn't want much to do with him, she always wanted Mom. Then with Ray, he said he thought things would change, but he was working even more to make more money. He wanted us to have the best and not go without, but he was not only working more he was pulling away from us, not just his kids, but our mom too. He said he had been talking to Mom, and they were working their differences out. He loved her, and she loved him, but they have forgotten how to be a 'We' instead of a 'Me'.

He said, she pulled back too because she didn't know what else to do. She had gone through times of depression as well, feeling alone, raising three kids with her her husband, who was gone from sun up until sun down. He said he now wanted to fix things with Alex and Ray. With Ray, it was easy, but Alex just walked away from him and wouldn't talk to him. "You touched me, and I so wanted to grab you and hold you, but I was afraid. I was angry with myself for losing all those years." He said. I hugged him again.

"Give her time, and don't give up." I said. He smiled at me.

"You know, it is because of you, that we are going to stay a family. Mom had just about had it with me. She was ready to leave, but you made the effort with her after we almost lost you." He put his hand on his heart, "Sam, those two days were the worst of my life. I wanted to die. I didn't care about anything else. You were the only one, I ever had that bond with as a baby, and I let you go without showing you, how much, I cared for you. I locked myself in my office for those two days and didn't speak to anyone. I was so scared, and then when we found out you were alive, I was angry. Mostly because you made us worry so much. I was angry at me, it s always me." I thought you tried to take your own life, you made us worry so much. I was angry at myself because if I had shown you the love you deserved you wouldn't have tried to kill yourself. I blamed myself and didn't

"Dad, what is important now is I love you. Today is my wedding day. You are going to walk me down the aisle, and I will know, holding your arm, that you love me. Do you know how happy that makes me feel? I said. "Thank you Dad." He had tears in his eyes again.

"It is a happy day Baby." We both smiled at each other.

"I wonder where my friends are, they are supposed to help me get ready. Ronnie went to get me some food, I'm starving."

"I heard the door open a while ago and then close. Whoever opened it must have seen us in conversation or crying I hope it wasn't Alex, it might make her hate me more."

"We all have to talk to her and encourage her to open up to you. It will be all right, I know it."

"Let me go see who tried to come in. I will make sure you get some food. I will see you when it is time." He kissed me on the forehead, stood up, and left the room. I touched the spot where he kissed me. I smiled.

Ronnie came into the room, "Well, I see you and your dad made amends."

"Yes we did."

"I didn't mean to bother you, so I left when I saw you two hugging. I brought you some food."

I snatched the plate of food away from her and started eating. "This is good; I was so hungry, thank you so much."

She laughed and said, "I am going to get your dress out and check for wrinkles and get your shoes and stuff all ready while you eat." I watched her hang my dress on a hook and place my shoes below it. She went to the bathroom, and set out my makeup, brush, and things for my hair. I ate all the cold eggs on the plate plus a piece of limp toast and it tasted great. I looked at the clock; we had less than two hours until I was to walk down that aisle. I figured it would only take me twenty minutes to get ready. I was beginning to get nervous.

Ronnie yelled out from the bathroom. "Edward is having a good time talking to everyone. He looks great; he is already dressed and ready. He said to tell you the wedding could start early, if it was okay with you."

I laughed, "I bet he did say that." She came out of the bathroom and looked so very pretty. She had put on her makeup and fixed her hair.

"It's not fair, Ronnie; you are going to be prettier than the bride."

"Oh like hell, you are gorgeous. You look beautiful even without makeup. Edward is a lucky guy."

Net came back in the room, she had her clothes with her and shut the door. "Can I take a real quick shower?"

"Sure, Net." She ran in the bathroom, and I heard the water. She must have taken ten minutes showering. I heard the water go off. I heard the hair dryer for just a few minutes. She came out in a pretty halter dress.

She opened the door, "Sorry, I was as quick as I could be."

"You didn't have to rush that much."

"I didn't want to be in your way, I know you have to have makeup and hair done."

"Net, we have plenty of time." She was fluffing her hair with her fingers. She began telling us everything was set up. "The chairs are lined up straight, and the tables for the reception all looked beautiful. They had centerpieces, in the middle of each table, with flowers and ribbons. The napkins had huge diamond rings, around them. Wine glasses, water glasses and champagne glasses are at each setting already. Ed and Vivian went all out. There are already so many people here, it is ridicules. Everyone came early to help." I ran to the window and looked out. There were tons of people milling around the yard and as far as I could see to the back, but. I couldn't see the deck or where the wedding ceremony would be held. I looked at the front and saw all the cars. I spotted Edward.

I screamed, "There he is, there is my Edward." Ronnie ran to the window and pulled me back.

"He can't see you, it is bad luck."

"He didn't see me, but I saw him. He looks so handsome. Oh, Net, he looks so nice. I am the lucky one." They told me to stay away from the window, I told them I would. I was so bored sitting in this room all morning. I should have been able to walk around upstairs at least. "Can't you make Edward stay outside for awhile and let me walk around?"

"Sure we could, but there are lots of other people in the house."

"Okay." I sat cross-legged back on the bed, right in the middle, and watched the two of them get ready. Ronnie helped Net with her makeup. They both had beautiful dresses. I checked my toes and fingers, and the polish still looked nice. I ran my hands down my legs, no stubble.

Vivian came in and told us to get ready. I jumped off the bed, shouting, "Already!" They all looked at me running around and laughing at me. I pulled my robe off and yelled for someone to help me. They just stood there watching me run around the room in my bra and panties. I saw everything was together, my dress hanging with my shoes below. Vivian said she would be back with a bottle of champagne.

Ronnie had me sit in the bathroom, and she put on my makeup. I was sitting there still in my bra and panties. I never did this, I was so modes. Net brought me a slip, and I stood up and put it on, it was just a half slip. I sat back down. Ronnie finished with my makeup and started on my hair. I asked Ronnie to cover my freckles, and she said she couldn't. They looked cute, I sighed, brushing on my hair. It was short and curly so it couldn't be changed much. She pulled the bangs back and put a Tierra on my head. I gasped, "I am not a princess, I am a bride." She told me to shut up. I watched her pull the sides back and pin it, and surprisingly it stayed for now. She curled it in the back and made the tight little curls straighten out some. I thought she was doing well. Vivian came back in with a bottle of champagne, and we all had a glass, trying to calm me down which worked well.

I settled down slumping in my chair. Ronnie kept pulling me up. Net was putting lotion on my arms and across my back and chest. She said it had a shimmer to it that would sparkle in the sunlight. I let her do what she wanted. Ronnie finished with my hair, and I looked half way decent. I had a hard time believing it, but I was happy with what she did to my hair. I wished she could have covered those freckles up.

They walked me back to the bedroom and had me step into the dress. Net zipped me up. I slipped on my shoes and they stood me in front of the mirror. I was shocked, to tell you the truth, and amazed that it was 'Me' in the mirror. I wore a white strapless white Satin gown, fitted at the top then flaring out from my waist down, and a short train in the back that drag about two feet behind me.

"Do you think Edward will like this?"

"Yes." Ronnie said.

"Do you think he will be happy he is marring me? I am not special."

"He loves you, and you know it."

"What if he changes his mind?"

"Sam, shut up." I did, I didn't say anything else. There was a light tap on the door. Net opened it; it was Mom and Dad. I started to cry, and Ronnie pointed her finger at me. I sniffed it up. Mom hugged me, and then she and Net went down stairs. Dad had tears in his eyes, and then Ronnie pointed at him, and he nodded.

Dad said, "Hunny, you look beautiful. You are the prettiest bride I have ever seen. I love you." Ronnie backed away for a moment

"What about Mom?"

"Don't tell her I said this, but you are so very much prettier than she was that day. She grew into her beauty, you know."

"Dad!"

"It's time to go." I looked at Ronnie. She picked up our bouquets and handed me mine and we walked out the door. At the bottom of the stairs, she turned around and winked at me. I heard the music. She walked toward the doors, Dad and I followed. She paused as she got to the doors and looked back one last time, and then started forward. The wedding march started and I stood in the doorway with Dad, holding his arm. We started walking, and everyone stood up when we got to the bottom step of the deck. We paused; Dad looked at me and me at him. He nodded once, and kissed my forehead, and then we walked down the aisle I saw Edward, and he was grinning from ear to ear, those beautiful dimples calling to me. I saw Edward and he was grinning from ear to ear, those beautiful dimples calling to me. When we reached the front, the minister said, "Who gives this woman?" Dad said, all teary eyed, "Her mother and I do." I looked at Mom and blew her a kiss. Dad kissed me on each cheek and then walked over and took Mom's hand. She held onto his arm with her other hand, as Edward took my hands in his.

The minister asked us to repeat our vows, after him, and we did. It was over so fast, I don't remember what he said. We said so many things to each other, but it was over. We were husband and wife. Edward kissed me, and then kissed me again, and yelled out to everyone, "Yippee." I was crying and he was brushing the tears away, and kissing my checks. We turned, and walked back down the aisle, together. Everyone stood up again. Mom and Dad came and stood beside us. Then Ed, Cook and Granger stood next to Edward. They had hired help today so, Cook didn't have to serve. She was one of the guests. Everyone came by us with congratulations. Some hugged, and kissed us. It was too good to be true. I was Mrs. Edward Anderson III. I looked at Edward and told him "I love you." He smiled and said to me, "I love you too, Mrs. Anderson." I giggled.

The photographer took pictures quickly. He took traditional pictures, and then he took lots of untraditional one where Edward was holding me up in front of him. He was looking up at me, and I had my hands on his shoulders looking down at him. He took one where Edward had me bent over backwards. I had one leg up in the air while Edward was kissing my neck. My head tilted back, and I was laughing. He took one with me on Edwards back, holding on to his neck, he was running away, and we were both looking behind us. He took one where Edward was trying to get away, I had a hold of his jacket, pulling him back, while my heals, dug in the ground. I bet these pictures would come out cute. He had many more great ideas. It was fun taking those pictures.

The guests started toward the tables, and Net was told everyone what to do and where to go. She led us to a table for the whole family to sit at. Alex was at my side, hugging me. Ray wanted to go play; he was complaining about his shirt, hating the clothes he had to wear. We sat down and were served dinner. Cook and Granger sat at our table too. Alex wanted to go sit with Net and her brother, so Mom let her go. Ray whined about it, so Mom let him go too. I kept looking back at Net. She had out done herself for what she did for us. I was so amazed with this girl. I was proud to call her a friend. She was the only real friend I had ever had besides the Quad. Thinking about them all of a sudden made me sad. There were only two of us here. No one knew where Kat was, and Abby was gone. Ronnie must have seen the look on my face, because she poked Edward with her elbow, and he turned to me. He leaned over and kissed me, and my whole attitude changed. I was so in love at nineteen years old. I knew I was young, but this man made my world go round. This man made the air in my lungs; this man gave me a reason to live.

We cut one of the cakes, which was beautiful. There were several in fact. Cook had made Edward's favorite cake, Ed's favorite, and my favorite. I guessed Edward had told her, and she made a special one for us to freeze and cut on our first anniversary and then one for us to cut for pictures. Everyone got their choice of cakes from the four served to the guests. They all looked beautiful. There was enough for everyone and then some. We had a champagne fountain everyone was having a good time. I drank and drank from the fountain. We were having a good time. I drank and drank for the fountain. We had wine, mixed drinks, and specialty non-alcoholic drinks for the kids and non-drinkers.

There were toasts from Edward's friends. They told naughty things he had done as a young boy. They told of his first tryst with a girl, not mentioning it was his dad's girl friend, but we all knew. They said funny things; and they said nice things that made us cry. Sal sang her toast, said it would be on her next album, and dedicated to us. I held my hand over my heart. Wow, that was a gift of all times. Thomas's toast was the nicest; it was beautiful, like a poem. He had it written down and said there was a copy in a card on the table. He hugged Edward, bent him over backwards and kissed him smack on the lips.

He stood back up, and then pulled at his clothes, and made this manly "Humph" sound as he walked back to his table. Maybe I should say, sauntered back to his table. Tory stood up and pointed her finger at him. He bent his head down, like a little boy and pouted. She kissed him on the tip of his nose. Everyone laughed except Edward. He was standing with his hands on his hips glaring at his friend, but it was all in fun. Edward grabbed me and kissed me a good one, bending me backwards and giving tongue. He stood and straightened his clothes and said, "Now that is the correct way it's done." Everyone roared after that. I enjoyed being the center of attention.

I saw a table full of gifts for us. We opened our gifts, which was rather embarrassing at times. We had so many gifts, and some things were a little private. His friends were real jokesters. We had condoms. We had a huge box that said 'Condoms' the the side, but when we opened it, it was a very nice crystal flower vase. But the vase was full, not of flowers, but condoms, gels, dildos, cock rings, and a plastic strip with little balls on it. I wasn't sure what t was for. Edward just told me to put it away and he would tell me later.

There were sheets, with little naked men and women; all over them, they were having sex. Oh my gosh, we had cookware, dishes, slinky little gowns. We had sex toys, and wanted to die when I saw them. Opening these things in front of Mom, Dad, Alex and Ray was quite embarrassing. We had edible lotions, and panties. We had cards with money, and gift cards. We had cards with naughty poetry in them, naughty little games you could play. Then, Mom and Dad gave us a Bible, each with our name engraved on them, and a beautiful cross for the wall. They also gave us five-hundred dollars for our honeymoon. Ed gave us one-hundred-thousand dollars to buy a home or as down payment. I was shocked. He said he had it why not give it to the two kids he loved the most? I couldn't believe it. I looked at Edward, then Ed and he said there were more surprises. He said someday this house and everything would be ours anyway; he might as well start sharing now. Why wait until he died?

I found out the other surprise. It was fantastic. Ed had talked to Dad about moving to Florida, as well as Edward. They had discussed Dad as being part of his firm, here so Ed could spend more time with Vivian, in Massachusetts, also traveling the world. He never was one to stay in one place long, but his firm was suffering. He had five other attorneys working for him, but Dad would take over Ed's place. He would have a huge increase in salary. They could stay in the boathouse as long as they desired and then, of course, buy what they wanted in time. Dad had accepted. Mom was very pleased with the move, and change for the kids. Alex and Ray were happy about the move as well, especially living in that boathouse. Cook would be at their disposal. This was too much to take in, all in one day. He offered, Edward a job at the firm as a first year, and eventually owning everything. Edward told his dad he appreciated the offer, but would have to discuss it with his new wife, though he was sure she would love the idea, and I do.

We finally were able to get away from all the excitement for a brief moment, and then the music started. The boys at the barn were playing at my wedding, and Sal was singing. This was a great-unexpected event. Everyone was dancing and having a wonderful time. We danced until I thought I would fall over. As we were dancing, Edward would kiss my face, touch my nose, and chin. I told him, I tried to get Ronnie to cover my freckles, but she couldn't cover them. He said he loved my freckles. Freckles were kisses from angles, and angles had made out all over my face. I laughed, that was the cutest thing I had heard.

I was so happy, my life was going in the right direction, and I had made peace with my family. Ronnie said she would like to spend more time here in Florida as well. We loved being here over the summer. We had good memories, and some really bad, but the good ones were the best of course. We missed Abby and Kat but we were happy.

A limo pulled up that I hadn't expected. It was long and sleek. There were so many surprises this day. Everyone walked over to us as we walked toward the limo. We looked inside and it was luxurious. Ed and Vivian brought out our bags; we had already packed for our short trip. She had my purse. She handed us each our phones. Edward opened the door for me, Ronnie ran up to me, hugged me, and thanked me for being her friend.

I said I am the one who should thank her. I told her how much I loved her. I told her we would be friends forever. BFF's, don't ever forget it. She was holding hands with J.T. Net came over and hugged both, Edward and me. I thanked her and told her I appreciated her more than she could ever know. I told her to expect the same help for her wedding in October. She told me to plan to spend lots of time with her, because she was going to be one of my new best friends. I told her I loved that idea.

We got in the limo. There was a bottle of champagne, and two flutes with our names and today's date engraved on them. As we pulled away in our limo, we were hanging out the window waving and yelling good-bye. Mom and Dad were happy, holding hands, which I didn't ever remember them doing.

Ed and Vivian were standing near them, holding hands as well. It was a wonderful sight. All Edward's friends were becoming my friends. I felt good, I felt safe, and I was happy. I wanted to live and I loved my life. I snuggled into Edwards's side, and he held me tight.

"We have a long happy life ahead of us, Mrs. Anderson"

"Yes Mr. Anderson, I believe we do."

73766809R00163

Made in the USA
Middletown, DE
17 May 2018